ONE SUMMER IN SICILY

ONE SUMMER IN SICILY

Nancy Barone

An Aria Book

First published in the UK in 2023 by Head of Zeus,
part of Bloomsbury Publishing Plc

9 7 5 3 1 2 4 6 8

A catalogue record for this book is available from the British Library.

ISBN (PB): 9781803284408
ISBN (E): 9781803284521

Cover design: Head of Zeus, Nina Elstad

Typeset by Siliconchips Services Ltd UK

Printed and bound in Great Britain by
CPI Group (UK) Ltd, Croydon CR0 4YY

Head of Zeus
First Floor East
5–8 Hardwick Street
London EC1R 4RG

WWW.HEADOFZEUS.COM

This one goes to my beloved newborn granddaughter,
Penny London.

Prologue

'Wake up! Today is the first day of the rest of your sex life,' my own recorded voice blared at me from the alarm on my mobile phone. A sex life that, in truth, was on its last legs, and not for the want of my trying. But I was going to give it one last go.

Six a.m. I stabbed at the snooze button and fell back under the duvet. *Tony*, I thought dreamily, stretching an arm toward his (empty) side of the bed, popping a puffy eye open. But as full consciousness took hold of me, I remembered that in that exact moment, he was in a hotel in Sicily doing, if I knew him at all, a last-minute practice of his presentation on avant-garde surgical techniques for reshaping saggy boobs.

And in the attempt to save my twenty-year marriage, I (who had refused his offer to operate on mine) had decided to defy my worst fear and board an actual airplane to fly out and surprise him. But crap, was it Tuesday already? I had a gazillion errands to run before I left today. I pried the other eye open, my mind way ahead of me and already in panic mode.

I tried to dart out of bed, but today of all days, when I was going to make the most monumentally romantic gesture of my life, I was absolutely knackered and unable to budge. My mind was now fully awake and held captive by my body. I wanted to move, was desperate to do so, but The Old Bod wasn't having it.

I *very gingerly* rolled over onto my side and balled myself up, trying to stretch my aching back. One more kilogram, one more cupcake and I swear my skeleton would buckle under my ever-increasing weight and leave me on the pavement in a heap of hefty hips and big boobs. I groaned and fell back against the mattress. Time to diet again. Time to change a lot of things.

Even this sex escape thing – was I, Methodical Mum, really up for this completely out-of-character, spur-of-the-moment gesture, at the tender age of forty? Well, almost forty – my birthday was in December, on the same day as my wedding anniversary.

And most of all, was I, who gets dizzy even watching *kites* in the sky or fish in the sea, really going to fly halfway around the world (on my own, to boot) for an improvised three-week vacation where clothing would (here's hoping) be unnecessary for most of the day (and night)?

Hell, yes. We had to get things moving again (pun intended). Get motivated, heat up the joint or whatever it is they say in sexy movies. But before I boarded the plane that would take me to warmer climes and the man of my life later today, I had quite the lengthy to-do list:

1. Help daughter Annie move her stuff into boyfriend Miles' flat before her move to Spain for her teaching job.
2. Remember not to sob while doing so.
3. Take Jumbo-Gemma, Annie's German shepherd, back to her flat after having looked after her for the week.
4. Finish baking the cakes I'd promised my bestie Martha for yet another one of our charities.
5. Finish helping old Mrs. Collins next door with the decluttering job we started weeks ago (good luck on that one).
6. Ignore my New Wrinkle of the Day and make myself hubby-ready, i.e. book waxing session.
7. Get sex life back on track.

Because – I admit it – I'd let myself go a little lately (yes, okay, for the last few years as it happens) but these days who wasn't busy, right? I mean, how many of us can say we have time on our hands to sit around and pamper ourselves? We have kids to look out for (because even if they're all grown up and have flown the nest you never stop worrying, do you?), jobs to do, bills to pay, husbands to deal with, laundry and ironing to do and oh – those dinners don't cook themselves, do they?

We had all of twenty-four hours in the day, minus let's say about eight for sleeping, and yet, we never seemed to manage any time for ourselves save the occasional late-night bath with candles during which, I'm not ashamed to say, I regularly fall asleep in the tub because I've been up since dawn.

How else was I supposed to get everything done around here, day in, day out? I ran my household with the efficiency of a Marine, keeping the place as clean as a whistle despite the gazillion possessions I'd filled it with over the last twenty years. I never tired of cooking, baking, hosting dinner parties for Tony's colleagues and sometimes even his eminent A-lister patients who wanted bigger implants or a smaller butt.

And especially today of all days, when I'd have relished the luxury of getting things done at a normal speed, it was looking tight. But in the end it would all be worth seeing Tony's thrilled expression. He'd be extremely proud of me for coaxing myself onto an aluminum deathtrap with wings without knocking down a few *gin-and-hold-the-tonics* first.

Three weeks of love, Sicilian sun, beaches and Malvasia wine, not to mention all the gorgeous food they have there. I know because even if I'm Canadian, my parents are Italian. Not that Ma ever cooked, mind you. She's probably the only Italian mother who's allergic to the kitchen. It was a good thing I loved cooking – albeit not as much as I loved eating.

And boy did it show. In the last three months I'd managed to go up a whole dress size. Either that or (alternative explanation, which I preferred) department stores didn't agree on the *definition* of sizes anymore. What was going on, a retail war? Was that how they managed to keep their customers, make dresses a size bigger without telling you, so that when you tried to shop somewhere else you'd be horrified at being a, say, size eighteen when elsewhere you were a sixteen? Just because I was an M&S size eighteen didn't mean I actually *was* an eighteen, did it? If only I could manage to squeeze into a smaller size in some other store I'd have made my point, but so far it hadn't happened.

The phone on my bedside table rang and I debated. If I didn't answer, it would serve me right if I'd later learned something tragic had happened to someone I care about. But if I *did* answer, it could be also be something completely normal but utterly time-consuming. Like listening to my friend Brends boasting about her brand-new boyfriend. And today of all days was not the day. Damn me for not getting call display. In the end of course curiosity got the best of me.

'H'llo?' I managed.

'Whahh...!' came a sob louder than my alarm.

I sat up. 'Annie, is that you?' My daughter was as stable and balanced as a tanker, her boyfriend Miles a trendy, ambitious yuppie and already ridiculously loaded at twenty-eight. The kind of man most mothers dream about for their daughters. I couldn't stand him personally, but if she was happy, I was happy.

'Gilly...!' came the strangled voice. It was Brends, going through another one of her moments, no doubt.

'What's wrong?' I asked. 'You sound horrible.'

'Never got to bed last night. Rick and I are over. *Over!*'

Well, at least no one had had a fatal accident. I threw my legs over the side of the bed and yawned silently while making sympathetic noises. Her twin Martha, incidentally my other bestie, didn't love drama, at least not her sister's, because it happened roughly every other week and she was sick of it. I was kind of her stand-in, secretly sick of it too, but being her friend and not her blood I *had* to show some degree of sympathy, otherwise what kind of a friend was I?

'Where are you?' I asked.

'I'm at his place. He's gone and I need to move out before he gets back. I never want to see him again!'

'Of course,' I answered, studying my hairy legs. Better get a move-on. The earlier I finished my chores the earlier I could get to the beautician's – no way was I showing up at Tony's hotel room looking like I'd escaped from the set of *Planet of the Apes*.

'Can you come round in your minivan?' she pleaded.

Ah. Bingo.

'Please? I'll never get my stuff out of here in one trip without you, and Martha's busy with the charity bake.'

There was my get-out card. 'So am I. I have to bake four cakes and get them there before four o'clock this afternoon, plus I promised to help my neighbor declutter and—'

'Please?' she whined again.

Ooff. If I said no, I'd be a shit. But if I said yes, would I manage to squeeze everything else in before my flight? I knew Brends; there was no getting rid of her once she started.

I groaned as silently as I could. 'Be over in twenty.'

'Gilly, you're an absolute star!' she chimed and hung up.

Not even out of bed yet and already my day was screwed.

'Be over in a bit, Mrs. Collins, promise!' I called over my shoulder to Ancient Agatha, the old biddy next door, who's as deaf as a doornail, as dried up as a raisin and half-blind to boot, with practically one foot and four toes in the grave but resilient as hell. She's always threatening to die, the ambulance visiting at least once a month but it would always be a false alarm, thank God. Whenever she was home she'd beg us to take her to the hospital and when she was in the hospital she'd beg us to take her home. But I don't know what I'd do without seeing her dear old face at the front window looking out onto the heath and watching the world go by, fantasizing a life she'd never had. Or maybe even remembering one she'd had. Who knew?

Centuries ago, I'd promised her daughter I'd keep an eye on

her to make sure someone was there when she eventually did keel over. And then, because I was apparently so trustworthy, in due time I'd also inherited her eight-year-old grandson Alfie whose parents left him there twenty-four seven because they couldn't (and still can't) afford summer childcare. You'd think with a grandmother living in Blackheath money would be no issue.

'What *took* you so long?' Brends squealed as I pulled up.

'Don't push it,' I warned her, my poor back already threatening to give out at the sight of all her stuff and my reserve of sympathy rapidly dissolving. 'Sorry-about-Rick-let's-get-going,' I huffed. 'I promised to help my neighbor declutter before I left for Sicily.'

We (meaning I) hefted her armchair from Rick's doorstep to my minivan while she followed me, pretend-clutching one padded chair arm. I was built like an ox, Brends having, au contraire, dainty, delicate bones that could shatter at the slightest effort.

'You're a real pushover,' Brends scolded me.

'You would know,' I grunted as I lifted the armchair into the back.

'Let her do her own decluttering,' Heart of Gold sentenced. 'Serves her right for hoarding all that crap all those years.'

'You would know,' I repeated. 'Why didn't you get one of your other hot male friends to help you?'

'Ha,' she retorted as I pushed the armchair in as far as it would go while she lit a cigarette. 'Men are only good for one thing.'

Was that a universal truth or what? Hubby excluded, of course. I swear, sometimes I wondered why Brends even bothered hooking up with someone new when all the guys ever did was break her heart. Probably because she knew I'd always be there for her. I know I never had a moment to myself, but what was I going to do if I couldn't be of help to those who needed it?

I also know my altruistic attitude was probably a not-so-knee-jerk reaction to my mother's lifestyle. She never gave a hoot about anyone, Dad especially. I would never want to be like her.

So yes, I did make myself useful. Maybe because I wanted people to love me because as a kid I wasn't very loved – all the sort of stuff a therapist would tell you at a hundred bucks an hour. But if helping others made me happy, where was the harm in that? And hopefully, it would be spread to those around me, especially Brends who needed to see the world beyond her own nose.

Did I just imply she was selfish? I stand corrected.

'Here,' she said tossing me a tiny plastic jar of tablets, which I caught in midair, courtesy of years of life-juggling. A woman's reflexes are paramount if she's going to survive in this circus of a world.

'What are these?'

'For your flight. I know you're terrified.'

'So you're giving me your tranquilizers?'

Brends shrugged. 'I can get some stronger stuff from my doctor friend. *Your* husband won't even prescribe you vitamins. Don't take more than two though, okay?'

'I don't need drugs to keep my cool, but thanks anyway,' I said, but she pushed my hand away.

'When you're on that runway and that engine roars into life, you'll be blessing my soul, believe you me.'

'Right,' I said, pocketing them and making a mental note to throw them out later.

Now only the cakes, Annie's suitcase and Jumbo-Gemma were left, meaning I had precisely one hour to turn into Mary Berry, Pickfords, and the fastest dog drop-off service all rolled into one *and* drive myself to the airport. And oh – mustn't forget my waxing appointment.

Cakes baked, cooled and finally iced, I threw myself in and out of the shower in six minutes flat, my wet hair dripping over my clean sundress and down into my neckline as I tripped over Jumbo-Gemma who broke my fall, which was rather fortunate considering I'd narrowly missed the stack of cakes already in their boxes by the door waiting to go. Phew. That had been close.

So there I was, dashing out of the house like a madwoman,

juggling extremely dainty boxes of pretty cakes, the last of Annie's suitcases, my own *Sesame Street* number on wheels (an old gift from my dad), Jumbo-Gemma's leash in my mouth, said Jumbo-Gemma attached to the other end and dragging me out the door like I was an armless water-skier.

I seat-belted the stack of cakes I'd secured with my huge kneading board so they wouldn't topple and fly all over the dashboard, tied Jumbo-Gemma in the back behind the safety screen, threw both suitcases onto the back seat and jumped into the minivan, flooring it to Annie's to whom I gave a quick hug and kiss with all the usual *keep-in-touch* and other motherly recommendations, unloaded the stack of cakes to Martha in record time, feeling immense satisfaction washing over me. I was done. Free to go and barely on time.

And then, as I pulled into the parking lot at Gatwick, it hit me. After all that, wouldn't you know it? I'd forgotten to wax. Which, as it turned out, was the tiny detail that turned my whole life completely upside down…

1

Ignorance is Bliss

The Aeolian islands, off the northeastern coast of Sicily.
'Lipari! Island of Lipari! Stay on board for Salina!'

Thank you, God. I had finally made it through a three-hour flight and a bloody boat ride without throwing myself at the airplane doors in a panic attack, courtesy of Brends' tranquilizers. It had been a battle of my inner wills, but when the engine screamed before take-off I almost did too and quickly washed at *least* a couple down my throat under the eyes of a snooty, slim woman in a business suit next to me. And they had worked a dream because when I came to, the plane had not only arrived, but was already emptying out.

And now I must have dozed off again in the catamaran from Point Milazzo to the islands because there were only a few stragglers left in the harbor. My white sundress was now so manky from perspiration and sleep and not even a boxful of wet wipes could save me. Grateful for *terra firma*, I slowly hauled myself to my feet, fished for my bag under my seat and followed the throng of vacationers out into the sun, breathing deeply of the fresh sea air.

Lipari! I was finally here, hairy legs and all. If I got to Tony's hotel before dinner I could sneak into his room for a quick shower and borrow his razor. And put on that lace cherry red number I'd been saving for ages...

But first – the fragrance of butter pastry *cornetti* and freshly made espresso coffee were bringing me to my knees. I hadn't eaten a thing on the plane as I'd knocked myself out with Brends' pills. Why don't airline staff wake you when they come round with the food trolleys? They should give us a *Please Wake to Feed* sign to hang around our necks or something. I still felt absolutely wiped out, almost as if I'd crossed the Atlantic by backstroke instead of just flown in the ITA Airbus. And believe you me – *bus* is the word. A bus with wings.

I'd never seen such a small plane – good luck finding bits of that thing in such a vast sea in case of a crash, assuming of course, we crashed in the Med and not on dry land. But we hadn't crashed and here I was, safe and excited, utterly proud of myself. I'd done it! I'd flown alone, although I hoped it would be the last time I'd ever have to do *that*.

Three luxuriously romantic weeks stretched ahead of us, sunning ourselves and bathing (not too deep, though) naked in the moonlight (I wondered if there were any private beaches?) and when we got back Tony and I would start the second (and hopefully sexier) half of our married life together.

And then I remembered my Ernie and Bert trolley. I'd forgotten it on the boat!

I whirled back and tried to fight against the waves of descending passengers to where all the luggage was stacked against a wall. I not-so-patiently waited for everyone in front of me to retrieve their belongings, wheelie suitcases, training bicycles and scooters. But a cursory glance told me my *Sesame Street* number was nowhere to be found. And through my tranquilizer fog, it hit me. *I'd forgotten it at the bus station in Catania airport in my haste to make the bus for Milazzo harbor.*

Crap! *Now* what? I had everything in there: my clothes, my shoes, my cosmetics, even my phone. Now, you might ask, who puts a cell phone in their suitcase? Did I mention that I'm a very organized person but not *quite* the seasoned traveler?

I waited, forlorn, as the ferry emptied completely and then had a pointless last look around lest Saint Christopher, patron saint of travelers, had had pity on me and somehow managed to unload Ernie and Bert from the bus and onto the ferry for me.

My entire arsenal of lingerie and party dresses was lost. How was I ever going to replace it? All my favorite *pièces de résistance* (meaning if he tried to resist me once again it would *pièce* me off royally) were in that damn suitcase, from my Monsoon cocktail gowns to my plus-sized lingerie. Some stuff I already had; other stuff I'd bought on a last impulse to boost my confidence. My marriage and subsequently my whole life were at stake here.

Now, standing amongst the dispersing throng of colorful and loud vacationers, I saw that the square off the harbor was in effect a circle. A roundabout, to be exact. Everywhere I turned cars were double-parking, picking up and dropping off tourists. And the heat? Unbelievable – like standing in the blaze of an open oven door. I ran my tongue over my already parched lips to moisten them and hitched my orphaned bag over my shoulder. At least I had my laptop with me.

Lipari town, as far as I could see, was tiny – a cluster of pastel-colored houses, really. In two steps I was in the center, among the cars and buses with people weaving through them, oblivious to the rules of the road.

I found Tony's hotel immediately and breezed through the sliding front doors, grateful for the rush of cool air and the taste of luxury already embracing me.

'Hello. I'm Gillian Dobson, Dr. Anthony Dobson's wife. He's staying here.'

The Sicilian girl in her white shirt and silk scarf looked up at me, pretending not to notice the sweat stains under my arms. 'Led me see – for de conference?'

'Yes.'

'Dobson... I see no Dobson.'

I leaned over the counter, swallowing, still sleepy and confused. How the hell was I going to find him: visit every single hotel on the island? 'There has to be. He said he was staying here.'

'Led me see again. Dobson... Dobson... ah yes. Apologies. Room 177. Here is your *kaycard*. It's de deluxe suite.'

Deluxe was to say the least of it. White marble-floored bathroom, Jacuzzi bath, shower with all the bells and whistles *and* a water bed. I thought water beds were a thing of the past. And the bathrobe? To die for – soft, white and plush, perfect for the cool temperature of the air-conditioned room, which oozed luxury, second-honeymoon sex. Well, soon – hopefully within the hour, if I had any say.

I immediately glugged down a half bottle of orange juice from the minibar and oh, what had we here? Cookies! A vast assortment, too! And did I see the familiar blue packaging of my all-time faves, *Baci Perugina* hazelnut-centered chocolates? Typically a Valentine's Day treat, for me and every woman in Italy with a choco-holism problem, *Baci Perugina* were practically a staple product in my diet. Diet – ha. Never did a word make me laugh that much. How are you expected to diet when you're surrounded by such scrumptious, gorgeous food, I ask you?

Now, while in the UK, Cadbury chocolate is my weakness, in Italy it's without a doubt *Baci Perugina*. Along with *Ferrero Rocher*, of course, and by the same brand, Ferrero Nutella. Can you even imagine life without Nutella? Nutella is the answer to every woman's problems.

Bad for you? Ha – how do you figure that the inventor of Nutella died in his eighties while inventors of medicine died much younger?

I should've written the slogans for Nutella:

Frustrated because you can't get a raise? Have yourself some Nutella.

Knackered by the end of the day?

Hungry but too lazy to cook?

Dumped by your man?

Nutella – the solution to almost every problem.

Forget the slogans. I should write an *Ode to Nutella* to thank it for all the slumps it had got me out of since I was old enough to twist the cap off on my own. My idea of hell? Chocoholic-proof Nutella jars.

When I'd fished the *Baci* and the *Ferrero Rocher*, I threw myself onto the salted peanuts and crackers, peering into the depths of the not-so-minibar. Was that *ice cream* I saw? Something told me I would be enjoying my stay here very much. Plus if I ate now I wouldn't be ravenous at the dinner table tonight and maybe, for once, I'd actually manage to pass as the dainty girl I used to be pre-motherhood, when Tony and I had no trouble whatsoever in between the sheets.

Before emptying the whole fridge and pissing Tony off, I jumped into the shower to wash the grime of seven hours off me (and to finally shave my legs). I would pamper myself with the contents of all those boutique gels and creams that I never bothered with at home, all the while humming romantic cheesy love songs.

The tranquilizers had been meant to knock me out for only a couple of hours but they must have reacted with something I ate or drank (the wine being a probable candidate) and even after that shower I was sitting on the edge of the tub in my pristine robe, slowly combing the no-rinse conditioner through my hair. Still a little woozy, I had just finished shaving one leg and was about to start the other when the hotel room door burst open, startling me.

'My sexy lady…' he drawled and I grinned. He'd come in with the energy of a full-blown twister. Indiscreet hotel staff. This was supposed to have been a surprise.

Perched on the edge of the tub, I turned to smile at him through the cinch in the door and rose, alarmed. At first I thought he was tripping backwards. But why would he be entering his hotel room backwards? And then because of his jerking movements and a huge, white vase crashing to the floor, I figured he had to be having a stroke. But when he turned I saw that he wasn't. But soon *I* would be, because guess what was attached to him? A woman. And even then (I swear to you) for a split second I thought they were wrestling, so remote from my mind was the idea that this could be happening. That he could be *kissing* another woman. Because there they were, mouth on mouth, hands grabbing and tossing off clothes like they were on fire.

'Oh, *Tony*...' the woman moaned.

'Oh, *Nadia*...' he echoed.

'Oh, *God*...' I screamed as the entire world stopped and he turned around, his eyes widening in horror.

'Gillian!'

A demolition ball had just swung its way into the room and straight into my chest as I tried to breathe, barely registering my surroundings now, trying to make some sense of it. The room swaying and my sight dimming weren't helping much either.

Wait, wait. Lemme get this straight. I'm in my husband's hotel room in Sicily after braving a three-hour flight, still sleepy from the tranquilizers and – that's it! I'm asleep – none of this is actually happening. It's just a... what do you call it? A figment of my imagination.

'What... what are you doing here?' the figment demanded.

Terrific question. What *was* I doing here, in this, this deluxe House of Shag? How had I even got to this place? I tried to remember, but my life just before this moment was gone.

I tried to focus on the face of the man I'd married almost twenty years ago, and all I saw was a blurry, fuzzy image. 'What *am* I doing here?' I asked him and, unable to think or feel, I instinctively turned and stumbled out of the still-open door, careening down an endless corridor in my (well, technically *his*) terry-towel robe and coordinated flip-flops, down a flight of stairs and out into the blinding light of the busy street.

★

Run. Run. Far. As far as I could from this nightmare. Why – *how* – had this even happened to us? Why was he sleeping with other women? Didn't he love me anymore? And if not, when did he fall out of love with me? What had I done to deserve this? Was I not caring and loving enough? Had we drifted that far apart without even realizing it? Or perhaps I was the blind one and he'd been planning this all along?

Don't you get it yet? said a voice inside me. *She's young. Fit. Gorgeous.*

Sick to my stomach, I dashed across the sweltering street into a bar and reached the bathroom just in the nick of time. There was no doubt that people's emotions were connected to their guts, but my gut was probably sitting on my heart instead. Or maybe it was my minibar splurge, who knows? The stomach has reasons that reason cannot understand.

I stuck my head down the toilet bowl for what seemed like hours as every source of pain tried to squeeze its way out of me along with my minibar sins. But before I could release it, the anguish pushed its way back down again, and I had to fight harder and harder to expel something that just didn't want to leave me. Because I knew I couldn't let go of the status quo that I'd been living with all this time. Grasping the reality of the facts had been almost impossible for me at this stage. Was she a one-nighter or were they having an ongoing affair?

'What *difference* does it make?' I wailed to myself. My husband was sleeping with someone else; wasn't that enough?

He didn't love me passionately and I wasn't the woman of his life after all. I was just an idiot. An idiot who'd sacrificed her life all these years for the love of her young family. And in one split second my whole world had shifted on its axis once again, inverting its trajectory completely. Another person had come between us, and I would not be able to forgive him. Ever.

And neither was I willing to be his doormat for another twenty years. Twenty *years* – bar a few months – we'd been married. Twenty years of *lies*? While I gave him my all, and more? How can someone who says he loves you, has shared a bed with you, actually *do* that to you?

I paused and tuned in to my body. My stomach seemed to have given all it would for now, having somehow plateaued out into a sense of equilibrium. And now it was my heart that was about to explode. Served me right to have a coronary in the john of a café gazillions of miles from home instead of staying put like the good little wife that I was and waiting (none the wiser) for my man to come home.

This was all Brends' fault. If I hadn't had to run off and help her fix her own life, I'd have managed to wax before my flight out, meaning I wouldn't have wasted all that time in his hotel room shaving, meaning I would've gone looking for him at the conference. Meaning that I would've surprised him in his hotel room, fully dressed and professional-looking, meaning I'd have probably never found out about *her*.

And now, what did I have, besides a cheating husband and one hairy leg?

To think I believed that now Annie had grown up, we'd be able to have some time for us – the rest of our lives. But now he wanted out. To think that all this time I'd tried to justify his coldness when I didn't live up to his standards with my shortcomings – the things I'd done wrong, done too late, too soon or not done at all. Not only that, the *frisson* of excitement was long gone. He'd found it with someone else who was much better than me in every way. All you had to do was take one good look at her and compare her to what I must've looked like all these years in my housewear and ponytails.

His implicit message was, obviously, *Don't get too comfortable around me*. Always be at your best, as if you were just bumping into me on a night out and not, say, in the corridor on your way to the bathroom. Because, while you might feel comfy and happy and safe and at home with me, I'm watching you and taking notes, tallying up all the times you look like shit.

Heaving a rattled breath like a dying nonagenarian, I splashed some freezing water onto my face and took a good look in the mirror. Jesus. My once happy (-ish) face had transformed into a blotchy mess with dark canyons under my eyes. There were new lines between my eyebrows and some even around my mouth now. My whole face looked like a geological experiment gone bad.

Hell, when had all this happened to me? When did I become this old? Had it been a slow, year-after year process that I hadn't noticed, all the while slapping expensive goo onto my face, trying to ignore every new wrinkle and thinking all was okay, as long as my family was solid? Or did it happen just now, the second I saw Tony with that woman?

Tall, slim, lithe. Long dark hair. An exotic look. Definitely a local. A gorgeous, young, sexy local. The exact opposite of me. And he'd "befriended" her in, what? Two weeks?

How many times had this happened before? What if this was a constant pattern? What if he did it all the time? How the hell would I know, sitting at home amongst my pretty things sipping coffee with my friends? How the hell would I ever know if he had one, two or ten lovers? I'd trusted him with my life – my *heart* – completely.

How can you have been so wrong? I asked the mess in the mirror with the eyes of a madwoman. Oh God, if this was how one aged overnight, I'd just broken the record. We were, I suddenly realized what doctors had been saying for decades, not only what we ate (which was more than enough to make *me* look like shit), but we were also what happened to us. And how we lived our lives, the decisions that we made. We wore our entire lives on our faces and bodies.

I dug into my pockets for a much-needed tissue, but couldn't find any. And there was no toilet paper to speak of. So I exited the bar and tore a couple of thin, scratchy tissues from the dispenser on one of the café tables while no one was looking. Only I'd grabbed a whole bunch and watched in dismay as they took flight on the afternoon breeze like seagulls gently gliding without a care in the world. Just like Tony's love, they scattered to the four winds, forever lost.

I swiped at my eyes and blew my nose with the tattered tissues. They completely disintegrated as I rubbed them over my face and as I picked the bits off, I wished I could also rub the unhappiness away with my tears, oblivious of the people who were staring at me like I was a nutter of some sort. Well, yeah – I had to be completely insane not to notice my husband was bonking younger women.

The sun could've fried an egg on my head and I'm sure my brain was already at a boiling point, but I charged on amidst the traffic, feeling sorry for myself and wondering how I'd managed to lose everything that had been dear to me. Oh, to see a friendly face now! I didn't even have my cell to call anyone back home. I'd never felt so alone in my life.

Still dizzy and now sick and exhausted, I stopped, confused and overwhelmed, trying to get my bearings among the cars whizzing by at a busy intersection.

'Gillian! Gillian!'

I turned in horror at the sound of Tony's voice as he ran after me, but he was still far behind. Obviously he couldn't have been in that much of a hurry to catch me. Tony had always been one for appearances, only starting to do something for me, only seeming to make unselfish gestures, like setting the table when in reality he was simply reaching for a bottle of wine and a glass for himself. Only thinking about himself. So now this gesture of chasing me was totally wasted on me.

'Gillian, stop! I need to talk to you!'

But I turned away, letting out a sob as I tried to put as much distance as possible between me and the immense pain ripping my heart open.

'Go away,' I cried over my shoulder as I ran, my flip-flops slowing me down (not that I was an Olympic sprinter by nature, mind you). And then an unnatural screech filled the air as a huge dark vehicle hurtled toward me.

2

Hotel Cassandra

Someone was shaking me by the shoulders, yelling at me. A man, red-faced and wild-eyed. Tony…?

'*Che cazzo fai? Sei pazza?*' the someone bellowed. No, not Tony, and I had no idea who he was, nor what he was on about. I was most certainly dreaming again. Soon I'd wake up, any second now, with the taste of sleep in my mouth, and this whole morning would disappear and I'd be back in my bed in the wee hours and this day wouldn't have even started. I wouldn't have answered the phone, forgotten to wax or lost my suitcase.

But it didn't happen. I didn't wake up. Because I wasn't sleeping, wasn't dreaming.

All I knew was that only hours ago I was baking cakes in London. On my own, yes, but at least in familiar territory. And then I remembered the minibar, Tony and his lover.

'*Ti potevo ammazzare!*' the man threatened and I covered my ears as his face contorted into the strangest shapes like in a kaleidoscope, a few Italian words clear to me in all that senseless babble.

Kill me? Why did he want to kill me? I didn't even know the guy. And then I turned, saw that traffic had come to a standstill, skid marks on the road, the stench of burnt rubber and the upturned rubbish skip and a blur of onlookers craning their necks, probably hoping to see a gory show. Had I been run over?

Was I hurt? I desperately tried to feel my body but my mind was hazy. I couldn't think or feel a thing.

I turned the other way to see a black Jeep smashed against a wall. Okay. I got it. The guy had swerved and braked to avoid me. I was, in effect, lying in the middle of a crash scene. The mad Italian was right – he could've killed me. But he didn't. I was still alive. And still cheated on, betrayed and lonelier and more lost than ever.

The mad Italian seemed to have calmed down and was now studying me like you do with wackos. He took a deep breath. 'Are you all right?'

I nodded, in the sense that I was alive, albeit far from all right.

'What's your name?'

'Gillian,' I sniffed.

'Where are your clothes, Gillian?'

I looked down and gasped at the spillage of my boobs like two huge scoops of vanilla ice cream and clutched the lapels to my throat, shaking.

'Gillian! My God, are you okay?' Tony wheezed as he reached us, holding his sides. 'What the hell, man? Are you trying to kill her?' he demanded of the Italian, like he really cared. As if. The guy was doing him a favor.

'Gillian, I'm sorry you had to find out like this,' Tony managed, his breath sawing in and out of him. 'We need to talk. Come back to the hotel with me.'

'The hell I'm going back there!' I cried, suddenly bawling – really going for it. 'Go away!'

Tony made a move to touch me and I instinctively screamed. The mere idea of his hands on me made my heart break a million times over. The Italian pulled me out of Tony's reach, suddenly protective.

'She doesn't want to talk to you,' he said in very good English. 'Leave her alone.'

'She is my wife!' Tony bellowed.

'Not anymore!' I sobbed, that being my only certainty. I didn't know what I'd be doing the next hour, let alone for the rest of my life which, under different circumstances, would have sounded like a big slice of freedom, away from my chores and duties. All my life I'd soldiered on, always with plans, something on my daily or weekly agenda. I could always look ahead and know exactly what I would be doing. I was linked to my life, well connected to it. I had my appointments and my to-do lists and plans that kept me grounded and going.

And now, like a dinghy's rope that had been severed from the master ship, I was drifting. Bereft. My home (or at least my idea of home) had been shattered. Smashed into smithereens.

The Italian took my face in his now gentle hands so I was looking up into his eyes. The crowd was still a faceless blur, which was just as well. Being caught out in public wearing just my robe, on this, the worst day of my life, was something I wanted to forget.

'Gillian? I want to take you to the *pronto soccorso* and have a doctor look at you. Is that okay?' the Italian asked.

'I'm fine,' I managed to sniff as I scrambled to my feet. The Italian was standing guard lest I should fall, but I managed to salvage the remaining shreds of my dignity.

'You're not taking her anywhere!' Tony yelled. 'I'm a doctor and I'll take care of her.'

But when Tony lurched for me the Italian stepped between us, his voice deep and menacing. 'Stay away. I'm warning you.'

I stared up at him, blurry-eyed, but I could see that he was angry, almost as if, by some strange form of empathy, he knew me and the agony of my humiliation, and then I glanced at Tony, who still had no idea of the damage he'd done to me. If anything, he stared at me as if *I'd* ruined *his* life and then he finally turned back in the direction of the hotel, still holding his side and shaking his head.

A siren announced the arrival of a police car and two agents descended, talking to the Italian who nodded and beckoned for me to follow him to his smashed Jeep. What else did I have to lose?

As he backed out of the railing one of the agents poked his head in and the Italian turned to him. 'I'll stop by later, Paolo,' he said and the agent dipped his head, not without eyeing me. Boy, I must've looked like a real prize in my robe and my hair all frizzy despite the conditioner. And now what was I going to do?

'I'm sorry to cause you all this trouble,' I whispered, my lower lip going for it again, sorry he hadn't killed me in the first place. As a matter of fact, maybe he'd just given me a great idea. I could throw myself under another vehicle (with my luck it would be a garbage truck) and get it over with. No more suffering, no more worrying. (Who was I kidding? The minute I saw a drop of my own blood I'd panic like a madwoman.)

He glanced at me. 'No trouble.'

'But I wrecked your Jeep...'

'It's fine. We need to get you out of this sun.'

And then I closed my eyes.

'...Gillian? Gillian, can you 'ear me?' came a gentle female voice. Martha? Brends? Was I home, sleeping on my sofa? Had none of that happened after all? Relief that Tony hadn't cheated on me and that everything was okay began to flood through me, but then I heard the voice perfectly clearly again. Only I couldn't form the words to answer her.

'She's in shock – a delayed reaction,' the other voice – a deep male voice said. 'She's had one hell of a morning.'

And then strong arms – they sure had to be – were lifting me and I heard a door swing open. And then I was warm, in my own bed again, wrapped up in blankets and something warm – a hot water bottle? – on my tummy.

'Drink this,' said the male voice, but I couldn't make his face out in the dim light. I opened my mouth and swallowed. Yuck. Brandy or something. I coughed but forced it down.

'Is she going to be okay?' came the female voice in Italian.

'She'll be fine.'

'Oh, the poor woman…' she whispered.

Then it was true after all. Tony had another woman.

'She'll get over it soon, I hope,' he replied.

Get over what, I wondered. Post-Jilt Stress Syndrome?

When I opened my eyes a female face appeared in my line of vision. Orangey-brown skin that had seen too many sun-tan beds, with coats of foundation spread across a pretty face that was closer to fifty than forty. Thick mascara framed huge green cat eyes and when she spoke her voice was so gravelly it sounded like she'd just discarded a dog-end and was going for the next any second.

''ello, 'ow do you feel?' she croaked in English.

Where was I? And how long had I been here? I was feeling like crap, too tight in my own burning skin, and my head was spinning. I probably had a lulu of a fever. I tried to lift my head again but she placed a cold cloth on it and gently pushed me back.

'Easy. You must lie down. You 'ave sun-strowwk. Don't worry about anything. Mattia 'as brought your bag and your dress.'

My bag. My dress. I'd run out of the hotel as fast as I could, leaving everything behind. Not that there had been much to leave. Just a marriage of almost twenty years. My head fell back onto an amazingly comfy pillow as tears welled up in my eyes again.

'Oh, poor you,' she said, taking my hand.

I soon found out that their names were Cassandra (Sandra) Anselmi and Mattia Spadaro. She was what I thought most sophisticated Italian women looked like – halfway between Nancy Dell'Olio and Monica Bellucci – who was Tony's not-so-secret passion. Sandra had a tiny wasp-waist and really groovy, short wavy hair dyed a million different colors at the same time and none in particular. It stood on end because she had so much of it. She was sexy and extremely confident. No husband was leaving *her*. In fact, as she chatted away amicably and spoon-fed me a bowl of soup, she told me all about herself. It turned out she'd left her *first* husband in Milan after he'd smacked her across the side of her head for the umpteenth time. She'd applied for an English teaching job in Lipari, which she readily got because no one else wanted to spend their winters here.

As the minutes passed by, even her heavy accent seemed to fade and I hardly noticed her missing *h*'s. And she was fluent in English, which was a blessing, considering that I, despite what I'd thought, wasn't completely so in Italian.

'Mattia told me about your 'usband. I'm sorry.'

I shrugged, drained.

''e is angry?'

'Ha,' I shot back. 'I'm the one who's angry.' To put it mildly, I was murderous. He should hope I never laid eyes on him again because I was sure I'd kill him.

'Is there someone else we can call?'

'No,' I almost shouted. 'There's no one to call. And he's not my husband anymore.'

'That woman he was with – I know her. Her name is Nadia Tomaselli.'

'Who, the tramp?'

Sandra looked at me with the same dismay that you look at your huge jar of precious Nutella that has fallen to the floor and cracked wide open.

'Nadia Tomaselli is the daughter of a world-famous surgeon. He owns a string of private clinics in Sicily, Northern Italy, Germany, Belgium and Switzerland. She herself is a corporate lawyer who works for the company. Everyone here knows about them. But I didn't know he was married!'

It figured. Did this mean she wasn't just a ditsy fling? This was his chance at living his Italian Babe Dream. And, apparently, she was also smart. What the hell chances had I ever had, in the light of all that?

So Lipari hadn't simply been a random choice. It was his love nest. If only I'd known he was cheating on me, I would've never scared the crap out of myself by flying and sailing over here on my own in hot pursuit of a cold husband.

Cold only toward me, though. I'd seen the way he kissed her, his lips milking hers as if she was transferring money through her mouth to him. Which, in fact, come to think of it, she was. (If she really was that rich, you don't even have to do the math.)

I was toast – had been for quite a while without even knowing it. The whole thing dawned on me like a big black cloud the size of an alien mother ship obscuring my once-sunny, hopeful horizons. But the shadow of it was too much to overcome. Numb as hell, I lay there, curling up deeper and deeper in the bed as Sandra gave me a gentle but thorough update.

They'd met at a three-day conference in London. (When?) My home turf. Hit it off immediately. Especially in bed that same evening, Sandra's sources had informed her. Nadia had prolonged her stay and in the space of a week they were an item.

'The wife is always the last to know,' I muttered.

'There's more—' Sandra bit her lip.

I groaned. 'Go on. How much worse can it be?'

Sandra's eyes softened. 'They're getting engaged.'

What? Not only did he have a new woman, they were *engaged*?

Yes, apparently. And he'd told her that before formally asking her parents for her hand, he needed time to set his affairs straight (me, ironically being the affair). Her family were filthy-rich Sicilian nobles who continued to make their own money in the medical field.

'Her father is absolutely smitten by Tony.'

Of all the sleazy, cheating husband-doctors in London, she had to pick *mine*? And here he was, about to start again afresh with her while referring to me as his *first wife*, the one that had got everything wrong, the one to be forgotten and thank *God* this Nadia tramp had arrived to fix his life. OK, maybe she's not a tramp. I'm upset, is all.

But what did she know about him? Only I could put up with his hang-ups and shenanigans. Just wait until this new girl came into contact with the *real* Tony – the one who left his dirty laundry (but let's not go there) on the bathroom floor. And picked his nose with one long surgical finger when he thought no one was looking. No, the glamorous gal would be running for the hills in no time.

Sandra was shaking her head. '*Cara* – it's not worth it. There is no stopping men like him. Believe me – I know his kind.'

I swiped at my suddenly flooded cheeks. I hadn't realized Tony *was* that kind.

'What are you going to do now?' Sandra asked.

Terrific question. What was I going to do now – *and* for the rest of my life? 'I don't know, I don't know...'

'Tell you what. You stick with me and Mattia. We'll take care of you.'

'Thank you so much, but I'm okay. I just need to find a hotel or a B&B.'

Sandra laughed. 'In August? That's very funny. No, you stay with us.'

'But I can't accept. My flight back is in three weeks.'

Three weeks? Had I just said three weeks? Was I staying *that* long? What the hell for? Books two, three, four and five of the *Tony Meets Younger Woman* saga? Why didn't I just get out of there before it really sank in?

'I can't impose on you that long. Unless I can pay rent.'

She smiled. 'You talk to me in English and we're even.'

'What? No, I can't accept that.'

'I'm serious. I need to speak more English. I teach English but you hear my accent? Even Mattia's accent is milder than mine.'

She did have a point, but nonetheless we agreed I'd pay a token sum and I made her swear not to blow my cover. I didn't want anyone to know I'd been deserted by my husband. Soon to be *ex*-husband, that is. It was embarrassing enough without the whole of the island's 10k population – plus another twenty thousand tourists, according to my guidebook – knowing about how pathetic old me had lost her husband to a younger, thinner, exotic babe.

'Stay as long as you want, Gillian. Get your bearings. You need time to heal.'

'Heal…' I whispered to myself. Now how the hell did one do that?

So we agreed. I would stay until my flight back (which I tried not to think about) and help her improve her English and cook their meals because judging by the soup she'd fed me, she could barely boil water, while Mattia looked like the kind of guy who enjoyed the best of life, food and wine included.

And in the meantime I had so much to figure out – how to tell Annie, first of all, and how to cope, how to start all over again and oh, yeah, *how the hell all this happened to us*. I couldn't just go home and wait for Tony to come back for his things. And say what, exactly? *Welcome back home, honey – did you have a good shag at the conference?*

And besides – with the Italian babe in his arms, would he even come home at all?

Without my husband of twenty years, what else did I have in the UK, apart from my two best friends, Brends and Martha? My daughter Annie would be living in Spain, so what else was there waiting for me? I had no career to speak of, was eminently unemployable at my age and had no prospects. I'd focused my whole life around my loved ones and now I had a big fat nothing to show for it. Just the thought made me want to curl up and die. Or, at least, sleep for the rest of my lonely life.

'Tomorrow things won't seem that horrible,' Sandra soothed. 'Try and get some sleep, now, Gillian.'

'Thank you,' I whispered obediently through droopy eyes.

In the middle of the night, I woke up. Exhausted but wired at the same time, I breathed in the fresh scent of the crisp, clean sheets and tiptoed down the dark corridor to the bathroom where a night light shone, which was lucky for me because the last thing I needed was to end up in Sandra and Mattia's bedroom by mistake, possibly, with my luck, while they were bloody doing it. Dropping in on someone else's sex scene twice in twenty-four hours – now that would be a record I challenge anyone to break.

It felt so odd, being in someone else's house in the middle of the night, a house that I could distinguish from my own with my eyes closed. Funny, how every house has its smell. I took a deep breath and examined the odors: predominant, the sea breezing through the open windows, like a light cloud, intermingling with the pleasant smell of a loved and lived-in house; some girlie deodorant that smelt like… oranges and lemons. And then a smell of some male shower gel. Which was faint but undeniable.

Here I was, an absolute stranger among their things, their furniture, their toiletries on the bathroom shelves instead of mine and Tony's. Obviously Sandra was the messy one, while Mattia's stuff neatly occupied only one shelf. Deodorant. A razor. Male shampoo. No Rogaine or similar to speak of. The guy did have a lot of hair, if I remembered correctly from the few confused moments I'd seen him.

I wondered how long they'd lived here, what Mattia did for a living, thinking that if they had any kids I'd have seen at least one by now. And yet it seemed like they'd been married for ages, so comfortable with each other and yet so fresh. Tony and I were like bread that had gone hard. So hard the minute you touched us we crumbled into a million pieces. We hadn't been able to stand the proverbial test of time.

But in my heart I knew it had nothing to do with familiarity breeding contempt or whatever idiocies they say to justify the end of a marriage. He just didn't love me anymore. The thrill was gone, yada yada yada. How thick had I been to not understand it? Had he tired of me, Gilly Wallflower (as he called me), because I didn't fit in with his crowd? Or because of the way I looked?

My body was not what it used to be. As a plastic surgeon, he was used to perfect breasts – or rather, *sculpting* perfect breasts.

I double-checked the bathroom door was locked and took off my nightgown to study myself in the full-length mirror. Face – still pleasant, although a hint of a double chin surfacing. Eyes, still green, although much sadder. Boobs – not too bad for a nearly forty-year-old woman who had breast-fed, but still, nowhere near the perfection Tony was now used to. His lover had twenty-year-old boobs that didn't even know what a stretch mark was, and she must have had a steel pelvic floor.

Thinking about it, he was brilliant at avoiding intimacy with me. Either he'd go to bed before me, claiming exhaustion and feigning sleep when I turned in, or he stayed up long after me, often sleeping in the guest room so he "wouldn't wake" me. When I'd removed the bed linen from the guest bed, he made do with the coverlet. Without saying a word, he had officially moved out of my bed.

And it suddenly dawned on me that our things would never sit together on the same shelf ever again, nor would we never actually sit together in the same room save for when around our daughter.

What was Tony doing right now, besides the obvious? Did he realize how much he'd hurt me? Why had he chased after me at all? Out of decency? No decent man did what he'd done to me. And what the hell could he have said to me that would make the thorns in my heart dissolve? I suppose he'd just wanted to alleviate his guilty conscience so he could live happily ever after. Make sure I was okay with it and all. Well, I was *not* okay with it in the least. I wished I'd never met him. If I could do that but still have given birth to Annie, my whole life would be made. Who needed him?

I closed my eyes and tried to stifle the sobs. The last thing I wanted to do was wake up these kind people in the middle of the night, so I tiptoed back to my room as quietly as possible and stepped through the open French doors onto the balcony. We were at least three floors high. (Holy crap – had Mattia carried me all the way? Tony could barely carry me to the bed. Though now, in retrospect, I realized he hadn't even wanted to.)

The flat was right on the corner of a narrow alley, but very central, as the next intersection up was the main drag.

It was fantastic that you actually didn't need to drive anywhere in the town center. As a matter of fact, not needing a car would be a great help for my finances, which, luckily, were not a problem as I had good old Nana's inheritance to fall back on. Everything I needed (knives, guns, crossbow and bazooka for any eventual jealous rampages) would be here and public transportation was very good, said my guidebook. A bus went round the island every twenty minutes. No place on the island was more than thirty minutes away. Yikes, that was *tiny*.

But what was I actually going to do here for three whole weeks? Why didn't I just fly home instead of hiding away here? Sooner or later everyone would find out anyway. I couldn't hide forever, right? But being me, I wasn't ready to face the music yet. Sandra was right. I needed time to heal, if that was ever going to happen at all. And when my three weeks were up I'd have to go back home. And do what, I didn't know. Get a job, for sure. And put back the pieces of my life. The question was: *How do you put a broken heart back together again?*

3

Size Isn't Everything

The next morning I woke up – still teary-eyed – to the absolute silence of an empty house. On the kitchen table lay a pot of hot espresso and a delicious selection of croissants and pastries filled with jam, ricotta, cream and Nutella. There was also a note:

> *Good morning!*
>   *At work. These are our numbers if you need us. Will be back around a quarter to two with lunch. Try and relax!*
>   *Sandra and Mattia*
>   *P.S.: Your bag is in your wardrobe.*

My bag? Thank God! I made a beeline for it, spilling out the contents onto the bed as if I could recuperate my entire life, or at least up until yesterday, when I was blissfully ignorant of Tony's betrayal and I thought I was a happy(-ish) woman.

Wallet, passport, house keys (ha), my turquoise scarf, a packet of almonds, a juice box, my laptop, pomegranate lip balm, a bottle of Jo Malone and a pair of oversized Chanel shades. And a packet of liquefied *Ferrero Rocher*, only the gold wrapping left, along with a gooey chocolate mess at the bottom of my bag. And, on the dresser, my white sundress and undergarments, clean and dry. Sandra was an absolute doll.

Luckily I had managed to get some euros in Catania airport.

That was a thing, now, like it or not. Tony and I shared a bank account. And I began to wonder just how much of our money had gone toward his lust-trips, because obviously this was not the first time.

We would now have to sell the house and split our assets down the middle. Luckily I had my Nana's inheritance to tide me over, but as I'd learned from my parents' divorce, the money goes faster than you can say *heartache*.

So I'd have to be smarter than them. I'd have to find myself a steady income that would leave my inheritance intact. The minute I started dipping into that, it was the end. But good luck finding a job at almost forty. Doing what? I hadn't worked since Annie was born, and even then I only wanted to be a homemaker.

Putting my financial worries to the back of my mind for now, I concentrated on the day ahead of me, the first of my single life. These kind people had taken me in when I had absolutely nowhere to go, so first thing, I had to get some supplies to cook up Sandra and Mattia a storm for dinner. I had promised to earn my keep. Food. Now why did that always sound like a great idea to me?

I walked out once again onto the balcony. Down below, off to the side, was a small orchard, the fragrance of lemon and orange blossoms wafting up to me. I inhaled deeply and realized that was what I'd smelt last night. What a gorgeous corner of the world this was. And to think I'd never thought much about the sprinkling called *Isole Eolie* on my ma's map of Italy. Tony had picked a great theater for his betrayal.

From where I stood I couldn't see the sea, but I had an amazing view of all the buzz of the main road. Now music was playing from a booth advertising – I could barely read the yellow sign – a shuttle bus? – and boat rides to and fro from the various beaches. I leaned on the railing and watched as two young girls in sarongs (didn't anybody wear any *real* clothes on this island?) sashayed across the road.

Beautiful people going about their business without a care in the world. Me, I barely made it to the dresser, so hard was my head throbbing and so tight was my skin bunching up my muscles and joints, like a bag too small for all my goods.

After a shower I slipped into my only clothes and went out for a walk around in the shade of the narrow back streets, avoiding the sun-drenched main *corso*. The last thing I needed to do was bump into Tony and his... *alternative* female company.

First thing I needed to do was track down my suitcase. Using the public phone by the kiosk selling bus tickets, it took me a good ten minutes to finally get through to someone at Catania airport despite the fact that I had jotted down the direct number from the website and had written it in my personal agenda.

'When did you fly to Catania?' the rep asked me for the second time. I smothered a huff and, pinching the bridge of my nose, repeated the dates to her. She had my flight number, name and everything. What was so difficult? As she tapped away, taking longer than the first draft of the Magna Carta, I literally suppressed a howl.

'When wos de last time you saw your lugg-*age*?' she asked. Next she'd ask me to describe it to her again and ask me if I had a recent picture of it.

'I forgot it at your shuttle bus station but I'm hoping someone brought it to the Lost and Found?'

There was a distinct silence. Even the tapping had stopped. 'Lost and Found?'

'You do have one, right?'

She sighed. '*Signora*, if you take de lugg-age outside airport, we can't 'elp you,' was the answer.

'But... but... isn't the shuttle bus part of the company?' I tried to argue, although I already knew it was a dead duck.

Another pause, during which I swear I could hear the cogs in her mind. Efficiency finally kicking in? 'No, *signora*. Bus company is separ-*ate*. You must call *dem*.' And with that, she thanked me for contacting the airline's help desk and hung up before I could get *any* help. And that was that.

Next, I dug into my bag and pulled out the receipt for the shuttle ride and dialed the number and waited to be connected. And that was when an automated message (in Italian of course) kicked in, offering me a series of options. But none were what I needed. I swear, as the female voice led me round the houses there was a distinct smugness in her tone.

I get impatient with this automated crap at home at the best of times – imagine what it was like trying to understand what the disembodied voice was saying as I hung on to the mouthpiece in the booth while cars, buses and taxis honked for dear life on the roundabout. Even ferries and boats belched out their baritone foghorns in the distance and I could barely hear my own voice. Absolute Italian mayhem. Why hadn't Tony chosen a quiet atoll in the Pacific to betray me?

When I finally managed to speak to someone it was to be told that nothing had been reported as found (as if), but in the event of the contrary (I'm translating directly for you here) I could be sure my *child* would have his *Sesame Street* suitcase back as soon as possible. Served me right, didn't it? Other people had classy cases, but not me, oh no. I had to go and be sentimental. That suitcase had been a gift from my father when I was a kid.

And speaking of life-long buddies, I dialed Martha's number. If I knew her, she'd be having coffee and Hobnobs in the garden with Brends and chewing her out about Rick.

'Hey...' I called down the phone when she picked up.

'Gilly – is that you?'

'Yuh,' I squeaked, cursing myself. *Steady, girl.* You must be really messed up if the mere sound of a beloved voice makes you want to bawl like crazy.

'I'm putting you on speakerphone. Brends is here. How's Sicily?' Martha asked.

Ack. I swallowed.

'Gilly? What's wrong?'

'Nothing,' I answered all too quickly. Who was I kidding? This was Martha and Brends, my longest-standing buddies. I huffed, trying to choke back the tears. 'It's Tony...'

'Is he okay?' Martha asked, and I could hear the scrape of a chair.

'He's done something, hasn't he?' Brends said. How did that one *know* every time?

I swallowed again. 'I... caught him...'

'Shut *up*...!'

'...and she's younger... *so* much younger...' and then I coughed, trying to fight the tidal wave of tears. The hurt, anger and rage made me physically ill.

'That bastard!' Brends pounded on something solid, possibly a table.

'Come home,' Martha said.

'And we'll hatch a plan to get back at the scumbag,' Brends promised.

'No, it's okay.' I rubbed my forehead but the weight wouldn't budge from it. 'I'm going to stay here for a while. With some friends.'

'Male?' Brends wanted to know. 'Because at this point, you're entitled to some of your own fun, you know?'

'Brends, will you shut up?' Martha said. 'Sorry, Gilly. Go on.'

'You guys would love them – she's a cross between the two of you.' But probably more like Brends, come to think of it.

'How long are you staying?'

I shrugged as if they could see me. 'I might as well stay the whole three weeks. I mean, I paid for it, didn't I? I need time to recover from this.'

Brends snorted. 'Good luck. You may never recover... What...? What did I say?'

'Never mind Brenda,' Martha said. 'You take as long as you need, sweetheart.'

'Do you want us to come out? I'll clock the bloody tosser for you,' Brends promised.

I tried to laugh but it came out in a strangled sound. 'No. That's okay.' But I sure wished I could take her up on her offer.

'What can we do?' Martha asked.

'To be honest, I'm still hoping to wake up and find it's all a nightmare,' I admitted, wiping my eyes while trying to keep my voice steady.

'Then you need to talk to him.'

'I suspect his lawyers will get in touch with mine.' I sighed. 'Which means that I'm going to have to find one first.'

'I'll email you the name of mine,' Brends promised.

'Thanks,' I said, my nose already filling up with the tears that couldn't come out of my eyes. 'I lost my suitcase. My phone was in there. But I have my laptop.'

'Oh, dear… Gilly?'

Too late, here they came, tears hot and gushing like waterfalls. I sniffed. 'Yuh?'

'Please keep us posted? Email us the number and address of where you're staying?'

'Okay,' I said obediently before I rang off. That was the way it was with unconditional love. Even if I'd called to tell them I'd murdered someone, they would always be there for me. Especially if I'd murdered Tony.

If I hadn't had the sniffles I would've called Annie, but I knew that the mere sound of her voice would break me, so I deferred telling her the bad news to when I was stronger, possibly in about ten or fifteen years.

I clung to the cord of the public phone, wondering if I could hang myself from it. The booth was conveniently raised on a dais. If I could wind the cord tight enough around my neck and throw myself down the steps in one mighty heave, my weight would do the rest. But I only considered this out of self-commiseration and just to imagine how Tony would feel. I'm way too chicken to top myself, really.

But I was mad enough to hire a hit man. Top *him* instead. Why should *I* have to die when *he* was the jerk? Even better, I could do it myself – invite him for a Closure Drink and poison him. Watch him writhe in agony as I slowly downed my own *vino bianco*. It would have to be a public place where someone else would take care of the body and I could pretend to be the shell-shocked, heartbroken widow. All I'd have to do would be to cry for a bit (that wasn't difficult lately) and pretend I didn't know a thing about the affair. Which was impossible, come to think of it. Half the island had witnessed my pathetic bathrobe-in-the-street moment.

Plus, I'd have to kill Sandra and Mattia as well, but they'd been so kind to me. No, I'd have to find a different way to get through this. But it felt nice to know I had alternatives. With a loud sigh I replaced the phone in its cradle and went on my way.

With no semblance of order of any sort, both locals and tourists alike emerged from and plunged into what looked like the main drag with a plaque reading *Corso Vittorio Emanuele*, consisting mostly of what I call young meat – the perfect playground for my cheating husband.

It was hard to find someone in their forties, I swear to you. All lean and tanned and draped in barely concealing sarongs of every color, I was lost in what looked like the set of *Baywatch*. Everywhere I looked there was not one soul built anything like me. When I thought I could get clothes in Lipari, I hadn't considered the *reality* of Lipari.

God, no wonder Tony wasn't interested in me anymore – compared to all these lithe, stick figures, I was a mammoth among gazelles – a bull not only in a china shop but every other shop I ventured into, where small spaces were stuffed with wares stacked to the rafters. I almost knocked a basket over, scaring the owner of one particular bazaar into following me around the whole time. Jesus, relax. Just because I was big didn't mean I was going to wreck the damn joint.

Everywhere I looked, there was an abundance of jewelry, lots of it black, ceramic pots, oversized Pamela sunhats of bright fuchsia and cool tealy-turquoise ones with enormous brims to keep you from frying to a crisp under the relentless sun. And speaking of frying, I was ravenous.

To get to the next eatery, which was only three doors down – thank you, God – I had to pass yet another infinite sea of tacky souvenirs such as magnets, fans, scarves and anything you can stick a *Lipari* label onto.

I'd never seen so much stuff in my life, not even in old Agatha's house. My eye fell on some smooth black stones topped by a handwritten carton sign in Italian that read *Liparite*, meaning, according to my travel book, magma that had been submerged and vitrified by seawater, resulting in a black, smooth, glass-like surface. It was also the local word for obsidian, a very close relative of rhyolite. It was beautiful, in its own strange, dark way. Several costly pieces of *Liparite* jewelry were on display. Maybe I could buy myself a big black heavy necklace with a sign that said, 'I'm wearing my heart around my neck.' Or use it to drown myself Virginia-Woolf-style. Or maybe I could duck into one of the side-street pizza ovens and do a Sylvia Plath?

On the left, another handwritten sign above a pyramid of gray stones read *Pietra Pomice*. Pumice stones. Very light due to all the air bubbles trapped inside what were basically balls of ash ejected from the volcanoes in the area. A bit like Aero chocolates. I picked one up. It really was light, almost weightless, like a film prop.

'Can I 'elp you?' came a shrill voice at my elbow. *Literally* at my elbow. I looked down at the tiny woman whom I'd in a split second dubbed Yoda, seeing as she looked at me as if she'd already christened *me* Jabba the Hut.

Could she help me? Not unless she knew how to kill cheating sleazy scumbag husbands or mend broken hearts, no. I eyed the row of T-shirts strewn under the ceiling like bunting, the middle one of which was huge with the writing, *I Love Lipari*. That would do for a start. I had absolutely zip to wear and so far, judging by the clothes in the fashionable shops, not many of them carried my size.

Not that it had anything to do with me anymore, but I discovered that in Italy they didn't do sexy lingerie stuff in larger sizes. What, only thin women had the right to at least *try* and seduce a man? Did they have a monopoly on them? What was a bigger woman supposed to do, wear a parka to bed? I don't know how many stores I ducked in and out of down the *corso*, but each time the response was the same, i.e. a surprised look that scanned my body up and down in a not-so-quick once-over that in some cases hid a sneer or a laugh, and then a contrite (as if) shake of the head.

'Can I have that T-shirt, please?' I pointed upwards and Yoda followed my gaze and blinked.

'That's not a T-shirt.'

I eyed her, then the T-shirt, a sinking sensation inside me. 'Not a T-shirt?'

'That is our *sign*.'

'Oh.'

Embarrassed silence. It was either get out of there ASAP before anyone else caught on to my lulu of a booboo, or get some advice. My desperation overcame dignity.

'Uhm, I lost my suitcase. I need to find some clothes.'

Yoda, just like every other living sales-creature I'd run into on the planet, quietly assessed me. I could see the numbers sky-rocketing in her head and let me tell you they were not the sums she'd make off me. As she mentally weighed me and sized me up to my full eighteen (well, okay sometimes twenty for fitted dresses) she heaved a little sigh.

'*Sisa*.'

'Sees all?' What did that mean? That they could see me down to my underwear? I didn't need anyone to give me that close a look, thank you very much.

Yoda shook her head. 'No – *Si-sa*.'

I thought that being of Italian descent would make getting around in Italy that much easier. Well. I was wrong. Good thing this woman was patient. She walked me outside, probably thanking the heavens she'd found an excuse to get the bull out of her shop, and pointed to a spot on the left side of the street.

'Sisa – the supermarket down the *corso*.'

Now, I'm no snob and have done my fair share of supermarket and flea-market shopping, but when I got to Sisa all I saw were a few racks squeezed into the back of a small grocery store. I lifted the tag of a blue and white striped jersey top. Size forty-two. How much was that equivalent to in UK sizes? I lifted the hanger. This would fit Annie. Actually, she might really like this style.

I stuffed it into my cart and looked around some more, moving the clothes in the front to one side. All the big sizes were always in the back, hidden away in shame, just like me.

Never in my life had I had a problem finding my size in North America or England. *Black lace baby doll? Size eighteen? Right this way, madam. Matching lilac bras and panties? XL? Satin or silk, madam?* Here instead they looked at me as if I was some sex-crazed woman escaped from a bordello for oversized women. And tights or thigh-highs? Forget it. Not that I'd ever have the guts to wear them here, of course. And for whom?

Back in the UK it had been a different story. I'd looked the saleslady square in the eye and said, 'Look, I need to jazz up the music in the bedroom,' to which she nodded knowingly and said, 'Right, pet. Follow me,' and I was introduced to not only something akin to Victoria's Secret but to those of practically every boudoir in the country.

As I looked desperately for something that I could get away with, another bright green top, Annie's favorite color, popped out at me. Again a size forty-two. Annie would love this as well. As I grabbed it a voice spoke sharply. *Mum! When are you going to stop telling me what to wear and let me make my own choices?*

I could almost hear her accuse me of smothering her, so I threw the top back onto the hanging rod. Dead center, of course.

She was right. I really was the Smother, always giving her my two cents. But, in my defense, in our family, even after Annie had moved out, I was the only one running the household. Making all the decisions meant that sometimes I didn't recognize the fuzzy lines between mine and Annie's. And, well, maybe even Tony's.

Was that why he had left me? Because I smothered him as well? I knew he hadn't been too keen on intimacy lately, only I hadn't wanted to admit it or delve into the whys and wherefores. I'd always secretly thought it was my butt, and this surprise trip was an attempt to change things. Only I hadn't realized I was too late. A whole *Nadia Tomaselli* too late. Slim, sexy, young and filthy-rich bitch.

To add insult to injury, next to me at the swimsuit rack stood an absolutely gorgeous exotic brunette checking out some bikinis the size of confetti. Just two tiny dots on a string for the top and a tiny triangle on a string for the bottom. Why the hell did they even bother spending the money? Why not just go naked? It was much more honest, no coy hide-and-seek, no *now you see it now you don't* games. I just didn't understand the logic behind it. But then, that was what most men liked, I guess. Or at least, men like Tony. How had I never realized it? Personally, I'd never been able to flirt, i.e. test the extent of my allure, not even when I was twenty and pretty. I've always been too shy.

I found a rack of large, dignified swimwear for women my age. Maybe they had my size? And if so, could I do it? How long had it been since I'd exposed my body outside my bathroom? Could I actually throw a towel over my shoulder and walk onto a beach (at least here I didn't know anybody) just like anybody else, without cringing at the idea of people's eyes on me, their mouths dropping into silent *o*'s at the sight of my milky-white, expansive body? Could I give it a try?

I caressed the swimsuit that looked like it might just about fit and checked the size tag. It read fifty-four Italian size. *Fifty-four?* Please God, make that be the price. No way was I going to wear anything that sounded more than double my English size. I hastily shoved it back into the rack. I hadn't worn a swimsuit in years. For two decades I'd stayed almost fully clothed – in and out of the bedroom. No, there was no way you were going to ever see me in one of those, especially now. I was just too *self-conscious.* Even back home the family never stopped reminding me of my looks – especially my mother-in-law, butt-kicker extraordinaire. *Too many cakes again this year, I see, Gillian,* Ma Sue would say with her upturned nose.

Now, you'd think every normal, traditional mother-in-law would be happy to have a daughter-in-law like me. Good cook, excellent seamstress and laundress and obsessed with cleanliness and running a proper home. But no. She criticized my love for food. For her and Tony, food was just fuel.

Luckily Pa Mike scoffed down all of my dishes as fast as he could, eternally hungry and with a slight paunch that Ma Sue always turned her nose up at. Poor man. He'd never have a decent meal if it weren't for me.

Imagine if Ma Sue saw me buying a swimsuit. She'd have a heart attack and end up stone-cold dead on the floor. So in the end I reached out and tossed it into my cart with a satisfied smile. Screw mothers-in-law.

In fact, to hell with them all – I loved the beach, albeit not deep water. And I didn't know anyone here. If I'd come all the way out here – why not go the whole hog and not give a damn about what other people – strangers, in fact – thought?

But I knew me. Even the slightest look askance my way would send my Hurt-o-meter soaring. Let's face it, being looked at with either pity or a sneer hurt like hell. Some people didn't do it to be spiteful. They just couldn't adapt to the idea that big people existed. Well, people – the news is, we *do* exist. And we have the same rights as you. We have the same dreams and aspirations and feelings. Only ours are hurt more often than yours, because we are constantly judged by our size. We may be fully insulated, but I for one am extremely thin-skinned.

I wished I could lose the weight and then go back to all those shops where I'd got frowns, just like Julia Roberts in *Pretty Woman* when she goes to Rodeo Drive to get a decent dress. That was all I wanted, too. A second chance to start all over again.

I imagined myself, much slimmer, going back there and make them take out the whole shop and still not buy anything. There. Who said big people were nice? Salespeople brought out the worst in me.

I added a new turquoise Pamela hat to my small pile of big purchases and a turquoise beach bag and headed for sleepwear, which was, in effect, two racks down.

As I expected, Sisa supermarket nighties were all in colorful cotton – not quite the lacy, silky numbers I'd brought with me and stupidly lost. Just imagine trying to seduce your man with one of these thingies that made you look like Krusty the Clown gone mad with a huge paintbrush.

Half an hour later and still not a stitch to cover me, I tried to shake off a rising sense of desperation. There was nothing here for me. It wasn't just the clothes. It was the feeling of not being accepted or wanted. Was I that different from everyone else?

By the time I got to the end of the shop I was sweating all over again, my feet and back killing me, and I still hadn't found any real clothes. Instead I'd accumulated an insane quantity of hygiene products, two pairs of flip-flops, some shapeless sarongs, a pair of sandals, a dozen pairs of beige knickers and bras from the old ladies' section opposite the bikini rack. And still no actual *clothes* to wear.

And just as I was about to give up completely, get changed back into my one sundress and slink back defeated to Sandra and Mattia's, I spotted *it*. Peeking out from behind a row of size Ms, *a size XL*. Whatever it was, I'd *take* it.

I stuck my head further out through the curtains of the changing room and, like in an Alfred Hitchcock movie, I tunnel-visioned it. A beautiful, beautiful blue dress with skimming lines. *With* sleeves to hide my arms. Something I could hide away in, but that was elegant without being too traditional. It was just perfect. Practically had my name on it. It was all I could see. Love at first sight.

Except that, story of my life, there was *another woman*, shuffling down the aisle with her own shopping cart *filled* with the last of the larger dresses. She had practically emptied the store, and now she was making a beeline for *my precious*, the only one left. Greedy lady. Couldn't I have at least one, to symbolize that there was hope for me after all?

She was big. But not as desperate as me. If I was going to leave this place with at least one decent item I had to make my move. She was going fast and I could see it was going to be a tough battle so I gave it my all as the instinct of survival kicked in and I made a desperate dash for my prize. She saw me coming and panicked, lurching for the dress. She was fast, but I was faster. Without thinking (and – here's the thing – without changing back into my dress) I lunged through the heavy curtains and out of the changing room. And collided straight into a brick wall.

I don't know how, but I was seeing stars and clutching at something hard as I spun through a multicolored universe in some topsy-turvy flight. I opened my heavy eyelids and found myself in the arms of a large man. Not fat large (which would've explained what he was doing in the plus-size section, if not why he was wandering around in *womenswear*), but *large* large.

Tall, muscular and, when I got a real good look at him after shaking my head of the cobwebs, I realized that not only was he quite the looker, with dark curls falling over dark eyes in a boyish manner, but that I actually knew him. He was, in fact, Mattia, Sandra's man.

'Shit.'

'Gillian…?'

'Sorry,' I whispered, my head spinning and still not quite all there. It was a good thing his arm was around the back of me, keeping me from collapsing onto the floor. That someone could bear my weight like that with one arm was awe-inspiring.

Winded and defeated, I realized my couture rival had taken advantage of my mishap and fled with the goods without even so much as a backward glance to check if I was still alive or not.

Mattia was still holding me, rolling my head to the left and to the right.

Now that I'd finally got a good look at him, I had to say he was not only handsome, but extremely manly and sexy, like the kind of guy you'd expect to see dangling from cliffs or jumping off flying jets. He exuded a rare sensuality that had seemed to have disappeared from the high streets. Strong muscled thighs in shorts and flip-flops, a fitted T-shirt stuck to his – I have to say – very fit body. A cross between Adonis and Aidan Turner. Lucky, lucky Sandra.

'Talk to me,' he coaxed and I tried to focus on his face, but it was hard in this position, dangling from his arm as if we'd just performed a dip in some funky dance studio.

'I'm okay,' I wheezed and suddenly he propped me up against the wall to see if I could stand on my own. I did a couple of knee bends but managed to keep myself erect with his help as the world whizzed by. 'Thank you…'

'Uh – no problem,' he said and suddenly stepped back with a cough, his face turning red. A man who blushed? What a rarity. I followed his line of vision down to my boobs – covered only in my bra. I jumped at least three feet into the air, letting out a shriek you could hear from the mainland as, to make it worse, heads turned in our direction, eyes wide. It wasn't every day, not even in hot and sunny Lipari, that you saw a woman standing in the aisle of a supermarket in her smalls. Unless you'd witnessed her running down the *corso* in her bathrobe.

God, would this man never see me with my clothes on? Now he was completely privy to the body secrets I managed to hide with big sweaters. I was really going to have to kill him after all.

4

Blame the Booze

With a pathetic excuse of some sort I dashed back into my stall, refusing to come out at his offer to give me a ride home.

'Is everybody still out there?' I hissed from behind the curtain as I poked my head through my dress.

'What? Of course not. People are always half-naked in Lipari anyway. Come out, Gillian.'

'Uhm, no thanks. I have… more stuff to try on…'

Silence. Not even *I* believed me.

'All right, then,' he called through the curtain. 'See you later.'

'Yuh…'

Two hours later, after I'd changed out of my only dress and into a new sarong (that was all I found in the end) I wandered through the streets with my Sisa bags and came across something that looked awfully familiar. A black Jeep, smashed up pretty badly. It was a miracle Mattia hadn't been injured himself. Hopefully I wasn't too late to pay for the damages.

And then, as I watched, a blue Vespa rounded the corner and – you guessed it – Mattia appeared again. Jesus, was this man everywhere or was this island really that small?

'*Ciao, Mario!*' Mattia called to the mechanic and ground to a stop so suddenly I thought he'd go flying. Obviously speed was his thing. One day he'd get someone killed.

They conferred for a few moments while I debated. I really

didn't want to see him again but there really was no use in delaying the inevitable so I straightened my shoulders and came out of my hiding place behind a van.

'Ah, look who's here,' he said with a smack-me-now grin. 'Nice sarong.'

I stopped in my tracks. So he was going to be like that, was he? And there was me thinking he was a nice guy. Poor Sandra was in truth married to a jerk.

The mechanic did a double take and looked back and forth between us. 'She the one who threw herself under the Jeep?' he asked in Italian. Sicilian, actually. I only got a few words here and there but it was enough.

Mattia didn't answer, but just looked at me with a big smile on his face. Seeing the damage to his car, I couldn't understand why.

'I did not *throw* myself under your Jeep. But you, on the other hand, almost killed me.'

'Almost,' he underlined, still grinning. 'Didn't quite manage.' The mechanic sniggered. Were they all the same, these Sicilian men? Smarmy bastards?

I crossed my arms in front of my chest. 'For your information I'm here to pay for the damages,' I informed them.

Mattia looked me up and down again, as if assessing my worth by my clothes. Good luck. With my huge Pamela hat, colorful sarong, sandals and little else, I looked like, with all due respect, a refugee.

He slowly shook his head. 'I don't want your money. Use it to buy yourself some clothes instead.' And then he added a whip-your-knickers off grin. 'Not that I'm complaining, mind you.'

Man – the nerve! If at first he'd been shocked by my boobs, now the memory of them must have made him bolder – and more arrogant – despite the fact that he had a gorgeous woman at home.

And another thing – did he think I couldn't afford to pay for his bloody car just because I hadn't managed to find any clothes?

If he only knew that it was my size that caused me to roam the island looking like this and not a lack of money. Although I wasn't exactly swimming in it and I was instantly reminded of how many things in my life needed getting back on track.

'I'm good for it,' I informed him.

Again Mattia chuckled. 'Yes, I can see that.'

Was it time to whack him on the side of the head, knock that arrogant smile off his face along with a couple of those absurdly white teeth?

White teeth, in a dark face, and eyes that burned holes in my already sheer, inadequate clothing. Sandra certainly had her hands full.

'For your information, I'm headed for the beach,' I lied.

'Well.' He chuckled again. 'In that case you're heading the wrong way. The beach is on the *coast*.'

Ha ha.

'How much?' I insisted, pulling out my wallet.

'Go home,' he said, his eyes twinkling, pinning me on the spot.

Without my clothes, my armor, I was, in fact, naked. Completely divested of my protection. What did he know about my life, about the pain and humiliation I was going through? How dare he judge me by the three minutes that he'd seen me. Who did he think he was with that proud head and shoulders, that utterly smackable face?

In any case, I wasn't going to look like this forever. As a matter of fact, when I got back home I was going to hit the gym and get fit and look the way I used to, many a kilo ago. And then Tony could eat his heart out for having cheated on me in the first place.

'You need a car to go to the beach,' he informed me.

'I'll take the bus,' I said through gritted teeth, still hanging on to my wallet, which I would have gladly shoved down his throat. 'If you can already give me an idea of how much it is I owe you...'

He put his hand on mine and I jumped as a bright blue electric shock coursed through his hand to mine. We both stared at the phenomenon. Then he looked up at me solemnly. 'You owe me nothing, Gillian. Put your money away.'

'I insist.'

'It was my fault. I should've looked where I was going.'

Ah-ha! A confession. 'Yes?'

'I was distracted.'

'By what?' I asked, once again, without consulting my brain.

He grinned, his eyes never leaving mine. 'Lots of things. There are lots of distractions on this island. Especially in the summer.'

How arrogant was he? Men were all Tonys in disguise. Before turning on my heels again, I nodded toward Mattia's Jeep. 'You know where to find me when the bill comes.' (Seeing as we lived in the same house.)

'Ah, come on, Gillian. Don't be like that. Hop on, I'll take you home.'

Home? With him? And on that contraption, to boot? I didn't think so.

'No thank you,' I declined icily and left him standing in the middle of the road. Normally, I'm a very nice person, but this guy brought out the worst in me, making me feel even more vulnerable. 'I'd rather walk.'

'Shame. I thought we could talk a bit.'

He meant "flirt" a bit, this one. Did he have no dignity at all? Or respect for Sandra?

Over a lunch of aubergine spaghetti, swordfish and *caponata*, Sandra was as chatty and happy as usual. I kept checking Mattia's face for any signs of shame, but there were none, his smile as broad and sexy as they come. Every so often, he'd look me straight in the eyes, and when I stared him down, he'd scratch the back of his head and look away. I looked at poor Sandra. Like me, she had absolutely no idea what a flirt her man was.

Sandra wiped her mouth. 'I have to pop into the school this

afternoon again, Gillian, but Mattia has offered to show you around and tonight we'll all go out to dinner. Mattia's treat,' she added with a wink and a smile in his direction. He reached over and ruffled her already crazy hair.

Look at them. I almost sighed. He *did* seem to adore her. Go figure men out.

Later, during a leisurely stroll with Mattia around town and up to the Upper Citadel to where the castle and museum complex were, he pointed out some sights of interest, particularly the necropolis where bodies had been interred in a crouching position in large jars. The perfect death for Tony.

The place was bursting with culture and in any other moment of my life I'd be taking pictures and notes like the nerd that I am, but today? I couldn't bring myself to care.

'Okay, Gillian, I know what you need,' he said, taking my hand as another – I kid you not – bolt of electricity shot up my arm. At this rate I was going to get electrocuted. I wrenched my hand from his, avoiding his gaze.

'I just need to get back now,' I stammered.

'Not until I'm finished with you,' he whispered in a low, sexy voice. Oh *God*…

I searched his face to find that twinkle in his eyes and that broad grin and opened my mouth to protest, but he nudged me forward. 'Come on.'

'Where?'

'To paradise…'

I swallowed. Unless it was the name of a tropical beach club, I was in serious trouble. But what could he possibly want with me in any case?

The answer lay halfway down the *corso* and precisely in a *pasticceria*, i.e. a bakery. Everywhere I looked, rows and rows of colorful pastries of every shape and size smiled up at me from behind a refrigerated glass partition, like a garden full of flowers, just waiting to be picked.

He grinned down at me. 'Eat something sweet, and I promise you'll feel better.'

This guy had me down pat. Dessert always made me feel better. I was not the kind of gal who felt guilty after a sweet session – on the contrary.

'*Ciao, Mattia,*' said the pretty brunette behind the counter, batting her baby browns at him coquettishly. '*Cosa ti do?*'

I knew enough Italian to understand the double entendre in that: "What shall I give you?"

'*Un momento per favore, Lisa,*' he said, allowing me some time to choose. But I couldn't, as there was just too much.

I looked up and he smiled. 'Shall I order a selection of the best?'

'Yes, please,' I breathed, practically salivating by now, particularly at the sight of the ricotta cannoli dipped in pistachio nuts. And the mini ice cream brioches. And the tiramisu...

Mattia guided me to a small table for two where he ordered two lemon granitas. 'To quench your thirst first, otherwise you won't enjoy the sweetness of the desserts as much,' he explained.

'Okay,' I agreed, not knowing what he was talking about. I always enjoyed the sweetness of desserts. If this was his way to make amends for being so flirty with me at a time like this, we could be friends for life.

When the selection arrived, a platter full of mini-pastries, I couldn't help but smile for a split second. Was I that much of a glutton that it overshadowed my grief at being deserted by my husband? Well, it was always better to be... *desserted* than *deserted*, wasn't it? *Desserted in Sicily*. I liked the sound of that. The perfect death, if I could choose.

'Try this first,' he urged, passing me a mini-thingy filled with strawberry and ricotta.

'Mmph...' was all I could say as the sweetness filled not only my mouth but my heart. It was beyond delicious. It was pure...

'Heaven, isn't it?' He mmhhed as he licked a drop of falling filling and I had to look away, feeling my face going beet red. And so we spent the next half-hour uhmming and eating as he described the ingredients and origins of some of the desserts.

'What's this one?' I asked, nodding at a small dome-shaped pastry with a red cherry on top.

'This,' he said, picking it up delicately, almost reverently, to let me try it, 'is Saint Agatha's breast.'

'Breast…?' I gulped, full-mouthed and wide-eyed and he laughed.

'It sounds amusing now, but there is a very sad story behind it.'

Sad story? Well, when in Lipari…

'There was a very young girl back in Roman times who refused the attention of a consul. To get back at her, he cut her breasts off. Legend says she used to walk around with them on a platter to show what had happened to her.'

'And someone thought it would be a good idea to turn her tragedy into a pastry?'

'Isn't that what we all do? Try to make the best of our sorrows?'

'I guess,' I admitted, looking down and thinking that this small pastry looked absolutely nothing like *my* breasts – that, actually, they were closer to a wedding cake. But he was right about making the best of life. It was a great idea, and one that I could stick to.

On our way home, just as I was convincing myself that not only was Mattia cultured, a fellow glutton, and pleasant to be with after all (if he didn't touch me), he stopped in front of a beautiful stone building.

Sensing he had stuff to do, I said, 'Thank you for a lovely afternoon, Mattia.'

'You're very welcome, Gillian. This is my office. I'm an architect.'

Ah, so he actually had a job. There was me, thinking he was a beach bum or something. 'Oh. It's very… nice.'

'Want to come in and have a look around?'

'But there's no one in there,' I observed.

'Of course not – it's siesta time,' he said with a grin.

The subtext was clear and I immediately sensed the danger. Siesta time, and a dark, closed office away from indiscreet eyes? And the hopeful look on his face? There was no way I was going alone into a married man's den. And there was me thinking we could be friends. What an idiot I was.

'Uhm, you know, I'm really tired. I need to go back and have a nap before dinner,' I stammered, feeling my ears burn with fury and embarrassment.

He blinked, his expression changing. He'd evidently received my subtext. He looked at his feet, a muscle in his jaw twitching as it seemed he fought to not look at me. 'Oh. Okay.'

We were both silent on our way back and I knew I'd made my resistance clear. Did he think it was okay to proposition me like that, with his own wife waiting at home for us? And what about me, not even twenty-four hours after I'd had my heart broken? Did he think I would actually agree to have a role in hurting another woman's feelings?

I locked myself in my room and pretended to sleep the rest of the afternoon, all the while fuming. What was it with men? Did they consider an extramarital roll in the hay *de rigueur*?

When Sandra came home that evening Mattia had gone out so I offered to make her an espresso in the hope of a chat.

'Mmph, I should marry *you*,' she moaned as she threw it back in one gulp. 'Go get changed. Mattia's coming straight to the restaurant.'

I panicked. The idea of sitting opposite Rudolph Valentino after the stunt he'd pulled on me? 'I can't come...'

'Nonsense.'

'I... haven't got anything to wear except for my sundress.' Which was true. How many times did I have to wash that thing?

'It'll do fine.'

'Why don't you guys have a night without me?' As if we'd wined and dined together for years.

'Absolutely not. We have to go out and celebrate.'

'Celebrate what?' I asked. 'My imminent divorce?'

'The joy of being *alive*,' she answered and poured me a tiny cup of the treacly brew. 'Here – drink up. I need you awake and perky.'

I got a feeling she was probably one of the happiest people on the planet, what with her *perfect* partner. Judging by the smoldering looks he'd given me earlier, he had *great in bed* all over his face. Good for Cassandra.

'To the joy of being alive,' I echoed without much conviction. Right about now a stroke would have suited me just fine. But I smiled and threw back the strong sludge and gasped at the harsh taste. 'What, no sugar?'

'Espresso is meant to be black and bitter.'

'Like my heart?' I quipped and she laughed.

'You'll learn.'

Later that evening, as we sat at a *trattoria* waiting for her man, Sandra and I ordered a bottle of Malvasia wine and checked out the menu.

'Do you know what you want?' she asked and I looked up.

'Aren't we waiting for Mattia?'

'I know what he wants,' she answered as she scanned the choices. 'Trouble is, what do *I* want?'

I wondered whether she was just referring to the menus or was trying to tell me something. If I hadn't known he was such a player, he would've come across as absolutely mad about her.

Lord, if only once, just once in his whole life Tony had looked at me the way Mattia looked at Sandra – the lazy, sexy smile, a knowing look in his twinkling eyes. I had to admit that Mattia really was a handsome guy. Younger than Sandra, it was obvious, albeit not that much, and it didn't bother her at all, I could tell.

Nor did it seem to bother him. They lived a relatively stress-free life with no garden or pets to speak of – just a turn-key flat that seemed to fit their lifestyle of being out and about.

Personally, I was more of a home, garden and pet type, although Tony was allergic to dog fur. Which was why I'd volunteered to keep Jumbo-Gemma while he was away. I missed not having a dog. Which was the first thing I was getting when I got back home. But before that, I'd have to find a place for said dog – and me – to live. My flight back wasn't for another twenty days.

Just how had Tony figured on getting rid of me? Would he have notified me via his lawyer? He'd have had to tell me in the end, seeing he was *getting engaged*. With a woman his daughter's age. And whom he'd known all of five minutes. Was that what happened to men during andropause? They lost the plot, were blown off course in their journey to middle age, unable to bear the thought of aging alongside the woman they'd married once upon a life ago?

And there was the financial aspect. Yes, I had my nan's money, which was quite a lot, but I never thought I'd have to use it to buy a house. God, how did it all come to this?

When I'd met him, I'd been on my way to success. Slim (believe it or not). Smart. Ambitious. And then I married him, had his child (actually, it happened the other way around) and became someone completely different in the space of one year. I'd become so taken with raising Annie, making sure she was happy and loved, putting my family before my marriage instead of alongside it. My priority had become being a mother. I'd practically lived vicariously through my daughter, thriving on her joys and accomplishments, so involved and hands-on that I forgot to be a woman as well. So he'd gone out and found himself another one.

'Gilly – stop that.'

I looked up to see Sandra's hand on mine, her eyes kind.

'The look on your face speaks volumes. He's not worth it. We'll find you a new man, don't you worry.'

I forced a smile for her benefit. 'Thanks, but the last thing I need is another man.'

'Sandra, *bellissima*!' came a deep male voice from behind me. I turned to see extremely broad shoulders, long golden hair (how is it that men can have way better hair than ours?), a hint of a beard, a smile *and* a body to die for. Not that I was ogling, mind you. But I do have eyes. First Mattia, and now this guy. What was it with this place? Were the hunks let loose all at once during the Female Hunt Season?

'Claudio, *bellissimo*!' Sandra cried back and it was kisses on the cheeks as he bent down to her and I glimpsed the hairiest chest I'd ever seen in my life. And he was practically jumping into Sandra's neckline, eyes, face and all. I wondered if Mattia would have enjoyed the taste of his own medicine?

'Claudio, this is my friend Gillian. Gillian, this is my colleague Claudio, the gym teacher.'

But of course. What else could he teach with that physique?

'Hi, Gillian, how are you? Enjoying your holiday?' he said with a kind smile. A smile that lasted about a fraction of a second before his eyes zapped straight back to Sandra's cleavage.

Come to think of it, every single man who'd come anywhere near Sandra couldn't help but ogle her, bask in the light of her sexy aura. And I was in high school all over again, trotting along behind my prettier friend who got all the guys while I got the dregs, i.e. the nerds or the losers like me, and the whole of Friday nights all to myself.

After about ten minutes there was still no sign of Mattia and Claudio reluctantly went. Our risotto of *pesce spada* – swordfish – arrived and so did a guy called Marco. Sandra introduced him to me but he only had eyes for her, of course. Not even an *Are you enjoying your holiday?* thrown my way. At least the Claudio bloke had bothered to ask me the token courtesy question.

After he went and the lemon and garlic-stuffed *spigola* arrived, another one called Fabio came up to say hello. And have his own good stare down Sandra's neckline, hungry, roaming, bold eyes taking in her gorgeous body, intelligent face and long slender neck. What was below the neck wasn't hard to imagine. I'd never seen a woman dress so succinctly. But then again, it was the summer and this was Sicily. And Sandra was Sandra – confident and sexy.

After a few more bottles of Malvasia and halfway into a dessert selection, Sandra looked past me and smiled. Who was it now? Franco? Roberto? Rudolph Bloody *Valentino*? Whatever – I was past caring and thanks to several glasses of Malvasia quite giggly, actually.

'Finally!' she chimed. 'Where have you been?'

Ah, speak of the devil. Arms spread out in an apology, Mattia kissed her, eyed me uncertainly and sat down. 'Sorry – I couldn't get rid of a client.'

'Dottor Tomaselli again?' Sandra asked and he groaned.

'The man is a pain in the ass. He always comes to me with plans for restructuring this or that house and he actually never buys any of them. He's just wasting my time. And how are you, Gillian? Did you enjoy your… siesta?'

Meaning, *Did you enjoy sleeping without me?* Cad.

And that's when I spotted them – Tony and his lover.

I choked on my wine, gasping for air, my eyes bulging. A large hand gently swatted me on the back and the few errant drops that had been tickling my tonsils slid down my throat pronto.

'You okay?' Mattia asked in his deep voice, looking at Tony over my shoulder and back at me with a soft expression.

The age gap between them was huge – so huge they looked like father and daughter out for an innocent evening dinner. Only there was *nothing* innocent in ruining a marriage. They'd ruined not only my marriage, but my entire life. What was I supposed to do with all that now? How was I supposed to survive after a blow like that?

Had he seen me? His smile froze for an instant as I feared for the worst. I wasn't ready for one-on-one (well, two-on-one, in this case) confrontation again. He laughed and leaned over to kiss her. He'd never held *me* like that before.

I'd never felt special, never been gazed upon the way he was now gazing at her. I still couldn't believe he was sleeping with another woman. That he snuggled up to her and pulled her close in his sleep, knowing full well, even as he lay comatose, that he was holding her and not me. He planned his days with her, ate with her and obviously had never had to arch his eyebrow at every bite she took like he did with me.

Did he ever think of me, even by mistake?

'Do you want to talk?' Sandra asked softly.

'No, thanksh,' I said through gritted teeth.

Maybe it was the wine, maybe it was, oh, I don't know, the absurdity of my husband of almost twenty years sitting two tables away looking like the happiest man on earth, but I giggled again. Uncontrollably. What the hell was wrong with me?

Mattia raised an amused eyebrow and Sandra waved a bejeweled hand in the air. 'Let her laugh – she's just a bit tipsy. Aren't you, Gilly?'

'Yesh,' I agreed. Tipsy and recklessly flippant. Because it was either that or nothing because as sure as hell I wasn't about to hang on to Tony's ankles, begging him to come back. So bring on the wine! God, I wish the table would stop turning and everyone would sit down still. And I wished I could stop giggling.

'It'sh not funny, you know,' I tittered and Mattia and Sandra exchanged glances when her phone rang.

'*Pronto? Alice? Che c'è, che è successo?*'

Mattia and I turned to Sandra as she listened, her face grim. 'I'll be right there,' she promised and snapped her phone shut.

'It's Alice – Renzo's left her again,' Sandra said. Or at least I think so – the Malvasia was working its magic on me.

She grabbed her handbag and rolled her eyes. 'She's all alone – I have to go. Don't wait up, Mattia. See you tomorrow morning, Gilly, and try to sleep it off or you'll have a major hangover in the morning.'

And with that, she kissed us and left.

'Where she going?' I slurred as Mattia took my elbow.

'Come on, princess,' he coaxed and I got to my rubbery feet.

'Where *we* going?'

'Home. Here, lean on me,' he said, sliding his arm around my waist. His wife had barely turned her back and already he was making his moves on me again. Man – the guy wasted no time.

'Where'sh your carrr?' I asked, looking at the deserted car park across the street.

'No car yet,' he said softly. 'It's wrecked, remember?'

'Uh. Yah. Shorry.'

He chuckled and got onto his Vespa. 'Come,' he said, patting the seat in front of him and literally lifting me onto it sideways so I was sitting between the handlebars and snuggled up against his chest. Before I knew what was happening, we were moving, a nice soft breeze in my hair contrasting with the heat on my face and breasts.

'Ooh. Shnug.'

He laughed, one hand tight around my waist and the other one, I hoped, on the handlebars. 'Gillian, Gillian. What am I going to do with you?'

And then all I could remember was getting to Sandra's, making a dash for the bathroom and throwing up into the toilet bowl as someone held my hair out of the way. Mattia. God, Lipari was sure doing miracles for me, wasn't it?

'Go away,' I rasped. ''m shick.'

'I'm not going anywhere,' came a soft reply.

Once the purging-of-the-sins hell was over, I rinsed my face with cold water and brushed my teeth, aware that, yep, he was still there.

'Better?' he asked.

'Better,' I answered. 'I'm sho shorry... thish shtuff never happens to me...'

He took my hand. 'Come. I'll fix you something to drink.'

'No more drink,' I pleaded.

'This is not liquor. It'll make you feel better. It's called *canarino*.'

I tried to focus on both his heads. 'You want me to drink a canary?'

Again, he chuckled, so low it was almost like a growl in his throat.

'It's just lemon and laurel in boiled water. It'll help you digest anything else left in there.'

'Oh.'

I let him help me onto the sofa where I lay face down, a plastic bowl on the floor next to me just in case. I began to shiver, hot and cold at the same time, as Mattia placed a throw over me and began to rub my back.

'That'sh nishe,' I murmured, enjoying the gentleness of his large hands. Then my eyes popped open in alarm. Was he at it again? I lay still, panic rising inside me. I didn't have the strength to move, so I waited, as vigilant as my muddled mind would allow me, but his hands never moved from my back to, say, my butt or anything. And when I let out a loud burp he chuckled and got to his feet.

'Come on, let's get you settled. You need to sleep it off.'

And he, believe it or not, lifted me up into his arms like I was a kid, strode across the apartment to my room and deposited me gently on the bed, removing my shoes and pulling up the sheets. I looked up at him doe-eyed. So he wasn't the jerk I'd thought.

'You're sho shweet,' I gushed as sleep invaded my mind, but not before I heard him clear his throat.

'Gillian…?' he whispered, his thumb on my jawline.

How could a simple thumb make me shiver like that?

'Y-yesh…?'

Silence. I opened an eye to see he was tormenting his lower lip. 'Nothing. Just get some sleep. *Buonanotte, bella…*' he said. Goodnight, beautiful.

I turned over as, with a loud sigh, he bent down again to kiss me on the cheek. I hadn't seen it coming and turned my face to him just in time for his lips to kiss mine.

'Oh...' I gasped, about to apologize as he continued to stare at me with the strangest of expressions on his face, probably mentally adding up the damage he had just caused Sandra. And while we were both tallying said damage up, he took my face in his hands and kissed me again. And again, pulling me close to him, whispering my name.

Which was so wrong – a repeat of the Nadia and Tony scene, only not as ferocious as we weren't ripping each other's clothes off nor moaning the other's name.

But how was it, this kiss per se, you might ask? Like being allowed to *only lick* chocolate. Undeniably tempting and unforgivingly delicious. I didn't know a kiss could taste that good and be so liberating. And so horribly unthoughtful of other people's feelings. Sandra had been nothing but amazing to me, and this was what I did to her? *Not* happening.

'No...' I pushed him away. But instead of backing off immediately, he lingered, hanging his head in shame. His hair smelled of shampoo and the rest of him smelled of clean, fresh male. Fresh was right. How dare he come onto me like that? Actually, he was more hot and dirty, if you'll pardon the pun.

'I'm sorry,' he whispered and catapulted himself off me and out of my room.

I lay in bed awake, chastising myself all night. What the hell had happened there? Mattia was off-limits. *Verboten*. Or as they say here in Italy, *proibito*. How on earth could I have done that to Sandra? Let her man kiss me? There was no excuse – not even all the wine in the world could justify what I'd done. I was no better than bloody Nadia Tomaselli.

When Sandra came home later that night I plugged my ears. I didn't want to hear them talking away in hushed tones – I couldn't stand yet another illusion of intimacy, whether it was mine or another woman's. I couldn't stand to hear another lie.

No woman should be tricked like that by a false lover. She was loving; he was a letch. And so was I.

So tomorrow morning, while they were out, I'd leave behind what I owed them in rent, a *thank-you* note, and a nice gift in return for their generous hospitality. And then get out of there like a bat out of hell.

5

Hotel Hell

The next morning, in my haste to get up and out of that house, my foot caught in the tangle of my sheets and I fell out of bed and onto my face – literally.

And when I checked my mirror, I groaned at the sight of my swollen, bleeding nose. And two black eyes. How the heck had I managed to do this to myself with just a bit of wine?

Well, I deserved it big time, after an evening of laughing (so I wouldn't cry) and drinking (so I would forget), now I had something new to forget. How the hell did I get myself into these situations?

Staggering to the bathroom sink, I splashed cold water on my face – are you getting a sense of déjà vu, I wonder? What an absolutely smashing (literally) start to the day, I thought to myself as I watched the blood trickling down the drain.

How the heck was I going to show my face in public with this honker leading the way like a beacon in the night? Why didn't I just go home already, rather than hang around here, getting live coverage of my marriage swirling down the toilet? Did I really need to see Tony and Nadia's love story unfold before me? Or was I supposed to sit in Sandra and Mattia's flat like the Elephant Man and watch the world go by from my third floor balcony? Not a bad idea, actually, since I still didn't have anything to wear except for my brand-new Mrs. Doubtfire bras and knickers.

But then there was *The Fact*. I'd let Sandra's husband kiss me.

And she'd been so nice to me, trusting me completely. Didn't I have enough problems without having a filthy conscience as well?

I spent all morning and half the afternoon looking for a place to stay, all the while running down the *corso* as fast as I could, not so much to find a hotel as to escape the broiling heat *and* all the culinary delights practically screaming at me from every direction, begging me to eat. And eat.

And then I spotted a lovely, leafy terrace. *Shade*. I would actually kill for some respite from this heat.

But in order to get to it I had to survive the gauntlet of two rows, one on each side, of pastries. It was Ambush Central all over again and I was done for. No going in for a simple glass of juice or a cappuccino, oh no. The *minute* you stepped in there you gained five pounds.

My plans of hitting the gym once I went back home were still valid, of course, but right now, right here, with all this food and me being so depressed and all, what was the point of even trying to resist? Why should I?

Come to think of it, why should I *be skinny* at all? Years and years of me dieting didn't prevent Tony from finding a younger, slimmer woman barely Annie's age, did it? So who exactly would I be making this sacrifice for now? If I was happy being rotund, why shouldn't I give in every once in a while (okay, a little more than that), especially now that I was here, in Italy, where life practically revolved around food?

And how does the saying go, *When in Rome?* Locals, especially during the summer, went to cafés at least three times a day. First, for their morning espresso and *cornetto* filled with either *ricotta*, cream, Nutella or jam. (No rocket science necessary to figure out which one I'd pick, right?) And after lunch it was an espresso and maybe a *mignon* pastry, just enough to chase lunch down, and then again in the evening for *aperitivi* (which I could easily give up for another portion of Nutella cake).

After having stuffed my face, I meandered through the *corso*, now distracted by all the narrow, winding cobblestoned alleys that seemed plucked out of medieval fairy tales and lined with two-story houses in every color of the rainbow, so different among themselves but at the same time so closely knit.

As I wandered aimlessly below freshly washed laundry and past people going about their daily routines, mothers with babies, children with grandmothers and cats – lots of big fat, happy-looking cats – I began to understand a bit more about the locals, the *real* people. Lipari town was, yes, a tourist destination, but, outside the summer, I could see how everything would return to its original pace.

Everyone was friendly, not too bothered about the chaos as they knew they'd get their island back to themselves soon enough and be all the richer for putting up with the likes of us, i.e., tourists like me who stuck out like sore thumbs as they were either still pale or already burnt to a crisp.

Much more stylish, the locals were not just fishermen and shepherds like in the days of old, but dynamic businesspeople, merchants, teachers, doctors, all driving around in eco-cars, leading normal lives. But bound together and surrounded by the sea – the perfect basis for a love-hate relationship.

So no, this probably wasn't the best place to recover from depression during a long winter, but it was summer now and I was already on the verge of a nervous breakdown anyway so what the heck – I might as well make the best of my time here and go with the flow. Chat with the folk, go places. Sort of like an *Eat, Pray, Love* thing in limited space.

If I'd thought finding some clothes was purely fictional, finding a *hotel* was pure science fiction, as Sandra had warned me. Still I searched far and wide, panting and sweating up and down the *corso* and all the side streets. I checked them all – Hotel Mea, Hotel Aktea, Residence La Giara, Hotel Villa Augustus and every other place under this blazing sun, finally arriving in Marina Corta, the small harbor for private boats as opposed to Marina Lunga, the larger ship harbor where I'd landed on the other side of the island. Between the two stretched the *corso* and all the other parallel roads.

So this was the famous place with its quaint little square on the harbor with a jetty and several cafés, churches and souvenir shops to browse in. And if I hadn't been so desperate to put a roof over my boiling head, I'd have stopped to breathe deeply of the sea air and watch the children throwing pebbles into the water as their parents polished their boats. I made a mental note to return here once I'd found a room.

Here, where the square squeezed back into a narrow road, I tried my very last hotel. No luck. But, moved to mercy by my sweaty hair plastered to my head, my perspiration-soaked sarong, added to the stoop of my shoulders, the good-willed receptionist tried other hotels and B&Bs for me. And with every call she became more and more upset as if it were her problem. I could hardly believe there were still such genuine people around.

'I'm so sorry,' she said. 'I continue to search, yes?'

I nodded. 'I'm so sorry to trouble you, but… I just don't know what else to do…'

In her early thirties, she looked more like a rosy-cheeked milkmaid who'd stumbled upon the receptionist's desk. All she needed was an apron and she'd be the perfect Sicilian mother, although much younger, rotund and with sparkling blue eyes. I loved her immediately.

'If worst comes to worst, you can stay on Milazzo and come back tomorrow,' she suggested. 'It's only an hour away, at the end of the day.' She wrung her hands, helpless. 'I'd let you sleep on my sofa but that's my eldest son's bed. I have four children, you see.'

'Four? Wow, congratulations.'

She beamed, although there was a hint of sadness in her smile. I imagined either a sick child or a difficult marriage or money troubles. Or all three.

'Thank you so much,' I said. 'How sweet of you to even

think that. I'll find something. Thank you for your time.' And with that, I turned to go.

'Maybe—' she began.

I turned back. Anything would be brilliant compared to sleeping under the arches or in the same house with Mattia. 'Yes?'

She scribbled on a piece of paper. 'This is my cousin Pina's number. She lives on Salina and almost always has an extra room if you get desperate. It's just ten minutes by boat.'

I accepted the sheet of paper like a lifeline. I already *was* desperate. Pina in Salina. Easy to remember. 'Thank you so much, ah…?'

'Maria,' she said. 'My name is Maria.' She scribbled again and gave me her phone number. What a sweet, sweet girl. So, taking advantage of the air con in the lobby and literally dreading the moment I had to go out and face the heat again, I called this Pina in Salina who was – you guessed it – fully booked.

By the late morning I'd already exhausted pretty much every avenue. And then, an hour later, when I was just about to give up to the idea of sleeping under a bridge somewhere, I found a card on a counter in a café.

Casa del Sole. And it was an entire house! I made the call. The owner, one Mimmo Subba, agreed to meet me at Marina Lunga in a red Fiat Punto. Like searching for one fish in the vast sea. Luckily, or should I say, unluckily, he found *me*.

He was an absolute mess from head to toe, wearing filthy, torn sweatpants and a T-shirt dotted with sweat stains under his armpits. I could smell him before I even saw him. Vulcano island's sulfuric egg-stink had been a bouquet of roses compared to the stench coming at me in waves.

'*Mimmo Subba, piacere*,' he introduced himself breathlessly (I wondered if he'd just caught a whiff of himself too?) practically grabbing my hand while his eyes swept over my bosom. '*Non ha bagagli?*' he asked, feigning a look around me for my luggage while squeezing in another glance at my neckline.

'I lost it,' I explained. 'In Catania airport.'

'Oh, that's a shame,' he tsk-tsked, and I began to wonder whether I'd end up like him in a few days, wearing the same clothes for evermore.

'*Andiamo* – let's go,' he suddenly prompted, taking my arm like we were old buddies and dragging me like I was his catch of the day to what must have been a car once upon a time. Because now it look like a smashed-up Coke can with more holes than metal. And because of that, once inside it, you wouldn't think it would stink, what with all that aeration, right? Wrong. It was so bad in there that once Mimmo shifted into first gear (upending a rubbish skip) and ran a ring around the roundabout, I was already gagging.

What am I going to do? I thought desperately as he rammed into third and then fourth and then fifth gear like a mad hornet. Throw up inside my purse? But then again, anything I did to this car would actually be an improvement on its present state.

I tried not to look around me, tried not to inhale the overbearing stench and hide the gagging, which was pretty embarrassing. Oh my God, how was I going to survive the next few minutes until we got to our destination?

Like in a horror movie, I couldn't stop staring at the ashtray that seemed to have a life of its own, cigarette butts jutting out and swaying at every turn as we began our ascent into the hills. Ash, like from a volcano, spurted out from between the butts and landed on my knee.

That's it, I thought. *I'm going to baptize this car with my very own colorful Kandinsky creation any second now*. I clutched at the clasps, threw my bag open in resignation and at the very last second spotted my Jo Malone perfume and a packet of tissues. *Bingo*.

Shooting Mimmo a sidelong glance, I sprayed the fragrance onto a tissue and brought it to my nose. God almighty, just in time. Thank you, Jo Malone, for all the loveliness you have brought this world. Thank you, thank you, thank you. When I got home I was going to actually send her a real thank-you note. I wondered if she would appreciate my story? After all, it was not exactly ad material, was it? Just imagine: anti-gag essence? Eau de Gag? Not the greatest selling pitch.

Although the ad concept had no future, I was already feeling much more chipper. All I had to do was keep my nose in the tissue. Forget about the hairpin bends as we climbed up. The post-traumatic effects of seasickness, upset stomach and motion sickness combined were nothing compared to what I was fighting against – Mimmo Subba in all his fragrant, infinite glory.

And speaking of infinite, how high up were we going? I knew the B&B was in the hills but we'd been going for at least ten minutes now, if the clock on the dashboard hadn't conked out in sympathy with the rest of the car. I'd have to arrange alternative means of transportation pronto because he'd agreed, for a fee, to taxi me around, but I sure as hell wasn't doing *this* ever again. I craned my neck around to look behind me and almost forgot his stench. Down below to the left of me, was the most breathtaking sight I'd ever seen.

Sparkling with a bright, translucent blue you probably only experienced once or twice in your life, was the Mediterranean sea, dotted with islands like copper-colored gems that seemed to have been dropped from the sky, so close you could almost reach out and touch them.

'That's Vulcano,' Mimmo said as he leaned close to me, his breath threatening to curl my hair. I pressed my nose further into my tissue and breathed deeply.

'We're stopping here now at *Quattrocchi* where you get the best view. You can get out and take a picture if you like.'

A picture? I needed an oxygen mask pronto. Plus I didn't know if stopping was a good or a bad idea because I couldn't guarantee I'd be able to haul myself back in here once I'd smelled fresh air. But I will tell you this: the island of Vulcano is a volcano in the middle of the sea and it looks like a mighty hand had sliced the top off, uncovering one hell of a giant crater. It was absolutely breath-taking.

Mimmo took out a map from the top of his dashboard and poked at it. 'This is where you came from the mainland – Milazzo, see?'

I nodded, already familiar with the geography.

'The archipelago spreads out like a "Y". First at the bottom you have Vulcano – the smelly one. It has sulfur.'

He was the one to judge.

'And then Lipari, followed by Salina. That's where the Italian movie *The Postman* was shot. To the west, Alicudi and Filicudi and to the east, Stromboli and Panarea. Ah, and then there's the tiny ones – Basiluzzo and Strombolicchio, the one that looks like a stone cathedral.'

And now he was at his car again, beckoning to me. I wondered if he'd accept the excuse without offense that I didn't want to leave this panoramic viewing point and that I'd make my own way to his house somehow? No, I didn't think so either.

Oh, how I missed Sandra and Mattia's nice, clean place. I missed Sandra, too, while I hoped never again to see Mattia.

'There is a private beach that you can't get to by land. You have to go by boat,' Mimmo explained, coming to stand behind me again, too close for my taste (and sense of smell) but he didn't really mean anything by it. He was simply unaware of the basics of social boundaries.

'It's beautiful.' I inhaled deeply, taking in (while I could) the spicy fragrances emanating from the juniper and other shrubs I didn't recognize. 'Have you ever been up to the top of Vulcano?' I asked.

'No. I've never left this island except once to go to Panarea. And I'm not doing *that* again. Too many rich, snobbish people.'

'Never been off the island?' I said before I could stop myself. Maybe his lack of social skills was contagious? But the poor soul shook his head with a great big smile, revealing the brownest teeth I'd ever had the misfortune to lay eyes upon. This man,

I realized, was really a boy inside. A lost, sad and lonely boy. Possibly still living with Mum and Dad, unemployed except for seasonal lettings, no girlfriend, no children, no real social life. Not that my life was much better than his, lately. Come to think of it, Mimmo and I were not worlds apart because I, too, had been wearing the same clothes for almost twenty-four hours now.

Because, let's face it, my *Sesame Street* luggage would be found by someone back in Catania, taken home and opened by some lucky big gal. I had Burberry Brit fragrances in there, plus a great Body Shop scrub and three new shades of lip gloss, not to mention my arsenal of silky, lacy lingerie and every single one of my glamorous Monsoon party dresses. I told you I'd pulled out all the stops to try and sex Tony up.

'Here, let me take a picture of you,' he suggested and I leaned against the railing, trying to smile and look like a happy tourist while all I wanted to do was cry my eyes out.

This was not how I'd expected it to be. Tony and I were supposed to have a happily ever after here in Lipari, bursting out of our skin in haste to get back to our deluxe suite with a balcony overlooking some other glorious bay. We were supposed to have made love like never before (that wouldn't have been difficult), waste the afternoon away in bed and finally, when we were completely love-sated, room service would roll in a sumptuous dinner that we would consume *al fresco*, on said balcony high above the sea, candles lit, shining in our loving eyes as we toasted each other and pledged our eternal love.

For the love of God, get a grip, you might say. Yeah, so would I if this was a story I'd made up out of sheer fantasy or if I'd been watching fictional characters on daytime TV. But you know, I had really *wanted* all that sappy, happy stuff. I deserved it. And now it was never going to happen again. With a heavy heart, I climbed back into Mimmo's car and to the place I'd call home for the next few days until I could talk myself off the ledge.

6

The Art of Survival

It was worse than I'd thought. Bear Grylls himself would have struggled in this place. The B&B was literally in the middle of nowhere, in open, abandoned (and wild) countryside with no other houses in sight, nestled among overgrown brambles and shrubs that did nothing to shade the drab exterior. At the same time the brambles obstructed any view of the neighboring islands which any other homeowner would have enhanced. All I could glimpse from the verandah was a rusty and misshapen gazebo stripped of its canopy sometime in the previous century.

Inside it was even worse. It smelled musty. It smelled abandoned. It smelled like... Mimmo himself. I reluctantly followed him in and threw open the windows, each time taking a deep breath as if my life depended upon it and praying for the reveal of a view of the sea from at least one bloody window, but it never materialized.

I followed him listlessly from room to room, all featuring naked, threadbare mattresses (and speaking of naked, yes, there was even a naked ladies calendar). Only one bed – a single – was made up, so to say, with a makeshift night table and an orange plastic lamp on top. A burn stain graced the surface. Single, derelict and burnt. We had quite a few things in common, this room and I.

The bathroom, sporting hideous brown tiles with a pattern mimicking water drops, had a moldy shower box, a cracked mirror and no bath mats or hairdryer to speak of. This was going to be like camping in the desert.

The kitchen, which was pretty much the entrance, was small and dark. As soon as Mimmo left I'd make myself an espresso, devour the breakfast food now as there was no way I was getting back in that car today or ever again to procure myself some dinner.

The breakfast would be strictly packaged goods. No chance of a full English, apparently. Oh, who needed bacon when I could have a chocolate-filled croissant and a jug of strong coffee all to myself?

'Okay then, call me tomorrow morning when you're ready to go back down?' Mimmo said, rubbing his hands, obviously in a rush now. I wondered what could be so pressing for him at home. A wrestling match, maybe, and not necessarily on TV, judging by the way he'd prattled on and on about his parents not getting along. It certainly wasn't laundry night. I tried to smile at the prospect of being left here alone. In this light, even Mimmo looked like a better option than complete solitude up here.

I walked him out, watched the automatic gate close after him and just a second too late realized he hadn't left me the electronic key.

'Mimmo!' I called, scrambling parallel alongside the property fencing, but he didn't look back, disappearing around the bend. I was stranded within the property until tomorrow morning, surrounded by a high fence all around, a cursory glance told me. But if I was locked in, at least thieves were locked *out*. Not that anyone would want to come inside *this* place. But what if it got around that a foreign woman was staying in the *villa* (as if) all on her own? Would I be in danger?

Locking the door once, twice and thrice behind me, I tied my hair back and peeled my dress off, carefully placing it across the back of a chair. How had I managed to get it so filthy? It had to be the Mimmo Effect.

With a grunt, I grabbed the yellow threadbare towels from

the back of the other chair and headed for the mold-trap of a shower, throwing myself under the meager trickle, grateful that I was able to wedge myself in through the narrow doors, and tried to stay clear of the walls. You never knew.

I longed for my own roll-top bath with my view of the heath, my candles and my foamy, lathery bath gels that seemed to dissolve any troubles at one whiff. If I was home, in our home, I would lie back and relax, giving myself a refill with a flick of my big toe when the water had cooled.

Resigned, I began to lather – and made the huge mistake of opening my eyes. A gazillion-legged furry thing the size of a hippopotamus was crossing the shower base, too large to be bothered by a naked woman jumping up and down in sheer horror. I tried to wash it down by pointing the shower hand-piece thingy at it, but the bugger was just too big and determined to live. I'd never seen anything so disgusting in my life, not even on The Discovery Channel.

Completely freaked out now, I turned the water off and ran to the bedroom, where I yanked back the covers in case the rest of its furry family was waiting for me there. It looked okay, except for the gray sheets. I leaned in and smelled them. They didn't exactly stink of Mimmo, but neither would you put yourself in between them. Who the hell could sleep anyway? I was way too wired, too overwhelmed by the idea of falling asleep and dying of some bacterial strain, or being halfway down the throat of some humongous and hungry insect.

What I needed now was an espresso. Winding the towel tighter around me, I flung the rest of the cupboard doors open. Even if the espresso was old, I'd still drink it. At the most it would taste stale, but by now my need of a caffeine hit was so dire that I'd have even drunk from coffee dregs, had there been any.

Had there been any being the operative expression. I opened another set of cupboards. Still nothing. Man, was this place for real? Ah, but what was that at the back of the cupboard – a stray *teabag*? Good enough. I stretched my arm up, far enough to reach it and sniffed it. It smelled like the cupboard. Musty and stale. Still, at least it would be something warm. A cup of tea would do me just fine right about now. All those hours in the heat and I was beginning to get the shivers. All I needed now was another sunstroke.

I turned the dial of the cooker for the flame to ignite. Which, as you can guess, didn't happen. Not even bothering to try again, I went straight to the source, i.e. the bottom cupboard next to the sink where the gas tank would have been kept. But of course there was nothing there.

So I went around to the entrance to look for the gas connection and, sure enough, there was the gas pipe, and connected to it was… absolutely nothing. *Niente*. How in the world could someone actually let out accommodation with no means of even making yourself a goddamned cup of tea? No gas, no hot water, no soap, no shampoo (good thing I had my Sisa toiletries), a bug-filled Iron Maiden for a bed and strange creatures freely roaming the premises – what the hell was wrong with this guy?

No, my inner voice snapped at me. *What the hell is wrong with you? What are you even doing here?* Why don't you just fly home and face the music?

Screaming the shack down, I checked that the monster was gone and jumped back into the shower again, almost fainting from the shock as ice-cold water ran into my hair, freezing my scalp and turning me into one giant goose pimple.

I briskly – *man*, you've never seen anyone move so fast – washed my hair and applied conditioner while I soaped up the rest of my body, howling and shaking violently now, gasping for breath, brain freeze and all.

It took me hours to get warm. I should've been in our six-bed detached in Blackheath, sitting by the fire, but instead all I found was a crummy blanket in the musty old two-stick wardrobe and swathed myself in it, regretting how tomorrow I would smell of Mimmo's blankets instead of the luxuriously fragrant Italian shower gel *Felce Azzurra* I'd bought, so I lay in the bottom part of the bed, shivering so violently I thought I'd be sick for the third time in the last twenty-four hours.

After having woken several times in the night to the sound of roosters (yes, roosters that had no idea what time it was, but that was okay because neither did I), dogs howling and God knows what else, I finally gave it up and jumped out of bed, still cocooned up and now sweating like fried onions.

I sniffed under my arms, decided I was not going to go through that hell all over again and applied a double dose of deodorant. Then I put my new sarong on (I'm a real prize, aren't I?), brushed my hair and splashed some water on my face and waited for Mimmo.

At the stroke of nine I convinced myself that not only was Mimmo terribly late, but that he wasn't coming at all. My guess was he'd completely forgotten about me. Well, that would make things easier. At least I wouldn't have to see his cow eyes saddened when I canceled my booking. I took out the thirty euros I owed him for the night, wrapped them up in a sheet of paper from my agenda with many thanks and set it on the kitchen/corridor table. With a little luck I'd never see this place again.

My last obstacle before I made it out of here was the chain-link fence surrounding the property and the gate to which I still had no bloody keys or remote. So with the determination I was known for, I lunged at it and began to scale the blasted thing. And got as high as my shoulders before it buckled under my weight, catapulting me into the middle of the main road. Well, at least I was out.

Picking myself up and dusting myself off, and boosted by the lovely day and the smell of freedom, the unreliable dimmer switch inside me turned my hopes back up, and as I sauntered under the hot sun down the path leading into the city I was actually whistling.

But by the time the sun had risen high above the houses, I

stopped, clutching at my spleen that was threatening to zap right out of my navel if I didn't take a rest. Fanning myself, I piled my hair atop my head and fastened it with a clip. Water. I needed water. And a bigger bag to lug my stuff around. I looked like a right *clochard*, or better, a giant snail with my home on my shoulders.

All that walking had exhausted me and I found I wasn't even hungry anymore. Plus, it couldn't possibly take that long to reach the town center, right? I'd been going for hours now. Where the hell was I? Was I heading north, south, east, west?

The tarmac had given way to loose gravel paths leading practically nowhere but into dried, sticky bushes and soon I was facing the horizon with its fiery-red ball in an immense fuchsia sky. Now, as romantic as that might sound, I was not in the mood. I stopped, confused, in the middle of the open countryside, unable to make out any details around me, just a fuzzy whirr of russets, browns and golds, when all I wanted was the blue sea with tiny little boats bobbing on its surface. Lipari was small – not large enough that I wouldn't find my way back down, right?

Had I made a left? A right? How the heck would I get back onto the main road? The more I twisted and turned like a Rubik's cube, the more I seemed to get lost. Trust me to struggle finding my way around on a rock that was barely thirty-seven square kilometers. I promised myself that at the next bend I'd recognize something, but when I didn't I decided on going until the next, and then the next, but still it all looked unfamiliar.

I had roamed for hours under the hot sun without seeing a single soul, my legs becoming heavier and heavier at every step. Where the hell was I? I could hardly keep my still-swollen eyes open, my mind becoming fuzzy and my body going suddenly from being boiling hot to shaking with the cold.

The sun had poached my brain, even with my Pamela hat, the wide brim limiting my line of vision, flapping around in the breeze and threatening to fly off and down into the sea, so I folded it back and held it there with one hand as the other soothed the pain in my side.

And then I braked to a stop. Not because I couldn't go on anymore, but simply because there was nowhere else to go but down into the sea. I was hovering on the very edge of the island, looking straight out onto neighboring Salina. I'd never seen anything so beautiful in my life. It almost completely distracted me from the panic that had been rising in my throat.

And then, as if by magic, two things happened: I caught sight of a large building. And at the same time I became aware of a low keening buzz. Was it the sound of a distant motorboat? I couldn't tell up here with the wind whipping around my head. I scanned the horizon where the sky met the sea in a bleeding of mauves and rusts, but there were only a few sailboats. Was it perhaps an animal? A wild animal, like a boar or a wolf?

I wish I hadn't skipped the flora and fauna section of my Sicily guidebook. Was I, at this very moment, being targeted by some wildcat with tunnel vision ready to pounce on me any second, leaving me shredded to ribbons and forgotten by all? Not that anyone knew I was up here. Not that anyone cared. Sandra cared, yes. But only until she figured out why I'd done a runner.

Maybe that was what I should do right now. Run. But to where? To my left was the sea, to my right the woods and straight ahead the house from where another cry originated, almost human, causing my skin to crawl. Despite my wiser instincts to turn and scram, I moved in closer. Now, I'm not the bravest of creatures, but there was no way I could now pretend I hadn't heard anything and go on my way.

As I inched toward the building smothered by shrubs and bramble and overgrowth, the lament grew louder. He – she – it? had heard me coming and seemed to be guiding me with its cries through a gap in the foliage where a small door hung on its last rusting hinge. It was a small animal, no doubt, judging by the feeble sound. The cries stopped as I climbed in and almost cried out myself.

Upon seeing me, a dog, mangy and bleeding, started to whine and pant at the same time. I kneeled by its side, ignoring the burrs digging into my kneecaps and the thorns scratching my face and arms.

'Oh, *look* at you...' I whispered, gently caressing its head, careful it didn't turn around and bite me, but it actually nuzzled my hand. The poor thing let me lift it as best I could, watching me with its eyes full of trust. I guessed he had no choice. If I didn't do something pronto, this dog was a dead duck. I pulled out my cotton scarf and wrapped it around his paw in the worst tourniquet in medical history.

'Don't you worry,' I whispered to give him – and myself – a shot of courage. Who the hell was I kidding? This poor old fellow was on his last legs. He must have been thirsty, starving and – oh! I reached into my bag and pulled out my juice box, (lucky for him I'd forgotten I had it or would've slugged it down myself hours ago), ripping the top off with my teeth. He lifted his old head and stuck his tongue inside, lapping it up in two slurps. I pulled out the bag of almonds and tried to feed them to him, but he didn't even sniff them. Not a good sign.

This poor thing was worse off than me. First thing I needed to do was get him out of the bushes. I nudged the side door of the building open, entering what looked like an empty garage, the smell of diesel instantly filling my nostrils. Could I leave him here and go get help? Fact was I still had no idea where I was. There was no way I could find my way back.

As I deliberated, he licked my hands. 'You are an affectionate little mutt, aren't you?' I cooed softly. That was it. Decision made. I took a good look around me and took note of every detail so I would remember how to get back and threw myself down the mountain path.

In the space of what must have been almost an hour, bush-scratched and sun-swollen, I made it into the town, absolutely mortified (but also relieved) to see it was so easy and wondering why I hadn't managed before.

'Vet!' I cried to a group of old men playing cards in front of a café. 'I need a vet!'

They all turned to me slowly, faces scrunched up in concentration. 'Anita Vetta?' one of them aped. '*Non la conosco*,' never heard of her, he said, shaking his head and checking with his mates.

Damn. How did you say vet in Italian? 'Veterinaree-o! *Per animale!*' I couldn't remember how to say dog, one of the first words you learn, dammit. So I howled to get my point across, but they all stared. And then laughed. And that's when I spotted it – the green cross of the *Farmacia* – right across the street.

'Please – *veterinaree-o!*' I called as I burst through the door. One more hour and he wouldn't make it. He was probably taking his last breaths as I spoke. 'Please – *animale!* A dog!'

One of the women in white coats rounded the counter, concerned. 'A dog bit you?' she asked in perfect English, the queue shifting as one to the furthest wall away from me lest I had contracted rabies.

'Oh, thank *God* you understand me! There's a bleeding dog up in the hills in an abandoned villa facing Salina. Can you please call a vet? He's really bad.'

But the woman shook her head sadly. 'There is only one vet and he is in Messina at a conference for the weekend.'

Damn. By the look of her there was nothing she could do. Bloody hell. Welcome to Italy. I'd have to take the matter into my own hands. 'Right. Can I have some antibiotics, antiseptic and some bandages? Where can I find some dog food? And some drips?'

I slapped some euros onto the counter. 'Do you want something for your scratches?' she asked.

'No, thank you,' I called before I dashed down the *corso* and into Sisa for some water, dog food, a small blanket with a paw pattern and two plastic bowls. And a chewy bone. I only hoped he was hanging in there.

*

'Easy, buddy, easy,' I whispered an hour and a half later, grateful I'd remembered my way back up thanks to the hairpin bend in the road and the tall magnolia tree that looked grateful for the abating sun. The poor mutt hadn't budged, barely lifting his head as I pulled out my supplies and grabbed an old crate as a table. I dabbed some antiseptic on his front paw where I'd made the tourniquet and he whimpered as I gently blew on the open wound and then poured the water into his new bowl and watched as he glugged the contents in one go, his eyes never leaving my face. When I was done I cleared the crate and sat on it, patting Wooffy's head. Yeah, I know, it's a horrible name but so what? He seemed to like it.

As the sun stretched across the infinite span of sea below and slowly dipped, plunging the horizon into a shockingly intense purple now, I sat next to my protégé. The antibiotics I'd smuggled into his water must have been working already because he peeled himself off the floor and gave the food a go, his eyes, much more focused, watching me.

'Attaboy.' As mangy and old as he was, he was sweet. Now to get all that crap out of his fur. I pulled out my only hairbrush and sighed. He needed it more than I did. Gently I brushed the burrs and all sorts of grass and sticky stuff out of his fur, expecting him to rebel any second. But he was a good dog, sitting patiently. It took me at least half an hour, and by the time I was done he was so fluffy he looked like he'd been through the spin cycle, poor mutt. I started to laugh and he yapped in protest.

Eventually, when he finished the bowl of food I knew we were home free. And speaking of homes, now was the time to have a snoop around the massive house before it got too dark.

Although old and derelict, the building stood absolutely magnificent, respecting the Aeolian tradition of flat roofs that collected rain water in the winter, whitewashed exteriors and enormous openings now boarded up. I couldn't imagine anyone abandoning it – and the view? To die for, high above the cliff facing the sea, the first evening lights already twinkling on the opposite shores of nearby Salina only a stone's throw away.

'You be a good boy and stay here for a bit,' I whispered to Wooffy – as if he could go anywhere in that state – and gave him a final pat. But he got up and limped after me through the side door.

'Well, you don't like being on your own, do you?' I cooed, gingerly picking him up and holding him against my chest. He licked my face as we went into the house, careful to avoid piles of rubbish and guck that had fallen in through the craters in the roof of what had once been someone's home.

Did I say home? It was more like a palace inside, with high, vaulted ceilings and thick walls made of large slabs of stone. Slowly we ambled from room to room, taking in the devastation wreaked by time and lack of love. This place must have been magnificent once upon a time.

Oh, the pain the owners must have felt to leave this place! Only death would justify abandoning it. Which was what probably had happened. I wondered who'd inherited it. If a lulu of a house such as this had fallen into *my* lap I'd never go out again, let alone abandon it.

Tired now, I returned to sit on the crate in the garage, which was slightly less damaged and thus cleaner, still holding Wooffy who was now sleeping on my lap. I, too, must've dozed off a couple of minutes, because when I opened my sticky eyes I found Wooffy licking my face.

'Thanks for that,' I said, patting its head which I could barely see now in the dying light. We were a moment away from total darkness, so absorbed I'd been with Wooffy's wellbeing and the building that I hadn't noticed the night falling so suddenly, like an animal pouncing on its prey. And speaking of which, was that a howling noise in the distance?

How the hell was I going to find my way down at this

hour? There wasn't one street light up here, although the lights from the town twinkled from down below. Not that I had anywhere to go even if I did go back down. So this was my lot? A cheating husband, an empty ruin of a house for shelter and a sick dog? Way to go.

Luckily there was a full moon rising, huge above the horizon, and bright enough to stop me walking off the cliff and plunging into the sea. I wandered outside again to admire how it illuminated the land and sea almost to daylight. But I'd never be able to make it back to town even this way. The countryside must have been (knowing my luck) riddled with all sorts of foxes and wild boar. No, better to stay here.

In the absolute silence of the night, I turned to face the other end of the sky that was less bright and gasped at the multitude of stars, so close up here that they looked fake in their luminosity.

It was like I was up high on a ladder, just under a painted dome of painted stars. I'd never in my life seen so *many*, and in an instant I realized that whatever happened to me in the future, I would never ever forget the magic of this moment. I would be able to recall the exact temperature of the sea breeze on my skin, the wild fragrance of the bush and the velvet immensity of the sky that I could almost pluck stars down from. Whatever happened in my future, this would be one of my life-mark moments that I might share with someone in words, but I would never be able to fully convey the beauty – the *uniqueness* – of the moment.

I made my way back through the opening that led into the garage heaped with stuff hidden under a tarpaulin that reeked of mustiness, diesel and all sorts of nasty things. Better than sleeping out in the open. I adjusted my body on top of the heap, making sure there were no sharp edges jutting out to poke Wooffy or myself, and settled down. Tomorrow was another day.

The stale taste of sleep lined my mouth as I opened my eyes and peeked outside through the crack in the door. All was quiet and the moon had risen high. What time was it? The cold night air had entered the garage and humidity permeated the room, sinking into my bones and freezing me from the inside out.

I wasn't feeling too good, now. Maybe it was the cold, the hunger or the fatigue, so I huddled closer to Wooffy who lay next to me, happily panting away, obviously feeling a little better, but still in pain. I shivered and turned over, my mind restless, my skin still tight across my face and shoulders, and settled down to worry about rats and wild dogs and all sorts of things, when Wooffy let out a bark.

I turned my head to see a projection of light race across the ceiling and then thread its way through the trees and bushes, followed by a rumbling noise. A car! I cowered in the corner of the garage, debating what to do. If it was the owners, I'd have a lot of explaining to do. If, instead, I'd stumbled on a criminal cove, there would be no opportunity to explain.

It reached the clearing where the house was and braked so abruptly I could almost hear each individual ping of gravel. Two doors slammed and I heard voices. Shit. Now what? Stay hidden? Make myself known? It could be anybody. As I was debating, Wooffy let out a bark and bolted through the door on his three good legs. I was trapped.

7

Hostage

'*Gillian, thank God!*' said a familiar voice.

I squinted, barely able to make Sandra out in the beams of the car, let alone look her in the eye. And then I saw *him* – petting Wooffy and hanging back guiltily – Judas the Third (Judas the Second being Tony, of course).

To anyone without the benefit of the backstory, he would have appeared to be just a guy who loved dogs, but even in the dark I could see the smoldering looks he gave me, his eyes practically speaking to me words I'd have never been able to repeat even to myself, as if Sandra wasn't even standing there between us.

But I wasn't imagining the way his eyes lingered on me, nor could I ignore the tingling sensations chasing all over my skin as if he'd just reached out and caressed me. And I had a feeling that if he'd run only his pinkie across my arm, I'd have melted. Not me, but my body. My mind didn't want to have anything to do with any of it. But apparently it wasn't communicating with my skin that was practically screaming at me to move closer.

Instead I stepped back, at a loss for words, shielding my eyes against the bright beams.

'What happened to you? Your face!' she cried.

'How... how did you know I was here?'

Sandra hugged me and again Mattia's kiss flashed before

me, the memory swallowing me whole. 'We thought you'd gone home, but then we bumped into Manuela, the chemist, who said a tourist was desperate to help an old dog up in the hills. It could only be you.'

At that, Mattia looked down at Wooffy, caressing his fur slowly, then looked up at me suddenly and I wanted to run.

'How… did you know where to find us…?' I asked.

'This is her hideout. No one knows why,' Sandra explained.

'Her? Wooffy's a she?' Boy, it sure showed me what I knew about sex if I couldn't even tell the difference between male and female.

'Yes. Diana. She's the town dog.'

'You mean she's not abandoned?'

'Abandoned? Of course not. She's been missing for a few days. Everyone will be thrilled to know you've found her. Where have you been, Diana?' Sandra cooed.

'And rescued her,' Mattia added, checking her paw and ruffling her fur and tail, which he (she) was now wagging almost violently. 'Well done, Gillian.'

He'd said it with that underlying tone, and I knew he wasn't referring to Wooffy's rescue, but my escape. What else was I supposed to do? Why couldn't he just leave me alone? Or, if he simply had to cheat, why didn't he go and choose himself proper cheating material instead of dumped, dumpy, frumpy me? Did he really think that just because he made my skin tingle with those long lashes and that generous mouth I was going to capitulate only hours after discovering my husband's betrayal? I was weak, but not *that* weak.

Mentally shaking my head, I stooped and hefted Wooffy, wounded leg and all, holding her to my chest like my own child, determined this little gal shouldn't suffer any more.

Sandra touched my shoulder. 'Why did you leave us like that? Did I do anything wrong? Or Mattia?' She slapped his shoulder. 'What did you say to her?' But he was silent, continuing to eye me, a little more furtively and yet a little more boldly. This was exactly what I'd wanted to avoid.

And then Sandra turned back to me. 'Please don't take any notice of him. He's all mouth but he means well.'

And kisses even better, I thought, immediately pushing the idea away in horror.

'I'm so sorry,' I faltered. 'I don't want to cause any trouble…'

Darling Sandra's brow furrowed. 'Trouble? Why would you be any trouble? Don't be silly. Now let's go back home.'

Home. To *their* home. With her man of the Wandering Lips? How the heck had I got myself into this mess? There was no way in hell I could stay with them. I would always think of that kiss and how it had made me no better than Tony or Nadia.

No – enough. Tomorrow morning I'd book a flight home. There was no point in staying here on this godforsaken island. For what? The Tony Ship had sailed and I didn't want to sink the Sandra and Mattia one. Plus the sooner I left Sandra and Mattia on their own the better. He'd always have other women, but I sure as hell wasn't going to be one of them. I just couldn't do that to another woman, especially a new friend who had in such a short space of time done so much for me.

Better go home and face the music now, before I'd be too down in the dumps to get my life back on track. Tomorrow I'd take a catamaran back to Milazzo, catch a bus to Catania airport and get on the first flight to Gatwick. Get the kiss-guilt out of my system. It had only been a brief moment, but *man*, a woman could lose her sanity with a guy who kissed like that. You think I'd be immune. *I* thought I was immune.

'Here, let me take her,' Mattia murmured, bending down over me and Wooffy, and I tried to ignore the magnetic pull.

'No – it's okay,' I said, not wanting to let her go as I climbed into the back seat of Sandra's car like a bad little girl, placing myself behind Mattia who was in the driver's seat.

'Can you take her in until she's better?' I asked.

'Sure.' Sandra patted her and sneezed.

'You're allergic, remember?' Mattia said and turned to me. 'I'll keep her. You can come and take care of her at my place now that it's ready.'

I nodded, distracted, then shot up in my seat as his words sank in. 'Your place?'

He gave me a funny, wary look. '*Sì.*'

'You mean you and Sandra… don't *live* together?'

Sandra snorted. 'Honey – a few weeks, I can take – but live with Mattia? You must be nuts. I don't know how any woman can stand to be near him for more than that. Good luck finding a wife.'

I stared back and forth between them, the strangest feeling sinking into my brain. 'You mean you're not married?'

'Me and Mattia?' Sandra snorted as he stole me a glance in the rearview mirror, the light of an oncoming car lighting up his face.

'But… but…' and then it dawned on me. 'You're not even… together?'

Mattia continued to eye me quizzically as Sandra cackled with delight. 'Together, with Mr. Perfection here? You must be joking. I'd sooner hang myself. No offense, darling,' she said, touching Mattia's cheek.

'None taken, nag.'

Well, I'll be – and I'd run away thinking… I hugged Wooffy, who licked my face. Okay, so Mattia was free. So let's take stock here. If he wasn't a sleazebag looking for an easy ride, what the hell was he doing kissing *me* then?

'Are you cold?' Sandra asked. 'Mattia, give her your jumper.'

I protested but Mattia slipped first one and then the other arm out of his white cotton jumper and next thing I knew Sandra turned to wrap it around me. It was warm with his own body heat and his unmistakable male odor. It was like being in his arms. I shivered again.

'It must be the shock,' she figured. 'Or you're coming down with something.'

Yeah, I mused. *A critical case of lust.*

Whenever we passed a streetlamp or a car, which up here was a rarity, I could see his eyes darting to mine in the rearview mirror, asking me silent questions to which I had no answer. Or maybe my sense of guilt was making me imagine it all and he was just checking the roads. *He* certainly had nothing to be ashamed of. He wasn't cheating on anyone, as far as I knew. He didn't have a girlfriend. Why, I'd never know.

The next morning I sauntered into the kitchen as Sandra was having breakfast.

'Oh my God, look at you – your face is still swollen.'

Exactly. Look at me. I was a joke, almost forty. A soon-to-be-divorced mess with a chocolate addiction and bingo wings to show for it. And I had actually believed that a man as gorgeous as Mattia could even remotely be interested in me, albeit for a tryst. And yet, that kiss... those *kisses* had flipped my insides inside out.

Instead of mourning over The Marriage That Never Was and all the years I'd invested in it, every time I closed my eyes I saw Mattia's solemn expression, his gorgeous mouth inching toward mine. And at night, when everyone was asleep and the house was quiet, all I could hear was the pounding of my own heart and think of how sexy he was, hanging his head low when I pushed him away.

I knew it was only a game for him. That's what men did – they played games, and if we were foolish enough to fall for them, too bad for us. Me, I wasn't falling for anyone else as long as I lived, come who may. No. I was done with love. Tony and I had been over long ago. I realized that now. Any effort to rekindle any feelings buried under the cinders had been useless.

'Gilly? Do you want to tell me what happened to you yesterday?'

I sat up, focusing on Sandra's kind face. Tell her what exactly, that I was a potential cheater? That Mattia had kissed me and I'd actually kissed him back, knowing (or at least thinking) he was with her, the woman who'd taken me into her very own home without batting an eye, out of sheer kindness? Yeah, that'd go down well for sure.

Having been cheated on gave me no right to perpetuate the sin like an eternal chain. Right? Of all people, I was the least inclined to behave like that. On what *planet* had I allowed this to happen?

'I'm okay,' I said as she took my hand, a kind, concerned expression on her face. 'I just fell out of bed and landed on my nose.' *And got lost up in the hills. And got sunburn. And scratched myself raw in the bush. All while trying to get away from your –* that *man. Yes,* I thought savagely. *It was all his fault.*

She watched me in silence. 'I know what's bothering you,' she said gently.

I lifted my face to look at her but faltered. I just couldn't do it.

'You are attracted to him.'

'Who? I am not,' I said, my cheeks on fire. 'I've got bigger fish to fry. My marriage is over.'

'Which is why you should move on and find yourself another man. I know Mattia very well,' she said. 'When I came home he was agitated and I instantly knew something had happened between the two of you, although he won't talk, the *stronzo*. So tell!'

I swallowed, but still couldn't speak. So she'd masterfully put the pieces together. 'He was flirting with you and you thought we were married, correct?'

Ouch. This was a new level of cringe.

'And that's why you left.'

No use in denying the bitterly obvious. My eyes swung to hers. 'I am so mortified,' I croaked.

She laughed, hugging me. 'Silly! Don't be. No harm done.'

'But I thought—'

'And you left – what an honorable woman you are. Many women would've stayed and enjoyed the ride.'

'You're not disgusted?'

'Of course not. But Gilly?'

'Yuh?'

'Don't play games with him. He's had enough problems in his life and I don't want him hurt. Unless you mean love – and I know you don't because you're still hung up on your husband – stay away from Mattia. If you want I'll introduce you to a ton of guys who just want some fun. Agreed?'

I stared at her. She was afraid *I* was going to hurt *him*? 'Okay,' I said obediently as if I understood. So he'd been hurt? I couldn't imagine him being on the receiving end. He looked like the kind of man who left you the morning after an incredibly hot night. Dearie me, when was I going to stop thinking of him like that? How old was he anyway, thirty? He could be my younger brother. Good thing I wasn't sticking around much longer.

'So! Don't tell me you spent the past few days camping out in the abandoned villa?' she said.

'No, but it would've been an improvement on the B&B I was staying in.'

'Which one?'

'Uh, the guy's name is Mimmo Subba, I think.'

Sandra laughed. 'Mimmo? You poor, *poor* woman! He isn't even registered and doesn't know how to run a bath, let alone a B&B!'

Well *now* they tell me. How the hell was I supposed to know? 'Hey, nice joke, by the way. Your English is improving every day,' I mused.

'Thanks, but I heard it on BBC. Listen, you don't have to worry about anything anymore. Mattia's moved out. If he bothers you that much you won't have to see him ever again – as much as that is possible on this rock,' she tittered. 'Come on, let me take you out to lunch.'

Moved out? Mattia was already *gone*? And he'd left without even saying goodbye.

8

Puppy Love

Da Pannuzzo was a restaurant I'd completely missed in my daily perusals. The owner was Alfonso Torrisi, a John Belushi look-alike from mainland Sicily. His brother worked in the family restaurant there while Alfonso came out to do the summer season here. The amount of flirting between him and Sandra was almost revolting.

'Isn't he *sexy*?' Sandra whispered. 'And he's loaded, too!'

Loaded, I could sort of tell by the vast assortment of gold crosses on chains around his neck, but sexy? In comparison to most men, he was not the best-looking. I studied his rubbery face, the sleek brown hair flecked with grays, the *pelvis-first* stance. He was very fit for an over-fifty, that had to be said, and must have been good-looking years earlier. Now all that remained of the man I imagined was bags under his eyes and the beginning of love handles. As if I was one to talk. I looked like Sandra's mom.

'So tell me,' I urged when two heaped plates of clams arrived and he left, not without winking at her. 'What's the story between you two?'

Sandra laughed. 'Story? We have sex every summer. You know, when he's here, but that's only for three or four months a year. There's no one else, you see, and I get bored with the same old faces.'

My jaw dropped but I clamped it shut again. 'You sleep with him out of boredom?'

'Oh, don't get me wrong. He's great. He's in love with me. And he really makes an effort knowing he will never have me permanently. Besides, he has a wife.'

A wife? I swallowed a clam and a bit of bread dipped in the delicious spicy tomato and parsley sauce as her words registered and my food lost some of its taste. 'Is that how it works around here?'

Sandra shrugged. 'You haven't been here long enough. You wait and see. Forget Tony. You'll be desperate for any man by the time the summer's over.'

'I won't be here when the summer's over.' I had a couple more weeks now that I didn't have to run away like a leper as I hadn't, in effect, cheated on anyone.

The day after Mattia had moved out, he called the house. 'So how are you, Gillian? Miss me yet?'

And already I could feel my cheeks burning again. He *knew*. And now everything, every word and every silence between us bore a different meaning. And the sound of his voice no longer came across as deceitful, but only sexy and inviting. And, technically, legitimate. There would be no one cheating on anyone. I mean, look at him – youthful, good-looking, single, successful and practically swarming with beautiful women.

To think that I'd kissed the guy made my skin sizzle. Yes, I was drunk, yada yada yada, he was gorgeous and I was weak. Period. It wasn't enough I had a broken heart and an almost broken nose – why was I getting myself into trouble so much lately? And why did I feel so awkward around a bloke I knew nothing about, bar the feel of his soft mouth and hard pecs?

Any other woman dumped only a week ago would be obsessed with schemes of winning her own husband back or, at least – which would've been closer to my personal style – topping him. But I neither wanted Tony anymore, nor did I hate him. Those thoughts had stopped forming in my mind, and I slowly came to the sad conclusion that not only had our love been one-sided, but that I had also tired of trying many years ago.

Even as I'd prepared for this second honeymoon, in the back of my mind there was always the fear of being rejected. Because I knew that physically Tony and I had stopped working long before we were a disaster *emotionally*. And with the desire gone, I thought we could at least make the best of what was left – respect, companionship and all that. But there was none of that left now. As sad as it was, there was no going back. I'd passed the Point of No Return. I'd passed the point of caring, period.

'Earth calling Gillian...' came Mattia's deep, deep voice, warming me down to my toes.

'Oh. Sorry. How's Diana?'

'Come over and see for yourself.'

Go there, to his home, me on my *own*? As if. I was already abysmally embarrassed by what I'd done. He probably thought I was some starved cougar on the prowl for her next victim. Still... to go or not to go?

'Uhm...'

He laughed. 'I promise to behave.'

'Oh.' Well, he didn't have to be *that* specific.

'See you in ten minutes?' he suggested.

'Er – sure.'

That hadn't exactly taken long, had it? Forty-eight hours of laboring honest intentions wiped out in two seconds flat. *Good going, Gillian. And stop grinning at the sole idea of seeing him again. You shouldn't be going anywhere near the guy.*

But I had a responsibility toward poor Wooffy – I mean *Diana*. Plus it would be nothing further from a date, with me showing up in this state, my face practically in shreds and still nothing decent to wear, right? I was doing this solely out of my love for animals. And looking like I did, I wouldn't be sending him any sex vibes for sure. It would be a completely innocent visit. So exactly ten minutes later, purple nose and all, I rang Mattia's doorbell and waited, my stomach flipping like a desperate fish in a dry bucket.

From inside I heard Diana's familiar bark and I smiled as Mattia appeared on the balcony, waved and buzzed me in, Diana already on the landing, prancing like a puppy, licking my face as I bent to hug her. I reached into my pocket and gave her the remains of last night's pork scraps. We watched as she swallowed every last strip. I took as long as I could so I wouldn't have to look at him without blushing in shame and... well, something else.

I still think the guy had no idea of how beautiful he really was, standing there in a pair of jeans and a white linen shirt, his hair still wet from the shower and his long black lashes practically dripping. He wasn't wearing any cologne or anything, but he smelled deliciously clean and fresh and... scrumptiously male.

'Coffee?' he offered, not mentioning the mess my face was, thank God, and I nodded, taking advantage to take a good look around. Sandra was right. The place was spotless. Even the mat in the corner with the tray and the two bowls I'd bought were immaculate.

'Are you okay with taking care of her on the weekends?' Mattia asked as he pushed coffee into the mocha machine.

'Why – do you go away every weekend?'

He slid me a wayward glance as he pulled out two cups from the top cupboard. 'Pretty much...'

And where the heck did he go? Did he have a girlfriend after all? 'I'm happy to take care of Diana, but what about Sandra's allergy?'

He reached into his jeans pocket and pulled out a key. 'You could sleep here. If you don't mind?'

Ignore the heat creeping up your neck and burning your ears to a crisp. Plus, I was so sunburnt he wouldn't notice a bit of blushing. *Would I mind?* 'Of course not. She's kind of my dog, too, now, in a way, isn't she?'

Mattia grinned and rubbed the back of his neck, clearly as

embarrassed as I was. The humongous white elephant in the room was not going away unless I did something about it.

'Look, I need to make something clear,' I ventured and he stood quiet, listening. So I swallowed. Was this embarrassing or what? 'I'm... very sorry – for what happened the other night.'

He looked up, his dark eyes twinkling. 'I'm not. It's not every day that I get to kiss a beautiful woman.'

I rolled my eyes. Me, beautiful? I knew he had the playboy gene, but I didn't expect the overkill. 'That's, uhm – very gallant of you, Mattia, but seriously – that's not at all like me. I don't normally drink, you know. Hardly ever, in fact. But I was drunk and sad and lonely and... I don't want you to think I'm that kind of woman.'

He grinned. 'What kind of woman do you mean?'

Hoo boy. Was it hot in his flat or was it just me? Added to the fact that we were alone once again, if you didn't count Diana, and I was again under his dark, Mediterranean spell. So I shrugged, helpless for words. 'The... kind who jumps from one man to another. My husband has just left me. I am not even remotely interested in... another man. So, I'm very sorry I kissed you.'

He cleared his throat. 'Oh. Okay, then. I understand. I apologize for taking advantage of you like that. You'll never have to worry about that ever happening again. It's just that you were so... vulnerable and sweet. Not to mention beautiful and sexy.'

Something was definitely wrong here. Vulnerable, yes, but beautiful and sexy? Maybe *pretty*, twenty years ago, pre-marriage, pre-baby, pre-middle-age, pre-smack-in-the-face-with-reality. But now? He must be going blind.

'Stop being such a playboy. I don't need chatting up. I'm too old for you anyway.' Of course I should've thought of that before I kissed him back, but hey.

'Don't be silly,' he said. 'What's a couple of years? Besides, I don't chat women up. Unless I'm interested.'

'Okay...' I whispered, wondering where this was going, like a Samuel Beckett play – purely nonsensical and yet... and yet...

'Gillian –we both acted out of character that night. I don't take advantage of drunk women.'

'Oh. Okay, then.' Which of course, it wasn't. What was *that* supposed to mean? That if I hadn't been drunk, he would've taken advantage of me? But then, if I hadn't been drunk, I wouldn't have kissed him back. Problem solved. So it was okay now. He was a decent guy and I was a soon-to-be-divorced woman who'd had a rough night or two. We'd made things clear. Wrong place, wrong time, wrong person. Friends like before. But then why could I not look him in the eye?

Mattia smiled, checked the coffee and put a tray of delicious-looking pastries in front of me and, glad to have cleared things up (sort of) made arrangements to take care of Diana.

But one thing still bothered me. Where the hell was it he went every weekend, and why hadn't he volunteered the information?

Back on the *corso* on my way home and away from Mattia's overwhelming presence, I let out a sigh of relief. Despite the coffee and pastries (I'd only taken one to be polite, and let me tell you dainty nibbling was not for me, because, like always in my life) I was still starving.

Left, right and center, eateries taunted me with their heavenly fragrances, and the big technicolor close-ups of today's specials weren't helping my self-discipline. Damn, would I ever make it to the end of the *corso* without giving in to temptation? Every other shop seemed to answer each one of my dreams: *Macallé*, cylinder-shaped doughnuts filled with ricotta cheese and cinnamon, and then sprinkled with sugar; lemon *granita*, chocolate *gelato*, Nutella *cornetto*, almond paste *biscotti* – where did it end? With my *own* end in the diabetes ward of a hospital?

As I lined up at the counter of my new-found bakery paradise, I was content to watch the world (well, the *town*) go by. Youngsters, the odd couple, then youngsters, youngsters and more youngsters and then oh – some women my age! Finally! I craned my neck. Where were they going? From across the street it looked like a beauty salon. Yeah. Maybe some other time. Possibly once my honker went back to its original size.

For now I was more concentrated on immediate pleasures, because this morning I had my heart set on *cannoli*, one with cream and one with ricotta cheese, both ends dipped in fragrant roasted pistachio flakes, the best Sicilian dessert in the world in my modest opinion. The flip side of being dumped was that I continued to be lavishly *desserted* wherever I turned. So there was no way I wasn't getting as much pleasure as I possibly could from this delicious island now.

Next to me in line were two very chic women around my age, one red-headed and one blonde, both fake, but extremely well-coiffed and wearing some amazingly expensive silk dresses and jewelry by the kilo. They were *marvelously Mediterranean*, in a league of their own as only Italian women can be.

And, in the shadow of these two goddesses, as I lined up totally undeterred by their physiques, waiting for my number to be hollered, my conscience nagged at me like someone jabbing me in the side with a toothpick. *Walk away*, a voice said to me. *Step away from all this food if you want the slightest chance of ever looking like these two.*

I don't know why, but the more I told myself that I'd have to stop eating tomorrow, *tomorrow* without fail saw me hungrier and hungrier. And in those earnest moments when common sense prevailed and I was telling myself that I couldn't go on this way, that was precisely when the person behind the counter would call my number, and I'd make a mad dash to be served. Yes, it had to stop, if I was ever going to get my life back on track.

So I decided to go on a diet – the minute I touched down at Gatwick again. Promise. I would change my ways. Keep busy outside the house. Find a job. But already that dampened my combative spirit – what kind of job could I possibly find at the tender age of forty? I'd been off the career scene for the past twenty years – all the good jobs were taken by younger, more ambitious people who were dying to start their adult lives. Me, my adult life had almost killed me. Plus, can you imagine me being office junior or assistant to some twenty-year-old? Neither can I.

And I'd have to move. No way was I sleeping at the house in Blackheath anymore. A woman had her pride. But where would I even live? Even if I did find a job, could I even afford to rent without digging into my nana's inheritance? Martha and Brends would certainly help me find a place. And then Brends would get on my case and badger me to find myself a man. Yeah, like that was happening.

How could I even think of starting all over again? And for what? Another slimy, cheating bastard? That's what all men were, right? Well, not all of them. Mattia hadn't cheated on anyone. I'd been wrong about him. Not that I was going to act upon the attraction that was growing, of course, but still it would've been nice to know that guys like that actually existed.

What was it he'd said? That he didn't jump from one bed to another or something like that?

A loud cackle coming from the two women at the next table made me smile to myself as they gossiped. Until a familiar name popped up, apparently very popular among female circles. *Mattia*.

At first I thought it was a coincidence. There must be plenty of Mattias around, but then the conversation got kind of specific and I knew it could only be him.

'He is so hot, I tell you,' the redhead said to the blonde in Sicilian, which I was picking up quite quickly now.

'Lucky you, you get to see him every day.'

'*And* night,' the other said. 'I'm seeing him this evening!'

Oh, was she? Apparently, despite what he'd said, the man was very... *busy*. It didn't surprise me, what with his lifestyle of roaming the streets on his blue Vespa like a young pup in flip-flops and shorts. And there was me thinking he wasn't interested in anyone. *Men*. You just can't trust them. Point proven, case rested.

'What can I geeve you?' Adriana, my favorite café counter girl asked. By now we were on a first-name basis.

'Two *cannoli* please, one with cream – ah – chocolate cream, and one with ricotta cheese.'

To which she grinned. 'Have you tried our new combination?'

My head jerked up. 'Combination?'

'*Sì* – chocolate ricotta. Try it – you'll love it.'

She grinned and pulled out the tongs and I pulled out my money, already salivating.

'*Buon appetito*,' she said as I grinned and took a huge bite.

'Hey, Gillian!'

Damn. My supposedly private foray into food was about to be aborted. Who the heck could it possibly be? On this island I knew all of what, two people? So I wiped my mouth and pretended not to hear. (I know, I'm a horrible person, but what would you have done with a stuffed face?)

'Gillian, over here!'

A male voice – not Mattia's. Well, whoever he was, he wasn't letting go. Caught in the act, I chewed and swallowed as fast as I could and looked up but couldn't find a familiar face.

'Remember me? The other night?'

Now *that* was something I'd never heard from a man before.

'It's Claudio, Sandra's colleague?' he offered.

I took a closer look. It almost *looked* like the Claudio from the other night – the good-looking one who'd actually asked me how I was. 'Claudio? Is that really you? I didn't recognize you.'

Indeed. He'd cut his hair and shaved. And still looked terrific.

'I'm trying to act like a grown-up,' he said, kissing me on both cheeks, Italian style. 'What happened to your face?'

My hand stole to my nose, as if I could in one gesture cover my bruised eyes and scratches as well. 'Long story.'

'I didn't know you knew the happy couple!' he said.

I blinked. 'Happy couple?' And sure enough, there they were, a bride and her groom, posing further up ahead at the top of the steps of Via del Concordato, she in an incredibly expensive – and tiny – wisp of white organza against the cobalt blue sky. It would have barely been enough for my headpiece.

The air of excitement and bliss enveloping the young (and of course gorgeous couple) was so tangible it hit me in waves. Happy and hopeful, they had their whole life ahead of them. Well, hopefully more than *my* twenty years. It figured that I'd walk straight from the end of my marriage into the beginning of someone else's happier ending. Good luck to them, though. I hoped they would be happy. Everyone deserves to be happy, right?

'Come on, let's go,' Claudio said.

I stepped back. 'Oh, no. I don't know them. I was just passing.'

Claudio took my arm. 'Well, now you have to stay and be my date. We're just about to go to lunch.'

Lunch? *Lunch?* You see? It wasn't my fault – food literally ambushed me – hunted me down. *Not* the other way around. So I stored my second *cannolo* (for now) in my bag and let him take my hand.

And then, still hiding my bruised face behind my shades, I wished I hadn't gone. The place was so romantic it looked like a film set for *The Great Gatsby*, high above the sea, with long tables covered in embroidered linen and dazzling crystal glasses rivaling the equally dazzling waters in the inlets below. The best china was laid out, and all the guests were singing and clapping, cheering the newlyweds on for a kiss every few minutes.

The poor souls couldn't get through a course without having to put their forks down, wipe their mouths and kiss. It was the kind of romantic I'd never seen, let alone experienced before. They were in love, besotted with each other. Why didn't I remember ever feeling that special, not even on my own wedding day? Were the positive memories in my distant past fogged up by my dreary present, I wondered?

I remembered the countless times Tony had snapped at me for no reason at all, or rather, for many reasons. I was too big for his liking, didn't dress like his colleagues' wives, spoke my mind.

Boy, did it all fall into place now. Tony was one hell of a man to please and I was surprised I'd kept trying for so long. Yes, he was a piece of work.

And then I saw *the other* piece of work sitting at the opposite end of the table. Mattia, ensconced between two gorgeous women – not the two gossipers at the table but two younger women – all over him as he silently watched me, as if amused. My hand stole to my nose, which I thought better to hide in my glass. As I was about to avert my eyes, he raised his glass and smiled at me. *God*, how I wanted to go home!

'Are you okay?' Claudio asked as he leaned in to pour me some more *vino*, the very thing that had got me into my Mattia-Mess in the first place. I was conscious of Mattia looking at me as I lifted my glass and then put it back down. I'd told him I wasn't a drinker. And yet I was getting the hang of it.

I turned to Claudio gratefully and gave him a mega-watt smile, which he returned, somewhat thrown, possibly. I don't know why I did that. It's not like I'm a teenager playing flirting games. I guess I just needed to not feel like a total disaster of a woman. Besides, Claudio was nice. And good-looking. A bit of an ego-booster, actually. Maybe he could be the distraction I needed – the guy I could have fun with without getting hurt. I could invent the *No-Hurt Flirt*. Ten days max and you're out. Brends would be proud of me.

Later, while walking home alone despite Claudio's insistence on accompanying me, stuffed and happy to get away from all the joy, a female voice called after me in English.

'Hello!'

I turned, expecting someone wanting to pimp out tickets to a show or something. But no. It was my friendly receptionist.

'Maria! How are you?'

She hugged me and double-kissed me on the cheeks, which I was kind of getting used to by now, and squeezed my hands. 'I was worried about you – I thought you might have gone back to the mainland.'

Yeah, me too. 'No, still here.'

'Did you find a place in the end?'

'I'm staying with Sandra Anselmi.'

'The English teacher? That's good.' She sighed dreamily. 'She looks like she knows how to have fun.'

'As opposed to me,' I sighed in return.

'And me,' she agreed. 'God, what I wouldn't give to look like her.'

'I know, she's gorgeous, isn't she?'

'And her clothes. I'd kill for something fancy. But where am I going to get stuff like that, and with what money?'

'Sisa?' I suggested and we both burst into fits of giggles. 'Hey – have you got time for a coffee, Maria?'

She glanced at her watch. 'I'm off this afternoon but I have to go start dinner for my children.'

'Just ten minutes?' I could see her fighting her inner sense of motherly duty. Sometimes even ten minutes can throw your schedule completely out of whack. I would know.

She grinned. 'What the hell – why not? It's not like I have a husband to answer to.'

Ouch. I'd been right about that, then.

'Divorced?' I ventured.

She shrugged. 'He never came back after our youngest was born.'

Was I in the presence of my twin soul here?

She took my hand. 'Come with me. This conversation needs more attention than a coffee. Can I invite you to eat with us?'

Eat? I'd just downed a seven-course meal. 'Only if you allow me to bring something,' I said. To which she recoiled in horror. 'Absolutely not. Come.'

And that was how we walked to her home, which was small, packed with children's clothes, toys and books. It was so warm and welcoming. Just like her.

'Tell me about your life back home,' she said, handing me

some potatoes and a peeler as she began washing some vegetables in the kitchen sink. I sat at the table and got to work. Funnily, it kind of felt like being in my own kitchen – not the room or fittings or anything – just the sense of home. Which was now long gone. I no longer had a kitchen or a home.

'My life? Well. I live in London.'

In a house that we're going to have to sell now...

'My... husband is a surgeon.'

Who left me out of the blue...

'Soon to be ex-husband, actually.'

Maria turned away from the sink to look at me.

'I just caught him with another woman. And I have a twenty-year-old daughter.'

Who doesn't need me anymore...

'Wow. I'm sorry. You have an amazing story.'

Yes. It's amazing I haven't jumped off a bridge yet...

'But you travel a lot, *sì*?'

'I'd like to.' *But I'm afraid of flying – and boats...*

'And you traveled all the way here, just to surprise him?'

I bit my lip. 'Yes.'

'That's tough. I'm so sorry.'

No. That was pathetic.

I shrugged. 'Life.'

She rolled her eyes and snorted her assent as she patted the vegetables dry and took my potatoes and we proceeded to dice them for her *caponata*. It was so strange, to be invited back to the home of someone I'd only seen once before, but somehow, it also felt right. This was Lipari, not London. And the locals were so friendly.

'I'd love to travel,' she sighed. 'See some European capitals. Lisbon. Oslo. Vienna. Maybe go to a concert of classical music. Wear a beautiful dress...'

It dawned on me that Maria was life-starved. Weighed down by money problems and single parenting, it must have been difficult for her. And yet, she always wore a smile on her face, no matter how hard she worked both at the hotel and at home. She was used to labor; I could tell from her small, red hands.

When her children came home, they all tumbled into her arms, from her preschooler to her teenage son, all there, showing their affection, happy to be home.

'Adriana!' I beamed when I saw my favorite café girl.

'You know my daughter?'

'Know her? She's practically my personal savior.' And when I told them about my love affair with her café, everyone laughed and Maria caressed Adriana's face.

And then my own Annie came to mind. She would've flinched at such a simple, loving gesture. Sure, she was a great daughter, but had never been particularly affectionate or, now that I thought about it, never particularly looked up to me or sought my advice. Probably because I always volunteered it.

After dinner and another coffee I offered to help with the dishes but Maria shooed me away with a promise to meet again.

Content, I strolled back down the *corso*, thinking how everything happened for a reason. This horrible man had left Maria destitute, but now there was no more fighting, no more cowering. Now she was free to live her life as she pleased. Well, almost. What she needed was a push in the right direction. Not to mention a few extra bob.

Enjoying the warm evening breeze coming in from the sea and not wanting to go back to Sandra's flat just yet, I lingered. If there was a time to nip down to the famous Marina Corta, now was it. So I made my way down the alley that spilled into Piazza Ugo d'Onofrio lined with sidewalk cafés and stopped, my heart *recognizing* him before my mind caught up.

Tony. In the flesh. And this time he was alone.

9

Facing the Demons

He stopped just in front of me and I was trapped like a white pawn facing a black pawn on a chessboard, waiting for death to be free. 'Gillian. I *heard* you were still here. Can I talk to you for a moment?'

I swallowed. He wanted to talk to me? Why, was it not working out between him and Younger Woman?

As I mentally tore her hair out of her roots and bashed him within an inch of his life, I wondered whether I wished I'd never known. Oh, but he would've told me soon enough. It looked like he was serious about her.

'I wanted to tell you I'm going home soon,' he said.

Did I want to board the plane with him? Was that what he was about to ask?

'Nadia is coming to the UK with me.'

Oh, goody... was this the part where I was supposed to slit my throat or throw myself at his ankles and beg him to reconsider?

'Have you spoken to Annie about us yet?' he continued.

'I thought you might want to do the honors,' I replied drily.

He shrugged. 'Okay, I can do that.'

'Good for you.'

'Gillian – I'm so sorry. I meant to tell you sooner but I didn't know how to break it to you.'

'Please,' I said. 'Spare me.'

He nodded, flexing his fingers as if he was about to perform one of his surgeries. 'Okay,' he said after a long moment. 'Shall we put the house on the market, then?'

And here we were. 'Unless you want to buy me outright,' I promptly answered, my gaze lost on some tourists stopping to observe the Chiesa del Purgatorio church.

He thought about it and discarded the idea immediately. The English *gentleman* didn't want to subject his new flame to his old wife's former home. 'No. I'll put it on the market.' More flexing of the surgeon fingers. 'Have you got a lawyer yet?' he asked.

'Damn right I have,' I lied. 'From now on you can talk to him.'

'Gillian…'

Gillian my foot. How much more did I need to be humiliated? Damn, damn, damn. No. I was not going to give him the satisfaction of seeing me cry. What had I ever done to him for him to treat me like that? For him to want to hurt me? When had I become the woman he no longer loved? And whatever had I done to be his enemy? Years of practically self-effacing love, putting my family before myself, catering to his every need, going that extra mile to prove to him he'd chosen well and that I deserved his love?

'Goodbye, Tony,' I whispered, walking past him without turning back.

And that was it. The end of my marriage. For good. What a joke it had all been, my whole life, all these years. A hysterical joke. *I* was a joke. I was hysterical. So I laughed. I laughed at the look I must've had on my face when I saw him burst into his hotel room with that girl in his arms, a second away from throwing themselves onto the bed and having furious, extra-conjugal sex. And I also laughed at the silly, sized-eighteen me who was so worried about waxing and looking fresh and relaxed for her husband when instead I could've fit three of her into my dress – with room to spare.

And as I laughed, I realized it wasn't so funny, and so discreetly, behind my shades, I wiped my eyes with my little finger, tasting my tears as they fell into my mouth, salty and cool in the evening air. I knew this was the deal – I'd come to terms with it. I didn't even *want* to be married to him anymore. So why the hell was I acting like a teenager with growing pains?

The cobblestones on the *corso* were too slippery for my heels and my ankles began to hurt, so I leaned against a wall and whipped them off. I didn't want to face the throng of tourists coming my way, so I made a right and began my descent up the steps of Via Maiolico leading up to the citadel. Very few people would attempt such a feat in this heat, I'd have thought, but as I climbed the steep stone steps dotted with stalls selling souvenirs of all kinds, it seemed that more and more people materialized the higher I climbed.

Damn, was there nowhere I could have some privacy besides my own room at Sandra's place? Back home you could walk for miles in a park without encountering a soul, but here? You couldn't swing a fish without bumping into someone you knew. Especially the one I knew and had loved the past twenty years.

I removed my shades and wiped the tears from my cheeks with the back of my hand. What the hell had I been thinking, coming out to this godforsaken island in pursuit of a husband who was no longer interested in me, only to receive the ultimate dose of humiliation? Stupid, *pathetic* me.

I limped through the citadel gates as fast as I could, under the long narrow archway into a clearing high above the sea past parents strolling behind kiddies on tricycles and trainer wheels, just happy to be alive and free. I wish I could've said the same for myself.

I passed the archeological museum, San Bartolomeo's Cathedral and the castle to Santa Caterina's church and then swung round and followed the steep descent via another lava-cobblestoned crescent, careful not to slip on the smooth rock, and finally joined Corso Vittorio Emanuele until I reached Marina Lunga to watch the lights of the huge ferries coming in.

Here, scooters, cars and taxis whizzed by me. A man (an old gizzard, it figured) even offered me a ride, but I swiped at my face and kept going, past the intersection and up a hill heading north.

How, how, how on earth could I not have seen what he was and had been for a long time now? How could I have been so clueless about my own husband? This was a typical situation, experienced by countless women around the planet. And yet, I couldn't bring myself to understand why (besides the obvious exotic/erotic reason) he would actually do that to me. Why would he betray my trust in him – Annie's trust as well? Did we mean absolutely nothing to him?

Gillian…

How the hell could he do this to me after a lifetime together?

Gillian.

How could he throw me out with the trash?

'Gillian!'

I swung around at the sound of my name, so relieved to see a familiar face. Mattia. Then I remembered I wasn't supposed to be so happy at the mere sight of him. Well, at least he had never betrayed me, lied to me and left me.

'I've been chasing you since the citadel. What's the matter?' he asked, his voice soft as he took a step closer.

'Sorry,' I croaked. 'I… uh. I'm not feeling very well…'

His great big hand came to rest on my back and guided me away from there as he helped me into his (newly repaired) Jeep, closing the door with a soft thud. In no shape for a conversation of any sort, I put my face into my hand and closed my eyes, uncaring of what happened next, whether he thought I was a baby or, worse, a psycho. *Go ahead, lock me up and throw away the key – what could anything ever matter again?*

My marriage was over. Of course I knew that. I'd known the second Tony and Nadia had burst into the hotel room, but now that it was a done deal it hurt like hell. I was officially The Deserted Wife.

And there was me thinking he'd be lost without me. That in a week max he'd be back, crawling for my forgiveness. Not that

I could ever take him back. And then what, see her face stuck to his every time he walked into the room? No thank you. I'd been married as long as I'd been single. What was I supposed to be feeling besides anger, hurt and loss?

Brends, whose specialty was sleeping with married men for some reason, had once told me married men were perfect for quick affairs because they never left the wife. Trust *me* to get the one bastard with the balls. And now that I was one of the injured party, I sympathized more than ever.

I don't remember much of the rest of the ride home, but I found myself at Sandra's door and Mattia by my side.

'Thank you,' I sniffed while fishing inside my bag for the key, but my hands wouldn't stop shaking and silent tears were still blurring my vision.

'Let me,' he whispered and I surrendered my bag to him, like I was being robbed. Hadn't I been? My whole life, or the few shreds that had been left of it, was now completely gone. Nothing else mattered anymore.

I was dimly aware of his arm as he guided me up the three flights of stairs and to the sofa, where he placed a soft throw around my shoulders. Are you getting another sense of déjà-vu?

'I'm sorry,' I managed in between sniffles. Which rapidly became a full-blown sob session. 'It's just so... *hard*...'

Mattia's jaw bunched and his eyes went even darker than usual, the color of obsidian, but he said nothing and pulled me against his big broad chest, which was by far the warmest place I'd been in ages. He let me cry, his body absorbing the shocks of my shaking, blubbering release. Oh God, how pathetic was I?

But luckily Mattia wasn't letting me go anywhere. I knew that while he was here, I'd be safe even from myself and that he wouldn't let anything bad happen to me. The realization that I was here crying my guts out to a practical stranger hit me like an eighteen-wheeler truck. I wiped my eyes with the balls of my fists that were now black with what was supposed to have been waterproof mascara and looked up, Mattia's image shimmering above me like in a sort of dream. I must've looked a sight.

'I'm sorry. Thank you. I'm okay now.' And then I burst out into a new howl.

'*Gesù…*' he whispered, wiping my face dry with his gentle fingers and I wanted to howl even louder but I didn't have any more strength left. Next step? A great almighty coronary, which would have solved my one impending doubt: *What Next in Life?*

Mattia was holding me tight, rocking me back and forth and shushing me like I used to do with Annie when she was little. He'd been patiently sitting there with me for so long, so I finally tried to move away and give him a margin of escape but he wouldn't let go. His body was like a big giant furnace and I wanted to wrap myself around him.

'Relax. Lie back. And tell me what happened.'

So I did. I told him everything, although it took me forever, what with the sobbing and blowing my nose and talking gibberish. But then, who knew the syntax of heartache? I knew the right words, like pain and anger and frustration – but to piece it all together and give it a semblance of logic, something that actually made sense? Pain was not a language you could learn until you've had your full-immersion experience in that region.

I could feel his body tense and his jaw bunch, especially when I got to the part about the weight gain and Tony becoming meaner and then finally deceiving me.

'I'm not even crying because it's the end of my marriage,' I blubbered. 'We didn't really love each other anymore. I'm crying because… because it's sad that it had to happen after all this time. Does that even make *sense*?'

He nodded. 'Yes. Yes, it does.'

'Ooff – I'm exhausted,' I breathed, trying to get up.

'Here, let's get you to bed,' Mattia said and before I could stand up, he whisked me up into his arms. Again.

'No,' I countered. 'I can walk.'

'I know. I just like to carry you.'

'Training as a weight lifter?' I quipped, wiping my eyes.

He looked down at me with the tenderest of smiles. 'Silly Gilly...'

It felt so strange, being carried by a man. And he showed no signs of breaking his back or collapsing a vertebrae under my weight. I just stared up into his face, doe-eyed, as he took me into my bedroom and delicately deposited me on my bed.

'Try to forget about him and think about good things. I'll be here when you wake up,' he whispered and gave me a light peck on the cheek, miles away from my mouth.

And I somehow believed him. Mattia, I felt it deep in my bones now, was not the kind of guy to just throw words around without meaning them. 'Thanks so much. It did me good talking to you,' I said and before I knew what I was doing, hugged him. And he held me close for a long, long time. It felt nice. Warm, cozy and yet... and yet... *exciting at the same time*. So exciting that, for a while, I really did forget about my troubles.

Mattia was not only kind, he was also manly beyond belief, every part of his body oozing sensuality. If it was true you (I) couldn't look at him without having naughty thoughts, there was also this other side of him that caught you (me) unaware. All my prejudices about gorgeous men just melted away after I'd actually made an effort not to only see him as The Bod.

He was sensitive. *Soulful*. He'd listened to me pour my heart out, tight-lipped and shaking his head when I got to the most painful parts. Somewhere along the line, we'd somehow managed to connect on a different level, as if it was the most natural thing in the world. And I had known the guy only a few days.

He slowly pulled back, studying my face. My body sent one kind of message but my mouth contradicted me completely. Go figure. I swallowed and straightened before I made another mistake, only this time I wouldn't have the booze to blame.

In response, Mattia took my hands and entwined my fingers with his in an all-too-intimate gesture. It wasn't studied, though, and came naturally, but it surprised me all the same and filled me with immense pleasure, thrumming through me like when you sink your tired, freezing body in a hot bath at the end of a long day. It comes as a bit of a shock but then you relax and let yourself go. But I didn't want to get too comfortable. I was nowhere near ready for a scene, especially with a man who was younger. There was already way too much competition out there.

'I think you're going to be okay, Gilly,' he whispered, his eyes never leaving mine.

'I am?'

'Absolutely. You're practically halfway there. Now go to sleep. I'll see you when you wake up.'

And so with the knowledge that I was being looked after for once in my adult life rather than vice versa, I curled up to sleep, wanting the time to go by quickly so I could start the rest of my new life. And, yes, see Mattia again.

'Jesus, what a monster,' Sandra commented the next morning when I filled her in on Tony. I left the Mattia part out, for some reason, though. It wasn't as if something had happened. All he did was make me some soup (way better than Sandra's, by the way) and sit with me until she returned. There were no innuendos of any sort, and for a moment I thought I'd imagined the sexual tension between us. But I knew I hadn't. There was something there. Whether it was Mattia responding to my unconscious signals or a conscious interest on his behalf, I didn't know.

She smiled. 'You know what you need? Some super-pampering!'

'No, I need to call a lawyer back home.'

So I contacted Brends' divorce lawyer, John Bennet, and explained my situation to him. He readily (after I paid him a generous retainer, of course) agreed that it would take months if not longer to get my money after we'd sold the house. Again, kudos to my Nana for taking care of me.

So I thanked him and asked him to proceed. I would be emailing him all the pertinent documentation to open my case.

'No, not red. It's the color of menopausal women,' I objected as I was shown all sorts of hair dye samples in the beauty salon.

Sandra and her hairstylist Gina, who was once upon a time a *Gino*, I'd been duly informed, barked with laughter as they sifted through my pluri-dyed hair.

Gina picked up a strand, studying it. 'Ash blond was your original color. We could try something similar,' she suggested.

I turned around in my seat, aghast. 'How did you know that? *I* don't even remember my natural hair color.' What with all those cheap store-bought dyes, I'd tried most of them and was never satisfied. I didn't want to look like my hair was dyed. I just wanted to have my old hair back. Correction. I wanted my old *life* back, pre-betrayal.

'And no biker-chick funky cuts either,' I added. 'I'm a traditionalist by nature.'

'Can she *wash* it?' Sandra quipped and I bit my lip. 'Sorry, it's just that—'

'I know, change is more difficult for some rather than others,' Gina acknowledged with a wink in the mirror. I loved her already.

'And some men try to stop you from changing,' Sandra added knowingly.

'And some men leave you if you do,' Gina said with a sigh and we all nodded.

I looked in the mirror, at my tired, aging face. The very weight of the world was there, in my every wrinkle, every crease, every drooping line. *This isn't just old age*, I told myself. This was the face of complete, absolute, utter misery. It was all fine and dandy starting a new life, but with *my* looks? Please.

Sandra patted my shoulder. 'Blonde it is, then. Can we get Sonia to do a French manicure in the meantime?'

'Actually,' I said sitting up, determined to start from scratch.

'Can I get something to rejuvenize my face? I had sunburn a few days ago and need…' What, exactly? A face scrub? More like a facelift.

'Great idea!' Sandra enthused. 'No offense. You're a beautiful woman, but you have this aura of rejection around you. Not to mention you need a good face treatment.'

No shit. In the space of a few days I'd bruised my nose, my eyes and got third-degree burns in this frickin' sun. 'And you think that a two-hundred-euro makeover is going to dissipate my negative aura?'

'Honey, by the time you leave this place you'll be a brand-new woman!'

And I was – after spending the whole afternoon – and a huge chunk of money – getting a pedicure, manicure, cut and dye and a glycolic acid face treatment, plus a complete wax from eyebrows to calves, i.e. ninety-five percent of my body – I am not kidding you; I may have been a natural blonde, but don't forget my Italian DNA.

I admired the new me in the mirror. Apart from actually turning into someone else altogether, I couldn't have done any more. Or looked any better. As a matter of fact, I looked like the old me from many years ago – at least ten years younger. Weight aside, that is. But hey – one thing at a time.

Because this was just the tip of the iceberg. I needed more than an afternoon at a beauty center. I needed a strict diet – and a new dose of confidence. Which, I had to say, was already starting to seep in as I passed my reflection in the shop mirrors down the *corso*. Sure, my shape was still the same, but something had changed and not only on the surface. There was a new bounce in my step. The knowledge that I could *change*, take better care of myself. Funny lot, we women were. If our hair is in good shape that day, we instantly stand taller and start flicking it around from shoulder to shoulder, feeling more confident and thus, automatically sexier. If we're having a bad hair day, we feel like complete shit and the rest of our qualities go down the drain.

'You know what you need now?' Sandra linked her arm through mine. 'New clothes!' she chimed.

As if. 'Sorry to disappoint you, Sandra, but I haven't found one store that carries my size. Not even Sisa can handle me.' I was destined to wear my daily sarongs forever.

She laughed. 'You're talking like you're a female Yeti. You make me laugh, Gillian.'

'But I'm telling you. I have been to every single place on the island. There is nothing for me here.'

She gave my arm a gentle pull. 'Come on, this way.'

This way was down a narrow alley off the *corso*, past the fragrance of fresh laundry, past Antonio's Trattoria to the very end where a gang of old tomcats hung out, so huge and feral even neighborhood *dogs* feared to tread.

She rang a bell and stepped back to check out the upper window, cupping her hands around her mouth. '*Cosetta! Sono Sandra, apri!*'

And like magic, the front door pinged open.

'Let's go,' she said, all excited.

Beautiful honey-colored, antique marble stretched over a long wide corridor that gave onto large sunny reception rooms on both sides, both packed with black and white and sepia family photos in silver frames. This place was like a Tardis. I wouldn't have even noticed it from the outside, and yet inside it was a delightful tribute to the days of old, with antique furniture kept spotless, shiny and lemony fragrant.

'Here she comes,' Sandra whispered and I looked up the stairs to see a tiny old woman the size of a ten-year-old shuffling down, perilously perched on a walking stick. I watched her every step, ready to dart for her lest she should slip, her tiny feet delicately tapping each step as she descended.

Cosetta was dressed in what looked like an original cream Chanel suit, her neck covered in strings of pearls. Her hair was stark white and her eyes the clearest, sharpest blue I'd ever seen, her lipstick the color of pale coral. She wore sensible but classy shoes and when she kissed Sandra and oh – me, as well – she smelt deliciously of *Felce Azzurra* soap.

'Cosetta, we need your help. My friend Gillian has lost her suitcase. And she's been left by her husband.'

What the hell did she need to say that for? Trying hard not to roll my eyes, I stood quiet and still as those old laser-blue eyes CAT-scanned me at length, the coral mouth scrunching up. Oh my God, what was she thinking? I really didn't need another person to tell me I was too big for normal clothes. Maybe this wasn't such a great idea after all.

'*Venite*,' she finally chirped and we followed her into a room at the far back where she drew the curtains and lit the lights and I almost died and went to designer heaven.

Not that I had owned anything designer in the past few years, but my memory was still good. Gucci, Prada, Krizia and Valentino peeked out from transparent garment bags – all hanging from a rod in this back room and suddenly Sandra couldn't contain herself.

'Cosetta, Gillian needs a complete wardrobe...'

'What?' I squeaked. 'I can't—'

Sandra held up her hand. '...but you have to *treat us right*.' Meaning Sandra wanted a discount, I guessed.

Cosetta waved her away and pulled me closer to the rod, swimming her way through the bounty. I was salivating, open-mouthed as the labels went by. Believe me, I was no vain woman, but what with the new hair, the new skin and all, I felt that maybe I deserved to buy myself something nice. Just one tiny thing. *And* put it on Tony's credit card. That would serve him right.

Actually, come to think of it, make it as many dresses as the bastard could afford. Payback time for what he did to me. I only hoped that something would fit. Because Sandra wouldn't have taken me here if this Cosetta didn't have my size, right?

Sandra smiled as I closed my jaw. 'Cosetta used to own a shop on the *corso* many years ago. She's our best-kept secret.'

So the next two hours were spent with Cosetta to-ing and fro-ing from the rod while I, stripped down to my new old-lady bra and underwear, tried everything that was thrown my way. Sandra busied herself like her life depended on it and together they'd stand back and assess me with a critical eye. And surprise, surprise, most of the stuff they brought me fit, if only perhaps a tiny bit tight.

'Perhaps some shapewear?' Cosetta suggested delicately.

Shapewear?

'It can shave off a few pounds easily,' Sandra agreed. 'Get rid of any lumps.'

I sent her a *Gee, thanks for that* look and she laughed, pulling up her own dress. I backed away instinctively but did a double take when I saw she was wearing an all-in-one girdle herself. Sexy and lacy, but still shapewear.

'You don't think women look slim without any help at all, do you?' She laughed at the look on my face.

So the time had come. Shapewear. Damn, hadn't I been in a prison of my own long enough? The last thing I needed was for a *girdle* to tell me when I could breathe.

It was like squeezing a watermelon into a dainty clutch, but in the end, huffing and puffing, I managed. If you asked me, I looked like a piece of haggis. Only bigger. Big butt, big thighs, big sigh. And yet, when they slipped a dress over my head, it settled nicely on my hips. Huh. What do you know, maybe looking half-decent was worth not being able to breathe for once. Gone were the bulges, the multiple roly-poly bits around my stomach that usually roamed free. Sure, my thighs were still humongous, but with these gorgeous, quality fabrics skimming over the bad bits, I almost looked… normal.

Actually, I looked better than normal, because my normal was baggy jeans, a sweatshirt and flats. I hadn't looked like *this* in years. Had it only taken an afternoon to transform my looks? A haircut, a girdle and a dress? Had I always been this close to looking normal without obtaining the effect? How dumb did that make me? It was like I'd been fumbling in the dark all these years when all someone had to do was turn on a light.

And now I had some quality dresses. Nothing too flashy. Traditional but easy. And elegant. Cosetta waved my credit card away.

'Just give her some cash,' Sandra whispered.

'Okay, but how much?'

'Here,' Sandra said, reaching into my purse and counting out two hundred euros.

Cosetta took it and bowed graciously.

'What? That's nowhere near enough,' I protested. It was daylight robbery, poor woman.

Cosetta shrugged. 'I don't need money. I've had this stuff in here for years. Treat it delicately. Like a baby daughter.'

'But Cosetta, I can't—'

But she grasped my wrist with her tiny hand. 'Sandra is like a daughter to me. And I like you, too.'

I blushed. 'Cosetta…'

'Some advice, if I may?' she persisted.

I nodded.

'Forget your husband. Find yourself a new man. One who will chase *you*.'

Yeah, like that was ever happening.

'I can't stop staring at you!' Sandra cried as we sauntered home. Well, she sashayed, I took tiny steps like a geisha lest my girdle should pop.

'Really?' Neither could I, actually. For the first time in the shop windows I admired *myself* and not the cake displays.

'Really. You look much younger.'

'Thank you. How is it that you and Cosetta are such good friends?'

'She's Mattia's grandmother.'

I stopped. 'Oh.'

'Yeah, we're good friends. Only... I'd rather you didn't mention it to Mattia, okay?'

'You mean to say that Mattia doesn't know you and Cosetta are friends?'

'Oh, he knows, of course. He introduced us, back in the day when all was well.'

'What does that mean?'

'That they're not exactly on good terms.'

'Why?'

She chewed on her lower lip. 'I'm sorry, I can't talk about it. Forget I even mentioned it, okay?'

I shrugged. 'Okay.' If she couldn't talk about it, she couldn't talk about it. And yet, it hurt that there was something huge in Mattia's life and I wasn't allowed to be privy to it. As if I actually had any right to know. Go figure.

But still, I couldn't help but wonder what the heck was going on. Why were they estranged? What had happened to push them apart? Had he done something wrong? Or was it her fault? I couldn't possibly picture Cosetta as someone who could anger anyone, let alone a loved one. Nor could I imagine Mattia not being respectful to his grandmother. He was too nice a guy. *And the plot thickens...*

10

A Call from Home

Mattia. I wondered what he'd say if he saw me looking like this. Would he compliment me? I wished he'd ask me out for a coffee or something. Thing was, I was scared and nowhere near ready. What was I going to do with a new man?

To which Sandra cackled in delight when I argued my points with her. 'You didn't really just say that, did you? What would you do with a new man?'

'I mean besides that!'

'Oh really, Gillian! It isn't all about sex, you know?'

If anyone knew that, it was me. 'I know. But do you?'

Sandra laughed. 'You referring to Alfonso? We do much more than just have sex. You can always go out and have a drink with a guy. A chat. Maybe even dancing and dinner.'

'I can do that with you, too.'

She took my arm and rolled her eyes. 'You're hopeless.'

I knew that. But was it my fault if I hadn't been able to heal and bounce back as quickly as everyone around me did?

'Come on,' she said, dragging me to my feet. 'We're going for a drink.'

So this was her strategy? 'Oh, no thanks. Not doing that again – that thing where you get me drunk and slink off and leave me alone with Mattia.'

'What's wrong with that?' she asked. 'You didn't seem to mind the last time. Mattia is a catch.'

'Yes, but I'm not fishing. Besides, didn't you tell me to stay away from him?'

'I told you to stay away from him if you weren't looking for love, but looks like love has found you.'

'What?'

'Gilly, I have reason to believe he has feelings for you. There's no *time* to go through the traditional mourning period. It's just a waste of time, especially when your husband's already moved on.'

Tell me about it. Men were still a catch even with gray temples, but God forbid we get a bit of gray ourselves. Life didn't have any mercy on dumped, middle-aged women.

'So move on.'

I stared at her. Was she now suggesting that I date Mattia?

She cupped her hands over her mouth and pretend-shouted. '*Mattia*. I'll get you paired off with him if it's the last thing I do. He is so the man for you – you'll see.'

'Sandra – listen to me. I'm going back to the UK soon.'

Sandra's mouth fell open. 'And you'd leave a man like him for someone else to snatch up?'

Good point. But Mattia and I had absolutely nothing in common.

'Sandra, I already did the guy with his secrets. I'm not getting embroiled with someone who is going to end up hurting me again. Besides, he's too young for me.'

She waved her hand, Italian-style. 'Nonsense. His secrets are something he has to deal with. Issues he has to solve. And stop it with this age thing. He's only four years younger.'

'I know, but it's more the outlook than our ages. I'm divorced with an adult daughter. He isn't even married. He's still living the life of the bachelor. I'm not one to take on a man like that. Plus, I'm still in mourning, you know.'

'Oh, please, you would be so perfect together.'

Oh, we would, would we? Then how come I imagined him with someone who looks like Nadia hanging off his arm? If even

Tony, who was in his late forties, had graying hair and wouldn't be caught dead on a Vespa, could be with Nadia, didn't Mattia, who still oozed youthful, boyish stamina, deserve someone like her instead of someone like me?

But one thing was true – with my nose and face slowly returning back to their normal color and size, I actually looked much better with my new haircut and new dress. Properly groomed. I had a good feeling the gods were on my side today.

And thus fortified, I decided it was time to face the music, embrace reality and deal with it. So I phoned my daughter Annie.

'Hi, sweetheart!' I called into the public phone with a gaiety I didn't feel. Emailing my daughter Annie on my laptop with false tales of how much fun Dad and I were having would have been easy compared to this, a one-to-one conversation, where she could hear my voice and instantly know something was wrong. It pained me that I'd have to be the one to tell her about our divorcing after all. Not today, though.

'Mum! How are you?'

'Everything is going great.' I could feel my nose lengthening, hitting the opposite panel of the phone booth, as I closed my eyes in sheer pain. If anything, I knew she'd be supportive and tell me to move on and get myself another man. 'So how are you, Annie? And work? Meet any interesting people there?'

'Mum – I *know*. Dad told me. I'm so *sorry*.'

Great.

'I didn't want to call until you were ready,' she added. 'How are you holding up?'

I rubbed my eyes. 'I'm fine.'

Silence.

'Really, Annie. I am. Dad and I just… don't have anything in common anymore. Besides you, of course.' Gawd, did I sound stupid or what?

Annie sighed audibly. 'But what are you still doing in Sicily then, Mum?'

Terrific question.

'Get out of there. Come to Barcelona. I have plenty of room here at my flat. We'll chill out and talk until you decide what you want to do.'

My heart warmed instantly. I almost felt a pique of guilt, although I couldn't place my finger on the reason why. Tony had left me and not vice versa. Still, I felt I'd been unable to keep my promise of giving Annie a loving, lasting family.

'Okay?' she persisted and I could hear the hope in her voice.

No, it was not okay. I was sick and tired of chilling out and talking. I'd talked and chilled all my life and look where it had got me. I'd known exactly what I'd wanted to do with my life but it hadn't worked out.

'I'm okay, honey.'

'I miss you, Mum,' she tried in a last attempt. Little sneak would do anything to get me out of here. Still, you had to appreciate her efforts.

'I miss you, too, sweetie. Why don't you come out here? My roomie won't mind.'

'You have a *roomie*?' A long, protracted sigh, and I was once again reminded of how much she and her father had in common. Both extremely judgmental. Don't you just love it when your children get to the stage they think you're the foolish one? When did the switch occur?

The thought of Sandra, the new friend who cared enough to drag me out of bed and back to a semblance of a life made me smile. 'Absolutely. You'll love her. She's great.'

A long, undecided silence. 'I don't know, Mum. All this time out there. What are you actually doing? Aren't you just wasting money and your life away on that rock?'

Prejudices, prejudices. 'Come and see for yourself. Book a flight for the weekend.'

'I don't think so. I'm very busy with work and all.'

'Oh. Okay, then.' I bit my lip. Of course. Annie was always busy with work and all. Never had time for relaxation. Again, just like her father. Until... he took off the rest of his life and buggered off on vacation with fresher meat. 'Talk to you soon?'

'You're not going home, then?' she insisted.

Home. Which home was she referring to, exactly? Ours no longer existed. Those days were gone, when we could sit around and have a barbecue in the garden, or cuddle around the fire in the snug, content to chat or bake cookies or eat popcorn in front of a DVD. I couldn't remember the last time I'd felt a sense of contentment. The brick and mortar in Blackheath still existed all right, but it had lost the flavor of home quite a while ago. As far as I was concerned, I didn't have a home anymore.

'No, sweetie. I'm not ready to come home just yet. I'm just going to relax here for a bit. But on my way back I'll drop by and we can spend a few days together, okay?'

Annie was silent for quite a while before she answered. 'How about starting over, Mum? Finding yourself a new bloke?'

As if. She had intended to plant the seed, hoping I'd mull it over in the meantime. Make sure I knew it was okay with her. But my terrain was no longer fertile for love. A fling, maybe one day. But love? I didn't think so.

11

Sweeter than Sugar, Hotter than Fire

August twenty-fourth was the *Festa di San Bartolomeo*, Patron Saint of Lipari and protector of fishermen. To celebrate, Sandra bought a new dress. Together we weaved through the town, absorbed in the hive of activity. The noise was unbelievable, what with paper horns and the brass band playing at the top of their lungs. I loved it. Maria was on the sidelines of the parade, waiting for her children to go by in procession with their groups.

'I've come to ask Saint Bartolomeo for a little miracle,' I barely heard as she cupped her hands over my ear.

You could do that, ask for a miracle? Not a bad idea, actually, if he listened to you. 'Did you ask for a lottery win?'

She snorted. 'That would be too much. Just a decent job. The hotel is closing for the winter months.'

Jesus. If Maria was out of a job she was in big trouble. 'Oh, Maria, I'm so sorry...'

She shrugged. '*Che sarà, sarà.*'

'Listen, Maria. I want to help—'

But she just looked at me with a tender smile and shook her head. 'Thank you, Gillian, but no. I can manage.' And then her sad eyes brightened as they fell to a spot over my shoulder. 'Oh, there's my little Susanna!' And with that, she squeezed my hand and ran after the procession.

How was she going to manage without a job? All those mouths to feed and not a companion to shoulder the burden with. Life just wasn't fair on the most deserving, most decent people. I would have liked to help, but Maria was not one to accept money. Such a dignified and lovely girl.

Maybe Sandra could put in a good word at the school for her? I could keep her two youngest while she worked the extra hours. Yeah, Sandra would freak. Despite being a teacher, she was not a child person. Or maybe I could pay Mirko, her eldest, to walk Diana? I already walked her twice a day on my own. She was practically my companion, but I suspected she wouldn't complain. Mirko loved animals. I'd obviously pay him double the going rate, provided he brought the bulk of it to his mum.

Sandra returned with two *macallé* pastries and looked about her. 'Not quite like a Stones concert, but it'll have to do. For now. Ooh!' she squealed, obviously spotting something way more interesting than the San Bartolomeo floats.

'I'll be right back,' she shouted over the din as she plowed her way through to Alfonso, and I nodded, already lost in my huge fluffy ricotta-filled *macallé*. God, this alone was a reason to stay here forever – all the best food you could ever want, beautiful scenery, lovely people and a quiet way of life. Except for tonight.

The town was festooned with elaborate streetlight decorations and the entire population had converged to thank and follow the statue of San Bartolomeo all the while taking turns in carrying it and the gold and silver ship miniature, *U Vascidduzzu*, or Little Vessel, the symbol of all the boats in the archipelago. I'd never seen anything so joyous and solemn at the same time. Certainly not in London, anyway.

I watched as Sandra flirted with Alfonso. Men. As if one couldn't live without them. Look at me. Wasn't I doing fine, sort of? Now that Tony was definitely out of my life, couldn't I be free to be me? No longer did I have to worry about his criticizing glances at my tummy or bingo wings and feel all the worse for it. Now I didn't worry about looking in the mirror anymore. So I took another victory bite, enjoying the nuances of flavor in the ricotta: a hint of lemon, pistachio and did I also taste cinnam—

A tap on my shoulder made me whirl around and, what do you know, Mattia himself was standing right in front of me, impeccably dressed in a sand-colored linen suit and a baby blue shirt open at the neck. He looked as good as my *macallé* pastry, if not better.

'Ciao,' he said with a grin. 'You're looking great. Sexy dress.'

Sexy – me? Well, he was looking good too, actually. In fact, I couldn't remember the last time I'd ever turned my head to look at a man. And Mattia was certainly a head-turner.

'That looks delicious. Can I have a bite?' he asked and in a split second I realized I had lapsed into a daze like when I was in my teens checking out the cute guy in the high school band.

'Oh. Sure.' I nodded and offered him my pastry and he ducked so that our eyes were level, sinking his teeth into the soft dough, all the while watching me with those dark-chocolate eyes. And suddenly this crazy, insane (albeit familiar) image of him taking my mouth instead caught me unaware, making me gasp.

Despite myself, I had to admit he was hot, hot, hot in every way, the ricotta cheese cream lingering on his full dark lips and – *whoa, don't give yourself a coronary, girl*. He could be your younger brother.

Not that he was exactly watching me in a brotherly way now, his dark eyes scanning my face as he slowly chewed, swallowed and licked the sugar off his lips. And suddenly I needed a nuclear explosion to drag my eyes away from them. And his Adam's apple, covered in dark, sexy stubble? Delicious. I wondered what it would be like to nibble on his throat?

Rather than licking my wounds over Tony, one dark, secret side of me would have much preferred licking the sugar off Mattia's lips. I took a deep breath to clear my head from the free flow of naughty thoughts I couldn't seem to stem. Was Sandra's style rubbing off on me? I stepped back in horror and he laughed.

'Sorry – did I take too much? Come, I'll buy you another

one,' he said, offering me his hand as people with huge flags and clusters of balloons passed by in droves, blocking the space above and around us, making it difficult to recognize exactly where we were standing. In every sense. Because for someone who understood my plight, he was doing one hell of a job to make it even worse. And for someone in my situation, I didn't look all too convinced I knew what I was doing.

I chanced a glance at Sandra still flirting away with Alfonso and decided that if I couldn't beat them I should certainly join them. To hell with everything. Go for it. Go with Mattia, wherever that (or he) took me. He was as sexy as hell and looked like the kind of guy who'd give you the time of your life. I hadn't had the time of my life in… well, never. Years, in fact. In any case, I'd be home in a week's time and my little nostalgic sojourn back into my youth would be over and behind me. So why not try my Non-Hurt Flirt Theory with Mattia after all? It wasn't like I was staying here forever, anyway.

But I looked up at him, registering the look in his dark eyes and instantly chickened out. You didn't flirt with a guy like him and leave unscathed. Everybody knew that. 'I – I can't. I'm waiting for Sandra to come back,' I managed.

Mattia followed my gaze and grinned. '*Sì, buonanotte*,' goodnight, he said. 'She's not coming back.'

'She's in love with him,' I said almost as if to justify her.

And then, without warning, a loud bang shook the island as a blaze as intense as a nuclear explosion lit the sky and the buildings all around us shook. I jumped and gripped Mattia's arm. 'Oh my God! An eruption!'

He steadied me and smiled. 'Calm down, Gilly – it's just fireworks.'

Fireworks? I stared blankly at him and he nodded skywards. And there they were – a sky full of burning colors. Wow. Gorgeous. I didn't know which way to turn, what with this handsome hunk of a man at my side, his reassuring hand still lingering on my back, his gaze lost on the missiles hissing skywards in squiggly trajectories, bursting into reds, greens, oranges and whites against the immense purple sky.

As everyone *oohed* and *aahed* around us, I kept my eyes glued to the sky as Mattia turned to look at me at length. I could feel his eyes lingering on my face. When I couldn't stand it any longer, my eyes met his, dark laser beams scanning my very soul.

'And you?' he said.

I started. 'Me, what?'

Another burst of color caught our attention briefly and he slid me another glance. 'Are you really sure you're no longer in love with your husband?'

A man with a child on his shoulders went by, nearly knocking me out with his trailing balloons. Mattia steadied me yet again.

'Why do you want to know?' I ventured, almost challengingly. When I felt threatened, I attacked.

He shrugged. 'I'm trying to figure out what you're still doing here in Lipari. How long are you planning on staying?'

I folded my arms across my chest. 'I'm not so sure,' I said warily. 'It all depends.'

He folded his arms as well and planted those obsidian babes on me. 'On what? If your husband takes you back? He just might have to after Nadia's family finds out he's still married to *you*.'

I glared at him, then shoved my *macallé* into the crook of his folded arms, when really I wanted to ram it up his nose. 'Here, you finish this. I'm not hungry anymore,' I said and left him standing there.

'I hope he doesn't!' he called after me. 'You deserve better, you know?'

As if. I knew I deserved to be loved. But by a decent man who would never hurt me, and not some Rudolph Valentino on a Vespa who thinks it's okay to flirt with a vulnerable woman who's just been dumped. If I decided to flirt with him, it was my decision, my move. Not his. If I wasn't ready, I wasn't ready, right?

Feelings or not, it was better steer clear of him after all. He was way out of my league anyway. Plus, at this point in the game, I couldn't afford another crash like Tony. And I'd promised myself I'd never be that vulnerable again.

I'd also made a promise to Wooffy-Diana, however. I was responsible for her alongside Mattia. So the next Saturday I ate humble pie and headed for Mattia's office to pick her up as usual so *he* could go off to God knew where. Because he'd never volunteered an explanation of any sort about his wayward weekends. I rang the doorbell and he poked his head from behind a partition wall, buzzing me in, much like he'd done when I went to his home for the first time.

'Hey…' he said, obviously happy to see me, and a wave of pleasure washed over me.

'*Ciao*,' I answered as Diana rounded the corner at full speed, making my face a licking-target as I shot a look around his office. It was gorgeous, with cream-and-caramel-colored stone walls, ensconced floor lights and large brown leather sofas. I wondered how many women had been seduced here, between these cool stone walls during a summer afternoon siesta?

'Nice…' I said.

'Thank you,' he answered, followed by an awkward silence. 'Do you…want a look around?'

I hesitated, as he looked harried, wanting to finish something in a hurry. 'No, that's okay. Next time.'

'Okay.'

Gosh, you'd think he'd insist just a little, out of decency. But obviously he was in a huge hurry, bags already in hand.

'Listen,' he said. 'I'm sorry about the *Festa di San Bartolomeo*. I was out of line.' Was he apologizing about the flirting or the butting his nose into my personal life? Either way he was uber-forgiven if he kept looking at me like that. Dark, dark puppy eyes with a wolfish stance – one helluva combination. And then I checked myself. Hadn't I resolved to keep him distant? And now I had a dog-share with him *and* slept in his bed, albeit alone. Go figure *me* out.

I shrugged. 'It's okay.'

'I should never have asked you about your husband. I do hope he comes back…'

As if.

'…if that's what you really want, I mean.'

I sighed. 'Thanks, Mattia – that's very kind of you. But I don't think that will be happening anytime soon.'

'Sorry. I just wanted to make sure… I thought—'

'Thought what? That we really might get back together again?'

He shot me a sidelong glance and nodded. '*Sì…*'

'Never – not even if he was the last man alive.'

And then he took a step closer. 'I don't want him to hurt you.'

'Well, thanks, but it's a bit too late for that.' Any reference to Tony made my stomach churn. 'Let's not talk about him anymore, okay?' I whispered and he nodded.

'Sure. Sorry.'

'It's okay,' I repeated.

'Okay,' he echoed and we stood around for another long awkward moment like two idiots before I reached out for his keys. Instead, he misunderstood and took my hand. Which was quite nice. Except nice can also be destabilizing. Because I knew what would happen next if I let him get any closer. I hadn't missed the gleam in his eyes. He was still a man, after all, and had nothing to lose.

And I was still a very lonely woman. One thing would lead to another and… and right now in my life I couldn't be any more off-kilter. One day I wanted him and the next I was terrified. Sooner or later I'd have to gain a balance of some sort, just so he wouldn't think I was a nutter or a terrible flirt, the two things coinciding in this case.

Of course, it would've been nice to not have any baggage and let go and enjoy the ride a much younger man was offering me, but I was eyeball deep not only in baggage but also in scruples. What would my daughter think if I started seeing someone who was more suitable for her age? Okay, let's not exaggerate. He was thirty-six according to Sandra, which made him sixteen years older than Annie. But still almost four years younger than me.

I looked down at our joined hands and coughed. 'Uh, keys?'

Embarrassing pause. 'Oh. Yes. Sorry.'

'It's okay,' I said for the third time and we laughed. 'Are you swinging by the flat before you go?'

He stuffed his hands into his pockets and looked at his feet. 'Uh, no. I have my stuff here. I'll go direct.'

'So where is it that you're going?' I ventured.

My question threw him. 'Just… away.' He shrugged, busying himself with the handle of his suitcase.

When it became clear that where and with whom he was going were definitely going to remain a mystery, I took his keys, wished him a good time and made my way to his flat with my new best friend.

Damn. What game was he playing? One minute he seemed interested and the next he couldn't get away from me fast enough. And then I suddenly wondered whether he and his grandmother Cosetta had fallen out because she wanted him to grow up and get serious about starting a family? It would be horrid of him to feign interest in me just to piss his grandma off, wouldn't it? An older, divorced foreigner with a daughter. Everything an Italian Nonna would want her grandson to avoid. Whatever the problem between them, that would be the ultimate revenge on his part.

'It's just you and me now, Doll,' I whispered to Diana as she curled up in her basket and I stretched out on yet another leather sofa, staring at the four walls as the sun went down. Yet another weekend on my own to kill. Sandra was with Alfonso and Maria was busy with her kids. I could always call Claudio, who'd left me his number and *begged* (these Italian men were real players) me to use it.

Now, someone like Claudio, I could handle flirt-wise. He

was fun and happy-go-lucky, without that Sicilian intensity of Mattia's that simply floored me every time I looked into those dark eyes. Damn, where the hell *was* he going? The mainland? Did he have a girlfriend Sandra wasn't aware of?

Not that I cared, of course. I cared so little that I went back to Cosetta's to pay her a visit.

This time there was no need to shout up to the balcony as Sandra had because as soon as I rang the doorbell, the massive door buzzed open.

And now what? What could I possibly say? "Hi, Cosetta, I was just passing by"? She'd see right through me, of course. And besides, what right did I have to stick my nose in her life? Why she and her grandson weren't speaking was their business.

'Gillian, welcome,' came the chirpy voice at the top of the stairs. Today she was wearing a pale yellow Chanel suit and a set of absolutely beautiful gray pearls. This woman had impeccable taste. And lots of money. But the big blue eyes didn't match her happy voice and I wondered whether it was the ongoing feud between her and Mattia that kept her miserable.

'I figured I'd see you again,' she said as she beckoned me in.

'Oh?'

She closed the massive doors behind me and grinned. 'You and I have unfinished business.'

'We do?'

She nodded. 'First, let's get you some shoes for your dresses.'

Shoes. She was right. I did need them.

'Thirty-eight,' she sentenced, looking at my feet. 'You need a size thirty-eight.'

I had no idea what my shoe size was in Italian, but she had a good eye. I followed her to the famous back room as she pulled the curtain aside and once again I felt a wave of happiness as she pulled out a few boxes. 'Try these on,' she said, offering me a box containing some gorgeous white leather sling-backs with a medium heel.

I slipped my feet in them and grinned up at her. 'They're comfortable.'

'Ferragamo. Excellent quality.'

'Have you got a matching bag?' I asked.

A quick rummage and she produced a beautiful white leather bag with a navy blue trim.

'I could spend all day here,' I said with a happy sigh.

At that, she smiled. 'I'd like that. We could talk about... him.'

My jaw fell open. 'Er, him?'

'Mattia.'

'Why?' I asked, my ears suddenly burning.

'Because I asked around. It seems you two are more than friends and I need an ally.'

'You must be joking.' I laughed her off. 'Mattia and I argue about almost everything.'

She beamed at me. 'Mattia loves a challenge. And so do I. Will you help me get closer to him again? Please?'

'But... why me? I hardly know him. Why don't you ask Sandra? In fact, why *haven't* you asked her?'

She waved me away. 'Sandra is just a friend. You, I think he'd really listen to.'

I wondered why that was, but decided not to go there. 'I don't know what to say,' I replied.

'Just talk to him. See if you can convince him, *sì*?'

I shrugged noncommittally. 'I can't promise you anything, Cosetta...'

'Just... try. Please?'

'Okay. How much do I owe you?'

'Nothing. They're a present.'

'Oh, I can't accept!' I warned her off.

'Consider it a thank you.'

'But I haven't done anything, nor do I think I'll be able to.'

'No matter.'

'I'm sorry, I can't accept.'

'Fine. Then just make a donation to the church for the poor.'

I eyed her. She really didn't need the money, and the poor did. 'Thank you. Done,' I agreed and said my goodbyes.

Imagine that! Mattia listening to me. Firstly, I had no idea what went down between them. Everything here was so hush-hush, but I expected the entire island except me knew.

SEPTEMBER

12

Lingering on Lipari

By the time August dissolved along with the hustle, the bustle and the noisy night-life and September rolled around, I was still literally lingering on Lipari along with the few stragglers left. And I was none the wiser about where Mattia went on the weekends. Nor had I made any inroads toward helping Cosetta befriend Mattia again.

In all honesty, I really didn't feel in a position to rock the boat.

Mattia was always flirty but more guarded than ever. It was as if he wanted to spend time with me, but a part of him was against it. He knew I would be leaving, sooner or later, but the exact date was a mystery even to me. Luckily I had an Italian passport, which allowed me to stay indefinitely. My departure day had come and gone and I still couldn't bring myself to go. I'd delayed my return to the UK, waiting for the moment I'd be sick of this place. It hadn't arrived yet. And actually, with every day gone by, it became more and more obvious to me that I didn't want to go. I'd been here for some time now and still I couldn't bring myself to leave. *Soon*, I'd promised myself. *When the sunny days are over. Before the winter sets in. Then I'll go back to the UK.* Go back. Rather than a return home – it sounded like an exile. With Annie living her own life in Spain now, I didn't have anything to go back to.

Sandra and I got along like a house on fire after a few initial teething problems caused by the state she always left the kitchen and bathroom in. It had fast become apparent that Mattia was the clean one in that arrangement.

I knew that despite her generous offer, we were both too independent to continue to live together. But I couldn't bring myself to book a flight back to Gatwick. Every time I tried, my hand froze over the mousepad. All I'd had to do was click on *Confirm*, but I just couldn't do it. Was the idea of leaving Lipari that painful? Or perhaps, was it the idea of leaving... someone else?

Although it was still hot, the tourists had rapidly dwindled and the locals had gone back to their everyday lives, the seven islands slowly closing in upon themselves, like a flower now too shy to show itself to the outside world. Many shops closed at the end of the summer (along with some of my fave eateries) and for the first time I saw the island stripped of all its showy finery.

Conversely, its bare, intimate beauty lay in the landscape, in the old limestone buildings and the dark eyes of the happy children on old battered bicycles who once again had the old cobbled streets to themselves. Everything had shifted to a smaller, almost family-like scale. People, mostly shop owners, the souvenir and bakery ladies included, began to recognize me around and about. And even if I stuck out like a sore thumb, I'd never felt more at ease than here. Here I had everything I needed.

And strangely, almost without realizing, every day I found myself waking up in a better and better mood, as if some giant weight had been lifted off my shoulders, and plans for the new day were always at the forefront of my mind. No longer was I wandering around aimlessly, stuffing my face and feeling sorry for myself, but I had made it my mission to get to know every nook and cranny of the entire island.

As soon as I got over my fears of water, I'd schedule visits to the other islands which were just as beautiful, if not more primitive and rustic. Alicudi and Filicudi, the remotest, I was told, didn't have any electricity before 1986, for example. There, people lived much more natural rhythms, much more elemental.

And I found I wasn't thinking about Tony as much as I used to and soon it became as if he had simply been an error of judgment and not the father of my only child. And every day I found it hurt less and less.

Sure, you couldn't erase twenty years of living with the same person, but I was doing my damnedest to put him behind me once and for all. He didn't deserve my tears, he didn't deserve my thoughts. From now on my thoughts would only be positive. I may have lost a husband, but I still had my daughter and my own self. Everything else that had made up my life was material and could be replaced.

Not that I needed much nowadays. None of the objects in our beautiful, former home had made me happy in the real sense of the word. Of course, Tony's profession had allowed us the best of the best, but now, none of it held any value – not the costly paintings that I had never really liked, not the glossy modern kitchen or even the roll-top bath – nothing. Actually, I felt quite free of it all now. Maybe in a previous lifetime I'd had much less and had been happier – who knew?

Still, I needed a home of sorts. Soon we'd sell the house and I could add my half to Gran's inheritance, although the money wouldn't go very far in the UK as I didn't exactly want to live in a rabbit warren. And going back home to Canada to where the houses were bigger and cheaper, thus putting an ocean between Annie and me, was out of the question. And so was me being on the same continent with Ma again.

Maybe I could, I don't know… move… *here*?

The thought hit me out of the blue, but in retrospect I think it was more like when you're desperate for a solution while staring it in the face. The thought of staying in Lipari – really staying, indefinitely – became less and less of a crazy idea and more of a serious option. Maybe I could buy something – a flat, or even a house? I know, it was by far the wackiest thought I'd had in years, but why not? Who said I had to stay in the UK for the rest of my days? I'd only moved there to be with Tony and even

Annie had moved away. Now (or soon enough) the world could be my oyster, as they say. And it had been years since I'd allowed myself the luxury of trusting my gut feelings. It felt crazy, but at the same time it felt *right*.

As far as money was concerned, my inheritance would give me a mortgage-free purchase, but of course I still needed to eat, pay bills, et cetera, so I needed a job ASAP. I wasn't too worried about survival, because if I could survive Tony, anything else would be cotton candy and a walk around Coney Island.

So I went online to see what was available on the local job market. And crashed back to reality. There were only summer jobs ending in September, and most of them were minimum wage, intended for youngsters, such as waitressing, scooping ice cream and everything else related to the tourist industry. I slumped in my seat. What was I expecting? Someone to roll out a red carpet for me, the *Americana pazza*, i.e. the kooky "American"? (They hadn't quite grasped that I'm Canadian.)

As it was, an hour into the search, the font suddenly shrank, so I enlarged it. And then it went fuzzy. Was there a glitch in my PC? Fan-bloody-tastic. I went into the dining room and opened Sandra's. Still the same, fuzzy screen. What was wrong with these things? God, I *hated* technology with a real passion sometimes.

'Sandra, there's something wrong with the computers,' I called. 'The screens are out of focus.'

She leaned on the doorframe and watched me squint at the screen, sniggering. 'It's not the PCs, silly. It's your eyesight.'

'What? My eyesight is perfectly fine.'

'Ah, you remind me of myself a few years ago. Difficult to come to terms with it.'

'With what?'

'How old are you?'

I knew where this was going, of course. 'Almost forty. Right,' I groaned, getting to my feet.

'Where are you going?'

'To the optician's before I go completely blind, where else?'

'Go to Nigro's – he's the best.'

I grabbed my bag, wondering what was next. Senility?

After a few try-outs and swapping of lenses on the metal contraption strapped to my head that made me look like a cyborg, I settled on a pair that were nothing extraordinary. Apparently Sandra had been right. I was now, courtesy of my tender age, long-sighted. Way to go.

Some people look great in glasses. Smarter. Posher. At this point, it didn't matter to me what *I* looked like. I would never look like *me* again, I realized as I studied my reflection. Get over it – people change – evolve, yada yada yada. Accept it and move on. Was this how it happened – middle age? You looked in the mirror one day, not being able to recognize yourself anymore? Your face took on new creases that made your expression change, just like that, out of the blue? No warning? And worse, did this discovering that you looked like your mother *after all* happen overnight?

I looked closer. As a matter of fact, not only could I see Ma, but I could see Pa in there, too, in the sad lines around my eyes. I'd always had nice eyes, but what good were pretty eyes if they oozed misery most of the time?

So I pocketed my glasses and walked back to Sandra's all the way wondering, *Now what?* How do I kick-start my life again? What kind of permanent work could I possibly find at my age, and on this tiny rock, to boot? Was I perhaps taking a greater risk than I thought? The sensible me pre-heartbreak would have never even contemplated such reckless behavior, but now? Why does this predicament not scare me as much as I'd thought it would?

Yes! I *was* going to do it! I was going to stay! I knew that now. I was going to rebuild myself a life from scratch – and all on my own this time. How exactly I was going to do that was another story, but I relished the challenge.

When I got to Sandra's, I bit the bullet. 'Sandra, I've decided I'm going to look for a place to live.'

She looked up from her laptop, a frown on her face. 'But I thought you were happy, here with me…'

'I am. I'm so happy that I'm going to buy a house and move here.'

'Oh my God, Gillian! Are you doing this… for Mattia? Have you told him?'

I laughed. 'Hold your horses there, missy. I'm doing it for myself. But I need a job.'

'A job, on this rock?' She shook her head, and then her eyes lit up. 'I know! You could do some afternoon English lessons at my school! We're looking for someone at the moment. It's only for a few months, but better than nothing, right?'

'Teaching, me? Thanks, but no thanks.'

'Don't say no just yet. You might not find better at this time of year.'

I knew she was right. And yet, I just couldn't see myself in a classroom. I wanted to be my own boss.

'So are you staying for him?' she asked again.

'I'm not interested in a relationship right now,' I assured her.

'That's crazy,' she countered. 'Who wouldn't want a man like Mattia?'

'I don't want any man. I just want…' I huffed. A life. And a man had absolutely no place in my New Life Plans right now, except maybe for a bit of fun.

'Sometimes if you get a man he gives you everything else,' she said, regarding me sadly and I remembered her stories of her rich lovers.

'I don't need a man's money. Men are expendable,' I informed her. Hey, I liked that one. Was I on my way to some universal truth? 'I can manage on my own.' That and my gran's inheritance, actually, but she was a woman too, so it didn't count.

'I wish I had met you while forming an opinion on men,' she whispered. 'I'd be a lot happier and less disillusioned.'

'Those who are happy are crazy,' I sentenced.

'Those who are crazy are happy,' she countered softly, and in her eyes I saw a wisdom I hadn't quite caught before. I'd always considered her a worldly and streetwise gal but I hadn't stopped to think she was the result of lots of suffering.

Now that I had made the decision to stay, I went out and bought myself a cell phone to call my peoples. Ma could wait as she wasn't exactly hanging on the edge of her seat to hear from me. She'd only tell me to forget the no-gooder and get myself off this rock. Only Martha and Brends understood me.

'Sweetie, how are you? You don't check your Facebook page anymore,' Martha said.

Oh. I'd completely forgotten about it. I couldn't even remember my password now, come to think of it. Who needed a virtual life when I could talk to my best friends on the phone or in the flesh? Up until then I had been preoccupied with my past life, watching it become more and more remote with each passing day.

'Gillian?' Martha called.

'I'm sorry, I've been really busy.'

'Doing what? When are you coming back?'

'What for?' I countered breezily.

Stunned silence. Then she tried a different approach, similar to Annie's style. 'We miss you.'

'I miss you too,' I said over the sudden lump in my throat. 'But I can't come back just yet. Not until...'

'Tony may never come back to you, sweetie.'

'No, it's not that. I'm not interested in him anymore.'

I truly wasn't, although for the life of me I couldn't figure out what else could keep me here. Summer was over and we were in for a rough winter, but somehow, I felt that a rough winter was the least of the sacrifices I'd have to make to get my life back on track. I knew tough times lay ahead of me and yet... and yet, I knew there was a hidden ray of sunshine somewhere behind all that. There had to be.

'Is there… another man?' she asked.

Was there? I hadn't seen Mattia for days and he only called to make arrangements for Diana. Besides, I wasn't making any more decisions based on a man. 'No.'

Martha understood. 'Do you want us to come out?' she asked.

Hell yes. 'No, that's okay. How's Brends?'

A sigh. 'Seeing another married man. I swear our mother is turning over in her grave just about now. Brends would get along swimmingly with your Sandra, I think. I can't put a harness on her, for God's sake. She's gone absolutely wild after her second divorce.'

Divorce. *Ahia*, as Sandra would say whenever she smelled trouble. There it was again, the legendary D-word.

'Do you think I'll go wild, too?' I asked, feeling suddenly lost for a minute, as if I depended on Martha to tell me I wasn't really lost at all, but perhaps just temporarily confused.

Good old Martha never failed me. 'Don't be silly. You just need time to figure it out. At your own pace.'

'Yeah,' I agreed.

'But Gilly? Find your way back soon, okay?'

The warmth of her affection always did that to me. 'I'll mourn faster.' As if.

I felt her smile.

'You do that. And keep in touch!'

'I will,' I promised, putting down the phone, a great big smile spreading across my face.

Sunday morning as Sandra slept in I decided that if I was going to try and fit in and not stick out like a sore thumb, I needed to work on my tan. So I put on my cossie (without faffing around too much in front of the mirror except to check I wasn't too overly bulgy in the thighs and butt area), threw on one of my gazillion sarongs and walked to the bus stop bound for *Spiaggia Bianca*, one of Lipari's most beautiful beaches. For September the weather was glorious and I couldn't wait to cool off in the sea.

As I was waiting I thought about reading my copy of *La Sicilia*, the Sunday paper, but next to me was a more valuable source of information. Gossiping girls. Like the local *Carabinieri* police, they always came in twos.

'So did you meet him last night?' one whispered to the other.

'Did I ever. Oh my God, Sonia, I almost passed out! Mattia is one hot guy.'

My ears pricked and I pretended to be absorbed in an article. And why were they always talking about Mattia? Were there *no* other men on this island? Granted, it was a small island, but come *on*.

'Don't look! Here he comes!'

Before I could stop myself I turned to see him coming my way on his faithful old blue Vespa. He stopped right in front of me, his eyes twinkling with mischief.

'Good morning, Gillian!' He grinned and then glanced at the two behind me. 'Girls…'

I folded my arms in front of my chest, trying not to glare at him. So much for a man who didn't play the field, right? In any case, what business of mine was it if he made women literally pass out? I could understand why – he could sometimes be arrogant beyond belief, but, truth be told, he was devastatingly sexy, especially when he wore shorts like now. I could only imagine what he'd be like in bed. Just the thought made my throat go dry.

Those legs were pure muscle, not too hairy, not too huge. Just right. His hair was tousled by the wind, a lock falling across his forehead. Had I been insane I'd have reached out and pushed it back off his dark ravishing eyes. Luckily I managed to hang on to the last shred of my dignity – and my self-control – as he flicked his head to clear his face, his boyish trademark gesture that made girls (and older women) swoon.

'Going to the beach?' he asked.

'Considering I'm waiting at the Cannitello Beach bus stop, I have a beach bag and am wearing a sarong, I'd say yes.'

He grinned and leaned in closer. 'You were never one for wearing too many clothes if I remember correctly.'

Ack. I'd hoped he'd erased from his memory my runaway bathrobe *and* my Sisa droopy grays. 'How lucky for me that you remember,' I said icily although for the life of me, I don't know why. To stay in control, I guess. Because the minute I allowed us to be friendly, I would want more and make an absolute fool of myself.

He grinned his awfully arrogant, gorgeous grin. God, I hated men like him. 'My dear Gillian, with or without any clothes on, you're waiting for the wrong bus.'

I was? I chanced a discreet look around.

'This one goes clockwise to Quattropani... and that one,' he said, pointing across the street, '...goes counterclockwise to the beaches.'

Busted as usual. 'Ah. Thank you.'

'I'm going to Spiaggia Bianca,' he informed me, nodding to the beach towel slung over his broad shoulder.

Canneto it was, then.

Behind me I heard whispers of contempt. All I caught was "older woman" and "dumpy". Mattia clearly heard too but ignored them. What a piece of work he was, having slept with the gossiper and eight hours later, he thought he could flirt with me? It was all I needed. I picked up my bag and took off. And of course he followed me at about one mile an hour, his Vespa softly chug-chugging alongside me. Damn, was there no escaping him? This island really *was* too small for the both of us.

'Gillian – wait. Let me take you.'

Just the idea of him seeing me in my swimsuit made me

want to hurl with anxiety. 'No thank you,' I said haughtily. 'I've changed my mind.'

'Don't listen to those girls, Gilly,' he said quietly, his eyes softening. 'They're just jealous.'

'How charming of you to blow your own horn like that.'

He laughed. 'No, silly. I mean they're jealous of you – you're a *real* woman.'

Me? Ha. 'Go away, Mattia. I need a break.'

He gripped his handlebars and leaned forward. 'Why are you so angry with me? What have I done now?'

What had he done? It was all the things he hadn't done. Like for example, why wouldn't he tell me where he went every weekend? And why hadn't he ever told me about his estranged grandmother? On the surface, he appeared to be friendly and understanding of my personal plights, but did he tell me anything about himself, his life, his secrets? Oh no.

I wanted to tell him that if you wanted to be friends with someone, you had to trust in them. Confide in them. Not keep them at arm's length like he did with me. Physically, he was raring to go. But emotionally? He was inarticulate in that area. I wanted to tell him all that, but all I could do was frown and blurt out absolute nonsense.

'Me? You're the one who's always... forget it. Anyway, tell your lady friends to stop talking about your sexual prowess in public. Contrary to what you believe, it doesn't make you look good – or reliable.' Especially since he'd practically sworn celibacy to me.

He frowned. 'What are you talking about?'

I jerked my head toward the two girls across the street. 'I had to stand there and listen to how – oh, never mind.'

He turned to look at them, then at me. 'You mean Alice and Giulia?' He chuckled. 'They are two of my workmen's daughters. I've known them since they were born.'

'Yeah, well, they're not so little anymore, are they?'

'What do you mean?'

Jesus, did I have to spell it out to him? 'I overheard one of them saying that you're so good in bed she almost passed out last night.'

His jaw dropped so far down I swear if I hadn't been so annoyed I'd have laughed.

'They said *what*?'

'You heard.'

'But they're only what – fifteen?'

'A bit more than that, Mattia. Don't you have eyes?'

'I already told you, Gillian. Only for women.' He grinned. 'Like *you*.'

'Oh, brother.' I sighed, actually quite relieved, between you and me. For more reasons than I care to confess. 'Well, you'd better get them straightened out before they ruin your reputation. Wait, no – it's too late for that, isn't it?'

Again that endearing/annoying flash of white teeth. 'You know, Gillian, if I didn't know you had a crush on me, I'd think you hated me.'

'Pshaw!' I hissed as a green moped sped past. Then, before I could stop myself: 'I don't hate you. You know that.'

His Vespa wheeled an inch closer to me. 'You don't?'

'Of course not. You piss me off, yes, but you have been very kind to me since I got here. After you tried to kill me, that is.'

Mattia threw his head back and laughed, his eyes twinkling. Then he inched even closer, his voice dropping to a low, caressing murmur. 'You know something, Gillian? You *are* an amazing woman. And your husband is an absolute idiot.'

Okay, that was it. One more look like that and I'd… He had absolutely no right to look at me like I was the most desirable woman in the world. Who was he kidding? I was *never* going to be his token older woman. Besides, he must've had loads of women of every age, shape and color available. Did he think I was the missing notch on his bedpost? Not happening. Even if he *was* positively mouth-watering. I was not about to jump into the sack with the first guy who smiled at me. Or was I? Tall, dark, handsome, incredibly sexy. No. He was no threat to me in the least. To prove it, I lifted my chin in defiance.

'Okay, you can come to the beach with me. But you behave yourself. No flirting.'

He grinned. 'Okay. Let's go.'

13

Falling Into You

'Hurry and park that thing away or we'll miss the bus,' I said. 'This bastard driver always speeds up whenever someone begs him to stop.'

He chuckled. 'That bastard is my cousin Piero.'

'Oops. Well, he still does it on purpose.'

'Maybe you don't shout loud enough.'

'Me? Believe me, I can shout loud.'

'Then why don't you?'

'What?'

'I've never heard you raise your voice. You're so quiet and delicate.'

Delicate, me? Had we met?

'Come on,' he whispered, patting the back of his Vespa and my eyes widened in horror. 'Oh, no, you're not getting me on *that* thing again.'

'You didn't seem to mind the last time you were glued to me.' He grinned and I stopped.

'You see? That's exactly what I hate about you.'

But the guy was undeterred and flashed me his trademark grin. 'Don't pretend you don't remember.'

I might have been drunk, but I remembered perfectly well the warmth of his chest, the clean smell of his skin. And how I wanted to lick him from head to toe. I eyed him, balancing himself on those two very slim wheels. No *way* I was going anywhere with him.

'Promise we won't crash?'

He opened his arms wide and I wondered what sort of woman wouldn't want to dive in between them. 'With my precious passenger? Never. I'll be very careful. I promise.'

To prove his point, and also because he saw the iffy look on my face, he took hold of my forearm to steady me as I gingerly swung one leg over the seat behind him, half expecting to fall over the minute I sat down, the feeling of someone else balancing for me very foreign.

'Ow! Seat hot, hot, hot!' I gasped and jumped straight off, almost taking the Vespa with me, but he had a firm grip on both. He threw his head back with a laugh.

'Here, put this under you,' he suggested, volunteering his towel and I soon found myself sitting solidly behind him again, my arms now around his slender waist (hoo boy) as he slowly took off.

'How am I doing?' he asked. 'Slow enough?'

I nodded. 'Good, thanks.'

And gradually – *very* gradually – he picked up a little speed, just enough so elderly pedestrians on Zimmer frames weren't walking faster than us, and wound our way through the streets of Lipari town center, not giving a hoot about what people thought.

And soon I was enjoying it, finally getting a different, accelerated version of all my travels on foot throughout this island, exhilarated by the wind in my hair, the whirr of colors and fragrances of the eateries reaching us as we passed, but I was not hungry in the least. At least not for food. There you go again, you dirty mind. What did you think I was talking about? This time I was hungry for *life*.

With his strong body warming the insides of my thighs and me laughing my head off for absolutely no reason (other than too much oxygen going to my brain all of a sudden) Mattia laughed along, telling me to hold on to my skirts in case we went flying into a fruit cart or worse, a display of obsidian.

I was beside myself with elation, forgetting my problems for just one day. Tomorrow they'd be back with a vengeance, but today – *today* I was free to enjoy this rush of bliss. Free to experience a little guiltless *frisson* of pleasure out of time and space. And completely out of my lifestyle.

The buildings gave way to a canopy of trees and soon the trees gave way to a graveled road and open country lanes and sunlight. I breathed in like I hadn't in years. It was like flying, the breeze whipping my face, the sun caressing my bare legs and back and I had not a care in the world, like when I was a child. And above us bright, solid blue sky.

'Are you comfortable?' he asked the shell of my ear and a little shiver ran down my spine as his lips touched the side of my face. I was *more* than comfortable. I felt beautiful, happy and safe, even as we were careening down a loose gravelly slope that a wrong move would've sent us crashing down into the sea below. With Mattia, nothing could hurt me.

'Look!' I gasped as we rounded a bend, and there, the landscape was white, almost lunar, sloping down to the whitest beach I'd ever seen in any magazine. Whiter than Florida, whiter than Cuba, whiter than Sardinia. And the colors of the sea? Unbelievably crystal turquoise waters that look like those old, artificially colored postcards, the entire vision beckoning to me so strongly I wished I could soar over the entire bay in one swoop and drink it all up at the same time. Today, for the first time in my entire life, I really did wish I could fly.

'*Bello…*' he called back and slowly came to a halt. 'Here we are.'

I looked at him, at where he'd parked on the steep slope of a cliff, and then at the beach below.

It was too sheer a drop to the beach for any vehicle to attempt. Oh, goody, we were going rock-climbing now, apparently. Yes,

I know I said I wanted to fly, but did I ever mention my fear of heights?

'Come on – you afraid?' he asked me.

Is Lipari an island?

'Of course not,' I lied through my teeth, flashing him a great big smile. 'Last one down is a rotten egg.'

And with that, I hefted my beach bag and before Mattia could stop me (and before I could change my mind), threw myself down the slope, realizing too late that it was too steep for me and that my legs were too slow to carry me as my body picked up momentum and speed.

'Gillian!' I heard him shout and then I knew I was really in trouble.

Oh God, I was going to fly right off the side of the mountain, break my neck and drown in the sea!

You know when death knocks on your door and your whole life flashes before your very eyes? I saw Annie, during every phase of her life – her first steps, her first words, the first time she said *Mummy* and her first day at school.

And then I saw myself lying dead at the bottom of the mountain, the waves lapping at my bare, scratched and broken legs, my butt exposed to the world and Tony standing over me to reassure the police and coroner that yes, it was me, but that we were divorcing so he didn't want to have anything to do with me, whether I was dead or alive, and that he was home free to live his life now as he pleased.

I suddenly hit the ground with such force it knocked the breath out of me. Only I hadn't crashed onto the rocks below. The cobalt blue sky was still an infinite, uninterrupted dome above me, and Mattia's face was now inches from mine. I lifted my head slightly. 'What...?'

He'd tackled me to the powdery ground, thus breaking my fall – and saving my life yet again.

I lay under him, still stunned out of my wits as he frantically checked my bones. I was battered and bruised all over. But alive. And *very* aware of him plastered to me.

'Thank God you're okay...' he breathed, his relieved face towering above me for a moment, and then his head dropped like a decapitated puppet's, over my breasts, although his body, supported by his arms, was clear of me as he tried not to squash me, seeing I'd just survived one trauma.

The sound of his deep breaths sawed in and out of his chest and I swear he looked like he was about to...

I lifted my head and it fell back with a thud as he and the sky beyond him began to whirl, the ringing in my ears drowning out the ebb of the sea below.

He gently tilted my face to the left, then to the right. 'Your neck looks fine. Can you move your arms?'

I flexed at the elbows, wincing in pain. But I could move.

'And your legs?'

I slowly lifted one foot and he delicately caught my calf, flexing my leg so my thigh touched my chest, then gently rotated it and did the same with the other leg, satisfied that I was still in one piece, his large warm hands protective. Just a routine thing you do when someone almost falls off a cliff. And yet it was one of the most erotic moments in my life.

'Nothing's broken,' he assured me with a grin, his eyes crinkling at the corners. Up this close I noticed he had these cute little wrinkles. Still, not bad for thirty-six. Great, actually.

'Do you feel dizzy?'

'I'm fine. Really. Thank you. You actually saved my life.'

Again he grinned. 'What are friends for?'

I made to sit up but he stopped me. 'Wait. There's no hurry.' And with that, he took off his T-shirt and shaded me from the blaring sun. It was the first time I'd ever seen his bare chest and let me tell you it had been well worth risking my neck for. Brends would've jumped his bones there and then, but I was, of course, a *lady*. Still, it was nice, lying in the shade Mattia provided, his eyes never leaving mine, his hand absently caressing my head as he watched my face, still concerned, but not afraid out of his wits as he'd been a few minutes ago.

'Can we go down to the water now?' I asked.

'Only if you're not dizzy,' he answered as he gently pulled me close to him as if he was about to, dear God, try and *lift* me bodily. Again.

'I'm not dizzy,' I lied. But I knew it had nothing to do with the heat or my near-death experience.

'Okay, then. Let's take it easy. Very easy.'

'Mattia, I'm fine, really. Just rattled.'

'Maybe I should take you home.'

'What? No, really, I'm fine.'

'You need to rest.'

'I will. But for now I just want to take in this beauty. Please? I'm dying to wet my feet.'

He seemed to consider. 'Just for a few minutes. It's too hot and you need to be in a cool bed now.'

Preferably yours, I thought. Gosh, what was happening to me? I could say it was the fall that had recalibrated my brain, setting it to Desire Mattia Mode and no one else. But you and I both know I'd be lying my butt off.

Slowly but surely, Mattia helped me down the cliff, using the footpath this time and not my crazy thin-air shortcut, until we reached the water's edge. The bathers hadn't seen or heard what had happened way above their heads, which was just as well. Mattia took off his jean cut-offs and I almost had a coronary at the sight of his powerful but lean and toned body barely covered by a pair of black Speedos. You might not like Speedos – *I* don't even like Speedos, but let me just say *God bless Italian men*.

He waded in until he was up to my knees and then held out his hand back toward me. 'Coming in?'

And take off my sarong in front of him? Never in a million years. 'No, uhm... I think I'll just watch – the *people*, I mean. You go ahead.'

'I'm not leaving you for a second,' he said, squatting down

into the shallow water next to me, splashing his arms and face. Jesus, he was sexy beyond words, his body so vibrant, his smile so alluring. I was afraid that any second I'd lose all control of my motor skills and my sanity and reach out to caress his broad, tanned shoulders, bend down and kiss his full lips, run my tongue over his jaw and taste the salt glistening on his skin. But being me, I didn't. Instead, I bent forward and splashed my face and shoulders. Screw not wetting my sarong. In this heat it would dry in a jiffy. Faster than you can say: *"Take off your clothes, please…"*

'I have been meaning to ask you something,' he said, still crouched in two feet of water and leaning in so close I could see the gold flecks in his dark eyes.

'Yes?'

'When I kissed you that night… why did you leave?'

I blinked, rising slightly so a gentle wave wouldn't wet my face. *Aw, shit…*

'Oh. *That.*' Wasn't it obvious? I shrugged, but he took my hands.

'You ran.'

'Yes…'

'But not without kissing me back first.'

'Uh…'

'You ran because you thought Sandra was my woman.'

Had he been talking to her about this? I swallowed. Boy, was my throat dry.

'Uh…'

'Admit it. You *are* attracted to me.'

Busted. So now what was I going to do about it? Act my butt off, of course.

'Don't be silly – you could be my younger brother, for Christ's sake.'

'I'm not that much younger than you. And what I feel is not brotherly at all.'

'Oh.' What else could I say? What the hell did I know about being a cougar?

So I said nothing and he studied me in silence and finally sighed. I know. I was a complete moron. I *deserved* to be alone for the rest of my life. Let's face it – I just didn't have that get-up-and-go gene.

The ride back was slow as Mattia wanted to avoid any bumps in the road (good luck with that). When he deposited me on my front door he insisted on walking me up to Sandra's apartment, but I declined, promising him I'd go straight to bed.

'Gillian?'

'Yes?'

'Are you okay?'

'Of course.'

He studied me and then nodded briskly as if I'd passed some test. 'Put some aloe vera on your skin and get some sleep. I'll give you a call tomorrow.'

'Okay. Thanks again, Mattia.'

I stood before Sandra's front door, thinking, *Boy am I neck-deep in it*, when he stopped in his tracks and turned back, his eyes riveted to mine, dark and solemn. Uh-oh – I recognized that look from that night when... when...

'What?' I said after a moment, the silence unbearable, my body remembering the hormone-storm the first time he kissed me. He wasn't going to do it again, was he? Please, God, make it be so...?

And for once, God listened and Mattia took me by the shoulders and guided me (finally!) to him as I stared, doe-eyed, his eyes darkening and his mouth, that magnet that attracted all my various particles like a lodestone, closing in on me. (Actually, his mouth was slightly parted and yum-yum-*yummy*.)

It was better than the first time. First, because I wasn't drunk, only frazzled. Second, because I had been hoping (I can tell you that now) that it might happen again and third, because it hadn't been an accident or an afterthought as one might think. This kiss was a real soul-trip, deep and thorough, so thorough I began to wonder how he, so apparently reserved about his life, had actually kissed me in public. But when the front door opened we flew apart like two teenagers on Daddy's doorstep.

'Cia-ooo…?' Sandra's voice died as she came to a dead halt in the street before us and painted her own picture. Me, I didn't know what to think or say. From what I gathered at a quick glance in Mattia's direction, he was even more flabbergasted than me. Before I could get my breath back, he squeezed my arm, face flushed, and left me there like a sack of potatoes, saying 'Ciao,' to no one in particular.

'Hello?' said Sandra, hand on hip and a great broad grin across her tanned face. 'That looked very tasty.'

Oh, it was.

'You want to talk?' she asked, but I could tell by her dress and stance that she was going on a night out.

'That's okay. Go.'

She shrugged. 'Are you kidding me? For this, Alfonso can wait!'

'No, that's okay, really.' Also, I was dying to go upstairs and think about his kiss on my own, relive it over and over again. That's what happened to dumped women with a new avenue, however short – they reverted back to being brainless teenagers whose minds are taken over by a hormone invasion and they can think of nothing else for days. Or nights.

Punching my pillow, I knew it was going to be what Italians called a *notte in bianco*, i.e. no sleeping. It was nothing more than a kiss of course, but I couldn't seem to step away from it, like when you're really thirsty and you think, *Just one more gulp and I'll stop*, but you just keep on drinking and drinking. The memory of that moment was sweet and intoxicating and… addictive. And now I wanted more.

As I turned onto my side to settle in for a nap, in my own imagined parallel universe I got out of bed. I pulled on a dress and sandals and walked to his home. There, he opened his door and said, 'Is everything all right?'

And without further ado he swept me up against that rock-solid chest (I got a good feel while he was lying on top of me at the beach) and knocked me out of my senses with a breathtaking, lip-searing, jaw-breaking kiss. And he told me that he had been in love with me for *some time now* (a girl's allowed to dream and because this is my dream I'm doing it my way, okay?) and he kissed me again and again until I was blue in the face. Which of course, wasn't enough for either of us so I'd *had* to stay the night.

Okay now, back to planet Earth. Was I completely bonkers or what? How could I even consider hooking up with someone like Mattia, a gorgeous, single Italian architect in his thirties? And with the reputation of a playboy? He was completely out of my league. And, despite what Sandra always said, not even remotely interested in a steady relationship. As if I was.

No, in that department, I can honestly say, I gave my all. And besides – what was he going to do with a woman who checks her face in the mirror every morning dreading new wrinkles, when *he* had a trail of lusty females ranging from sixteen to sixty-six?

Granted, I was still a woman with needs (loads of them) that hadn't been satisfied for some time (too much time), but how long was I really going to allow myself to be lulled by my crazy imagination? Look at me, constantly changing my mind. One day I was hot, the next I was cold. I needed sorting out pronto. Plus, I had things to do. No time for dreaming the night away. And, above all, no guts for a sentimental detour with someone like him. Claudio, I could handle, for he was sturdy, flat terrain, but Mattia? Pure quicksand.

Funnily enough, the next day Claudio called me. He wanted me to tutor him privately in English.

'Uh, you're better off with Sandra,' I suggested.

'No. I want a native speaker. Please say yes, Gillian. I'll buy you dinner every night.'

Here we go again. But yes, he could be a safety net. Someone I could have a fling with and not emerge totally shattered.

'You don't give up, do you?' I said with a laugh. God, he was the kind of guy made to break some women's hearts. But not mine. 'No dinner, Claudio. But I'll tutor you. If you promise to study.'

'Promise. From now on I'll be your slave.'

All in all, the man was harmless. Gorgeous, but harmless.

Later that week Maria came calling to tell me she'd found a job as a checkout girl at Sisa, of all places, and we had a good laugh over a cup of coffee (and all right, I admit it – a couple of ricotta cheese *macallé*).

'Well, I might not be checking people in anymore but at least I'm still checking them out,' she said jovially. 'And I'm bringing money home.'

I beamed at her. 'You know, Maria – I admire you so much.'

She rolled her eyes. 'Please. I admire you.'

'Me?'

'Of course – look at you, the way you bounced back from your broken marriage. I was on antidepressants for months before I could get out of bed after Stefano left me. And even then I was dragging myself around. But I had to.'

'Exactly. You pulled yourself out of a deep hole. You deserve to find a nice man who… what is it? Why are you looking at me like that?'

But she just kept smiling. And then bingo – I got it. 'You found a man?' I gasped.

She shrugged, blushing. 'It's too soon, really. We'll see.'

'Who's the lucky guy?'

'His name is Leo. He's a landscaper. Oh, he's so cute! And he doesn't mind that I have children, you know?'

'Oh my God, Maria, I'm so happy for you!' I hugged her. 'I wish you all the best!' She deserved it.

'About Claudio,' I asked Sandra when I got home that evening. She was at her laptop, typing away at a report. She took off her glasses and grinned.

'Ah, his magic is already working on you? What about Mattia?'

She never let go of anything, this one, did she? I rolled my eyes. 'Silly. He looks like a real playboy, doesn't he?' Like someone else I know.

'That's an understatement,' she said as I plunked myself down onto the sofa. Whenever Sandra took a pause from work, a story always came with it. 'My colleague teaches Italian at the school. She has been in love with Claudio from the first day she arrived three years ago.'

'Did she ever stand a chance?' I asked, although I already knew the answer. Loners like us never got the guy. Or, if we did, it never lasted.

'Oh, you know him – he's a real flirt with all the ladies. No one ever had a chance with him though because he was married and absolutely crazy about his wife.'

'Was?'

'Last spring she left him.'

What was this, Divorce Island? 'Why?'

Sandra shrugged. 'Who knows? Maybe she missed the mainland. She left and no one's heard from her since. Claudio was devastated.'

'That playboy, devastated?' Who knew?

'Absolutely. Almost got himself killed, throwing himself off a cliff in his car. It was Mattia who found him and hauled him out before the car exploded. Barely made it – you could see the flames around for miles.'

'That was brave.' So Mattia had the rescue gene in him. Which made him practically perfect. *Big deal.*

'So now Claudio's back on the shelf.'

I'd always hated the expression *on the shelf*. Like we were hanging in there, like cuts of meat waiting to be picked up by someone. *Anyone*, just as long as we weren't alone anymore. Horrible.

'All divorced men go back on the shelf immediately, while women take longer to get back out there.' She sighed.

'So if Claudio is still on the shelf, why didn't you pick him up?'

'I told you – the man still loves his wife. And second, never shit where you eat.'

'Charming.'

'I'm serious. How awkward would it be to have to sit across from him at meetings after I've slept with him and sent him packing? Awkward for him, I mean.'

'Maybe you wouldn't have sent him packing. Maybe it could've worked out.'

'I'm not taking any risks,' she sentenced.

'Isn't love about taking risks? Look at me.'

'Uh – exactly. No thanks. I don't need the extra aggravation. Besides, I'm really hung up on Alfonso now.'

'I thought you just used him for sex.' I knew the truth, of course, but loved provoking her. And she loved falling for it.

'Am I? Then why do I miss him when he's not around? He's so wrong for me but could easily be the love of my life. I mean, look at him. He wears gold chains, for Christ's sake, he left school when he was twelve to work in his father's restaurant, and he smokes cigars. And yet, he's so... *wonderful*.'

'Yeah, and he's also so... *married*. Move on. Isn't that what you told me?'

She cocked an eyebrow. 'And was I wrong? Look at you now – you've blossomed.'

It sounded crass, but I had to admit she was right. I was actually relieved (now) I'd been dumped. A sort of yoke had been lifted off my shoulders. I no longer had to worry about jumping through hoops to please Tony and the sensation was utterly liberating.

'Anyway, we both know who *your* type is,' Sandra continued. 'What was that all about, the two of you on my doorstep the other evening? The sexual tension was thicker than fried polenta.'

God knew I'd been seen enough times in public with him to get people speculating. The drunken Vespa ride, the day at the beach, not to mention me flashing him at Sisa. After that it had been a wonder he even wanted to be seen anywhere near me.

'Nothing,' I lied, although I don't know why. I'd had a gazillion chances to tell Sandra about my growing... inclination toward Mattia. But I feared the minute I admitted it, it would become real. *A real problem.* 'I've had my share of cocky men, you know.'

She rolled her eyes. 'With all due respect, you've only had Tony.'

'And it was enough,' I assured her. 'The last thing I need is to lose the plot again for someone new who will, eventually, dump me. Because that's how it works. I know that now.'

'Now look who's talking about not taking risks.'

'Oh, I'll take risks,' I assured her. '*Calculated* ones. But there's no way I'm getting mixed up with someone like Mattia.'

'He's sex-y...' she sing-songed.

As if I didn't know. 'He's also trouble.'

Sandra leaned forward and put her slim hand on my knee. 'The man's a real alpha male, I tell you. And he's the man for you.'

'But he's too young for me, Sandra. Besides, I'm not ready for another relationship. I'm still finding my own feet.'

'Forget about your feet, Gillian. By the time you're ready someone else will have snatched him up.'

I rolled my eyes in mock exasperation. 'If he's such an alpha male, why don't you go for him, then?'

'I already did.'

What? I sat up, already feeling my insides twisting. So I had been right. There had been something between them after all. 'You... *slept* with him?'

She sighed. 'The truth? I tried. Ages ago. Luckily, we've both forgotten all about it.'

I leaned forward, my eyes ballooning inside their sockets. 'Shut up. What *happened?*'

'Well, it wasn't one of my finest moments so please don't tell anyone.'

'Who am I going to tell?' I promised. This was getting weirder and weirder. Mattia, uber-hunk, refusing a cat like Sandra? I just couldn't picture it. The idea made the world seem like *The Twilight Zone.* It just didn't follow any logic. 'I'm listening.'

'It was a million years ago. He was in this very kitchen taking measurements of the flat for my landlady, Donna Angelina. I did everything I could to get his attention. I offered him coffee, food, booze, but nothing. He wouldn't take anything from me. So I asked him to help me hang my curtains. When he came in, I made sure I was up on the chair in my shortest dress.'

I rolled my eyes. 'Yep, that sounds just like you. Then what?' I was dying to know.

'He stopped short. So I got down, walked over to him and kissed him.'

A strange sensation ran through me. Jealousy? 'You didn't!'

'Oh yes.'

'And what did he do?'

'Nothing. Just stopped me, made me promise I'd never try a stunt like that and went straight to—' She slapped her hand over her mouth.

'Where? Where did he go?' And then I knew it. 'This has something to do with his mysterious weekends, doesn't it?' I didn't need to be a rocket scientist to put two and two together.

She bit her lip. 'I can't tell. It's a secret.'

Bingo. Mattia had a secret. A secret that Sandra knew and that, despite her promise to him, she was *dying* to tell me. What could it possibly be? A secret lover, or worse, a wife who didn't know what he's up to? The possibilities were endless. He could be in Lipari for work, and then got back to her on the weekends, and she was probably completely oblivious to it all. Weren't the wives always the last to know? Look at me.

And it all made sense. I'd asked him about it and he'd dismissed the topic altogether. It was something he didn't want me to know. Why? What was he hiding? And why did the fact that he didn't want to share it with me hurt like hell? He wanted me to be myself with him. But did he do the same with me? No.

Whichever way I looked at it, it didn't sound too promising for me. Now *you* try to get a good night's sleep after that.

14

Running with the Runs

The next day I got a call from Cosetta. She wanted to know if I'd had any luck.

'The truth?' I replied. 'Mattia and I aren't close enough to talk about things like that.'

Silence.

'Does he know about your husband's indiscretion?' she asked. I balked. 'Yes. But—'

'That's being close, wouldn't you say? He knows all about you, while you know nothing about him. What a strange relationship, don't you think?'

She could say that again. I may have known him as a person, his likes and dislikes, and what he would say in a particular situation. But I didn't know anything *about* him. With him, familiarity was a one-way street, and he just wouldn't let me in. Cosetta was absolutely right.

'I'll see what I can do,' I all but snapped, and rang off. I know I'd agreed to help an old lady, but to me it seemed that she was the strong one in this situation. She was maneuvering me like the best of puppet masters, and there wasn't a thing I could do about it, because I was dying to know more about Mattia and his secrets.

Later that Sunday morning I climbed the steep steps of *Via del Concordato*, or what I call the Giants' Steps, to wander through the citadel in peace and quiet, only I'd forgotten that it was

Sunday and mass was in full attendance. Which was why Sandra was in a deep sleep at home, absolutely knackered after a whole week at work with her mob.

I stopped to watch some street artists drawing with colored chalk, all hunkering under a long banner reading *Spontaneous Street Art* as the congregation – including Girl Guides, Boy Scouts, the choir and the band – all spilled out of the church in one happy, liberating heave. I noticed one chunky girl stood out from the gaggle of youngsters, self-consciously tugging at her sweater to cover her round bottom. As if it ever could. Nothing – *nothing* would ever hide our extra bits. She would soon learn. I felt a wave of knowing sympathy. Deep down she pushed the pain and embarrassment aside because she thought she'd grow out of her baby fat. In many cases we didn't. I had, but then I'd had Annie and gained the *baby weight*. Except for a brief period before marrying Tony, I never really became the beautiful swan, never morphed into the graceful butterfly like Daddy had promised.

This youngster had one sad wake-up call ahead of her. Life didn't always get better with adulthood. If anything, it was the end of the dream. When you grew up, you didn't actually have it all, unless by *all* you meant the heavy thighs, the bingo wings and the roly-poly hips. And less sex.

It had been so long ago since – you know – that I couldn't even remember. I had some faded images of a night, one night, but I couldn't remember any details. The few times we'd had sex in the last few years had seemed to overlap into one endless session and frankly there was nothing for me to hold on to. No special moment that I'd pinpointed and said, *Ah-ha! This is a moment I will never forget. This moment I will cherish forever.*

Sad, I know, but I'd become so used to accepting second best (not that I had anyone to compare him to) so I'd just got on with it, resigned to the fact that there could be other things, better things (besides my darling Annie) in a marriage. How wrong I'd been.

At my age, my next important pit stop or milestone in life would probably be, with my luck, Alzheimer's, Parkinson's or, if I was extremely lucky, both. And oh – why not throw in, while we're at it, a hearing aid and adult nappies?

And speaking of which, I needed to *go* all of a sudden. Badly. It was maybe the heat and all the iced water I'd guzzled on my way up, but I was getting more and more desperate by the second as my insides began to twitch and squeak. I mentally calculated a quick dash home but I was way too far to make it. Shivers ran up and down my spine and I swiped a hand over my cold, wet forehead. Any second now and I would be embarrassing myself like never before. What could I do? Where would I hide? There was no escaping the throngs of people in the streets whose favorite activity is to people-watch. Well, they certainly wouldn't miss the spectacle of *me*.

I hobbled across the cobblestoned sacristy, grateful for the respite from the blazing heat, thinking that maybe the cool interior of the church would calm my body and fill me with some peace of the senses. But there was no peace to be had by a body in the throes of the runs. I looked around. Surely there had to be a bathroom in a church? What were the congregants expected to do when instead of the Divine, human nature called? In case you were wondering, there are no bathrooms in churches in Italy. None that I could see, anyway.

Has that ever happened to you? You're on holiday somewhere in the sweltering heat and after having drunk a bottle of ice-cold water, your stomach decides it can't cope with it?

I had no choice but to make a mad dash down the steps, take a short cut to the *corso* and—

'Gillian!'

Dammit, did every *single* person on this rock know my name?

'Gillian!'

Oh, God – Claudio. Could his timing have *been* any worse? I cowered at the thought of not being able to get away from him in time.

'Hi!' I chimed, trying to sound chipper and hoping my face wasn't as contorted as my intestines felt.

'I need to talk to you,' he said.

Oh, man. It sounded serious. And *lengthy*. 'Oh, it'll have to wait. I've got some errands to… uhm, run.' And that word was dead apt.

'I'll come with you.'

'No!' I cried. 'Why… don't I meet you down in *Marina Corta*, at the bar?'

His eyes narrowed. 'Are you meeting someone else?'

'Of course not. Meet you there?'

'Which bar?' he asked.

How was I supposed to know? I could barely think straight right now. 'The one with the guitar hanging on the door?' I volunteered. I was horrible with place names.

He smiled. 'Okay. How long do you need?'

Terrific question. Another gut-wrenching spasm shot across my abdomen and it was all I could do to not double over in pain. Oh, boy. Not good.

'I'll call you,' I called over my shoulder.

'Gillian – wait,' he said.

'Later!' I managed as I ran down the steep stairs of the hillside, each foot pounding heavily on the steps that were too far apart for comfort. Each time I landed on the next step my stomach lurched, and I pictured myself spraining an ankle and flying, completely out of control, bowels included. Now how would that be for some Spontaneous Street Art?

Would you bloody believe it, by the time I crawled into the loo, I didn't have to *go* anymore? The urge was gone – completely vanished into thin air. How the heck did you explain that one? I only hoped that when it came back – and it would with a vengeance – that I was already home. This meeting with Claudio would have to be a short one, just in case. I couldn't afford to be out of the safety of Sandra's walls.

As I was leaving the stall, my cell phone beeped with a message:

Meet me at my place tomorrow for aperitivi? Eight o'clock?

Mattia! Inviting me back to his place. Which could only mean one thing. Step Two of The Fling? But hadn't I decided he was too dangerous for me? But before I could stop myself I texted back: *Who is this? Only kidding – I'll be there!*

To which he answered: *Fantastic! I have many delicious things waiting for you…*

I gulped. Too late to change my mind. I was on my own, now. I exited the bar and found Claudio right where we'd agreed, sitting under the large square parasols, his feet sliding in and out of his sandals and propped up on the stone barricade between the *piazza* and the quay facing the sea.

Boats came in, unloading families with sun-beaten skin and excited voices. I wondered how long a ride lasted? Not that I'd ever go – you know my sentiments about not being on dry land – but it was nice to see such carefree, flushed faces.

I should have taken a page out of their book. Take now, for instance. I was in the company of someone I liked very much and who flirted relentlessly with me and I couldn't bring myself to enjoy the moment. There must be something seriously wrong with me, apart from my bowels.

'Are you okay?' Claudio said, leaning in to touch my forehead. An innocent gesture, but it bothered me. Nope. Not fling material after all.

'Sure, I'm great.'

'You seem… *strange*.'

'I am strange, remember?'

He grinned. 'That's true, but you're a nice strange.'

I laughed, feeling my stomach rumble. Why didn't he get to the point? Maybe some warm water would help me? Or better, something solid?

'Can I offer you something?' he asked as if reading my thoughts. 'An ice cream? Have you had lunch yet?'

'Lunch?' meaning we'd be here at least another hour. I didn't *have* another hour.

'Sure,' I found myself answering despite my screaming intestines as my Italian mobile rang.

'Excuse me... Hello?'

'It's me, Sandra. Don't come home for a bit, okay?'

Oh, Christ. She had Alfonso over for a Sunday morning romp. *And* I needed the toilet again. 'Okay,' I said, hanging up and getting to my feet. Just the thought of not being able to go home to the toilet had triggered another session.

'Please excuse me,' I whispered to Claudio, hoping he didn't think I was avoiding him as I ran across the tables to the loo again. And by the time I got there, I was fine again, so I washed my hands and took a look in the mirror. Not bad. I didn't look too frazzled. Maybe I could still make this a nice afternoon after all.

'I'm so sorry,' I apologized as I sank into my seat again. 'I'm all ears. What did you want to talk to me about?'

And that's when he leaned forward, took my head in his hands and kissed me smack dab on the lips and sat back with an expectant grin as if to say, "What do you think about *that*?"

What would *you* have done or said?

I mean, Claudio was gorgeous, friendly and kind. Great company on a night out with friends and all. Just the ticket to get any woman out of her blues. And just as I was thinking about what to say, my body decided for me.

'Excuse me one more time, Claudio,' I apologized and disappeared back into the bar.

15

Confusion

'Whaddyou doin' down dere all dissa time-a? Go home!' Ma screeched over the phone. *Home* – again that foul, four-letter word. If I heard it once more I'd scream.

'Why don't *you* come out, Ma? See the old country again.' I threw her way, knowing she'd never in a million years come back to Italy.

'A you kiddie me? Whaddam I gonna do inna Sicily? Florida gorra everyting. Sunnashina, restorants. I no wanna be a poor woman inna Italy no more!'

'But it's not poor – it's beautiful.'

'Beautiful don't mean rich,' she countered, and I figured that in a way she was right. Lipari's only wealth was from tourism. I couldn't wait to see what it would be like when the winter set in. Was it really as cold and boring as Sandra said?

At the end of the day, I'd be happier to live here, even if it was only a rock in the sea, where you could actually get around without stop-starting at traffic lights every three minutes while the entire city swooshed by at a dizzying speed. Here, on the other hand, people stopped to say hello or give you a ride when you were too drunk to make it home on your own. Or save you from certain death by throwing themselves atop you to stop you from hurtling off a cliff…

I guess it was no secret as to where my loyalty lay, right?

But should I tell Ma that I was moving here? That I was using my grandmother's inheritance to buy something here? No – I really didn't want her to fly across the ocean to make sure it never happened. Ma hated my grandmother but she loved money. She measured everything by how much money you had – success, happiness. Everything. I was so glad we were not alike.

The next day, my intestinal crisis now completely over, I was laying low, lest Claudio pushed me for a reaction to his kiss. I'd thought about it and thought about it. But you can't rationalize feelings, right? Either you have them or you don't. And I didn't. Not for him, at least.

Plus, don't forget I was meeting Mattia for an *aperitivo* at his place. But it seemed *he* had, because when I rang his doorbell and practically ran the whole three flights up, I found him with a woman. An *older* woman.

'Hi – you're early,' was all he could say.

Immediately Cosetta's words flooded my mind and I clammed up, insanely furious for… what? He wasn't my cheating husband, nor a sworn lover or even someone who'd said, 'I might be interested in starting a relationship with you, let's talk about it.' None of the above had happened. A kiss, no matter how delicious, didn't mean anything nowadays.

When was I going to get with the program? All I'd got were vibes, mostly flirting vibes coming from my internal hormone storm. I was lonely, and I was attracted. But he hadn't committed to anything. So why was I absolutely devastated? Why didn't I just go home, forget about Lipari completely, and find myself some monkey job somewhere back in England?

'Gillian?' Mattia said. 'What's wrong?'

Good question. I must've been mad to think I actually had a date with him. *Aperitivi* meant absolutely less than zero. And to think I'd snubbed good old Claudio so I could be here instead.

I took a breath and stopped as the woman appeared at the top of the stairs behind him and squeezed past me, ignoring me completely, waving to Mattia over and over again.

'Nothing.'

I waited until the woman wound her way down the stairs and until I heard the massive door close with a thud.

'Oh, I know that look. You're angry because you found me with that woman.'

'*What?*'

'You heard.'

'What do I care? You can sleep with as many women as you want.'

'Sleep? She's a client. I'm doing an extension for her.'

I hesitated. Was he lying? How would I know? What did I know about him? I hadn't even figured my own husband of twenty years out; how was I expected to know what was on a complete stranger's mind?

'What you do in your own home is your own business.' I shrugged and he took me by the shoulders.

'Okay, I think it is time for you and me to talk seriously now. Come inside, Gilly.'

When I hesitated, he took my hand. 'Gillian, I think there's something between us.'

'I'm sorry, but you're wrong,' I lied. 'I'm not interested in dishing out to a younger man who will boast about how he got yet another cougar into his bed the very next morning without a care about what she feels.'

He blinked at me. 'Cougar? What cougar?'

I rolled my eyes. 'It's an English expression. It means an older woman who likes a younger man. I'm an older woman. You're the younger man.'

There. I'd said it. Now there was no turning back.

'Gillian, what are you, thirty-eight? So you're two years older than me.'

Almost four, actually.

'Listen,' he insisted. 'I don't care about your age. Why can't you just believe that?'

Because... because men like that just didn't become serious

about women like me. And in any case, I wasn't looking for ever-lasting love. All I wanted was… a flirt. A scene.

'I'm not ready for another man yet.' *Especially one so good-looking who'd be a constant reminder of what I no longer was.* 'And anyway, you are not what I need.'

Man, did that sound horrible or what? He looked at me as if I'd slapped him.

'Maybe you're right,' he said. 'I won't bore you anymore.' And then, without another word, he left me standing there and went back inside. Did I have a knack for pushing men away or what? I had never meant to offend him or anything. I just wasn't ready to let my guard down. He seemed honest, but every time I turned around he had his finger in the cookie jar. Who the hell wanted to live that way?

He'd left the door wide open. All I had to do was cross the threshold and call his name. Apologize for being a twit. But I just couldn't bring myself to do it.

So with my heart six feet under and a mouthful of tears, I descended the stairs, only to roam aimlessly around town. Boy, lucky I had my bug-eye shades so no one had any idea of what was going on inside me. Heartache? Just throw on your shades and walk tall. No one can see what's happening to your insides.

Strolling past the *Anime del Purgatorio* church down the jetty in Marina Corta and watching the boats coming in was now my favorite hobby in the world. So was bargain hunting, so the next morning I decided to treat myself to a chocolate and orange ice cream and do both, browsing for something to send to Annie and my ladies.

And that was when I saw it. In the window of a real estate agent's office, between an art gallery and a souvenir shop, was – the biggest, most humongous announcement ever:

Vendesi/For sale, località Quattropani. € 220.000.

I recognized the area and the house in the photo immediately – the magnificent abandoned villa where I'd found Diana. Only two hundred and twenty thousand euros? How could that be possible? In London you couldn't get a run-down *shed* for that price. Had my gran's inheritance money finally found its resting place?

I took stock of what I was seeing in the three pictures as I remembered it quite well, especially its massiveness and the breathtaking views of the sea, a *stone's throw away from Salina*, so close you could touch it. Good, solid period stone building. Three stories. There were what, nine, ten bedrooms in total?

And then I knew. It could only be one thing. A bed and breakfast. That was it. I'd found my calling. My place in life. I was going to have, in one lucky strike, a home and a business of my own. It had been waiting for me to discover it before going on the market – how exquisitely lucky for me?

Without even hesitating, I made a note of the phone number of the real estate agency and called immediately. *I really must be nuts, tucking myself away to lick my wounds on a tiny island, no bigger than a speck of sand*, I thought to myself, laughing in sheer glee. *Absolutely mad. Absolutely priceless.* Was fate deciding for me?

'There is a lot of interest in that house,' the agent informed me.

'I'd like to see it as soon as possible then,' I countered.

With Mattia a dead duck, I might still have a shot at a modicum of happiness now, instead of the dark abyss that used to stretch before me like Faustus' ugly gaping hell. It had been only a few hours and I missed him terribly.

But now I could do my own thing – buy the house, do the work. Put aside some money for Annie's down payment whenever she decided it was time to put her foot on the perilous property ladder. Save the rest for a rainy day. B&Bs did extremely well here in the summer. Entire families survived on summer income throughout the year comfortably. So yes. I was staying. Rebuilding my life from scratch. This would be my brand-new Sicilian Life.

And then it struck me – when I'd lost my way on the country roads leading to that house, I had actually and unwittingly *found* my path in life.

Although the outside of the building was decent, inside it was an absolute mess. Worse than I'd imagined, even worse than Mimmo's place, starting with the roof that actually had prickly pears and capers growing through the gaping holes where the pan tiles had collapsed.

How the hell was anybody going to make this place habitable (and rentable) ever again? And most of all, how much were renovations going to cost? I was no rich dame who opened businesses for pleasure. I needed to invest securely, run a sure-win summer business that would tide me over for the entire year.

So the trick was to get the house as cheaply as possible, do it up as cheaply as possible and furnish it with as little money as possible. And then invite the Easter Bunny over for tea.

'I want to show it to someone,' I told the agent the next day. She was a woman of about my age, all smiles and teeth.

She checked her agenda. 'The day after tomorrow would be best. I have another viewing in three days.'

Awh, crap. Just my luck.

'I think I've found a house I want to buy, but I'm already in competition,' I said to Sandra the next morning at breakfast.

She looked up from her cereal. 'Buy? You mean you're really staying?'

I beamed like an idiot. 'I think I just might.'

'Excellent! But why buy? You can stay here with me.'

'Thanks, Sandra, you are amazing and I love you to pieces, but I really need a home I can call my own. And a business. I want to run a B&B. And I really don't want to work for anyone else at this stage of my life. Who'd even hire me at my age? No. I need that house.'

'Okay, you're not thinking straight, *cara*. What are you going to do all winter when storms batter the island and there's nothing to do?'

'Live,' I answered, taking a sip of my espresso. 'Live and be happy. Take whatever life throws my way. If I survived Tony, I can survive anything.'

She put her spoon down. 'You *do* want to stay because of Mattia, don't you?' and then she gasped. 'You *are* in love with him! I knew it!'

My jaw dropped. 'What? No!'

'Yes!' She clapped her hands. 'I'm so glad it was you who bagged him! Good for you!'

I waved my arms to silence her. 'Sandra, stop. There is nothing between us. No more men for me. I'm absolute crap at relationships. Plus, we had a fight and now he's not even talking to me.'

'A fight? About what?'

I huffed. How could I even put it logically? I tried, but it didn't even convince *me*. 'I like him, he said he liked me, but I don't trust him. Not because of anything he's done, but because I don't have enough confidence to believe a guy like him could like a woman like me. Plus if Tony left me after twenty years, what does that say about my lovability?'

'Don't be ridiculous,' she scolded. 'One failed marriage doesn't mean you're bad at relationships.'

'No, but neither does it mean I'm brilliant at them. Anyway, you want to come and look at the house? See what you think? I need your advice.'

She studied me and smiled. 'Of course. Where is it?'

'Where I found Diana.'

Sandra's face fell. 'Oh God, Gilly, that huge old wreck? Why don't you find a nice flat in town near all the action?'

I shrugged. How to explain that fate had decided for me? 'I'm a country girl at heart, Sandra.' Besides, houses in the town center were outrageously expensive and they were small. Gardens were very few and far between, too. 'No. I want a big house with some land and a view. A place where my guests—' I shivered in delight just saying the words '—will be happy to stay.'

'Okay, but don't expect me to come up there very often. I want you down here for the weekends so we can party, *sì*?'

I thought about the weekends, and how Mattia always disappeared. If he was out of the picture, at least I had lovable, dependable Sandra. '*Sì*. Thanks, Sandra.'

The next day the agent and I waited outside our front door for Sandra who was getting in from work. As she strolled down the street toward me, she waved. When I waved back, she didn't stop waving. I got a sneaking suspicion and turned around. Behind me, from the other end of the *corso*, Mattia was approaching. Jesus, what the hell was *he* doing here?

Sandra reached us first, all smiles and little jumps of excitement. 'I called Mattia!'

'What for?' I groaned.

'He's the architect after all, isn't he?'

'Hello, Gillian,' he said softly before I could retort. And then to the agent, 'Ciao, Carmela.'

The agent gushed. Good grief. Another one who'd fallen prey. *Don't get your hopes up too high*, I wanted to warn her. I also wanted to bite her head off for smiling at him like that.

'When did you decide to stay?' Mattia asked me without taking his eyes off the road as we followed Sandra's car and The Gusher's. It didn't make sense to take three cars. I could've gone with Sandra but she'd hurried away leaving me alone with Mattia, of course. Would she never stop strategizing in my favor?

'What does it matter? The house is perfect for me.'

'And there's no other reason?'

I shot him a glance. 'Meaning?'

'Meaning you're buying this to be closer to your husband. Everyone knows he's coming back to live here. Just come out and say it.'

Oh. So that was his beef, then. 'It's not. Tony's staying in the UK as far as I know. What's it to you, anyway?'

He scowled at me and I realized he was way too intense, too serious to be a flirt. He was not the type of man you could just sleep with and walk away from. Because I knew the memory would be too overwhelming. If just kissing him had caused all that emotion in me, can you imagine what it would be like to just let myself... love him?

He shrugged. 'Absolutely nothing, as we agreed. Your life is your own.'

'Thank you.' I huffed. 'Why are you even here?'

'Because Sandra said you needed me.'

'Huh. And you came.'

'Why wouldn't I? You're the one who's mad at me. Not vice versa.'

'I'm not mad at you. I was... mad at myself. It had nothing to do with you.'

He turned. 'You sure?'

'Absolutely.'

'So we're friends again?'

'Absolutely.'

To which he turned and suddenly grinned at me, his eyes twinkling with newfound mischief. 'Good. Because you're not getting rid of me just yet, Gillian.'

What a relief. I didn't like the idea of not having him in my life anymore. I turned my attention back to the winding road.

Mattia's affection, or interest or whatever you wanted to call it, was new territory for me. I had no idea how to behave because I'd never been here before. I know it's petty, but I had started comparing him to Tony the minute we met, while I was sprawled on the pavement of the *corso* in my robe and Mattia had stood in between Tony and me. He didn't even know me but he nevertheless was ready to go up against another male to defend me, like a buck protecting his doe. And even today, by coming here, he'd made a statement. He cared. In what way, it didn't matter.

'Here we are,' he said and turned to look at me, his dark eyes soft and warm and I had the feeling that he would forgive me for much greater offenses. Not that I planned on ever hurting him.

'Thank you for being here, Mattia,' I said as we descended from his Jeep.

'It's my pleasure,' he answered, holding out his hand. I slipped my hand into his, and all was good again.

I stepped back as The Gusher gave him the key along with a radiant smile. Me, I was content to watch the muscles in his back work under his T-shirt when he turned to grind the key in the ancient lock, using all his strength. With one hard shove he pried it open and we followed him inside.

In broad daylight, I could see that the ground floor was massive, opening onto a huge space, with four more large rooms connected via a corridor. The kitchen, or what was left of it, faced the back of the house. As he pulled one of the boards off a window I gasped and jumped forward in delight. A picture-perfect view of the island of Salina filled the window, so close I could see the houses scattered along the opposite coast.

We got to the top of the stairs and Mattia pushed open all the windows, one of the shutters falling straight into his arms. I coughed as dust floated around us in silvery-golden specks and a dead pigeon fell from a hole in the ceiling, just missing me. It was all I could do to not shriek.

'I haven't been here in years,' Mattia said as he propped the shutter on the floor against the wall, almost as if in awe. Yeah, I was in awe too. Of the state of the place. How much was this all going to cost with the renovations?

'Well, what do you think?' Sandra asked him, breaking my sorrowful train of thought. 'Is it a good deal?'

'Absolutely not,' he sentenced and my heart sank. 'But I'll talk to the owner, see if I can bring the price down.'

'Do you think you can do that?' I asked. 'I'd really appreciate it.'

He didn't answer, but continued to look around every nook and cranny. It was unnerving. What did I know what to look for? All I saw was cobwebs, fallen beams, upturned tiles and dust. On the outside it looked almost pristine, but the interior was a war zone.

'Look at this!' Mattia said. Sandra and I moved forward at something on the floor. Not a dead rat, hopefully.

Mattia nudged the floor with his boot. 'This,' he said, 'is *pece!*'

He said it like *paychay*. Which sounded a lot like paycheck to me. 'What is *pece*?' I asked.

'It is a precious tar fossil stone used only in the houses of rich people. You can't find it anywhere else except for old churches and very important buildings.'

Rich people might have used them but all I could see was a dusty, dark floor. Mattia rubbed a larger surface to reveal some more. It was almost black and very shiny. 'It looks intact!' he exclaimed, getting even more excited.

Sandra grinned at me and raised both thumbs and although I had no idea what they were on about the feeling was transferring to me, too.

We followed him from room to room as he checked all the floors, which seemed to be the only thing he cared about, but then he ran his hands along the walls, each and every one of them, and turned to us.

'The walls are solid stone. All they need is a good clean.'

He smacked the dust from his hands and wiped them on his jeans. He was a sight for sore eyes, the real manly man type who wasn't afraid of getting grubby or scratched. He was, in fact, the opposite of Tony with his surgeon hands. Mattia's hands were so big he could swat ten men to kingdom come in one single blow. Well, maybe that's a bit exaggerated. But they were strong.

Like the holy trinity, we followed him into the next room, cracks crawling all over the vaulted ceilings. Here he stopped and groaned softly.

Sandra and I exchanged glances as my heart fell.

'How bad is it?' I asked.

He ran his fingers along the surface as, with bated breath, I waited. I had everything riding on this.

'Pretty bad.'

Damn.

And then he turned and smiled at me. 'But not impossible.'

'How much is it going to cost?'

'Depends on what you want. I can have a few scenarios for you by the end of the week.'

I wanted perfection. Only I couldn't afford it. Okay, time to wake up. In the end, it was all about numbers. If they didn't add up I was screwed. Once again.

'Okay, then. Thank you for your time,' I said and we all headed downstairs and back out into the sun, me leaving a piece of my heart in there and wondering if I'd ever make it back inside.

'Would you like to go for a coffee?' Sandra said to him, giving me a nudge between the shoulder blades.

Of course. Manners. 'Please,' I chimed. 'Maybe we can even get some of those *macallé*,' I suggested, cursing myself for remembering the evening of San Bartolomeo when he'd practically made love to my pastry.

'My treat,' The Gusher butted in and Sandra and I both turned to look at her. Who the hell had invited her? We were like hens in a farmyard preening before the head rooster.

'Uhm…' Mattia looked at his watch. 'Sorry, I have to get back to my boys and finish the day.'

'Oh,' Sandra, The Gusher and I said in unison.

'Another time,' he said and lifted his hand in salute. 'Are you okay going back with Sandra?' he asked. Did I have a choice?

'Sure,' I said, my heart sinking. Why didn't he want to be alone with me? What kind of mixed messages was he sending me?

The Gusher also made her exit in a timely manner, seeing as the rooster had left the building.

'Wow,' Sandra said as we watched him disappear into his Jeep down the narrow drive.

'I know, it's a great house opportunity, isn't it?'

'I was talking about the fact that he's really got the hots for you.'

I huffed. 'Stop fooling around and just tell me what you think of the house.'

'You know how I feel about the house.'

'Why? It has great potential.'

'So does he. You should give him a chance.'

I laughed and linked arms with her. 'You're hopeless. Come on, I'll buy you lunch,' I offered, steering her toward her car.

16

The Price of Going Home

Antonio's Trattoria, one of our favorite haunts whenever Sandra and Alfonso weren't talking (as was the case now) was just off the *corso*, entering the narrow alleyway that smelled of fresh laundry. After a few meters the fragrance gave way to something even more heavenly. Great Sicilian food.

'My favorite girls,' Antonio cooed. And then, he ducked to speak in her ear. 'Fight with Alfonso again?'

Sandra nodded and he shook his head appropriately, clapping his hands impatiently. 'Luigi!'

'He knows?' I whispered as we sat down.

She shrugged. 'Everybody pretends, but we all know everybody's business.'

Luigi came round with the menus and we ordered a bottle of white Inzolia wine – just one – and agreed we would share an enormous sea bass with grilled vegetables.

'So what do you think about the house?' I asked as I flattened the napkin over my thighs.

'You know what I think. I don't want you to go. I like you living with me. Besides, who's going to cook for me?'

'Alfonso, if you get back together. Personally I'd rather he left his wife first,' I answered.

Sandra stopped and grinned. 'Look at you, rooting for the opposite team!'

I shrugged. 'If a man doesn't love his wife anymore, what's the point in staying?' I knew that much now.

As we waited, Sandra leaned over and took my hand. 'I have something to confess, Gillian.'

I put my drink down. It sounded serious. 'I want to stop fighting with Alfonso. So I'm going to go back to accept his invitation to live with him in Catania.'

'Wow, why didn't you tell me he left his wife?'

She took a sip of her Malvasia. 'He hasn't.'

I blinked. 'Sandra – no...'

'I love him too much, Gillian. I can't help it.'

'But he's married. You'll always have to sneak round behind the wife's back. You deserve so much more. You deserve a man all of your own.'

Something about the coal and the kettle flashed through my mind, but this was different. Alfonso was never going to leave his wife if Sandra bent to his ways. This was a recipe for disaster.

'You should try and get Alfonso out of your system once and for all.'

But Sandra was shaking her head. 'It's too late, Gilly. He's in my blood. I can't forget him.'

'But you will never be happy playing second fiddle.'

At that, her eyebrow raised and I explained. 'It means you will always be second to another woman. And you'll never be able to marry him.'

She shrugged again. 'So? Look around you. Look how marriages fall apart.'

I didn't need to look that far. I was proof of what she was saying. In this day and age keeping a marriage alive was a *job*. Keeping above the drudgery of everyday life, the animosity and resentment away from the bedroom was a herculean effort. I knew.

'So what are you going to do, just sit around and wait for him to call you when he is good and ready?'

'No. We'll travel a lot on weekends. He goes to Milan very often. I'll go with him.'

'But what about work? You can't just run off whenever he snaps his fingers.'

She was silent.

'Sandra?'

She looked up at me and pursed her mouth. 'I'm going to quit.'

'What? No! Sandra, you can't do that – are you nuts?'

The fish arrived and we leaned back from the table as Antonio himself served us, his eyebrow arching as if he'd heard the tail of our conversation, but he said nothing. Sandra was about to make the biggest mistake of her life and I wasn't going to let her do it.

'Promise me you won't quit your job,' I begged her when we were alone. 'You told me that in Italy when teachers leaves their job, they can never get back into the system again.'

'That's true,' she admitted wistfully.

'So you can't even leave for a while to, say, have kids?'

'You can take maternity leave like in any other civilized country, but it only lasts so long. If you leave the system to explore other careers, other avenues, goodbye job.'

'That's also absolutely stupid – and scary! It's like... like *Hotel California!*'

Sandra raised an eyebrow and grinned. 'As in, you can't leave, but you can check out whenever you want?'

'Exactly! It's anti-family, anti-*everything*.'

'That's the way it is. In many ways this is still a third-world country.'

There was some truth there. 'But you absolutely love your job, right?'

'Yes,' she snapped, exasperated. 'But I love life more.'

'Oh, Sandra, you are such an amazing woman. You can do much better with your life. Please reconsider.'

She snorted and I shook her wrist. 'You know I'm right. The bank manager. He'd kill for you. *Signor* Mancino, the jewelry store owner. Any man you want, you can have. Forget about Alfonso. Besides, he's too old for you anyway.'

'Again with the age differences. He's only ten years older.'

'Yeah, but there's already a big difference visually. You're gorgeous and he looks like your father, for Christ's sake.' Okay, I was pushing it a bit, but I had to do everything in my power to make Sandra see reason. 'And in a few years he won't be able to perform and you'll still be a vibrant woman in your prime. What are you going to do then, stay home night and change his diaper like Mimmo does his parents? Huh?'

Sandra laughed, but her eyes clouded. 'Eat your fish,' she said. The woman was a hardhead.

'Promise me you won't leave your job at least,' I insisted.

She was silent.

'Sandra…'

'I promise I'll consider not leaving my job.'

Knowing how pig-headed she was, that would have to do for now.

The days progressed slowly that week and still no word from Mattia. Would he be able to bring the price down from two hundred and twenty, I wondered? And would I be able to make a go of this business? *Of course you can*, I told myself. *If anyone else can, so can you. You're no fool.*

I wasn't? Then what the heck was I doing here, in a foreign country, on an island – a mere rock in the middle of the Mediterranean – all on my own, embarking on a financial adventure like this? Sure, I'd have the sale of our house to pay for the work and keep me going, but what if it didn't work out? I'd have squandered all Gran's money on the proverbial cathedral in the desert. Then what was I going to do, penniless and jobless? Sit by my window and look at Salina all day, wondering how I was going to pay the bills if no one was interested in staying here?

Just as I was in a downward spiral that would probably

end up with me convincing myself to back out of the purchase and hightail it out of there back to the UK and to my buddies Martha and Brends, there was a providential knock at my door. Mattia – bearing a huge bag in one hand and a laptop in another. And a grin so sexy it would melt any woman's clothes off instantly.

'*Ciao*. Brought some food while we work.'

Work?

'I have some good news. And food for three.'

Three? Well, what did I expect? 'Oh. Come on in. Sandra's out.'

He fired up the computer while I set the tiny table on the balcony with Sandra's nicest tableware, the fragrance of eggplant, sausages, cheese and God knew what else was in that bag literally weakening me at the knees (okay, it was mostly Mattia's proximity, but that wasn't why he was here). He was here for business. To make my dream come true, if I could afford it.

'Did you speak to the vendor?' I asked as I sat down and began to open the containers, fragrant steam puffing out from beneath the aluminum lids. It felt odd to be sitting opposite him like we were bosom buddies sharing a meal. Or… lovers.

'I did. He is willing to come down fifty thousand euros if you buy it before the end of the year.'

I eyed him. 'Why?'

Mattia sighed. 'He and his wife are divorcing. This money will be her settlement, but he needs it as soon as possible.'

'Would you… do the work for me?'

He grinned. 'I thought you'd never ask.'

'How much would it cost me?'

'What's your budget?' he asked, out of the blue.

Now normally, if a builder came up to me with a question like that, I'd turn around and say, "*Not so fast, buster. First you tell me what my wish list costs.*" Because I'd had my fair share of scammers and was wary as hell. But Mattia? I found I actually trusted the guy. With my money, at least, if not my heart.

Yes, I know, I'd trusted Tony and got a kick in the teeth in the end. But this was different. This was purely business. Never mind the *frisson* I got whenever Mattia walked into the room or the sense of loss whenever he left it. He wasn't seriously aware of the effect he had on me, so technically, without this very important piece of information, he had no power over me.

But somehow, he was that kind of man whose hands you could put your life in. Like someone you've known a gazillion years and who will never ever betray you.

'Budget? I'm not sure. I want it to be simple but elegant. A modern version of old Sicily. Does that make any sense?'

Mattia studied me and his lips curled into a smile as he nodded. 'It makes perfect sense. Here are some sketches I made – take a look.'

As I munched on my *melanzane alla parmigiana*, I flipped through the sketchbook. And swallowed hard. It was the most beautiful thing I'd ever seen. Black *pece* shone on the floors that contrasted with white stone walls with light sconces and large low windows looming over scattered leather sofas in pastel shades of blue echoing the shade of the sea visible through the huge picture windows.

He watched my face and I saw the beginning of another smile. 'Like it?'

I put my fork down and reached for a napkin. Preferably to wipe my eyes and blow my nose at the same time. A huge knot in my throat was making my eyes burn but I pushed it down. *Businesswomen don't cry*, I told myself. 'Like it? I can't believe how lucky I am to have found the place.' *And you*, I wanted to add, but kept the lip zipped.

He took a sip of his Nero d'Avola wine and studied me with those dark eyes. 'Good things happen, Gillian. All you have to do is believe.'

And just then a damn tear ran down my cheek and I swiped at it. 'Is it really going to happen?' I asked as if he was an oracle or a Greek god.

Mattia chuckled, the thin sheet of ice between us completely gone for good. 'Don't worry. You'll get the house and I will build you the most beautiful boutique B&B ever.'

'Boutique it is, then,' I said.

At that, he reached out and squeezed my hand. Was that just a friendly gesture? In any case, it was sending delicious shivers chasing down my spine, warming me more than the wine. Gawd. If his hand on mine could send my mind reeling, I didn't dare think of anything else.

I only wished that he would open up to me. I needed this, if it was anything at all, to grow into something. Because at the moment, what with Cosetta waiting for information I was not getting from him, I was at a complete stalemate. In every sense.

'Guess who's left his wife?' Sandra flicked a hand through the sophisticated jungle that was her hair and grinned as we were having lunch the next day.

'What? No way!' *And another family bites the dust. I hoped his kids were old enough to cope.*

'I'm moving in with him for the rest of the summer. Sure you don't mind living here on your own?'

It was only going to be for a few more months until I got the house anyway. 'Of course not.'

'Okay, good. But I'll talk to my landlady and get her to bring the rent down.'

And then a thought hit me. 'Are you sure you want to move out permanently?'

She rolled her eyes. 'Don't start on me, now, hear? Your mom should've named *you* Cassandra.'

'Sorry. I *am* happy for you.'

'Me too, so let me enjoy it. Alfonso was worth working on. Which is what you should be doing now.'

Was Cassandra right after all?

★

'We have competition,' Mattia dropped by to tell me the next day. 'And stiff, too. Dr. Tomaselli wants your house.'

Tomaselli? Why did that name sound familiar? Ah. My ex-husband's future father-in-law.

'Maybe I shouldn't be telling you this, Gillian...' he said cautiously, studying my face.

'Shoot. Nothing can kill me now.'

Mattia hesitated. 'He wants it for his daughter's summer home. As a wedding present.'

Which meant that Tomaselli wanted to close the deal fast. Well, that wasn't happening. This was my house. Tony had taken everything else from me – no way he was taking my dreams as well.

One would think I still had a beef with Tony. Truth was, I couldn't care less. It wasn't about him and Nadia. It was not a competition at all. It was simply time for me to get what I deserved. He didn't even have to know I was in competition with them. If he ever got wind that I wanted to buy it he'd delay the sale of our house for sure.

Better get Mattia to keep my name out of it until I managed to seal the deal. The question was, how was I going to pull it off?

'You're kidding me!' Sandra screeched when I told her who my competitor was.

'I know! What am I going to do?'

'Exactly what you were thinking of doing.'

I eyed her. 'Meaning?'

'Oh come on, Gilly. Not even *you* are that naïve. Surely the thought hasn't occurred to you? You talk to the old man, tell him who you are and that Tony is still your husband. He doesn't even know you exist.'

Well, now that she went and said it... 'I had thought of that, actually. But I don't work that way.'

'Well, then you better change or else goodbye *villa* along with everything else.'

'Sandra...'

'*Cara* – you won't ever achieve anything if you don't get your claws out. A Sicilian saying goes, be a sheep and you will get eaten.'

Yeah, that was pretty much me summed up in a nutshell. All my life I'd been meek, unassuming. But I couldn't bring myself to do something like that, even if it might get me the house of my dreams. I could never in a million years stoop so low as to call the in-law up and spill the beans.

'I know,' I admitted. 'But I can't do it.'

'I'll do it for you.'

'You will do no such thing, Sandra.' *Damn me and my goody-two-shoes-ness.*

'Why not? Don't you think the old man deserves to know Tony is still married?'

I was battling with myself. How badly did I want the house? How badly did I want my own happy ending? And how badly did I want to stay faithful to my principles when my whole life was at stake? Terrific question.

But one thing I knew for sure. Nadia Tomaselli deserved to know what an arsehole her "fiancé" was.

The week dragged by like nails on a chalkboard. When I thought I'd go mad with waiting, Mattia finally called to meet me at Lorenzo's café.

He put down his menu and studied me. 'We have a problem.'

My gut dropped to my feet. 'The seller changed his mind?' Was he getting back together with his wife after all? The one time I wished someone to be happier than me in love and it worked *against* me?

'Tomaselli made a definitive offer. Above asking price.'

OCTOBER

17

That's Amore

The weather had turned on a dime and autumn had arrived with a vengeance. The wind was everywhere – whipping the sea up into a froth from its torpid summer slumber, blowing down the narrow medieval streets, stealing in through chimney breasts, rushing down the school corridors – and in through Sandra's old, single-glazed windows.

With Sandra gone, the place seemed not only colder, but older as well. I no longer slept with the windows open, nor air-dried my hair, and began to wear socks (you've got to love cheap old Sisa) around the house and made myself hot mugs of tea to keep me company in the evening when I curled up in bed with a good book as opposed to a good man.

My landlady hadn't invested in anything that would remotely keep the place warm and welcoming, and what hadn't mattered in the heat of the summer, like high ceilings, cold ceramic tiles and the lack of any source of heat, made the place now feel like a stark, unwelcoming warehouse and nothing more. Even the modern furniture now seemed fit only for a summer home, and the thought of my skin touching the glass or granite surfaces made me wince.

The cold weather had caught me by surprise. One day I was walking down the beach barefoot and the next I was huddling in the damp space that was my room. The only good thing was the visit I got from Mattia.

'Congratulations, Gilly – you have a house.'

I stared at him as his words slowly sank in, and I almost knocked my chair over as I leapt up to grab his forearms. 'But you said he'd offered more than me?'

'He had.'

'But how did I get it, then?'

He squeezed my hands, eyes twinkling. 'You just got it. *And*… fifty thousand euros under the asking price.'

'But how? How on earth did you—' And then it dawned on me. 'You didn't! You and Sandra!'

'What?' he asked innocently.

'You didn't,' was all I could say again.

He studied me, his eyes enigmatic, his face unreadable. 'Let's say he is no longer looking for a *villa* for his daughter and son-in-law.'

Holy shit. 'You… blackmailed him?'

'Of course not. He came to ask about the renovation work like he does for every other house with a sign on it. Sandra had stopped by the office and we agreed to simply tell him that Tony's wife was in the area.'

Tony's wife. It sounded surreal – and utterly menacing – even to me. 'What did he say?'

'Well, first he turned white and then pink and then by the time he was purple he said *thank you* and that he'd think about it. Sicilians like that don't show their weaknesses, you see.'

I saw.

'And the next day he called me back and said he wasn't interested anymore. And that's that.'

That was that. 'So he doesn't know about my interest in the house?'

'Absolutely not.'

This guy and Sandra were my miracle workers, no bones about it. I felt my eyes water and my nose filling up with unshed tears. Again. Just call me waterworks. 'Thank you so much, Mattia.'

My dream home seemed more and more secured every time Mattia was in the picture. The guy was definitely a keeper.

'I have to watch out for my friends,' he said, taking my hand in his. Uh-oh. *Major* blood-rush alert, whooshing straight to my heart. There was no oxygen going to my brain. In fact, now I was going to kiss him. Smack on the lips. *Stop me, somebody stop me before I make a raving, idiotic fool out of myself.* Yet again.

But Mattia didn't look like he wanted to stop me from doing anything. Instead, he leaned in close and... kissed my forehead. Fantastic. My friggin' *forehead*.

Well, what the heck did I expect? Hadn't I said I wasn't up for trusting a guy ever again? Let alone one who looked like Mattia? But I absolutely loved him for being on my side after all.

'Thank you,' I sniffed. Steps two and three – home and business – accomplished. My love life, still galaxies from even starting.

He lost his smile and put his glass down, taking my hand. 'Will you do me one little favor, Gillian?'

I wiped my nose. 'Yuh?'

'No more tears. I told you – this is the beginning of a new life.' Dared I hope that much? I grinned. 'So where do I sign?'

He threw back his head and laughed. 'Dotted line – next week.'

I looked at him, the handsome face I'd grown fond of. Who was I kidding? I *trembled* in his presence. Even now, I couldn't stop crazy images flashing through my head. Images that would have sent previous me screaming while running for cover. Candlelight and flashes of flesh (his dark and taut) rolling around on dark silk sheets. It was a delicious thought that kept me company.

I practically ran to tell Sandra. 'I don't know whether I should be mad at you or hug you to death,' I breathed, still wheezy.

'Give me a hug – we deserve it!' she sing-songed. 'And oh – on the way home I bumped into Nadia's cousin who told me everything. Her father is *livid*.'

My hand stole to my heart. 'Oh God...'

'He confronted Tony who tried to deny it at first by saying you'd both agreed to a divorce and that it was only a matter of time, blah, blah, blah.'

Only a matter of time – hadn't he been right, in the end?

'*And...* she says it's over.'

'Over?'

Sandra nodded. 'Nadia was lucky her father didn't kick her out. She shamed his family's honor.'

'Wow,' was all I could say. Poor Nadia. In the short space of a couple of months, Tony had managed to break two hearts. Now that was a record, especially for him.

Now that I was buying a house and a future business up in the hills, I needed to be mobile. What with my recent and future expenses, I couldn't afford a car – not just yet. So I came up with a brainstorm of an idea. I would buy myself one of those three-wheeled agricultural mini pick-up *Ape* things that the island was riddled with, and with good reason.

Remember the Tasmanian devil? This little vehicle made the same noise and hugged the hills like a Himalayan pack mule. And they were relatively cheap. I'd get a second-hand one, have it spray-painted with my new logo that I hadn't had designed yet. What was the color of optimism?

The next morning I went to the garage where Mattia had taken his Jeep. The mechanic winced when he saw me. 'What can I do for you?'

'I want to buy an Ape.'

I swear to you the guy did a double take. 'You want a what?'

Bloody Italian chauvinists. 'You heard. I want a Piaggio Ape.' I took pride in pronouncing it correctly – *Ah-pay* – to show him I knew what I was talking about. 'Make it diesel,' I announced, proud to know that diesel engines were particularly reliable in bad weather. See? Always thinking ahead.

'Are you sure you want to *drive*?' the mechanic asked me, having been told of my road awareness. Couldn't blame him, though, could I, after I'd almost got Mattia killed in the attempt to not plaster me against the bus ticket kiosk. It seemed like ages ago now.

I folded my arms in front of my chest. 'Do you know anyone selling a second-hand one or not?'

He shrugged. 'Maybe. How much do you want to spend?'

That was easy. 'As little as possible.'

He wiped his hands on his overalls and nodded. 'Okay, leave me your number and I'll call you when I find one.'

'Soon, yes?' I didn't want to depend on anyone ferrying me up and down the mountain. I didn't want to depend on anyone, period. Not anymore.

I could see he didn't think much of women by the way he answered my questions. It was obvious he considered my gender only a pleasure toy and nothing else. So, assured that within the week he'd let me know, I practically skipped down the street.

18

Aphrodite on an Ape

The next Sunday morning, I dragged Sandra out of bed and up the Giants' Steps to Upper Town Lipari to visit the archeological museum in the citadel. It overlooked the terracotta rooftops of Lipari, practically giving you a bird's eye view. The last time I'd been here I was with Mattia a thousand years ago and I had missed the entire archeological experience which, much to Sandra's horror, I was making the most of now.

What an amazing museum, what an amazing site. I never thought I'd see something so gorgeous. We stopped to catch our breath and gazed out over the bastions to the open sea, a multi-pixel puzzle of greens and turquoises and transparent patches lapping against the stone walls below. I breathed in deeply of the salty air, wishing I could just soar over the sea like a seagull and dip into the waters to refresh my sweating, overheated body. I wanted to drink in the entire sea, eat the entire landscape and keep it inside me forever. It was one of those views you never forget.

'Why didn't you let me sleep?' Sandra groaned.

'Because this is culture and you've never been here before. Shame on you – this is one of the most amazing museums I've ever seen!'

'But it's too much work, hiking all the way up here…'

'Lazy girl,' I scolded her. 'But, if you play your cards right, next time I'll drive you.' And I let her in on my Ape purchase.

She squealed 'A three-wheeled tractor? You must be absolutely nuts, but I love it!'

'Shush,' I said, conscious of the locals milling around and eyeing us curiously. They already thought I was *pazza*.

Sandra beamed at me. 'It's such an original idea – so *you*! Most women wouldn't be caught dead in an Ape, but you – you don't give a shit!'

I shrugged. 'I've never been exactly Miss Fashion, you know. Plus, it's practical. And cheap. I'll paint it a bright color and add a logo on it to be recognizable.'

'Excellent!'

'There's only one problem,' I admitted. 'I don't know how to drive those things.'

She shrugged. 'Ask Mattia to teach you, no?'

'What? No, I can't ask Mattia that,' I said decisively. God knew he'd single-handedly sorted out half my life already. The last thing I needed was for him to take over the other half that I was still free to screw up, Gillian-style.

'Can't ask me what?' came Mattia's voice from straight ahead. I looked up and there he was on a ten-speed bike, walking Diana who was panting away happily on her leash. When she saw me she lunged and Mattia gave the leash some slack.

'Hello, beautiful,' I greeted her, ruffling her fur. I still managed to take her for a walk every weekday morning and paid Mirko, Maria's son, to take him out afternoons, much to Mattia's pleasure. She was, after all, my dog too, even if I had nowhere to put her for now. She spent her mornings at Mattia's office behind his desk, waiting for me to appear.

'I can't wait to settle in the new house so I can bring her home,' I told him. 'I *miss* her.'

He grinned. 'She'd love that. But then *I'd* miss her.'

'You can come and see her whenever you want,' I said, swallowing as I felt my face go red hot. 'How long is it going to take, the reno?'

He grinned. 'You impatient?'

'I just want to have my own place and get on with it. I can come up and help you with the build,' I offered.

'Sure. But it'll be a while before the house is habitable.'

'We can rough it, Diana and I.'

'She's even bought an Ape but she needs your help to learn how to drive it,' Sandra contributed, unable to stay quiet for any length of time.

'I do not,' I argued and Sandra slapped my arm.

'Shut up. You do,' and to Mattia: 'She does.'

He shrugged. 'No problem. When are you picking it up?'

'Next week. From your buddy's shop.' I couldn't pass that place without remembering how he'd damaged his car and had refused my money. We'd sure come a long way since then, I realized with some satisfaction.

'Mario? Why didn't you tell me? I could've put in a good word for you. It's still not too late. I'll give him a call.'

'No, that's okay. It was cheap.'

'How cheap?'

'A thousand euros.'

'A thousand euros for a second-hand Ape? Never. Let me take care of it.'

'See?' Sandra said, jabbing me in the gut.

'Ow. Okay. Thank you. I really appreciate it.'

He shrugged. 'Happy to help.'

I sighed inwardly. With relief. Every cent saved was a cent earned. Plus that meant I'd be seeing him soon again. Now if only I could stop salivating at the mere thought.

Two days later we got our appointment with the *notaio* to purchase the house. *My* house. It sounded so strange to be saying that. *My house, my house…*

And this new life that I was slowly and painstakingly carving out for myself with a little (well, okay, a lot of) help from my friends was mine, too. My business, my future. Mine, mine, mine. Gran would be so proud of me, spending her money in Italy again.

I only hoped it went well. Starting over was always a big risk to say the least. What the heck did I know about running a B&B?

'We can start Wednesday right after we have lunch.'

I blinked. 'Lunch?'

'Of course. We'll be done at the *notaio*'s around noon. Then we have to celebrate your purchase, no?'

'Of course. Celebrate my purchase.' *And possibly tie myself to the chair so I don't jump your bones.*

Sandra clapped her hands. 'This is so great! Too bad I'm at work or I would have joined you.'

As if she ever would. This woman was so determined I spend as much time alone with Mattia it was ridiculous. It was as if she wanted to make sure we ended up together. She was a great friend, but a little unrealistic at times.

Not that I didn't think about him all the time. He was definitely the best in my book anyway, forget about that knicker-stealing smile and pecs you don't need any imagination to see through his T-shirt. Yummy yum-yum. I wondered what he was like in bed. Was he as warm and passionate as he was in day-to-day life? As fun and playful? Did he take his time or…?

'So see you Wednesday?' he asked and I tore myself away from another fantasy that was just forming in my mind. Alas, I would never have the answers to all my naughty questions.

'Can't wait to become an Italian homeowner,' I said with a grin.

'It'll all go well, you'll see,' he assured me.

But the night before the purchase, true to my old insecurities, I lay in bed wide awake, my mind racing, thinking of all the scenarios that would become concrete with this gigantic move. And all the risks it entailed such as:

a) The B&B might not be successful.
b) It might be successful but I might not like it after a while, which meant:

c) I'd be stuck on a rock in the middle of the Med with no way to go home unless:

d) I sold up. But if I couldn't sell:

e) See c).

Midnight chimed and I was nowhere near sleeping. Was I up for it? Could I do it? Was this the first step toward the rest of my life? Or was I absolutely bonkers, buying the first thing I saw and that would anchor me definitively, more or less, to this island? What had I even seen in this place to warrant me staying? Was it the weather, the landscape, the beauty of the island and the people? What was it? Was it all enough to do this? Or, let's be honest, was it also, if not mostly, the hope of seeing Mattia every day? But even that would sooner or later die, as the man was not a monk. Oh, if only he really was interested in me. But even if that miracle could be conjured, I would never be able to let myself go again.

These thoughts kept me busy until the clock chimed three a.m. I gave sleep up as an impossible feat, threw the blanket off me and padded into the kitchen without any slippers. Big mistake. The marble floors were freezing and by the time I got to the cooker I had foot-freeze.

That was what was keeping me awake all night. I was having a nocturnal case of cold feet. That was all. Tomorrow, by the light of day, I'd be okay again. The night was always a time of doubts for me. All I needed was a good night's sleep.

So I put the kettle on and rummaged through the cupboards for some chamomile, although only elephant tranquilizers would work at this stage.

Through the open shutters in the kitchen the moon reflected on the thin glass panes. Unlike this place, my new house would have double glazing. Definitely. And a fireplace. And gas heating. And a huge kitchen. I slipped my cold feet under me and added, *and nice rugs*.

So tomorrow – in a few hours' time – I'd wake up (assuming

I could ever get to sleep) and strut into the *notaio*'s office with all the confidence in the world that yes, I did deserve this house and the chance to start anew. So there.

I took my hot mug to bed with me and opened one of Sandra's magazines in the hope it would lull me to sleep. Fat chance. When I heard four chimes from the church bell, I smiled to myself. Only a few more hours and one huge decision now separated me from The Rest of My Life.

A few hours later, I still couldn't stop smiling and it was contagious. Mattia gave me his arm with a happy grin and together we strolled (when I actually wanted to run but there were people about and you know what it's like in small towns) down Via Umberto Primo and then west on Via Garibaldi to the *notaio*'s office in the piazza of Marina Corta.

This was a perfect day – the sun was warm in the bright sky and the sea was calm and quiet again, gently lapping against the harbor quay.

This was it. After years of disappearing into the background (not for nothing Tony used to call me Gilly Wallflower) and weeks of wondering what would happen to me, I'd finally taken the bull by the horns. It was a big decision to move, no lock, no stock nor barrel, seeing as I owned nothing here and it suited me fine, to a place I'd never heard of before.

But Lipari and I understood each other well and promised to live happily ever after. I had no doubts whatsoever this time. I belonged here and was slowly making friends everywhere, thanks to Sandra and Mattia.

And that's when, coming from the other side of the piazza, I noticed a familiar figure – Tony's lover – and an elderly gentleman, presumably her dad, Dottor Tomaselli.

On spotting us, he stiffened, his body language betraying him. He just wanted to get away from us, or rather, me, before Nadia recognized me. But instead, remembering his ingrained social-stage politeness, he nodded to Mattia, esteemed as an equally respectable man, meanwhile shooting flaming daggers at me.

All this before Nadia looked up from her feet and saw me, her face a mask of sorrow. I wanted to reach out to her, to tell her that I wasn't angry with her in the least – not anymore, even if previously I'd have gladly ripped her hair out of her scalp. But it wasn't her fault she'd met a jerk. Her heart had been broken, too. This was more than obvious in her slouched posture, her huge, red-rimmed eyes and air of defeat.

But how would she take the gesture? From what I had learned, Sicilians were very friendly but also very dignified, and would never appreciate a public display such as atonement or forgiveness.

'Come,' Mattia whispered, steering me away from the piteous scene and through an enormous two-story green wooden door with a shiny brass plaque reading *Notaio Giunta*.

'She'll get over it,' Mattia said.

'I hope so. For her sake.' No woman deserved to suffer for love. How the hell was she supposed to know Tony was a douchebag? And a married one, to boot?

Contrary to common belief about Italian bureaucracy, the purchase went smoothly and only took an hour in all. I was the owner of a beautiful, huge, dilapidated wreck, and I couldn't have be happier! After we all shook hands and exchanged contracts, we left the palazzo and Mattia steered me toward *Il Buongustaio*, a restaurant just fifty meters off *Marina Corta* and with a view that funneled out into the open sea.

'My treat,' I said as he pulled out (I swear to you) a chair for me at one of the sidewalk tables.

'No way. I'm an old-fashioned man. No woman of mine pays for anything.'

'Except for building work,' I said with a laugh and he grinned.

'So, what are you having?'

A scene with you, I wanted to say. *I want a scene with you…*

We ordered *spaghetti allo scoglio* and Inzolia wine, followed by a *fritto misto di mare*, so fresh the fish were practically still swimming in our plates. After lunch he wiped his mouth and practically pulled me out of my chair. 'Okay, time to go.'

Oh. He had stuff to do. Of course. He could only spend so much time with me. Time was money and he had to get back to his office to make more of it. So I put on a polite face to hide my disappointment. 'Well, thank you, Mattia, for all your help. I'll see you when the work starts, then?'

'Not so fast,' he said, putting a hand on my waist.

I looked at him blankly.

'Your driving lesson, remember?' he said.

Yikes – I'd completely forgotten about that. A shame to ruin such a gloriously triumphant morning with my driving.

Ten minutes later, as I did my best to follow his instructions, he mock-cried, 'The brakes, the brakes!' when I launched my brand-new second-hand little yellow Tasmanian devil downhill at the speed of lightning while he feigned (at least I think) a look of horror and went through the motions of bracing himself, his frame huge inside the tiny cabin. With my butt as well in there, it was a miracle we'd fit at all.

Tony, I remembered, had turned my driving lessons with him into such a bloody nightmare that I had simply refused to drive with him in the car. He always had a way of making me feel stupid and inept. But with Mattia, I laughed and laughed, sure my sides were going to split, as I rammed down a gear to climb the next hill, the little but powerful motor *mam-mamming* like a mad hornet. I can't remember ever having such a good time, his eyes in mine despite the winding road, our thighs rubbing and his proximity making me giddy like a teenager with her first love.

When the sun began to go down, he showed me how to switch on the lights and we exchanged places. As he got into my seat, he studied me at length, his arm outstretched behind me, his eyes roaming over my face, slowly leaning in. And then his smile disappeared and his obsidian eyes delved into mine.

Ohgodohgodohgod, I thought. *He is going to kiss me again. Am I ready?* I swallowed, trying to hide the sheer panic rising in my throat, threatening to smother me. I wasn't ready. This was not how it was supposed to happen, in the road by the side of a wild field as the last rays of the day turned everything to gold, just him and me, looking into each other's eyes.

So – big surprise – I panicked. 'Ah, thanks so much for putting your life at risk – once again – for me.'

He pulled away, but grinned.

'I'm a real accident waiting to happen, aren't I?' I tittered.

'Nah. You are divine. Aphrodite on an Ape…'

That was possible the nicest thing any man (Tony included) had ever said to me. And if I was Aphrodite on an Ape, he was most definitely Valentino on a Vespa. *Bellissimo* on a Bugatti. Alpha male on an Alfa Romeo. *Figo* on a Ferrari. A macho on a Maserati, a…

'I had a great time, Gillian. You are such a laugh.'

That was it? That was really it? No changing his mind about us? No *I'm sorry but I can't stay away from you despite my sincere efforts*?

It was hard to hide the shock, but man, I was good. 'Thanks, you too,' I answered noncommittally, primarily to break the spell he had woven around me all afternoon.

In total silence, he dropped me off as close as possible to Sandra's flat and I alighted, my heart beating out of my chest as I stepped back to let him pass.

'Gillian?' he called softly.

I turned. 'Yeah?'

'Where do you want me to park?'

Oh, right. That thing was *mine* now, wasn't it?

'Uh, I'm not quite sure,' I whispered.

'You can leave it in my lot behind the office, if you want. I only have the one car,' he offered.

'Oh. Right. Thank you. And the fee?'

He grinned and shook his head. 'How are your building skills?' he asked me out of the blue.

'Zero.' I laughed. 'But I'll do anything to help.'

'Excellent. Now, are you ready for the rest of your life?'

I looked at him and grinned. 'You betcha.' I now had more than a couple of reasons to stay.

I took a step closer. 'Are we starting tomorrow?'

'Might as well. We've got to get you into business as soon as possible.'

'Oh. Right. Thank you.'

'Good night, Gillian.' And with a wave, he took off.

That was it? No caresses, no hugs? I had imagined the Return of the Flame. Not even one measly little kiss?

When I got in, I went straight to the bathroom and sniffed my armpits. The buckets I'd sweated in the last few hours would've challenged any deodorant, but luckily my Italian pharmacy-bought Derma Fresh had held. I smelled fine. Then why the hell was he in such a rush to go?

And then I caught a glance of myself in the mirror. All that wild cry-laughing at his faces and jokes had given me panda eyes. No wonder he'd run for the hills.

19

Renovation, Insulation, Infatuation

The next morning Mattia and I started our first day of work on the house. I was up before dawn, biting my nails even while I showered and dressed. The sky was a bit cloudy, not quite that vibrant cobalt blue anymore. The weather was still warm between ten and two, but as soon as the sun went down it was Run for your Socks. To think I'd gone months and months on end wearing just flip-flops while back home it would already be coat-weather. Now this was what I called living it up.

In ten minutes I was driving my Ape up the uneven gravelly road, only to find Mattia had beat me. His Jeep was in the drive and Diana was already sniffing around.

'Hello, beautiful,' I murmured as she sauntered toward me, slapping her tail against my shins. 'Welcome to our new home.'

The door was wide open and I could hear scraping sounds up on the top floor. He was up a ladder, singing to a tune on a portable battery-powered radio and inspecting the roof, all that was visible to me his long legs and, well, a rather nice butt. He looked great in cut-offs, his strong legs hairy but not so that you'd take him for a caveman or anything. They were a perfect hairy. Nice calf muscles, too.

'Hi!' I shouted, thinking maybe I shouldn't have sneaked up on him while he perched precariously atop a ladder. I held up his cappuccino.

He ducked and smiled. '*Ciao*. That for me?'

'Come and get it.'

Mattia slid down, landing on two feet like a gymnast. What a bod. '*Grazie*. Mmph...' he murmured, uncapping the cup and sipping slowly, eyes closed as if he was savoring the most delicious thing in the world. What could be more delicious than his own lips? With that sudden thought, I almost choked on my own coffee.

'How, uh – bad is it?' I asked, grateful I had something else to concentrate on besides his sinews.

He swallowed and looked me in the eye. 'Actually, it's better than I thought. Most beams are salvageable. All we really need to do is put a layer of insulation in and relay the pan tiles. It'll be done in less than two weeks, and I'll do the en suite right after that so you can move in if you want while we work downstairs, if you don't mind a house full of sweaty, loud men and dust.'

I brightened up immediately. I was going to be living here! All year round!

'And I'll get you a good deal on the insulation, don't you worry,' he promised with one of those sexy grins.

Hoo boy. Here I was, in way too deep. Get back to business pronto, Gilly Morana.

'How good?' I challenged.

'Less than half the price if we go and pick stuff up ourselves.'

'And you're willing to do this for me?'

He took another sip of his cappuccino and closed his eyes in pleasure again. It took me lots of concentration to think about insulation.

He opened his eyes and pierced me with his gaze, more and more intimate by the moment. 'You deserve it.'

Which, to me, was unheard of. Never had any man told me I deserved something good. So I decided to stop questioning his motives and just take the good of everything as it came.

'Are you sure you don't want to wear something more comfortable?' he asked, eyeing (hurray!) my little (-ish) blue (designer) dress.

I looked down. 'What, this old thing?'

'Suit yourself. Here, hold this,' he said, giving me a bag of plaster that almost sent me reeling.

He stepped back, eyeing me critically. '*Tutto bene?*'

'I'm great,' I reassured him, making a mental note to wear jeans and sneakers, if not a combat outfit, the next day.

As I helped him and his team out without actually managing to get trampled or trundled on, it became apparent not everyone was concentrating on their work. The blacksmith, who walked with a limp, kept stealing me funny glances.

'Hey, pretty lady…' he drawled, his eyes flashing and for a moment I swore he was going to reach out and grab me.

'Gino – stop making a fool of yourself,' Mattia scolded.

'Why, what did I say? She's a pretty lady, no?'

'Just get back to work, will you?'

And then, to me: 'Don't mind Gino. He's all bark and no bite.'

'He's scary-looking,' I whispered to Mattia as the man limped away.

At that, Mattia stopped and looked down at me. 'You have no reason to be afraid of anything. Not as long as I'm breathing.'

Now, how would *you* have interpreted that one?

NOVEMBER

20

A Sinking Sensation

Having worked on restoring the roof for two solid weeks, by the first week of November the house was well under way, the attic floor, as Mattia had promised, already weather-tight and the top-floor bedroom and bathroom hooked up and habitable. I wasted no time at all moving in with my three shopping bags, one of which contained my brand-new duvet set, all I owned in the world now, if you didn't count a B&B in the making. I guess I had to start over from scratch to appreciate the things I'd taken for granted in life.

'Roughing it, I see,' Mattia commented with a grin as I parked my Ape in the driveway amidst carpenters, plumbers and stonemasons and moved my possessions upstairs.

'I was dying to spend the night here,' I explained, mirroring his grin. *Possibly with you. Wake up with you next to me, your strong arm around my waist, your face in my collarbone...*

'Well, be patient and it will happen soon enough,' he promised and I started, having lost the thread of the conversation.

'Forget soon enough. I'm sleeping here tonight.'

He shrugged. 'Have it your way.'

But the next morning, my first morning waking up in the house, when I opened my eyes I instantly knew something was wrong.

The house was completely quiet. Not a hammer banging, not a saw sawing, not a scraper scraping. It seemed like the night before Christmas. They couldn't all be out to lunch, right? Besides, it was only ten o'clock. So I threw my cardi around me and got up to investigate.

Just as I'd thought. The front door was closed, Diana wagging her tail at me for her breakfast.

Thinking it was probably some sort of religious *festa* again – God knew there were about three different celebration times during the year for San Bartolomeo alone – I padded into my makeshift kitchen and boiled the kettle, reaching into a bag of chocolate *Pan di Stelle* cookies while eyeing the jumbo-sized jar of Nutella I'd bought myself in a fit of self-love/self-hate. Tony always shook his head whenever I brought home a jar, because he knew it was one of my most reliable emotional crutches. He always said one shouldn't rely on food to feel better. It was a shame that not all of us could rely on sex, the next-best thing.

Diana stood to attention as I reached into her bag of bickie bones. 'Sit,' I ordered in English and she fell to her butt, eyes watching me like a hawk. So I rewarded her, which felt great for the soul. It would've been nice if life had been like that for people. Easy rewards.

Humming, I spotted Mattia's radio on the counter and switched it on, busying myself with breakfast (no, of *course* bickies aren't enough!) while dodging the unopened bags of cement and grouting, wondering what could keep Mattia and his team away from work, when I realized that it was Saturday. No builder worked on a Saturday.

Okay – house to myself. Great. My day alone was now positively bursting with possibilities. I would lounge around, stick my nose in the work although I'd already seen the high quality of it, kit out my bedroom and oh, maybe go for a stroll and pretend to bump into Mattia. Diana really missed him. And then I remembered he normally went away on the weekends.

But now with Diana living with me permanently Mattia didn't need me to sleep over to watch her and I was no longer privy to his travel plans. Now I'd never know what he got up to. Where did he go? Who did he see, what did he do? And most importantly, were we at the point that I could ask him again and actually get an answer from him this time?

The unidentified Italian tune playing faded out and the first familiar notes of "Livin' on a Prayer" filled my kitchen alongside the smell of fresh coffee and I belted out the lyrics at the top of my lungs, playing the electric broom in the corner. That was one of the perks of living in the countryside. No neighbors.

I took my food to the conservatory facing east and sat down. And then I noticed some spots on the floor and bounced right back up. I wouldn't be able to sit and look at *that*. Anal to the point of self-effacement, I went through my cleaning stuff under my makeshift sink looking for the bucket and mop. Where had I put the Lysoform?

I burrowed myself deeper into the cupboard, sure I'd left it there. Bloody workers must have used it. Mattia made sure they left the place spotless after a day's work. Oh, well, you couldn't complain about that, could you? Maybe I should hire *them* to do the major cleaning before I opened for business.

'Gillian!' came a shout from behind me and I sat up inside the cupboard, banging my head against the piping. Damn. And then I realized that but for a pair of knickers, my butt was practically naked and sticking out into the open room. Too late. He'd already seen. *Bloody hell.*

I sat upright and pushed my hair out of my eyes, trying to play it cool, but only managed to slip on the washing-up liquid that had in the meantime spilt all over the floor. I grabbed the side of the sink and hefted myself, gooey knees and all, to face his amused expression. And played it as cool as I could and *man*, you would've been proud of me.

'Oh, hi. What are you doing here? It's Saturday.'

'Hi, sorry, I didn't mean to startle you,' he said cheerfully, but nothing, not his tone, nor the polite averting of his gaze could hide the fact that I was practically naked. 'I just remembered I'd left the water pump off. I didn't want you to be high and dry all day.'

I blinked, pulling my cardi closer around me as if it could actually cover my butt or erase the spectacle imprinted in his mind. 'But – I've got water. I just had a shower.' As if it wasn't obvious enough.

He grinned. 'Yes, but that's coming from your reserve tank. By tonight you wouldn't have had any left.'

'Oh. I'm so sorry you had to come all the way up here on the weekend. You could've called and told me how to do it.'

At that, he grinned and helped me to my full height, which wasn't much to begin with, but I'd been hunching to hide The Ample Bosom, an old trick you learn early in school when they start calling you *Boobies*.

He coughed. 'Silly. You know I care.'

He cared. In what way? I wasn't an idiot. I knew he liked to flirt – was damn good at it, too. I'd reached the conclusion that his interest, if we could even call it that, was simply due to the fact that I was a foreign woman all on my own and had sparked his male sense of protection. Of course. You had to admit he was always hanging around for some reason or other. I could understand him being helpful Monday through Friday, but Saturday? His day off? And speaking of which, how come he hadn't gone away this weekend?

I ran my gooey fingers through the hair hanging in my face. What a sight I must've been. Maybe when the house was finished I could invite him over for a roast dinner, to thank him for... looking out for me? Maybe a nice North American meal of meatloaf, pumpkin pie and... yeah and maybe even a belly dance for him as well, just to make sure he never returned.

Stop kidding yourself, Morana, I said to the weakling still lurking somewhere inside. Despite all my resolve and all I'd achieved so far, I still couldn't bring myself to even dream I had a ghost of a chance of him being interested in me.

'I'm just watching out for you,' he reassured me.

So there you had it – see? Suspicions confirmed. He was *just watching out for me*. The guy was just being helpful. Of course. Why had I even for a split second indulged in the fantasy that he could actually, *really* be interested in me...? He was only being *helpful*. God, kill me now? Anything so I wouldn't feel this insane pull.

'Did you really sleep here on your own?' he asked and my mouth fell open. 'Sorry,' he said. 'I didn't mean – don't look at me like that.'

I parked my arms in front of my chest. 'Like what?'

But he only grinned that damn, take-me-now grin and my knees, which were already gooey enough with washing-up liquid, turned to absolute Jell-O.

'Sandra is sure going to miss having you around. You're a barrel of laughs, you know?' he said.

Gee, just the compliment I'd been waiting for all my life from a man like him.

And you? I wanted to ask. *Do you miss not having me around?*

'Don't give me that look again, Gillian.' He grinned. 'I meant that in the best possible way, you know.'

How lucky for me. As I turned to go get dressed, just because he was watching out for me, he offered to help me hang curtain rods and tie-backs, spending pretty much all morning of his precious Saturday. I wondered how he'd managed to get out of his still-a-mystery-to-me weekend commitment.

During the next few weeks Mattia and his men relentlessly worked their way downwards through the house and I followed in their wake with my mops, dusters and a new vacuum cleaner I'd purchased at a hardware store next to one of the souvenir shops. Soon I was able to take pictures of at least a couple of bedrooms and the communal area and the gardens on which I personally was working like mad with the help of Leo, an old school-friend of Mattia's. I wondered if it was Maria's Leo?

My gardening experience though was of no use here because I was used to English plants. Here they were different, the seasons off-kilter and everything practically out of whack. So I went back to the hardware store (that had everything *including* kitchen sinks) and bought myself three books on Mediterranean gardening, one even in English. How hard could it be?

As I was scrubbing the dry specks of cement off my stupendous new bedroom floor on all fours, Mattia knocked on the doorframe. Can anyone see a pattern here? Well, at least this time I was actually wearing clothes.

'Come in!' I chimed, unable to contain my excitement.

'Hey, you're fast,' he mused. 'I should hire you to work on my team.'

'I'm not sure that you could afford me,' I quipped, dusting myself off and getting to my feet.

And to show him my valor, we worked non-stop until lunch – a quick onion and cheese omelet I whipped up along with a tomato, basil and rocket lettuce salad. And after that the hours flew by. Every once in a while he'd look up and search my gaze, which I'd avert just in time because my eyes were always plastered – you guessed it – to him.

'*Andiamo*,' he said finally as we stood by the kitchen window sipping on a nice mug of coffee and enjoying my enthralling view of the island of Salina.

'Where?'

'For a *passeggiata* down the *corso*.'

Passeggiata? A walk – in public – with me, down the *corso*?

'But... but I thought you didn't waste your time walking up and down the strip.'

He looked down at me and grinned. 'It's not a waste of time if I'm with you.'

Was he for real? Sex-god Mattia Spadaro wanted to be seen in public with me? What for? It didn't make sense, not with his fleet of women floating around him, like tiny dolphins riding a wave.

But if I wasn't careful that wave could have the devastating effects of a tsunami on me.

Because whenever he looked at me with those piercing eyes I always felt... *strange*. I was familiar with the falling-for-a-guy jitters, the erratic heart-pounding, the cold sweats. But it had taken me a while to recognize these symptoms as part of my feelings and not some usual *Turn of the Month News* in my body that indicated I was yet another day or month or year older. You know, one day an erratic heartbeat and the next a major coronary or worse.

How long had it been since I'd experienced these feelings? I didn't need to wonder. I knew the answer to that. Twenty years. Harking back to when I was young, foolish, happy and in love.

And then, somewhere along the way, I wasn't young or happy anymore. And then, not only was I no longer "in love" with Tony, I'd actually stopped loving him altogether. But when? I couldn't recall the precise moment, but it certainly must have been between him introducing me as Gilly Wallflower to one of our new dinner guests, i.e. an investor he was hoping to ensnare and fool into helping him open his own clinic, and snarling at me because my dresses weren't as small as those of the wives of his competitors.

Had I stopped and not even realized it? Had I stopped loving him years ago but chased him all the way to Sicily out of... pride? Had my decision been a knee-jerk reaction, the last chance to resuscitate a dead relationship?

Because I had been unhappy when I was with Tony. Sure, there were some peaks of happiness, but they all depended on external factors and never on the supposed love between us as a couple. Annie getting her degree, Annie finding a job – all her victories made us happy. But besides that, nothing had bound us together as man and woman anymore.

Not only that, I'd ascribed my lack of happiness to boredom (mine), andropause (his) and a general sense of not belonging.

But now, after all these years I'd realized that he'd never made an effort after I'd put on the weight during my pregnancy. And I had still continued to think that we were happy, though admittedly stressed.

I'd realized it was like he'd suddenly looked and seen a woman he didn't recognize. He should've kept loving me for who I was, not the trophy wife he'd expected me to be in the eyes of his colleagues and clients. But, and there you have it, he had never loved me for real. And all that time I'd loved him as best I could, despite the fact I was getting nothing back. Save for a daughter I loved with all my heart, of course. But my love for Tony had slowly – *very* slowly – dissipated.

But to start over with a new man? That was a completely different ball game. Yes, there was the great feeling of novelty and the hope and all, but who could guarantee that it wouldn't be worse or as bad as the first heartbreak? That with Mattia, provided this thing would ever take off, it wouldn't all come crashing down? I had *everything* to lose this time. But, I could also have everything to gain. If I only threw myself into it, no reservations.

'So – what do you say?' Mattia prompted and I started out of my reverie.

Right, the *passeggiata*! 'But – I can't go like this,' I protested. 'I'd have to get changed. It's evening now.' Besides the fact that I was wearing my old bra performed no miracles for me. If I was going to be at all presentable, I needed a li'l *pick'em up*.

'You're right. We'll do this the proper way. Go upstairs and have a nice shower in your brand-new bathroom. I'll be back to pick you up in an hour.'

And he left me standing there, in the middle of an empty room with nothing but a new mattress on the floor and a head full of dreams. Through the open attic window, I saw him get into his Jeep and go. He was whistling.

I called Sandra who was there in ten minutes flat, loaded with all sorts of tricks as I mad-dashed through my designer duds looking for something appropriate to wear.

'I'm in trouble!' I cried.

'Why?'

'Because I'm not cut out for this!'

'*Madonna Mia*, again with the same litany! Come with me.' She beckoned me to sit down on my mattress and began slapping stuff all over my face.

'Not too much,' I protested as she rubbed and rubbed her fingertips over my eyelids and cheekbones. I didn't want to look like the clown from the movie *It*. I was scared enough for the both of us. Was this an actual date, then?

'Should I be scared?' I asked as she scrunched up her mouth and wiped some stuff off.

'No, I'm doing a great job, you'll see.'

'No, I mean – why would Mattia want to be seen out on the town with me?'

'Because you're funny, sweet and kind?'

'That's not enough with a guy like Mattia,' I managed before she attacked my lips with a small brush and then stood back.

'Oh, trust me. Mattia could have any bimbo he wanted. But he wants a real woman. Someone who is kind. Compassionate. And funny. In a nutshell, you. Besides, not that it would matter to him at all, but have you not looked at yourself lately?'

I blinked. 'Why would I want to do that?'

'Because what with all your overalls and T-shirts you've been wearing on this bloody building site, you haven't had the time to wear proper clothes. Surely you've noticed the difference?' Sandra said.

Difference? It wasn't like I spent my days preening myself in the mirror. More like pushing wheelbarrows full of cement up the hill to Mattia. I did feel strong and more wiry, though.

'Look at yourself,' she urged, pulling me toward the glass door so I could check out my reflection. You understand, of course, that I didn't own a full-length mirror like she did. Except for the one in the shower that Mattia had installed in my en suite, the bastard.

I'd have liked to think that was some devious plan of his for future encounters, only the idea of my butt reflected in that mirror made me shiver in horror. But hang on a minute. I looked closer, and sure enough, my huge hips had deflated somewhat to a nicer, more slender curve. I blinked. I knew I was slowly losing weight by balancing my desserts with huge amounts of physical exertion on the site, but I hadn't realized how much.

Hello, cheekbones! I pulled back my neckline and found a collarbone as well. Who knew I had all these bones screaming to come out? How could I have not noticed it? Because for weeks I'd been rolling out of bed and straight onto a building site, working all day. That *had* to have an effect on my body and my muscle tone even if I ate the world for dinner afterwards.

Let's not kid ourselves, I was still curvy, but at least now I had a shape that resembled the average woman and not, say, your average Zeppelin. And to think that all these years I'd avoided stepping on scales and glancing at mirrors and ignoring my once-ballooning dress sizes.

Years ago I'd stopped checking and made a break for the very last item at the back of the rack, always in black and flowing lines. With the result that I always looked like a tent. And I had lost the strength to even care. Because the only purpose of clothes was to cover my body. I had seven drab dresses, one for each day. I never went anywhere. What was the point of pining over a size twelve when it belonged to a galaxy far far away from me?

But if I could look better and build up some confidence, my whole world would be made. I'd also strategically avoided mirrors like the plague. And now, when I least expected, was ambushed by one. Two, actually. That one behind me revealed secrets I'd have never believed. I couldn't keep my eyes off my butt. It looked like the one I had when I was in high school, bless my soul.

How could I have not seen the pretty girl buried deep inside me?

'And I think that tonight he might finally tell you how he feels.'

I rolled my eyes although my heart did a quick *ba-boom-ba-boom-ba-boom* jump in my throat. 'Be *quiet*.'

'I'm serious! Do you know what it means for a man like Mattia to walk alongside a woman in public? And on the *corso*, to boot?'

'Uh, no. But I'm sure you're going to fill me in.'

As a response, she attacked my hair and fluffed it around, raking her fingers through it as if tearing at jungle leaves.

'Ow...'

'This is huge – an unprecedented event!'

'Sandra, I hate to burst your bubble but thousands of people walk down that *corso* a million times a day and it doesn't mean a thing. It's the only way to get from one side of the island to the other, that's all.'

'Not in the evening! This is a real date! Do you have any idea how many women would *kill* to be in your shoes? Even if I'm wrong – and I'm not – why not just let yourself go and have some fun?'

I rolled my eyes, desperately wanting to let go to a new possibility that had been inching its way into my heart before I even knew it, but too afraid to let myself go to complete, full-blown, hopeful thoughts. Thoughts that, once thought, I couldn't take back, not even from myself. Things like this just didn't *happen* to someone like me.

'I'm telling you – in the evening, the *corso* becomes a cat-walk – a stage. He wants you and everybody else to know how he feels. He wants to make a statement.'

How could Sandra actually think *that*? Plus, the only statement *I* was making was that I had precisely ten minutes to get dressed now. And to put on my good bra.

'Here,' Sandra said dumping something onto my bed – one

of the nude-colored girdles Cosetta had thrown in for free. It was the closest thing to a Sherman tank. No spillages from that big mama.

'Oh, no – I'm not wearing *that*.'

'Why not? Don't you want to take his breath away?'

'His, not mine. I can hardly breathe in that thing, let alone the fact that it takes me forever to get into it. If I so much as open my mouth to breathe it'll pop. Besides, you just said that he doesn't care about my looks.'

She grinned. 'No, he doesn't. But remember how good you looked in it? It's just for show – you're not getting laid tonight if I know him. He's a classy man.'

I crossed my arms in front of my chest. 'What else do you know about this man? His PIN? His inner leg measurements?'

'Silly. I told you – he's like a brother to me now. And I want *you* to score him – not that woman who's—' She stopped. 'Anyway, try this on.'

I turned to look up at her. 'What woman?'

She shrugged and turned on the floor fan. 'They all just want him for his looks. And his money. Now put this on – quick, before he gets here. Stand in the breeze so you don't sweat all over. It's an unusually hot evening even for autumn, isn't it? You want to remain fresh and cool.'

Sandra really knew her stuff. With a whole lot of huffing and puffing that in this heat would've warranted another shower for the effort, we finally squeezed me, breasts, butt, gut and thighs into the girdle, my skin still remarkably cool and my hair whipping around me like a luscious supermodel in a BMW commercial. The Haggis Effect was notably reduced. Even my girdle wasn't as tight on me!

I chose my favorite purchase – a light blue linen *Krizia* dress with high-heeled shoes to match. It somehow brought out my light tan, making it look deeper. I looked good, actually. I looked healthy. I also looked like I was crapping myself. What woman exactly was Sandra talking about?

'You need to tell me now, Sandra. Is there someone else in the picture?' I asked her. 'Because if there is—'

'Oh, *Madonna mia*, how long are you going to obsess?' Sandra threw her hands into the air. 'The man wants *you*.'

'Yeah, but what about after *The Morning After*? And as a matter of fact, what about *all* those mornings after? What comes next?'

But she just shrugged. 'Who knows for sure? *Che sarà, sarà.* Surrender to life, already!'

Surrender to life. Easy for her to say.

'And *smile*!' she said, giving me a light shove as she reached into her bag. I knew she'd tell me if he was already taken, or worse, had a secret lover or something. 'Here, put this on. Not that men notice these things anyway, but I've been saving it for a special occasion – and this is it.'

It was a simple but effective necklace of pale turquoise stones. Not too long, not too short, nestling right in the newly discovered hollow of my collarbone.

Sandra fussed with it and stood back to assess me. 'Perfect.'

I looked up at her through misty eyes and gave her a great big hug. She was such a doll to me. 'Thank you, Sandra. For all your help. Always.'

She smiled, getting misty-eyed herself. Who knew she had it in her? 'Go and do me proud, Gillian Morana.'

I was ready for my mind, if not my heart, to open up to new possibilities, however temporary they'd be. Maybe Sandra had been right. Maybe it *was* time for me to have some fun.

21

Walking the Plank

I'll spare you the turning of the heads, the popping of the eyes, the elbow jabbing and the whispering.

'Who's that? Mattia's got a new woman?'

'Is that the Englishman's wife, Nadia's rival?'

'Well, she sure got her own back!'

I stopped, riveted to the ground. If words could dig holes I'd have been a colander right about now. And a very shaky one. My knees wobbled and Mattia laced his arm around my waist. It was as if we were picking our way through a CG still-frame, a sea of bewildered faces. No one breathed, no one moved except for us. It was official. Lipari now knew that their favorite architect and heart-throb had lost his mind. I looked up into Mattia's face. His eyes were all happy twinkles. It was obvious he did like me.

But even *if* he was interested in me, how long would that last? How long would he stay with me? I know I hadn't planned anything permanent, but I was almost forty and wouldn't be getting (or looking) any younger. In fact, every year was one step closer to looking like... like *Ma*. I'd barely gotten used to enjoying the effects of being slimmer, and already now I had to deal with the age issue *as well*?

It had never really been a problem before, but now? Now that I'd had recovered my long-lost femininity, I was beginning to enjoy it again. I wasn't all that ready to lose it by sleeping with someone younger, thus reminding me of how quickly time had gone by and, by extension, of how much I'd missed out on.

But as I strolled by his side, my eyes dropped to his tanned, strong forearms, following the muscles twitching, young and vibrant. Mattia was in his prime. Four years may not have been a lot to most women, but they were to me.

'Everyone's staring,' I whispered as he led me down the *corso*. Sandra had drummed the meaning of this outing into me well and now I was paranoid. And shaking like a leaf. Who knew I'd care about what other people thought?

'Let them stare. They're admiring you.'

'Or you, you mean.'

Mattia looked down and laughed. A carefree, boyish laugh. It became him tremendously. 'Ah, that's where you're wrong.'

And as we got to the end of the *corso* that opened onto Marina Corta, he suddenly stopped, amidst all the traffic of people, his face as solemn as Sunday morning mass.

'What?' I said. 'Am I talking too much?'

But he just shook his head and took my face in his hands. And kissed me. Long and hard, his tongue gently caressing its way into my mouth, neither demanding, but still questioning, testing my response. Which came all too quickly. I let myself fall into that kiss and everything – the locals, the white and orange fairy lights hanging from restaurant awnings, and the different types of music at every different corner – disappeared. Nothing existed but his lips on mine.

When, a moment – or ten years later – the kiss ended and I emerged a happier woman, I pushed my hair away from my face and stared up at him like a dazed teenager.

'Wow,' was all I could say. I felt like a seven-year-old kid whose favorite famous astronaut had just landed in her own garden.

He grinned. 'Couldn't resist. You are something, you know, Gillian?'

At this point, I had to be. That kiss had been a real ego-booster.

Of all the women around, he'd chosen to kiss me. I felt like a million dollars. No, make that euros.

'Where are we going this time?' I blurted out in the usual Gillian style as Mattia closed the car door for me the next evening.

I want to see you again, he'd said at the end of yesterday's date.

I'll see you on Monday morning, I'd answered. (Right about now you must be thinking, *Jesus, this chick deserves to be alone*. And you'd be absolutely spot on.)

He'd chuckled. *Why should we have to wait for Monday morning?*

Why should we, indeed? Especially when he was looking at me like he was now, his eyes twinkling in the slowly dying light. Boy, did he sure manage to wield that magnetic pull on me. Who could say no to this man?

'First, a nice dinner, and then…'

And then? And then what? Oh God. Sex? With him? Him with… me? Sandra had rightfully predicted that it wasn't going to happen on our first date, but the second…? Just how did it work in Italy? In North America the three-date rule was still in act as far as I knew. So what the heck was I waiting for? *I was no spring chicken and the clock was a-tickin'*, granted, but wasn't Date Two still too early for a romp in the hay? Was he really going to seduce me? Or was I expected to seduce him? I didn't know up from down – what was I going to do with a man like him?

'Anything you want,' he answered my question from moments ago and for one horrible moment I thought I'd voiced my fears aloud. 'We can do anything you want.'

'Anything?'

He took his eyes off the road to slide me an uber-sexy grin. '*Anything*.'

Howl. Ohgodohgodohgod. I wasn't imagining it. He *was*

referring to sex. Even now, as he swung into the parking lot of a restaurant and opened the car door and circled my waist, I jumped. 'You are so beautiful, Gillian…' he whispered.

'No, I'm not,' I blurted.

'Hey, that's my date you're talking about,' he said softly, his sexy lips curving into a smile.

'Awh, that's okay. She can take it.' I smiled up at my date. *My date*. Look at me – I was finally learning to fly.

I was quiet all through dinner, just enjoying the sea breeze and trying to ignore the passing swarms of beautiful women looking like they'd just leapt off the pages of some hip fashion magazine. Brunettes, blondes, redheads, tall, pretty, delicate-boned. The choice was endless, all looking like a stiff breeze would blow them over the terrace rooftop and down into the sea below. All so chic and effortlessly beautiful. And so *young*.

'Friends of yours?' I asked, trying to keep the ice out of my voice as I sipped my Malvasia, careful not to overdo it with the booze again as the consequences could be disastrous this time.

He shrugged. 'In Lipari everyone knows everyone. Everyone's related to someone. Plus, there aren't many people to talk to.'

'Right,' I said when, to my surprise, he stood up and offered his hand.

'Care to dance?'

Dance? Mattia, I found out, couldn't dance to save himself, swaying and making funny jerky movements. But he had me laughing all evening. I had never had such a brilliant time in my whole life.

'Ever think of leaving this island?' I asked as he dipped me, caught me, swirled me like a weightless rag doll, all the while stepping on my and other people's feet. He was an absolute mess.

'I'll have to if I keep colliding into people,' he said with a laugh. 'Leave? Nah. I travel all the time for work. Conferences, conventions.'

'I meant leaving permanently.'

'What for?'

Good point. 'A real city?' I suggested.

'You mean a place where they have theaters, cinemas and stuff?'

'Yes.'

'We have all that here.'

Great point.

'If we want more, we can always go to the mainland. Milazzo is a lovely city only an hour away.'

'But in the winter you can get cut off by storms.'

'Yes. But we can survive independently here. Plus why would I want to share amenities with hundreds of thousands of people on the mainland when I can share them with my nine thousand and ninety-nine friends?'

Excellent point.

'If I want to see Paris, I fly to Paris. If I want to go skiing, I go to Saint Moritz.'

Could it be so simple?

It was almost, I kid you not, dawn, when we got to my house and he held out his hand for my key. Even last time, he'd seen me in. It hadn't been a gig to get his foot in the door but, as he'd once put it, just taking care of me. Watching out for me. And now he was towering over me, my door (and heart) wide open.

'I had a great time, Gillian. I can't remember laughing so much. Ever.'

'You're the one who provided the entertainment,' I answered, wondering if tonight he'd take it a step further? Surely I should offer him a coffee, a nightcap or what was it they did in the movies, just before he kisses her and they glide seamlessly, in one long, passionate embrace, to the bed? But I only had a mattress on the floor for the moment.

As I watched, he reached out and delicately ran a strand of my hair through his curved index and planted those magnetic, *magmatic* obsidian eyes on me as my body suddenly switched into overdrive.

'God, Gillian, you're so damn sexy...' he whispered and I stopped short. 'Pure woman...' and he leaned in, his mouth barely an inch from mine as I was practically salivating worse than Diana whenever I presented her with a treat.

I swallowed as he drew even closer, still not kissing me quite yet, making me realize how much I wanted him to kiss me.

Hoo boy. I *did* want to slide into his arms. But I couldn't afford to. I wouldn't be able to survive another blow, that was for sure. I moved back, tearing my eyes away from him, putting my lips out of reach. But it wasn't getting me anywhere. He had me propped up against the wall.

'But... but...' I mumbled, trying to distract him. 'You haven't even experienced your mid-life *crisis* yet.' The guy had never been married, no kids. And not even a hint of a bald patch or a belly. How could I cope with that?

He looked at me and chuckled. 'Gillian, I'm thirty-six years old. I'm not a boy. I'm a grown man.'

'But you don't even know how old I am,' I protested. 'How could this ever work? Look around you. Look at women your own age, and then look at me. You—'

He took me by the shoulders and whispered, 'Gillian, shush. You are... heartwarming. Beautiful, inside and out. The way you make me feel? I can't explain it, but next to you, any other woman just won't do.'

'How... how... do you mean?'

'Look at what you've done with your life. You've bounced back brilliantly. You're starting a business. You don't need a man, but I'm hoping you will be with me.'

Ah, the things a guy would say for a good session. And to the point exactly, just look at what I'd done with my life. I'd raised a kid who'd run off as far away from me as possible the minute she got a chance and oh – so had her dad, incidentally.

But before I could voice any more of my qualms, his mouth descended on mine and the message in his kiss took me completely by surprise. Different from the others, this kiss was less delicate, *utterly* delicious, mind-boggling. I met his tongue stroke for stroke, anxious to be as close as possible to him.

He was so beautiful, so perfect, like in a classical portrait, his body powerful and yet so harmonious. He was strong... and yet gentle as he put me on my bed (well, mattress) and I thought – I don't think I was able to think at all, just... enjoy the anticipation.

'*Bellissima...*' he murmured into my ear as he laid me back and I could feel myself letting go as he raised my arms high above my head, caressing my sides as his hands stole upwards, taking my dress along, his lips covering the same ground, and I shivered, my brain mush, trying to get us both as naked as possible as he kissed me, raising himself on his arms, my fingers frantically pulling at the buttons on his shirt, which he finally discarded somewhere, a blue whir on the fringes of my mind.

As he pulled me atop him I turned to liquid – like a jar of warm Nutella that has been left in the warm Sicilian sun for too long. The very same Nutella that had honed my body, along with cheesecake and cookies and desserts of every kind and that were now lodged under my skin. I could point to any given part of my body and say for sure, down to the month, when and what it was I'd binged on to cause it.

You think I'm joking? Just to prove it – belly. Third grade – peanut butter and jelly sandwiches for a year. The list was endless, as was my insecurity. And here I was, a result of many similar years. And delusional to have thought for even a split second that this gorgeous guy kissing me actually saw me as attractive? Sure, we had fun together and I made him laugh, but come *on*. How long can you keep laughing once you become... intimate? My bra-covered breasts were crushed against his bare chest, and any minute now he'd be making to remove my skirt and he'd see my girdle-less stomach pouring out under his hands and he'd literally freak.

And my boobs? They were not what they used to be. They had kept count of each passing year, of the effects of breast-feeding, of the merciless laws of gravity and… I couldn't let him see me like this. Not now, not ever. And before I could stop myself, I was pushing his large, delicious hands away from me. He stilled, searching my face, surprised at what he saw there. Refusal.

'Gillian…?' he whispered.

'Go away,' I said. 'Please.'

'Sweetheart, talk to me…'

'No. Please go.'

He finally got to his feet. 'I don't understand, Gillian,' he whispered. 'Did I do something wrong?'

'No. Please go,' I repeated, not willing to share with him this, the lowest, most humiliating point of my life so far.

As he pulled his shirt back on, he was clearly stunned and hurt as if I'd kicked him over the head. In a sense, I had. He'd never seen it coming. Truth be told, neither had I. I was having the time of my life – I never remembered being that happy and excited and elated. But I should've known it was never going to happen – not with my hang-ups and paranoia of being judged and refused. But this time I hadn't needed him to refuse me. I'd done all the dirty work myself.

22

Didn't We Almost Have It All?

A whole week had gone by since my miserable show. Mattia's team worked on the renovations round the clock, but I'd caught only brief glimpses of him when really I wanted to get him on his own and explain without all the builders around us.

So on Friday afternoon I worked up my courage and dialed his number. I'd apologize for being such a screwball. Explain, as neatly as possible, the mess inside my head, all my uncertainties, all my fear. And ask him to stay if he could ever forgive me.

God, was I here again, depending on what a man said? My past experiences had taught me that nothing good could come of it. But I was in too deep now. What was the worst that could happen – he'd say no, right?

Wrong – the worst that could happen was that he didn't answer. His voicemail kicked in and I kicked myself. Leave a message? *Hi, Mattia, it's me, the mess, sorry for what happened – or didn't happen the other night. Shall we try again?* Easy-peasy – in an ideal world.

In reality, I hung up. It was high time I stopped kidding myself, using the build as an excuse to see him twenty-four/seven. So I was attracted to him. Big deal. So was half the population here.

Disgusted with myself, I put my phone away and proceeded to pore through some furniture catalogues. This was supposed to be the beginning of the fun part, but all I could think of was

244

Mattia and the important role he was playing in my life at the moment.

Of course. This attraction was a sort of transfer. Like a patient falls in love with their shrink, thus I was in awe of my builder who was also, let's face it, my life fixer-upper at the moment.

So yeah, of course I needed to speak to him very often. But from now on it would be only about bathrooms, tiles and window fixtures – nothing else. Unless he called me back and we sorted ourselves out.

A few minutes later my phone rang. My heart in my throat, I made a mad dash, almost dropped it and breathed a hello without even checking the caller ID. It was Sandra.

'*Ciao!* I've got a class meeting tomorrow night so I'm afraid we have to cancel dinner. The principal's bent on making one of his endless speeches.'

I groaned. I hadn't spent a decent evening with her for ages now, what with Alfonso in the picture again.

'Unless you want to do it tonight?' she asked.

'Sure! I'll cook.'

'Great! Remember – no onions or garlic. I might be seeing Alfonso later tonight.'

'Right,' I said and put the phone down with a sigh.

But three seconds later she called me back and I rolled my eyes. 'Yes, I know, no peppers either – they give you gas.'

Silence. And then I looked down at the caller ID. Of *course* it was him. Who else could it be when my guard is down?

'Gillian?' Mattia said uncertainly.

Oh, crap.

'I found your call?'

'What? Oh, yeah, that.' Well, if Sandra was going out with Alfonso maybe I could invite him over for some *Please forgive me drinks* and pizza as a late-night snack? Dinner was too intimate anyway, right?

'Did you want something?' he prompted.

Ouch. Did I want something? You could say so. I wanted to

stretch out on his wide chest and bury my nose into his pecs and stay there for the rest of my life.

'Uh…' *Now or never, Morana!* 'I'm making pizza tonight. I was wondering if you wanted to stop by and share some?'

There. I'd done it. Now it was in or out.

An almost tangibly embarrassed silence ensued, during which I was already contemplating retracting my invite. Or I could say that Sandra was going to be there so it wasn't a *tête-à-tête* thing. Give him time to retreat and save my dignity. I could hear the cogs turning and then catching in his mind as he tried to make some sense of my call.

'Ah, I can't,' he finally said. 'I'm away all weekend.'

'Oh. Okay.' So I'd see him on Monday at the site – as usual. Him, me, and at least a dozen men with plumber's bum.

'See you at the site, then,' I said, something akin to a major disappointment washing over me. Like a headache starting from the top of my head and swooping down all the way to my feet. *Damn.* Well, what had I expected? The guy was practically naked in my bed and I pushed him away. What the hell was wrong with me? I'd been lucky he hadn't sent someone else to finish the build. If I could only figure out how to bring us together, conquer my fears and discover where he spent his secret weekends.

The next day as I was driving back up from the town from running some errands, he called. Had he changed his mind? Was he going to forgive my unforgiveable *faux pas* and… maybe ask me out again? *Please God, let it be so. I promise I won't screw it up this time. Just give me a shot at this – this incredibly difficult game they called Starting Over.*

'Can you come back to your house?' he asked, and I could tell it was a pressing matter, yes, but highly unlikely a booty call.

'Oh God, is there a problem?'

Silence. 'No. But just come.'

'All right. I'll be there in fifteen minutes.'

*

You know when you're absolutely positive something has happened – that strange feeling you just can't shake? Luckily most of the time you're wrong. Everyone's okay, alive and well but it's just a pipe that's burst and you welcome it with enthusiasm in exchange for the safety of your loved ones? I loved many people here.

When I pulled up the drive and parked, Mattia was lingering with someone hidden by his massive bulk. At the sound of my Ape he moved and I saw her.

'Annie!' I cried, rushing to her side and pulling her into my arms, happy but motherly instinct already checking her out. She looked all right, except for the red-rimmed eyes. Mattia had made her a cup of coffee and had been lingering so as not to leave her alone.

I was barely aware of him disappearing out back as I tried to imagine what could have brought my daughter here so suddenly without even a phone call. Was she ill? Would I have to rush her to the mainland? Mattia would've already arranged for that, I was sure. I knew I could count on him for something like that.

'Hi, Mum,' she murmured and I knew that whatever it was, we would be okay. If she was ill I'd fight tooth and nail and get her the best treatment. If she was ill; I was ill. If she bled; I bled. She was my daughter – my blood. Just as long as she was alive we would tackle anything that came our way together.

'Annie – what's wrong?' I whispered as I gently pushed her hair off her pale face. God, it felt good to have her in my arms again, like when she was little and ran to me for help. But that had been a long time ago.

'I only popped over for the weekend – I'm due back at school on Tuesday.'

'Okay…' I answered, waiting.

And then she buckled. 'Oh, Mum – it's a total mess!'

'What is? Talk to me,' I urged as I led her inside and onto the sofa.

She stuffed her hands in her pockets and I recognized Tony's trademark gesture for when he was frustrated. 'I think I'm pregnant…'

She was alive and well. Nothing else mattered. Which was what I whispered to her over and over again as she sobbed into my chest, in broken words about how she didn't have the courage to tell Miles for fear of having to curtail the career she'd just started, let alone her *life*.

'You're the only one who would understand – please don't tell Dad!'

As if. 'Of course not, darling.'

'Oh God, what am I going to do?'

I took her gently by the shoulders and spoke softly but firmly. 'Now listen to me, Annie. You are not alone. You have me. I will be right behind you every step of the way. Understand?'

Annie's face crumpled up again, but she fought against a new onset of tears, sat up and nodded.

'Good girl. It's all right to cry and be confused. But by tomorrow you'll have a different feeling about this.'

Which she did. Already by the evening, when Mattia had cleared the decks, (not without an uncertain glance in my direction) Annie and I were watching DVDs and pigging out on every possible kind of food, such as pizza, almond paste cookies, chocolate and pistachio éclairs, chocolate and orange ice cream, butter pastries, from savory to sweet and back again. All stuff I'd rounded up on a quick trip while she napped, more or less filling the back of the Ape with enough supplies to last me (and an army) a whole winter.

When I'd got back she'd showered and changed and was padding around in her jammies like when she was a little girl and knew on some level that no one would ever harm her. That she was, no matter what she did, loved. I wished I'd been that lucky growing up. Our mistakes, well, we carried them on our backs for the longest time. Annie would have to learn to discern what she could and couldn't do.

I downloaded *Freaky Friday* on my laptop and we laughed so

hard until she turned to me and sighed. 'Mum, would you switch with me if you could?'

Meaning, would you be okay having a child with no man in sight? In a sense, I did. Only I'd already done the hard part (always on my own). And if I could do it, anybody could.

'If I could, I would take your worries off your shoulders. But this, sweetie, is something you have to tell Miles.'

She bit her lip. 'I know, but he'd want me to marry him immediately and give up work and all and I'm not ready to become…'

Me. She wasn't ready to become me, make my same mistakes. Which was a good thing. I only wanted what was best for my daughter. I didn't want her to be unhappy as I had been. Miles was a Xerox copy of Tony in the making. In a few years he'd be even more successful. He was already arrogant. Which was why he and Tony saw eye to eye. And why Miles would push her to have the baby.

She looked up as if suddenly aware of her new surroundings. 'You've changed so much in the last few months, Mum. I can't believe you've bought a house.'

'Neither can I.' I grinned.

'I guess you're definitely not coming back, then?'

'Only if you need me, Annie.'

She thought about it. 'I can't blame you for staying here, the way Dad treated you.'

'Thank you, love.'

'Mum? Are really going to run a B&B?'

'I already have August next year all sold out.'

She beamed at me. 'Look at you, in the space of just a few months! And that Mattia looks like a nice bloke.'

I swallowed. 'He is.'

'Are you just friends?'

'Annie – of course.'

'Are you sure? He looks at you like he wants to swallow you whole.'

'Annie!' When had my daughter and I *ever* talked about sex? She'd never been comfortable with the issue. Like mother, like daughter.

'Don't be shy, Mum. I can tell a mile off he likes you.'

'You don't even know him.'

'Well, we had a quick chat over coffee. The way he talks about you… I could just tell there's more than a little something there.'

'He's younger than me.'

My worldly daughter shrugged. 'Who cares? It's not like he's your toy boy or anything. From what I gather he's got his own company and certainly doesn't need your money. I think you should let him know.'

'Know what?'

'How you feel.'

Huh. Is that how it was done, nowadays? I was out of practice.

A few hours later, Annie's shrieks shook the house down. 'Mum – Mum! I got my period!' she hollered from the bathroom and I instantly reached for the hot water bottle I'd bought only weeks ago. Annie had always had raging cramps.

I tucked the hot water bottle in with her and kissed the top of her head.

'Thanks, Mum,' she said. 'I don't know how I would've managed without you.'

I grinned. 'Sweetie, you don't need me anymore.'

'But I do,' she argued softly. 'I need to know that I haven't pushed you away.'

It felt good to know she was aware of the gap that had been expanding between us since she'd moved away to be with Miles. A mother who loves her children has to set them free, of course, but it's always nice to see them look back every once in a while to wave.

'Of course you haven't, Annie.'

'Thanks, Mum. Maybe I'll give you a grandchild one day after all. But not so soon.'

'Some day, maybe, Annie,' I whispered as I pulled the covers up to her chin. 'Now get some sleep. I'll be downstairs if you need me.'

''Kay…' she whispered, closing her eyes.

Phew. That had been close. Now we were back on the straight and narrow. From now on I was confident she'd make extra sure she didn't end up in a situation like that until she was good and ready.

At midnight I put my book down and climbed the stairs to the second floor and stopped in passing her door, suppressing the urge to drop in and check on her. She was, after all, a grown woman. And I'd come this close to being a grandmother. Go and tell Mattia *that* bit of news. Not that it regarded him anymore.

'Mum?' she called softly, and I poked my head into her room.

'Mmh? You better, Annie?'

'Can you come in a second?'

I stepped inside, still not wanting to invade her privacy or cramp her usually standoffish style. She was snuggled up against her hot water bottle, looking for all the world like my six-year-old of yesteryear. I missed her being little and needing me.

'Thanks. For always being there. And for not judging me. Ever.'

I smiled. Evidently the little things parents do under the radar stick after all.

'Goodnight, sweetheart.'

'Goodnight,' she sighed and added with a giggle, '*Smother*.'

And so tragedy averted, the next Monday morning I drove her to the harbor to pick up her life where she'd left it only days ago. When she hugged me goodbye, I was looking into the eyes of a newfound daughter. There had been a monumental shift in our relationship, where I'd finally become the savvy mother and she the daughter in need of help. And now she was once again happy, her usual confident self, having happily accepted that I, too, had changed.

But unlike Annie, I was still miserable. After a week of Mattia avoiding me despite us being alone in the house several times for hours on end – it must have been the *I'm barely older than your daughter* effect. He was hardly talking to me, let alone thinking about asking me out again.

I wondered whether, besides my pathetic show that night, having an adult daughter had scared him away definitively after all the times he'd told me that age was not a problem between us and that it was only in my head.

The next Saturday morning, during my usual early stroll in the harbor, I suddenly spotted him – brown arms glistening in the morning sun – carrying two suitcases (one very feminine) into a motorboat.

Instinctively I hid among a throng of people, waiting for the owner of the suitcase to appear. It was – *had* to be – a woman. Because it didn't make sense that a guy like that didn't already have someone. Even last week – and the weeks before, he hadn't been around. I remember scanning the streets for a glimpse of him, but *nada. Niente*.

But when he turned the motor on and slowly maneuvered out of the tiny harbor, he was alone and in that instant I realized he was going to meet her on one of the neighboring islands or maybe even the mainland. I'd come this close to believing he could actually be interested in me. What a joke I was.

'*Mamma mia, è delizioso!* Sandra exclaimed as she bit into my pizza masterpiece two days later. Her thing with Alfonso had lasted all night.

'Do you know what Mattia's doing next weekend?' I asked her matter-of-factly as she took another bite, eyes studying me.

'Forget him for now, Gillian.'

I sat up in my chair. 'What? Why? First you practically pimp him out to me and now – not that I'm interested, mind you—' I huffed. 'What's happening with him? I saw him in Marina Corta the other morning. Getting into a boat. With two suitcases. Where does he go?'

She wiped her mouth and shook her head, her eyes apologetic. 'I told you that I can't tell you.'

'You can't or you won't?'

She shrugged. 'I promised not to tell. I'm good at keeping secrets.'

I raised an eyebrow at her.

'Sure, I like a little gossip. But I'd never tell my friends' secrets,' she explained defensively.

Fair enough. But the curiosity was eating away at me.

'What *can* you tell me?' I persisted.

'About Mattia? He's a good guy. The best there is.'

'No woman on the horizon, then?'

She started and gave me a sidelong glance. 'Delicious pizza,' she repeated. 'Pass me another slice, please. Oh, by the way, would you like to go to *Salina* next weekend? We can take a dinghy; it's not far at all.'

I stared at her as she crammed another corner into her mouth, all innocent-eyed. She couldn't have been any clearer. Salina. Mattia went to Salina every weekend. I slid a glance out my kitchen sink window to said island, only a stone's throw away. I bet Mattia could swim that. I bet he *would*, to get to whomever was on the other side of this stretch of sea, so bent he seemed on getting there. But why?

DECEMBER

23

Secrets

With the slowly dropping temperatures, the quality of the light in Lipari had changed as well. Up here in the hills it may have been cooler and more pleasant in the summer, but the winter was proving to be a different story already. So I went to see Cosetta for a jacket.

'How have you been?' she asked with a grin as she pulled back the curtain protecting her wares. 'Congratulations on your purchase.'

'Thanks. I'm spending every free moment on the build.' I sighed.

'Only the build? I hear differently.'

'Oh?'

'You and Mattia. Word has it he's smitten by you, and I can see why.'

What could I say to that? Except for that I wished it were true. 'We're just friends.' Or rather, *were*. I shrugged into the jacket she held out for me as she smiled.

'He's a tough one, our Mattia. But inside – melted *gelato*. I should know. I raised him. His parents died when he was a boy.'

Ah. Finally some mysterious family history. He never talked much about himself. In fact, he didn't talk about himself at all. It was simple – he didn't want me anywhere near his grandmother. Hell, he didn't want me to be anywhere near *him* anymore. At this point, even the friendship had gone. Which hurt so much more than I'd anticipated. The days were dark and long without him popping by, his warm presence filling my home.

Sometimes I'd dart past his office in the *corso* while shooting the glass-faced entrance a fleeting glance in case he was at the front desk and I'd be rewarded with a glimpse of him, but he never was, always rushing from one building site to another, or squirreled away at his draftsman's table, making someone else's dream home come true.

'There's so much pain and anger inside him, Gillian. He needs time – and your love – to get over it.'

'Get over what?'

'You don't know?'

I shook my head.

'Well, maybe you should wait until he tells you.'

'Why would he tell me? I told you, we aren't as close as you think.'

'Then why would you want to know?' she countered. But it wasn't a defensive countering inasmuch as an inquisitive one. Why would I want to know if I didn't care? But how could she assume I did? Or perhaps she was used to women asking about him. The only certainty was that they were not close, far from it. How could he be hostile toward this little woman?

'You won't give me a clue, Cosetta?' I urged.

She shook her head. 'I can't. But I'm sure he will, when he's ready.'

'Yeah.' I half-shrugged as I reached into my wallet. When he was ready. Ready to trust me, to open up to me and to maybe even love me. That was going to be one helluva wait.

As I was driving up the dirt road on my way back home, there was a loud bang and my Ape almost went flying. It took me an enormous amount of strength (summed up by the fear of going over the cliff and straight into the dark Mediterranean) to get the wheels straight and to brake.

I got out and checked the tires first thing. And bloody hell – who gets *two* flats at once? I must have left town with one, not noticed it and my luck had let me down. Now what? I looked around me. It was nine o'clock in the evening. All the farmers had gone to their homes hours ago. No reason to be out on a dark night like this. Only mad dogs and Canadians.

So I called Sandra. She'd come up in a jiffy, even if she hated the countryside. I let it ring. And ring. And ring. And then her voicemail kicked in. She must have been with Alfonso and couldn't hear her phone. Damn. Who else could I call? I didn't know anybody else well enough besides Maria, who didn't have a car. And then, the only other possible name came to mind. Mattia.

Could I? Could this be the moment we could bury the hatchet and become friends again? Would he be willing to help me? Of course he would – he'd help any woman stranded on the side of the road. One hoped.

Well, there was only one way to find out if I was right. I dialed his number. He answered on the fourth ring, just as my heart was doing its thirtieth leap in my chest.

'Hello?'

Shit, he sounded like he'd been asleep, his voice low and gravelly. And sexy as hell. At this hour? I could picture him stretched out on his bed, his hair all mussed, bare-chested and warm from slumber, looking absolutely scrumptious... with *her*. Whoever she was.

'Hi, Mattia!' I was so glad to hear his voice I'd sort of screamed his name. I cleared my throat and tried a more friendly approach. 'How are you?'

A pause. Then a distracted 'What is it, Gillian?'

Oops, that hadn't sounded very promising. I suddenly cursed myself for being so brave. I should've chickened out as usual. Chicken-ness sometimes saved your ass.

'I was going home. And I got a flat tire – two flat tires,' I tried to explain without cringing, but, nope, I cringed. 'I called Sandra but she's nowhere to be found and I don't have anybody else's number – not anybody I feel comfortable calling and—' I stopped, realizing how pathetic I sounded.

More silence, and I could feel him drifting – no, *zapping* – away from me at the speed of light. And another man had bitten the dust. Man, how *did* I manage to do that?

Please don't be a jackass, Mattia, I wanted to say. *Let's talk about this. Tell me what you're hiding, and I'll explain my fears to you. We can make it right.* But the words just wouldn't come out. I'd had my fair share of cheats.

'...call Pino. Bye,' he said and hung up.

Call Pino? Who the heck was Pino, and how was I supposed to find his number stranded up here? Stupid, idiotic me. Would I never friggin' learn? It served me right to be alone. Never trust a man again. Especially if he was like Mattia, i.e. he looked (and felt) too good to be true.

Sighing, I knelt down for a better look under the Ape. Not that I could see much in the feeble light of my torch, something Mattia had advised me to keep in there at all times, along with a new packet of batteries.

I winced. One wheel, I could've managed to change on my own. It wasn't that difficult. But two? I only had one spare. Maybe I could change just the one and hobble home? No, that would damage the axle, I thought I remembered someone saying. It made sense, I guess. So I leaned back with my butt against the stone wall by the side of the road and tried to come up with a brilliant idea. Walking home seemed like the best, at this point. The Ape wasn't going anywhere.

And then the plumber who lived a few miles down the road drove past. I waved and he stopped. 'Ciao,' he said. 'What happened?'

'Two flat tires. Do you think you could lend me a hand?'

He got out of his own Ape to have a good look underneath. 'It's a miracle you made it this far up.'

Go figure. I was one lucky gal.

In the space of five minutes he replaced the front wheel with my spare and the back one using his own.

'I'll take your wheel down to town to fix tomorrow,' he promised.

'What if you get a flat before that?' I asked. 'How are you going to manage?'

He shrugged. 'What are the odds?' he said as he got back into his Ape. 'Go on ahead, I'll escort you.'

'Oh, you don't have to do that.'

'Of course I do.'

'Thank you so much. I owe you one.'

So that was how a girl got saved and escorted home by someone she'd just declared one of the nicest people in town, Mattia having lost his place in pole position.

But the more I thought about it, the more it infuriated me. He'd left me to fend for myself. Some *gentleman*. Even if his grandmother was of the opposite opinion, despite the fact they were estranged. What was going on? So I called my only source of island info hoping she'd answer now that I didn't need her anymore.

'Sandra, I have to ask you something. What's the deal with Cosetta and Mattia?'

She laughed. 'And you keep telling me you're not interested, *ehi*?'

'Are you going to tell me or not?'

Silence. 'I can only say that they don't quite see eye to eye.'

'But why?'

More silence. Jesus, what was this, The Third Secret of Fatima?

'Mattia's parents died in a car crash when he was a little boy.'

'*Mattia never told me.*'

'And, as you might have guessed, Cosetta is absolutely loaded...'

'*And...?*'

'But Mattia doesn't want a euro of her money.'

'Why? It would all go to him, right? Isn't he an only child?'

If he had a brother or a sister I'd have seen them by now on this rock, right? Unless they lived somewhere else.

Sandra hesitated. 'He had an older brother, Renzo, who died a few years ago. Mattia will never forgive Cosetta for it.'

'Why, was it her fault?'

But she went quiet again. So I played my trump card.

'Sandra – I'll be honest with you. I do have feelings for him, even if it's too late now – he probably never wants to see me again, but I still want to see him happy.'

'Well he's happy without Cosetta. A little less happy without you, though.'

If only. If he was half as miserable without me as I was without him. 'Please help me understand, Sandra.'

She sighed and I could feel the female solidarity emerging. 'Okay. But I can't tell you everything. That's his job. All I can say is that when Cosetta kicked Renzo out years ago...'

'She kicked her *grandson* out?'

'And Mattia followed his brother. In every way.'

'What does that mean? Why did Cosetta kick Renzo out?'

'That I can't tell you, Gilly. But Cosetta went through with it, Renzo died and Mattia kept his promise. He moved out, opened his own practice on next to nothing in capital and slowly worked his way up. Today he's the most sought-after architect of the whole province of Messina. He's done most of the hotels, most restaurants. He's positively loaded.'

'So he doesn't need her money.'

'Not anymore, he doesn't.'

'But that was years ago. Why can't he just forgive her and get on with it?'

'And that's the million-euro question,' Sandra concluded.

'You can't tell me more?'

'Gilly – you have to talk to him. Tell him how you feel. Let each other into your respective lives.'

I wished I could. But he wasn't interested in me anymore. He was helping me attain my goal because he was committed professionally, but wanted nothing more to do with me emotionally. Meaning, he would fix my house, but as far as fixing my heart was concerned, I was on my own.

And to the point, on Monday morning Mattia was back at work, avoiding me as usual. Of course. He didn't need to talk to me. Not for the build, not for anything. So when he appeared in the kitchen as I was doing the dishes, I panicked.

How was I supposed to react to a man who had refused to help me in a time of need? Any man should want to help a woman out, let alone one he'd wanted to sleep with. So what the hell was wrong with this guy? Had I overestimated him that much? He was nothing but a prat. A phony, all sexy grins and no reliability whatsoever. I was absolutely furious with him. So I attacked. Any way I could, with whatever weapons I had.

'Oh, by the way, thanks so much for not coming to my rescue,' I said. 'I understand you'd rather be in Salina with some hot chick. How dare you come onto me whilst hiding a relationship from me. And you knew what I was going through!'

At that, he stopped and stared at me for the longest time and finally shrugged. 'You made it crystal clear you're not interested in me,' he countered. 'So what do you care where I go?'

I stopped in my tracks and reversed a few steps so I was looking high up into his face. 'You could've told me you were seeing someone else rather than let me make a fool out of myself.'

Having heard the commotion, a couple of his men momentarily paused in the doorway. But I didn't shy away. Let 'em look. Let 'em look while my barely put-back-together-life fell apart all over again. Besides, I was already known as the wacky woman, the *pazza* of the island.

Mattia sighed. More of a groan, really. 'I've never lied to you about my feelings. I do care. Very much so. And I'm not seeing anyone else.'

'Lies. Every weekend you go away. Where do you go, Mattia,

if not to some hot lady? Is she older, too? Has she just been dumped as well?'

'I would never cheat on you or abandon you.'

'You did just that when I called you asking for help with my flat tires,' I snorted. 'You left me abandoned by the side of the road.'

At that, he threw his arms into the air. 'Who do you think called Pino to come and rescue your ass then?' he said.

I blinked. 'What?'

'You heard. If I was this horrible man you make me to be I wouldn't have cared about what happened to you on the side of the road that night and sent you Pino.'

'Sent me Pino? I was lucky the *plumber* drove by, otherwise I'd still be there. And who the hell is this Pino guy, anyway? How was I supposed to call him?'

At that, he crossed his arms over his chest. 'Pino is the *plumber.*'

'Oh.'

He sighed. 'First of all, I didn't tell you to call Pino. I told you *I'd* call him.'

'No, I distinctly remember you saying, "*Call Pino.*"'

'No, I said, "*I'll call Pino.*"'

'Oh. But if you cared so much, why didn't you come in person?'

At that his jaw snapped shut. 'Because I was in Salina.'

'Exactly. With another woman.'

He groaned. 'Gillian – you and I have got to learn to trust each other a bit more. You've been biased about me from Day One. But all the same I've come back to talk to you. To apologize and explain.'

'I already told you I... what? Did you say you came back to apologize?'

He grinned sheepishly. 'And to invite you to come with me to Salina on Saturday morning. Stay the weekend with me. And learn about my... so-called secret.'

Was this too good to be true? Had I missed something here? He cared for me. He wasn't seeing anyone else. He was letting me into his life by revealing his secret. He wanted to take me to Salina.

'I'd love to,' I gushed, and he took my hand.

'Good. We'll have a great time, you'll see.'

'Uh, Mattia? I'm so sorry about... that night. That was a horrible thing to do to you. But I can explain.'

But he shushed me, his eyes once again tuned in to me and it was as if nothing bad had happened between us. Hopefully, it would be as if I hadn't made the mistake of pushing him away.

'You don't have to explain, Gillian.'

'I want to.'

'We both have issues. And this weekend we can talk about them. Honey, I understand.'

Honey. He'd called me *honey*. In the space of five months I'd managed to be someone's honey. When in the past twenty years I'd become nothing but The Ball and Chain.

The next morning I woke up early and showered, taking extra care with my appearance. I flung my new jacket over my shoulder as I walked down to the marina, enjoying the fragrant salty sea air on my face. It was an incredibly warm morning for December, the sky clear, the sea so still it looked like a veil of baby blue gauze chasing the horizon.

I was meeting Mattia in the harbor of Marina Corta, where he always departed from. I knew he was giving me another chance. But there was something elusive about it all. I couldn't quite place my finger on it, but today all these mysteries were finally about to be dissolved. He was really ready to let me in. I wanted to do the same for him.

'*Buongiorno!*' I called when I spotted him, knee-deep in the water, his jeans rolled up, and my heart began its familiar jive.

In answer, he raised his hand, a wide grin on his face. Jesus, it had been ages since I'd felt anything like this for any other man. A lifetime, in fact.

I stopped at the water's edge. At least ten feet separated us, and when he came close and bent to lift me, my eyes widened.

'You still can't get used to someone carrying you, can you?' he murmured as my hands clasped behind his neck. Damn right I could. Only then it would be hard getting un-used to it. As always, he smelled clean and fresh, his hair damp at the back of his neck. Was this day as important for him as it was for me? Please, God, let it be so.

As if I weighed next to nothing, he carried me over the water and gently put me down onto the seat inside his boat. Now I needed to let go of him. There was no excuse for hanging on to him so tight. Well, except for two. Both of which, I hoped, wouldn't be obvious to him. I closed my eyes, thinking that if I could hold on to him throughout the entire trip, I wouldn't care about the boat threatening to tip over at every wave.

'Don't you like boats?' he asked gently.

I would've shaken my head, but I was already queasy enough as it was. 'Mh-mh,' I managed, sitting stiffly and looking straight ahead as he pushed off and leapt into the boat, me hanging on for dear life as it rocked under his weight. Forget any crazy ideas of getting a nautical license to ferry my guests around. I'd pay *double* the amount to not be in this damn thing.

Mattia rolled down his jeans bottoms, studying me. 'Why didn't you say so?'

I dared to turn my head to meet his eyes. 'How else was I going to learn your secret?'

He chuckled. 'The things a woman does.'

For love, I almost added. Almost. And then I braved a look around. Marina Corta was becoming tinier and tinier until we rounded the bend and then it was the open sea. Oh, boy. I swallowed hard, not daring to move an inch on my seat although I was already uncomfortable.

'Hey...' he said softly.

I looked up and tried to smile.

'Do you trust me?' he asked, taking my hands in his and leaning forward, his eyes on mine.

I eyed him, then returned his warm gaze fully. Did I trust him?

He'd done nothing but help me from the very start. I swallowed and nodded. I *more* than trusted him.

'*Brava*,' he said with a grin as the boat hit a bigger wave.

'Whoa!' I cried, the breeze whipping my hair around my face. 'How far is it?'

'Just over two nautical miles between Lipari and Salina. A little longer if you consider from harbor to harbor. Relax, sweetheart. I would never let anything happen to you.'

So I tried to relax, soaking up the incredible views of the rugged coastlines, looking down into the water where several schools of fish frolicked. 'Look at that!' I cried. 'They're so beautiful!' But Mattia only looked at me, his eyes twinkling.

And then Salina appeared, right around a bend, towering high above us like a giant movie screen seen from front-row seats. From the altitude of my kitchen window it had looked a little smaller, but now it dominated us, absolutely massive and verdant.

'What's that?' I said, pointing to a triangular stretch of water just beyond the narrow shore, almost as if the land had changed its mind and given way to the sea again.

'That's the salt lake, *Lago Salato*.'

'A lake on the sea?'

He grinned. 'Exactly. And that—' he pointed at an old stocky tower '—is the lighthouse.'

It was breathtakingly natural and simple. Once on the shore, Mattia rolled up his jeans again and brought me safely to *terra firma*, my hands on his sturdy shoulders. There were people milling about, but much fewer than on Lipari. Salina was, as far as I could see, much more remote. Wilder. And absolutely gorgeous.

As we reached the beach, tottering perilously toward us over huge black pebbles, was a toddler in a white dress. I was about to comment on how beautiful she was, but then I noticed her obsidian eyes – a mirror of Mattia's.

24

Tesoro

'Hello,' I said, bending once Mattia had put me on the ground, my heart pounding. Mattia's daughter. They were like two peas in a pod. So this was his huge secret, the one that Cassandra couldn't possibly let out of the bag. And this was where he went every weekend. Mattia had a child – another life on Salina.

And then, behind the baby girl, her mother – thin, beautiful and listless.

'Gillian, this is little Martina, my brother's daughter, and her mother Elvira.'

The woman stepped forward and offered her limp hand. I blinked. This was his niece?

'*Martina, questa è la mia amica Gillian. Saluta,*' he said, taking the child in his arms and giving her a great big kiss on the cheek.

But the child just stared at me, transfixed as we walked up the beach to a small house where Mattia opened the holdalls revealing all sorts of groceries, clothes, toys and shoes. Elvira put the groceries away quietly, and it made more and more sense by the second. Every week he went grocery shopping and spent two days here with them. And on Monday morning he was back in Lipari, working like a dog so he could drop everything and come back the next weekend. This was his life. He was, like it or not, this family's man.

Mattia was supporting his brother's family. And keeping them away from Cosetta. He considered his grandmother guilty of Renzo's death, although it still remained to be explained why. Also, Elvira – it was so obvious – considered Mattia her man, her territory.

Martina reached out and gently grabbed a lock of my hair without pulling. I kissed her knuckles and she smiled. I must have looked like an alien to her, with my blonde hair and fair skin.

'No, *tesoro*, no,' Mattia scolded gently until she let go of my hair.

'It's okay,' I assured him and looked up. 'What does that mean?'

'What?'

'That word you just said – *tes…?*'

'*Tesoro?* It means sweetheart. Literally, *my treasure*. And she is my treasure, this little girl.'

Tesoro. I liked the sound of it. And I loved this new side of Mattia, so different from the arrogant playboy I thought I knew so well.

'Are you okay?' Mattia asked and I looked up with a grin.

'Absolutely…' And to Elvira I said, 'You have such a lovely home.' Which was true. Although it was small, it had been expertly – no doubt by Mattia himself – renovated, with double-glazing and gas heating and all the conveniences of a modern home. So his family would be protected from those winter nights while he was away. Mattia had taken on his dead brother's responsibilities seamlessly. You had to love the guy to bits.

'Gillian, would you like to take Martina for a walk on the beach?' Mattia asked, but I knew it wasn't a question.

'Sure,' I answered all too cheerfully to hide the turmoil of emotions inside me and scooped the little girl up in my arms.

As we made sandcastles in the shadow of the lighthouse on the shore of the salty lake, I mused on all the sacrifices he was making. Mattia was practically everyone's protector. He was a self-made, selfless man who worked his butt off for those around him. He'd suffered a lot, obviously, although I was still missing some key pieces. If that didn't make him even more desirable I'd be damned.

'She loves sandcastles,' Mattia mused as he approached us, watching us muck around in the black, volcanic sand.

'Who doesn't?' I laughed.

He studied me in silence for a while, and I knew the time had come. He was ready to talk.

'I want you to know everything about me, Gillian. Because you are important to me.'

I swallowed. 'So are you, Mattia...' Wow, that sounded... *terrific*.

'The night my brother Renzo and Elvira found out they were pregnant, he went to tell Cosetta, who was absolutely furious. She told Renzo she didn't want him to have anything to do with Elvira who came from a family of fishermen. Cosetta always was a snob. She comes from very old money and hasn't got a clue how hard people have to work to survive.'

He came from old money, too, only he'd shunned it completely for a matter of honor. This man was revealing himself to be a quality guy more and more each day.

He looked at Martina in her white dress who was now rolling joyfully in the black sand, pure bliss on her chubby cheeks, and a shadow passed across Mattia's face. It was like the sun had hidden behind a dark, sad cloud.

'Cosetta threatened to cut Renzo out of her will if he married Elvira. But Renzo didn't care. He and I were starting our practice and we had our whole future ahead of us. We never wanted the old bag's money from the start.'

I nodded at what I already knew, careful not to betray Sandra's confidence.

Mattia's fists tightened and his voice cracked. 'It all happened so fast. On the way back to Elvira's, Renzo's car flew over the edge. He died instantly. Oh, Gillian – you can't imagine the horror, the desperation...'

I reached up and embraced him as hard as I could. He held me close, his ragged breath in my ear as he fought to keep control of his emotions. Emotions I never knew could be so deep and noble.

'This little girl is my blood. All I have left of my family.'

'It is a horrible tragedy, but Martina is so lucky to have you,' I whispered back.

Martina placed her tiny hands on the sides of his face and puckered her lips and kissed him. He hugged her to him fiercely and let me tell you, the love between them was so strong it left me reeling.

'She's such a beauty...' I breathed.

He looked up, his face bright again. 'She is, isn't she? Looks exactly like Renzo.'

'What about your grandmother? Wouldn't she like to be a part of the baby's life?'

'Absolutely not. I don't want her anywhere near them.'

'But she's just an old dear...'

'Who's made too many mistakes, Gillian. I begged her to stay out of it. But she was bent on keeping them apart. It's her fault my brother is dead. Her fault my niece doesn't have a father. I will never be able to forgive her. I'm not a forgiver, Gillian. You need to know that about me.'

I nodded, thinking how similar we actually were, and that he didn't have to fear me ever hurting him. I'd have to be nuts to lose someone like him.

Martina smiled and held her arms up to Mattia again who scooped her up and cuddled her close to him, whispering sweet endearments into her ear and covering her with kisses. The child giggled with delight. For all intents and purposes, he really *was* her father – the only one she'd ever known.

'I've been thinking long and hard, Gillian. I want Martina and her mother to move to Lipari so we can be closer.'

I nodded. It was a great idea. Martina needed to be near her father figure every day. But he did need eye-opening regarding

Elvira. That woman depended on him completely, and my female instinct told me she loved him, and I didn't want anyone to get hurt.

'Gillian. Are you okay with all of that? It is extremely important to me. *You* are important to me…'

I was grinning from ear to ear. Well, had he just made my whole life or what? 'Yes,' I whispered and he took my chin in his hand and delicately kissed my lips.

'Are you ready to head back to lunch? Elvira has cooked us some nice *zuppa di pesce*.'

I nodded and he wrapped his arm around me, pulling me close. Martina in his other arm, he led us down the beach, back to the house. I would never get used to feeling this special.

The Elvira issue would have to wait.

25

Mixed Messages

The next day back on Lipari, my cheap Italian cell phone decided to conk out. No amount of shaking or pushing all the buttons was going to do it. With a sigh, I got into my Ape and headed down into town to get it fixed. It turned out there was no fixing it, so I bought an Android with all the bells and whistles to use for business as well.

'Nothing lasts forever,' I snorted to myself as I held the new contraption, no sign of any buttons like my old one but a super-modern touch-screen you can't actually see in the sunlight. Did I mention I wasn't exactly a techie? Good luck making an emergency call under the hot Sicilian sun.

'How did your weekend in Salina go, dear?'

I jumped at the voice at my back and whirled. 'Cosetta – you scared me.'

The little woman took a step back, startled herself. 'I'm sorry, I didn't mean to. How are things?'

'Good, thank you. And you?'

'Have you made any progress?'

I scrabbled around for something to say, but she read the look on my face and realized I knew her secret. Everyone considered her guilty of Renzo's death.

With a soft sigh, she reached out and put a hand on my arm. 'Could you talk to him for me, Gillian?'

I hesitated. 'I already did. It's no use.'

She hunched her little shoulders. 'Could you try again? Please? Find a way to let me see Martina.'

'What? How do you expect me to—'

'You'll find a way. He trusts you.'

'He trusts me because I've never betrayed him.'

Cosetta's startlingly blue eyes shone with unshed tears. 'I was wrong. Terribly wrong to refuse Elvira as part of our family. I thought I could protect my grandsons from making mistakes. And my pride cost Renzo his life. I want to make amends to Mattia, but he won't even see me long enough to let me apologize. I want to take care of Elvira and Martina. Make up for my mistakes. My family is important to me. Please help me…'

I huffed. Mattia had been clear. He didn't want Cosetta anywhere near them. But then Cosetta was an old woman who wanted a second chance in life. Didn't we all deserve one? Martina was her blood, too. And the child needed to know her grandmother. Right?

'Okay,' I promised. 'I'll talk to him.'

Cosetta squeezed my hand and patted my cheek. 'Thank you, Gillian. You are a good woman. Mattia is lucky to have you in his life.'

If I was lucky enough to have him in my life, his family should as well. So the next day as Mattia and I were having a break from the grouting, I threw in my bait.

'About your grandmother…' I began, instantly regretting it when I saw the look on his face.

'*Si?*'

'She's old. Very old. One day Martina might ask you about her family, and what are you going to do? Present her with this sad story of a feud?'

He huffed. 'I'll think of it when the time comes. For now Martina is still a baby.'

'But you're deciding her future for her, just like Cosetta did to Renzo...'

'This is different, Gillian. Martina is too young to protect herself.'

'But one day she will be an adult and you'll have to face her anger toward you.'

He eyed me and put down his trowel. 'You've been talking to her quite a lot, haven't you?'

Busted. I'd never make a career in the Forum. I lowered my head in shame. 'Not really. But she goes straight to the point.'

He groaned. 'I thought I'd made myself clear about this. No Cosetta anywhere near us.'

I nodded. 'You're right. But I feel so sorry for her...'

'Sorry? What about my dead brother and his orphaned daughter! Feel sorry for them instead!'

I knelt back. He was right. 'Forgive me, Mattia...'

He leaned forward, filling the void between us. 'No, forgive *me* for snapping at you like that. But I want to be able to trust you completely.'

'You can, Mattia.'

'Good. So please promise me you will stay away from her. Okay?'

I nodded. 'Okay. You have my word.'

And that was the end of that.

The next day during the lunch hour when everybody had gone home and Mattia had gone to get the new kitchen faucets, Elvira appeared in my driveway. She must have taken a fishing boat from Salina and then hitched a ride up here with one of the locals.

'I came to speak with you,' she said, standing stiffly.

She was in a foul mood – I could tell immediately. Not even

two days and the Elvira issue had already reared its ugly head. 'Of course, come on in, sit down, Elvira.'

But she shook her head. 'No, I can tell you here, on two feet.'

Uh-oh, here it was.

'Mattia is *my* man,' she said clearly, in case I was slow. 'Everyone on Salina knows that. He's a father to my daughter. He only *works* on Lipari, but every weekend he comes home to me. And to Martina.'

'Elvira, I—'

'It was horrible when Renzo died. But then Mattia took his place. We were happy before you arrived. So please stay away from him.'

It was not my place to say anything to her about us. 'Mattia loves you both – I know that.'

She nodded. 'Yes. We are his family. One day he will love me as much as I love him. I need that to happen. So please stay away. For Martina's sake.'

'Elvira, I am not a threat to your family. Mattia will always love his niece like a daughter.'

'Yes, I know that. But I don't want you to get hurt again either. You look like a very nice person, Gillian.'

Hurt again? Mattia had told her more than was necessary, apparently. What right of his was it, to tell her my business?

That night, I waited for Mattia to come over for dinner as he'd promised. I wouldn't mention Elvira's visit. It seemed much kinder not to do so. I completely understood her desperation in losing a man like him. A man capable of such sacrifices for the good of others was a keeper.

Had there actually ever been anything between them? Was Mattia not telling me something? I just had to wait to find out.

But by nine he still hadn't arrived so I called him, ending up with his voicemail. I tried a few times again later but still nothing. So I left his office phone a message. Still nothing.

By eleven o'clock I was out of my mind with worry. What if something had happened to him? What if he'd been hit by a car?

Or had driven off a cliff, just like his brother? What if right now, he was lying unconscious somewhere? Who would know, at this time of night, if he'd crashed and his headlights had gone out? No one was expecting him but me.

So I called the one woman who knew more about him than anyone else.

'Sandra? I need your help. I can't find Mattia anywhere.'

Silence. 'Did you call all his numbers?'

'I've left him messages everywhere.'

'I'll text you Elvira's cell phone. That's the only place I can think of. You never know. Call me the minute you find him.'

'Okay. Thanks.'

A moment later Elvira's phone was ringing. She answered it on the fourth ring, her voice sleepy.

I swallowed. 'Hi, Elvira, it's Gillian. I'm sorry to bother you so late,' I said. 'I was wondering if... do you know where Mattia is?'

A pause and then muffled voices. 'He's here.'

What?

'Is that her? How the hell did she get your number?' he boomed and I envisaged him snatching the phone from Elvira. 'How dare you betray me again! Forget you know me. Forget my name!' And then he hung up.

Bile chasing up whatever I had inside me, I put the phone down. He'd found out about my promise to Cosetta. That explained it all.

And then my phone rang. Was absolutely nobody sleeping tonight? 'Gillian. Sorry it's so late. It's Cosetta.'

I rubbed the space between my eyebrows. 'What is it, Cosetta?'

'Did you hear?'

'Hear what?'

Pause. There was definitely a silence pattern tonight on my phone.

'Mattia is going to marry Elvira. You have to stop them, Gillian.'

I swear I almost had a heart attack.

Marry Elvira?

It didn't make any sense. He didn't love her. At least not the way a man loves a woman, I didn't think. How could he do this, make this huge decision from one day to the next, after all he'd said to me about how important I was to him?

I sat down with a thud. The answer was simple. Once again, I'd been had. That was the only explanation. Because Mattia's sense of duty toward his family was too strong. Stronger than any feelings he may have had for me. No point in insisting. Only more heartache awaited me if I went down this road and I wasn't ready for that. I was done chasing men who didn't love me.

Had my love stopped Tony from running off? No. And now Mattia was sick of my meddling and wanted to marry Elvira? In the end she'd convinced him it was the right thing to do. And that Renzo would've wanted it that way. I knew Mattia didn't love Elvira in that way, but obviously his love for little Martina had proven to be more important than his own love life. Who was I to blame him? I'd put Annie before my own happiness any day. It's what you did. The little ones first, no matter what. It was right. Even Tony had stayed married to me for Annie's sake.

I didn't expect a guy I'd just met to abandon a little girl and her mother for me. It was his one shot at a sense of normalcy. A family of his own. The playboy had finally found his resting place. I understood. It hurt like hell, but it made sense. Yes, I deserved his anger for breaking my promise to him. But I expected him to at least tell me in person rather than ignore me. If not for anything, to avoid the embarrassment of running into him in town and expecting to pick up where we'd left off.

'I'm not stopping anyone, Cosetta,' I managed. 'And it's time you learned from your mistakes. Goodnight.' And I hung up, totally numb.

It was the story of my life – I trusted a man with my heart – and then it went pear-shaped for some reason or another. This time it was my fault. Only now I was breaking record time. It had taken Tony twenty years to break my heart, but Mattia only a few months.

26

Bye-bye Baby

A few days later Sandra had literally come to the mountain, dragged me out of bed and down into Lipari town for a cappuccino, which was all I could swallow. She'd ordered trays of pastries but I couldn't bring myself to eat. It all reminded me of how Mattia had desserted me to death with the various *macallé* pastries. Now I was only... *deserted*.

I'd sworn I'd never cry over a man again but there you go. It was obviously my role in life to do so.

'Cheer up, Gilly. There has to be an explanation,' Sandra said, obviously not too convinced about Mattia either at this point. She knew how important the baby was to him, but he'd never been gone this long. So it must have been true. But Christ, to not even bloody tell me? What the hell was wrong with him?

'Yeah,' I snorted, wiping at my eyes again behind my huge shades. 'I scared him right off the island. Trust me to be the only woman capable of *that*.'

'Ladies!' Claudio called, sitting himself down at our table. 'What are we celebrating?'

Sandra and I exchanged glances before she said, 'Nothing. Why are you looking so happy?'

He beamed at me. 'No reason in particular. Staff is going for a pizza this evening. Coming?'

'Ugh, count me out. I had more than my weekly share of pizza last night,' Sandra said.

'Gillian?'

'No, thanks, I'm not in the mood. Plus, I'm not staff.'

'Oh, come on, Gilly!' Claudio coaxed. 'Enough of this sad little face. Come on! I'll buy you a Nutella pizza for dessert?'

Despite myself, I stopped in my tracks. 'A what?'

He laughed. 'You have never had a Nutella Pizza?'

I shook my head, already salivating. Man, I *deserved* to be big.

'Nutella instead of topping. And maybe a sprinkle of hazelnuts if you behave yourself. What do you say?'

'Go on, Gilly,' Sandra said. 'You have to try it. Make this man here happy.'

'Well…'

What else was there left for me to do? I'd been sitting home Mattia-less for days now, licking my wounds. He was, for all intents and purposes, gone, and rather than face yet another night sitting home alone crying while swearing myself off men for good – and for *real* this time – I needed to come up for air every once in a while. But on my *own*.

So I turned down the invite and on my way home bought myself a tub of pistachio-almond ice cream at Subba's (probably a relative of Mimmo's) as I anticipated another long, lonely night. When twice-deserted in Sicily… dessert was always the solution.

It turned out Sandra wasn't maxed out on pizza after all. She was going out with some guy to snub Alfonso because they'd had yet another argument regarding his ex-wife who was actually visiting him from the mainland when Sandra was at work. I won't even go into that. Suffice to say that these islanders are a screwed-up lot. Maybe they got bored too easily on this rock and found all sorts of diversions from their otherwise straightforward, simple lives and loves.

When Sandra called me that evening she sounded miserable. 'Sure you don't want to come with me?' she asked.

'What, on your date with this new guy? Thanks, but no thanks.'

'Please? Just for a coffee or something.'

'Sandra, if you don't want to go, don't go. Tell him you're ill or something.'

'But it's too late for that now.'

'Well then go out with him and don't think about Alfonso.'

'Ha,' she said. 'That's like asking you to not think about Mattia.'

Ouch.

'All right, then,' she surrendered. 'But if it doesn't work I'm sleeping over at yours tonight, so save me some food!'

And then she made kiss-kiss noises and hung up. That was one heck of a quick recovery. I envied her. She could have any man she wanted. And she had this resilience factor that I wouldn't have in a million years. Because I *missed* Mattia. Getting over him wasn't going to be as easy as getting over Tony. Which was so odd, right? I'd been married for almost twenty years, and yet here I was, mourning another guy and The Relationship That Never Actually Was.

'Where are you? Please come,' Claudio begged over the phone. 'I am here alone and let me tell you it's not much fun.'

I laughed despite myself as I swirled my ice cream around my tongue, taking whatever solace it could give me. Then, with absolutely no shame, I drizzled some melted Nutella over it, turning the bowl and watching hot decorate cold. Whoever said food was better than sex knew what they were talking about. 'I'm home. Too tired.'

'Even for me?'

I spilt some ice cream down the front of my T-shirt. *Shit.* And then his voice registered.

'*Excuse* me?'

'Can I come over when I'm done here? Bring you dinner?'

I looked down at my sweatpants and woolly socks as panic crashed through me. 'No – I'm not feeling very well.'

'But you have to eat. I'll bring you something in a bit.'

'Uhm, no, that's okay. I'm just going to bed.'

'Alone?'

There we go again. Apparently ignoring him had not been enough. Sandra had warned me he'd try it on, sooner or later, but I never thought he would. I mean, look at me. Actually, better not. I was an absolute mess tonight.

Laughter. 'Sorry, Gillian – just kidding. See you in a bit.' And he hung up. Was it me or did the guy not know how to take no for an answer?

So I jumped up, hid my carton of ice cream back in the freezer and threw myself into the shower, more for myself than him. I certainly wasn't interested, but that didn't mean I was allowed to open the door with Nutella stains on my T-shirt and greasy hair. Claudio was sweet but it ended there. I was too depressed trying to understand what had happened between Mattia and me.

There was a knock on my door as I wrapped a towel around me. Damn, if I opened up to Claudio now, it would look so set up, like in one of those soap operas you see on daytime TV. I didn't do clichéd.

My hair dripping on my shoulders and down my back, I padded downstairs through the piles of unopened stuff I was squirreling away for my B&B and walked over to the door and opened it a crack, never feeling so embarrassed in my whole life.

'Hey, *bellissima*,' Claudio said, kissing my cheek as he put the pizza down on the bureau by the entrance. Uh-oh. He was in conquering mode for sure, all sexy smiles and expensive cologne (which was very strong, by the way).

'Hi. Uhm – sorry I'm not dressed yet. I'll be right b—'

'No need to dress for me,' he said, taking me by my shoulders and leaning in to maybe kiss me or something, and I was so painfully aware of the fact that I was buck naked under my towel. Contrary to what he might've gleaned in his mad thoughts, nothing was going to happen here tonight, or ever, except for maybe having a slice of that delicious-smelling pizza, and me sending him packing afterwards.

As I ducked out of his way, I pushed out a hearty laugh to put emotional distance between us as well, in case he hadn't got my message. After another couple of half-hearted attempts on his behalf to corner me, I verbally tackled him. 'Right! Sit down, Claudio, and tell me what's wrong.'

To which he opened his mouth to protest, closed it and opened it again. And then burst into tears. I'd never seen a grown man cry – not even my dad when Ma left him – so I was kind of at a loss. What did one do in these situations?

'I'm sorry,' he sobbed. 'I don't cry. Ever.'

I put my hand on his. 'What's the matter, Claudio?'

His broad shoulders shook and he rubbed his face and head. 'You must think I'm an idiot.'

'Of course not...'

And then he looked up, his eyes glazed over. 'My wife. She left me last spring. And now she wants a divorce. I can't forget her, but she says she can't trust me anymore. But I swear to you, Gillian – I never cheated on her. I love her too much.'

Now, you'd think I was the last one to be able to judge a guy. But you could tell he was honest. Oh, how I sympathized.

I put my hand on his shoulder and he embraced me in turn. 'You're a good woman, Gillian. Mattia should wake up and see you for what you are.'

As if. He thought I was a *quote*, miserable, scheming, calculating bitch. *Unquote*.

I debated on whether to pull out my ice cream to cheer him up, but decided it was more of a pull-out-the-big-guns job and reached for my home-made tiramisu I'd saved for tomorrow's lunch with Maria's mob and Sandra. But hey, if I couldn't rely on it to mend someone's broken heart at a moment's notice, then what had I made it for? I dished out a generous double-whammy portion for him and already his lips upturned.

And that's when the doorbell rang. Sandra. So her date with Luca had turned out to be a disaster, after all. Well, she'd fit right in, especially tonight, here at Relationship Fiasco Central.

'Hi,' said Mattia, as I opened the door and jumped back in surprise. Surprise? Make it utter shock.

I swallowed. 'Mattia...'

'Looks like I'm just in time,' he murmured as he bent to kiss my collarbone. I moved away although I'd missed him tremendously and would've done anything for another chance. And yet, as I looked at him, pale and weary and even more handsome than I'd remembered, all I could think of how I'd let him hurt me and humiliate me for absolutely no reason.

'Is that all you can say after all that?' I said softly, not wanting Claudio to hear.

He started. 'I'm sorry but I've been in the hospital on the mainland. Martina had bloody meningitis.'

My mouth fell open. 'Oh, my God, is she okay?'

Mattia held me still by the shoulders. 'Better now. God, I've missed you. I wanted to send for you but I couldn't get a hold of you.'

'Why didn't you call?'

He blinked. 'I did. Your voicemail kept kicking in. Didn't you get my messages?'

Messages? Oh. 'I got a new phone but I don't know how the message thingy works.' Was I a disaster or what?

'I even tried Sandra but she never picks up, so lost over Alfonso, that one. No matter. I'm back. And I'm going to make it up to you, starting right now...' he said, drawing me into his arms, his hot breath making me shiver even despite my anger and I pushed him away. 'Why did you say all those horrible things to me?'

He blinked. 'What horrible things?'

I gulped, a huge knot in my throat. 'You said I was a horrible scheming bitch.'

'Wha-at?'

'When I called Elvira's phone.'

He stared at me and then paled. 'Jesus, that was *you*? I thought it was Cosetta! Elvira said she kept calling and I just assumed – oh my God, Gillian, I'm so sorry!' he moaned, pulling me into his arms and kissing me.

'You're telling me you thought it was your grandmother?'

'Of course! Why would I talk to anyone else like that? Don't you understand how much I care about you, Gillian? That you're the first woman I've ever really trusted my whole life?'

And despite myself I once again believed him. 'Elvira has made it clear to me that she thinks you're hers.'

He ran a hand through his dark curls. 'Elvira – I can't believe she just let me think it was Cosetta. Jesus, am I blind or what? We have a problem with her, sweetheart. I'm going to have to talk to her, reassure her that I'll still be there for them no matter what. But I'll make it clear once and for all that you are my woman. No one else.'

I swallowed and tried to smile in the face of impending doom. Never mind Elvira – I had a disheveled, gorgeous gym teacher in the next room. How to get out of this one without any casualties?

'Mattia, I thought you'd *left* me…'

At that, he reached down and took my face into his. 'Left you? I'm so sorry, Gillian. You should know by now how I feel about you…'

'Cosetta said you were marrying Elvira.'

His mouth dropped. 'You see? You see how scheming she is?' he argued. 'That thought has never even crossed my mind!'

'Ever?'

'Ever.'

'Was there anything ever between you?'

'You think I'd actually sleep with my brother's wife? That

would be betraying his memory, Gillian. Why would you even think that for one minute?'

'But you never really...elaborated on... *us*.'

He grinned. 'I never did really, did I? You're right. But I can't wait to show you how much I *missed* you,' he whispered and I cringed, fully aware that I was buck naked under my towel *and* that I had a gorgeous male visitor in the next room.

'I thought we were over,' I cried in anguish.

'Over? We haven't even started yet, Gilly, and I'm going to wear you out,' Mattia said as he reached down and lifted me up against him and headed for the living room, his hands under my butt, making sure I knew exactly how *much* he'd missed me. Ooh, he most definitely had and I couldn't wait to hear and see more about it, but for Claudio in the next room. For modesty's sake I protested as Claudio got to his feet, still disheveled and flushed.

Oh, crap – a blind man could have seen this awkward *momento* coming. 'You, uhm, know Claudio, right? Silly question around here, I guess.'

Mattia's eyes rounded at the sight of Claudio's messy hair, rumpled shirt and wild eyes.

There was an awkward silence as Claudio pushed his hair away from his face and Mattia turned to me, his face pale.

'Sorry. My mistake,' he rasped.

'No, Mattia, you've got it all wrong,' I assured him as, without so much as looking me in the eye, he brushed past me and slammed the door on his way out.

And welcome to my daytime television life. Again. God, was there no escaping it? Why couldn't I have a normal, boring-as-hell life for once?

Helpless, I followed him outside as he marched down the steps to his Jeep.

'Wait! You're kidding me, right?' I called after him. 'What are you *doing?* Mattia!'

But kidding me he was not. As a matter of fact, he gunned his engine and disappeared in a cloud of dust that rose high in the outdoor lights without so much as a glance back.

'What an idiot he is,' Sandra said, shaking her head the next day. 'Call him, no?'

'You must be joking.'

'But why?'

'Because I've been here before, Sandra. No more begging.'

She sighed. 'You are a *testadura*. A hard head.'

'Look who's talking,' I retorted.

'Call him.'

'No.'

'*Call him.*'

'*No.*'

'You will be sorry tomorrow morning when you wake up alone.'

She was wrong. I couldn't be any more sorry than I already was.

'Mattia loves you. I can tell a mile off.'

Sandra was a dear friend, but she had no idea what she was talking about. She claimed to know men, to know Mattia. But there was no way she was right about his feelings for me. If he loved me, he would trust me completely, but obviously we had never really reached that stage. It had taken me ages to get his life story out of him, and the minute I did? We were happy for what, five minutes? But it was also my fault. I should have not made any promises to Cosetta, the very source of all his problems. He'd warned me he wasn't a forgiver.

And now we'd completely destroyed each other's trust.

27

Hysterical Housewives

As the days grew colder, darker and shorter, they seemed endless without Mattia. Gone were the summer dresses, the evening strolls and the afternoon siestas that broke the long hot afternoons, giving respite from the heat and constant activity on the islands.

Now the town was quiet, and its people made a point of getting their errands done in the morning so they could be home and dry before night set in at four p.m. Even the ferry service had dwindled. And so had Mattia's appearances – to fleeing sightings of his back as he disappeared round a corner, or amongst the crowd at the harbor, getting onto his boat on Saturday mornings as usual, doing his own thing.

He was everywhere but at the building site, and every morning when his men arrived I couldn't help but peek out my window, hoping he'd finally returned with them.

The house was almost finished but for a few minor details, which Mattia's men were dealing with quickly and efficiently. Minus the blacksmith, Limping Man, who still scared the bejeezus out of me with those savage looks he threw my way, like he wanted to undress me on the spot and then gobble me right up. And he looked like it wouldn't take him long, either. Two bites and I'd never be found.

You never have to be afraid while I'm around, Mattia had once said to me. And I'd believed he would be there. To love me, wake up with me and share my life. Why did men always conk out toward the end of a project, or worse, a relationship? Why couldn't they be steadfast and reliable until the very end? I should've been used to it by now. But it hurt like hell. Without Mattia, I was miserable.

So I'd recruited my best gals, Martha and Brends, for a working winter holiday. They were due here in three days and would help me clean the place up and act as my dummy B&B guests in order for me to catch any glitches right away. Besides, what with Maria available only by phone as she had her own tribe of four to run, Sandra back with Alfonso and Mattia permanently out of the picture, I needed all the friends I could get.

So I was back to square one again. *Still* at square one, truth be told. Starting over? Lots of my friends had done it. But they'd done it in the UK, with their friends and family to help them. This here was a one-woman job I was undertaking, in a land far, far away, without my environment as a safety net and my support group to help me out, except for this one week.

The rest of the time it would be only me. No one else to lean on unconditionally. Because here in Sicily, let's not kid ourselves, it would take me a while to be up and running on a completely sufficient basis. Who would I be able to depend upon? Sure, Sandra was a great friend, one I wish everyone had, but she had her own life.

And if I needed help in the middle of the night, who could I call? Who would come running? Maybe Mattia, once upon a time, but not anymore. I was absolute toast in his book now, forgotten forever.

As I made a list of all the things I needed, Mattia's foreman put in the rest of the grouting in the kitchen tiles, warning me at least ten times not to go in there. He didn't provide an explanation as to why my project manager had suddenly dropped off the face of the earth and I didn't ask. Besides, I already had an inside informer in Sandra.

According to her Mattia was already working on a 'big

project' on Salina. As if I couldn't imagine what it was – maybe an extension to Elvira's house, possibly an extra room for a baby.

The next day the rest of the beds and the furniture arrived. They were absolutely gorgeous, all in different colors of wrought iron (mine being cream), very refined and made in Italy by Letti Cosatto, and cherry-wood night tables and dressers. Italians, especially islanders, love their colors. Someone explained to me once that it was because in Italy the intensity of the sunlight and the weather conditions, especially near the sea, made the most of colors.

Come to think of it, cold countries did have an abundance of grays and taupes in and out of their homes, but they never went crazy for, say, a bright turquoise or an emerald green. It was obvious I had Italian blood running through my veins.

I would've liked to have watched the three men assemble the furniture, but I had the plumber downstairs installing my – *finally* – new kitchen. No more makeshift stuff for me. Nothing too grand, just a white IKEA model with shaker doors I'd ordered online from the store in Catania. It had arrived via ferry and cost me an arm and a leg, but still much less than an Italian one. You have to stay a little international, right? This was my only compromise. Everything else, from my cutting board to my sofas, was Italian.

It felt good to rebuild myself a home. It was like being reborn (or getting married again, minus Mattia – I mean minus *a man*).

Tony was probably still in our home back in the UK, waiting for me to retrieve my stuff. Well, he'd have a long wait. Although initially I'd loved every stick of furniture in that house, felt protected by all my possessions and surroundings that represented my marriage, now I couldn't care less if it all rotted away – our king-sized bed first on the scrap list. The only thing I cared about were the rest of Annie's photos and artwork, which she had at Miles' flat. So I emailed her and told her to help herself to my half of everything.

★

'*Cor*, Gilly, you sure got yourself a real palace here,' Brends chimed as she and Martha crossed the threshold like two pack mules. Apparently their luggage had arrived without a glitch, as opposed to mine, which was long gone.

'So,' Brends said, her high heels clacking on the ceramic tiles. 'Where's your new man?'

I could feel myself go poker-hot red, remembering how I'd spilled the beans of my attraction for a younger man. 'Well, um, actually…'

Brends put her bags down with a thump, mouth wide open. 'He's left you already. Christ, Gilly, what do you *do* to them?'

My sentiments exactly.

'Brends,' Martha warned her.

'It's all right, Martha. She's right,' I said miserably as I moved into the kitchen to check the shrimp and zucchini risotto. The aubergine swordfish was almost ready, too. 'I just never learn. Sandra warned me.'

'Sandra, the man expert?' Brends wanted to know.

'Yeah.'

'Tall, thin, crazy hair, but classy-looking at the same time?'

'Exactly. I never described her to you, did I? How—'

'She's limping up your driveway with a suitcase. And she's in tears. Some man expert.'

'Shut up, Brends,' Martha said again.

'Just saying.'

I eyed them and looked out. Sure enough, Sandra was trudging up my drive, swiping at her cheeks. I flung open the door. 'Sandra, what happened?'

She sniffed and dumped her suitcase on the welcome mat and gave me a hug, clinging to me. Normally it was her comforting me. I hated to see her like this.

'Alfonso – we had our last fight ever. I'm done, Gilly! Oh, you have guests. I'm sorry. I'll come back another time.'

'Don't be silly,' I said. 'This is Martha and her sister Brends from London. They're my friends, not guests.'

'Hi,' Martha said, holding out a chair for her as Brends poured her some wine.

'Better get some booze in you. Gets it all out quicker.'

Sandra accepted the glass, guzzling half of it down. Brends smiled. 'Attagirl. Now spill.'

'There's nothing to say. His wife has a financial grip on him.'

Now, in *my* case a husband sticking to his wife would've been preferable and less painful. In Sandra's case, not so good.

'And he has kids,' she whined, and then she burst into tears all over again.

'Oh, don't they all?' Brends agreed sympathetically as Martha silently patted her back as if they were bosom buddies. Female solidarity knew no borders. We had these Anti-Jerk Coalition skills. Brends more than anyone else. She beat the table with the flat of her hand. 'Tell me about this asshole.'

And so she did, as Martha pulled out another plate and I dished up. Luckily I always made extra, which was a good thing because Sandra ate like an army. Especially when she was down in the dumps. I'd always wondered where she put it all.

'What am I going to do?' she sobbed.

'First of all, you'll stay here with us,' I said handing her a plate heaped with risotto.

She grabbed a napkin and blew her nose.

'It'll be okay,' said Martha, the only one among us who was happily married.

Sandra lifted her head. 'Will it? I don't think so.'

'Give it time,' I said, and because I knew her well, added, 'Eat before it gets cold. You'll feel better.'

'Hello, anybody home?' came a sing-song from the door. I looked up as Diana made a dash for Maria, her lovely round face filling the window pane. 'I thought you might need some help cleaning this place out,' she said, producing all sorts of bottles and spray-cans. And there was even stuff at her feet.

'Come in, you!' I chimed and made all the due introductions. And then Maria went out to her brand new Fiat Panda and returned with a big oven tray.

'What's in there?' I asked.

She grinned. 'Focaccia. And cakes.'

'Yum!' Sandra squealed, never one to be sad for too long if good food was around.

And so we ate as Sandra told us all the ins and out of their relationship while Brends egged her on. Martha, Maria and I listened, adding the occasional word of encouragement as Brends continued her one-woman crusade against all men, living and dead. Not even Mattia, whom she didn't know, was spared, and this time Sandra was in no spirit to defend him or any man.

Brends had been left by two husbands, me by one and by Mattia, Sandra by a husband and by a lover. And from what I got from Martha's droopy mouth things weren't going very well at her home either, which was a surprise. And with a marriage that had been dragging on forever, even Maria had been in love with the idea of singledom, but had a family of four to support on her meager salary.

I looked around the table. All of us, at one point or another, had been in an unhappy relationship. Maybe instead of a B&B I should open a community center and call it Hopeless Housewives, or Let-down Lovers. Or better yet, Desserted in Sicily. Maybe even get an 0-800 toll-free number. *Whatever your fancy-gone-wrong, call us. We'll pick you up, feed you, booze you up and give you hope. We can't guarantee he'll come back, but sure as hell you'll have some good laughs with your kind.*

Not a bad idea at all, actually. I wondered if I should patent the concept.

Fed and warm again, Sandra looked around as I cleared the plates and brought my famous Heart Attack Pie to the table. No, it wasn't Italian, but it was an all-time fave in my family, made with – you guessed it – Nutella. And crunchy peanut butter, which had cost me an arm and a leg to order, and coffee ice cream.

'Gilly,' Sandra said, wiping her eyes. 'The place looks great. Absolutely fantastic.'

'Thanks. Martha and Brends came down to help me get it ready.'

'Why didn't you ask me? I'd have helped. Don't say it, I know, I see it on your face – Alfonso took up all my time. But from now on, friends first. Right, ladies?'

'Absolutely,' Brends chimed. 'Gotta tell you Gilly, you've made the right decision buying here. From what I saw down in the town, the men are gorgeous.'

Were they? I hadn't noticed anyone outside Mattia. And oh, Claudio of course, the reason I was in this mess after all.

'And *married*,' Martha cautioned, to which Brends shrugged and Sandra went all gloomy again.

'Ladies, you know what we need?' Brends asked, smacking her lips.

'Oh God, what now?' Martha asked, bracing herself.

'A night out.'

'I'm in,' I said.

'Me too,' Sandra chimed while she licked her spoon. 'Show that weakling I don't need him.'

'I'm designated driver,' Maria sighed, resigned.

'You have to be. The four of us won't fit in my Ape.'

Needless to say we hit the town bent on self-destruction. Well, Brends and Sandra were, while Martha, Maria and I played staid mother hens, and later that night when I helped a tipsy Sandra into bed, she grabbed my hand.

'It'll all be all right, won't it?' she asked, her eyes wide in the lamplight, and for a moment she reminded me of Annie, her slender form disappearing amidst the bedding for fear of the world crumbing down on top of her. She also reminded me of myself only a few months ago, when I was certain it already had. And Sandra had been there for me. And Mattia. But I just couldn't feel sorry for myself tonight.

If only I had known then what I knew about myself now. If I'd known my potential, I wouldn't have wasted my life and hopes away on a little man like Tony or even a great man like Mattia. So was Sandra going to be all right?

'Absolutely, *cara*,' I assured her. And with that, she was asleep.

The next few days of Martha and Brends' stay were spent cleaning windows, doors, shutters, stripping factory seal tape off the white goods, which was never-ending, considering I had seven en-suite bedrooms. Soon the rest of my new, Italian furniture would be arriving. And in exactly five months I'd be receiving my very first guests. Online booking was a blessing, and so was my fabulous website I'd called *South to Sicily*.

Martha and Brends helped me with the work as Sandra, for the very first time, did the catering, i.e. bought take-aways from the various restaurants all across town, blatantly avoiding Alfonso's, of course.

And all too soon the working holiday was over. Amidst tears and hugs, my UK girls promised to return and see how I was doing. I clung to them, realizing that I had passed the point of no return, and that I'd made my bed. And now I had to sleep in it. *Alone.*

28

Alone Again

The Saturday after that, December seventh was – or *would've been* – my twentieth anniversary, along with my fortieth birthday. I tried hard to remember what we'd done last year, but all I got was broken images of Tony working late and me sitting, all dressed up and going nowhere, in every sense, waiting by the phone for him to call.

As I fed Diana that evening, my mind on everything and nothing in particular, my cell phone rang.

'Hello, pet,' came Martha's voice, uncertain. 'How are you?'

Of course she'd remembered my anniversary. She always had. Only this year she didn't know how to act. Better put her out of her misery.

'I haven't thrown myself off the cliff in my Ape yet, if that's what you mean.'

I heard her smile, obviously relieved. 'One never knows, the way you drive that thing.'

'How's Brends and everyone?'

'God, don't remind me. Now she's got the Botox bug. That was all we needed. Have you seen the girls lately?' Meaning Sandra and Maria.

I rolled my eyes. 'They don't know today would've been my anniversary. It's not like I'm wearing the T-shirt, you know.'

Martha chuckled. 'Right. So what are your plans for tonight?'

Terrific question.

'Ah, nothing. Just chilling out, really.'

'Okay, then. You have a nice evening and if you get lonely just give me a call.'

'I will. Martha?'

'What, sweetie?'

'I've been meaning to ask you for some time. How... how are you and Michael?'

Silence, and then a sigh. 'Sometimes good, sometimes not so good. You know...'

'You should do everything you can to be happy, Martha.'

'I know. You're right. But not everyone has your courage, Gilly.'

Oh. So it was that bad. 'Do you want to talk about it?'

Noise in the background. 'Maybe some other time, love.'

'Okay.'

'Night, sweetie.'

'Night, Martha...'

Was *that* what she thought? That I had courage? Granted, I never thought I'd be living on my own without my husband, never thought I'd bounce back from the end of our marriage. Nor that I would've left the safety of my home to start a business I knew absolutely jack squat about. So maybe she was right. Maybe I had been brave, if not reckless. Who else did I know who had left her old life to start a new one with only a turquoise beach bag containing almonds, and a small bottle of Jo Malone?

After I made sure the fire in the hearth was well under way, I put up the fire guard to protect my beautiful new rug and raced to my bedroom to put on my new duck-egg winter jammies, soft woolly robe and bed socks. All new. My very own new start. *My* scented candles. *My* female colors, *my* silly doormat reading *Benvenuti, Amici*, welcome, friends. And my new life. I'd slowly filled what had been a shell with soft furnishings to make it a home. I'd slowly filled the shell of my life with warm friends.

Here in Lipari I was beginning to find a tiny little niche to nestle and just be myself, much more than in any other place I'd been so far. I let the pleasant feeling settle and grow in my heart without fighting it or acting upon it. The fact that I had Sandra and Maria was a bonus. Now if only I could win Mattia back. But it was too late. Even if Claudio tried to defend me, Mattia would never believe him, judging by the way we looked that night.

I made myself a bowl of cornflakes and settled down with the remote (all mine, too!) in front of the TV with my dinner and – wouldn't you know it – they were showing my favorite movie, *Unconditional Love.*

In Italian (good thing I knew the story already), Dan Akroyd announces he's leaving wife Kathy Bates because he feels she's stopping him from attaining his dreams.

Practically the story of my life. Only Kathy Bates hadn't been abandoned in favor of fresher meat and I didn't have Rupert Evert to cozy up to, albeit innocently, without even the remotest chance of an orgasm caused by him, throughout all my trials and tribulations.

Idiot, said a voice out of nowhere. *You could've had Mattia. He could've been yours if only you'd let yourself go. And you could've had orgasms galore. Who cared if it was only a sex thing with an expiration date? You could've had some of the best sex of your life. Hell, of anyone's life, come to think of it.* Or, more to the point, I could've had his *love.* No, better not to think of Mattia and what I'd lost.

And here I was, a failed marriage under my belt – plus a Could've Been relationship with the best man I'd ever met in my entire life. Now Mattia was part of the past, albeit a brief, not-to-distant past I wished I could just reach out and grab. But that was fantasy and this, my twentieth anniversary all on my own, was reality.

Enough feeling sorry for myself. I had a promising business already. Bookings were coming in like crazy, but still I searched for more and more ways to stand out. Gorgeous pictures on my website. Courtesy shuttle (the mad hornet Ape, which was still way better than Mimmo Subba's wreck of a car) to and from the harbor. Maybe extend it to day trips or something. In any case, I had to find something to give *South to Sicily* an edge.

Maybe I could get a fisherman to ferry couples around the islands for romantic picnics and anniversary (ha!) specials. But why would he do it for me when he could do it himself and not split the dough? It would make more financial sense if I didn't depend on anyone. If only I could do it myself – steer a boat. But you know me by now, terra firma and all that.

The cornflakes forgotten and now soggy and Kathy Bates once again a happy camper, I looked around me at the empty room. Now what? A board game with Diana?

And then came a honk in the driveway. Mattia! Had he come to retrieve the last of his tools? Or to tell me he really cared after all and could we work this out? Or at least be friends? Or maybe that he wasn't marrying Elvira anymore? Highly unlikely.

'Some guard dog you are,' I muttered to Diana who helped herself to my cornflakes as I peered through the peephole.

This time I would tell him I was sorry, that what he did was his business and could he please forgive me and be my friend like before, if nothing more?

It wasn't Mattia, though. The honking continued, followed by laughter and people piling out of a car. I turned on the porch lights. Sandra! And Maria and her three daughters.

'Surprise!' they shouted in unison and I rushed out to help them carry in trays and bags full of food. It seemed all they did lately was feed me.

'What are you guys *doing* up here?' I asked, hugging them.

'Just another Saturday night,' Maria chuckled.

'Alfonso's at work. Do you mind us crashing?'

Alfonso again? I never knew whether they were speaking or not, those two. Such a riotous romance. In any case, perfect timing. I grinned, suddenly reanimated because I wouldn't have to spend this crap evening on my own. 'Come on in.'

'We know it's late, but we hope you haven't had dinner yet?' Maria wanted to know, already fiddling with the dials of my oven. 'And by the way – shame on you, for not sharing your fortieth birthday with us,' Sandra chided playfully.

I raised my eyebrow in question and she rolled her eyes. 'Brends called me.'

I shrugged. 'It's no big deal. It's not like I'm twenty anymore.'

'Are you kidding me?' Sandra countered. 'Forty is the new twenty!'

I thought about it. If forty was the new twenty, then my life was supposed to be at its peak. But it wasn't. Granted, I had carved out a new life for myself here on Lipari. A new business, a new home, some fantastic new friends to cherish along with the old ones, but what I really wanted – *love* – was nowhere in sight. I would spend the rest of my nights alone. And if being forty meant being settled, then I had to accept settling into my new single life.

Maria rubbed her hands. 'Ten minutes and food's ready. Sandra, pop the wine!'

As we ate and laughed, I marveled at how these two women, who couldn't be any more different, had become friends. They were, in a way, a replica of Martha and Brends, the way they chided and mocked each other. Who knew they could ever have anything in common besides a broken heart?

The next day, after finishing my rounds of shopping and errands, I dropped by Alfonso's before going back home. He and Sandra, she informed me, were once again like two lovebirds now that he'd left his wife for good. It was amazing, the happiness that could derive from someone else's desperation. I would know. Twice over, in fact. I wondered about Elvira, and if she was finally happy with Mattia. Because that's where he'd gone, for sure.

'Did you hear the radio? Our first storm is due this evening. It's going to be very bad. Spend the night down here in town with us?' Sandra begged me over a cup of espresso. 'I'd be much happier knowing you're safe.'

'I'm more than safe up there. Mattia built me a sturdy house.' It was just a terrible shame that Mattia and I couldn't build a sturdy relationship as well.

'Do you miss him?' she asked.

'Who?' I lied.

She rolled her eyes.

'Nah. Besides, I've got Diana. She's waiting for me.'

'I wish you wouldn't go. I worry about you up there on your own in the middle of absolutely nowhere.'

'But I'm fifteen minutes away!'

'But you're alone!'

I shrugged. The story of my life. Even the times Tony had been with me I had always been alone.

A few weeks ago, I'd tried calling Mattia to make peace. To try and at least be friends (not that we'd ever been more than that, really.) He hadn't even bothered to answer me or give me the courtesy to tell me to go and jump in a lake. So yes, I was alone. But maybe, for the very first time in my life, it was a good thing.

'Silly. I'll be fine.'

But Sandra was determined to worry. 'Call me when you get home?'

'Yes. Can I go now?'

She hugged me. 'Yes. Hurry before the storm arrives. And don't drive fast.'

I turned and gave her a *How am I supposed to hurry without driving fast?* look and waved as I got into my trusty Ape. Now I knew how Annie felt when I s-mothered her.

Yes, the sky was a thick wooly blanket of gray and black,

heavy with rain, just about to burst. Luckily I had my trusted little diesel steed to take me home. Everywhere I went people now recognized the bright yellow with a rainbow on it. Adapting from Toronto to London had been a cinch. Living in the UK was stimulating and sometimes challenging for a Canadian girl like myself, but Lipari? With all its challenges, Lipari represented all I wanted – a close-knit community, a lovely home with an extra room for Annie whenever she wanted, and my very own business.

A business I had literally carved out of a rock cliff, hauling this monumental building out of the ashes. I'd worked alongside Mattia day in, day out, erecting fallen walls, underpinning collapsed floors and acting as a girl Friday for everyone on the premises. Had I had grown some balls or what?

Sure, I had years and years of hard labor ahead of me, God willing, catering to people's every need and changing beds and making breakfasts and scrubbing toilets. But, truth be told, wasn't that what I'd been doing all my life, only for free? Might as well get paid for it and even receive the occasional *thank you*, which never hurt, either.

And the Italian bureaucracy? If I'd lived through all the red tape necessary to buy the damn place, I could live through anything. The stacks of paperwork and running up and down the steps of the town hall to obtain the ever-growing list of permits no longer scared me. I could do this blindfolded, one hand tied behind my back.

Annie was only a couple of hours away and if and when Miles decided he had time to visit, they'd have a whole floor to themselves here.

Yep, after twenty years, I was living on my own again and now made my own choices, from what to have for dinner to what color to paint the walls.

And speaking of, now for some fun – decorating. I'd bought sheets, pillows, mats, curtains – everything I needed – and I couldn't wait to get home and play house.

Sometimes, (okay, I admit it – always) as I wound my way up the bends to my home, my mind would drift to Mattia. He and I had not been a good fit. At this point even being friends would be difficult, but he had to at least acknowledge me. He couldn't possibly avoid me during the winter months – on this island there was practically no one else to talk to.

Meeting him in the street was always awkward and although he never pretended not to see me, he didn't go out of his way to come up and say hello either, which happened only if we met face to face or at the most across the street. It would've been nice to talk to him, ask him about Martina. Was she doing well, growing up happily? And was Elvira making him happy, keeping him warm when he went back there at the weekend? And were they now finally a couple?

When I pulled into the driveway Diana was waiting for me just inside the door, her ears radar-straight. Well, at least I wouldn't be completely alone. I needed to get all this stuff in before the storm hit, as I was assured by Cassandra the soothsayer it would.

By the time I'd unloaded my Ape with my food, supplies and knick-knacks for the B&B, the first drops began. This was it. My very first Sicilian storm. I couldn't wait. I gave Diana a treat, ruffled her fur and proceeded to tear open all the cellophane wrappers from cushions, sheets and duvets and all my soft furnishings, which would add warmth to the place, much needed tonight especially. Had I been in the UK, I'd have gone onto the Internet and John Lewis-ed the hell out of Tony's credit card and had the stuff delivered straight to my door rather than haul everything up here myself.

For now, the important thing was to make my personal living quarters comfortable. Excitement shot through me like the wind in the rushes. First thing, my bedroom.

I made the bed with my brand-new luxurious white and duck-egg duvet and cover, reveling in the silly things like scatter cushions and scented candles (avoid vanilla if you're on a diet – the scent will make you constantly hungry) and artwork. It was finally time for me to enjoy the little things in life, and if I was at the point that standing at the door of my now finished bedroom, observing my work filled me with joy, then maybe I would be okay after all. The fact that my bed had a huge Mattia-shaped hole in it was another story.

Next came the bedroom that would be Annie's when she visited. I lovingly assembled some of her baby pictures in one giant frame above the bed, grateful I'd had the foresight to keep it in my bag and not in my *Sesame Street* suitcase, wherever that was now. Annie's favorite color was green so I scattered some colored accents against the white duvet and rug. I'd even bought her a chaise and a tall boy for her big boy. They would always have their own private area with en suite whenever they wanted to come and see ol' Ma, assuming she could drag Miles out here.

Come to think of it, maybe her baby pictures right above the bed was a bit s-mothery of me. So I hung them up behind the door, for her to see only when she wanted. Above her bed I instead put a ravishing view of the beach out at Porticello with its rickety bridge jutting out into the wide turquoise and white bay. I put down a fragrance dispenser and took one last look before closing the door with a satisfied smile.

The kitchen and living room took me the longest as I arranged all my cooking utensils into my new drawers, my kitchen linens, cookery and crockery, all locally sourced and in the colors of the sea. I'd made practically every artisan and retailer on this island better off financially, but it was worth it. I'd also, in these past few months, found friends in them. They'd stopped seeing me as the Crazy *Americana* (it still hadn't quite sunk in that I was actually Canadian) and had come to appreciate me as one of them, finally.

I boiled the water for tonight's specialty, fresh aubergine ravioli topped with parmesan cheese and *yum* – grated pistachio. Enough for seconds and thirds. Great with a glass of Malvasia. It was going to be a long, cold night. But at least I had Diana. She enjoyed sitting in her brand-new, multi-padded basket in the corner of this, my favorite space, as the fire began to whistle and pop, the pleasant essence of wood oils from oak, almond, lemon and carob logs filling the room.

In a few minutes the chill of the house was beginning to dispel and it already felt as if I'd been living here for years if not for my sense of excitement at new beginnings.

A gust of wind shook the house as rain – *real* rain and not just wimpy drops – began to lash the window panes. Showtime. Finally. I could've closed the shutters but I liked to watch as water hit the glass and wiggled its way down, crystal-like in the light of the outdoor lamps.

Diana whimpered and I patted her head. 'Come on, you silly sausage,' I said as I turned the channel to the *Telegiornale* just in time for the weather report when a crash of thunder made me jump and the TV screen fizzed. The storm was coming from the north, bringing in icy winds and, judging by a glance outside, a biblical downpour. Who cared? All hell was breaking loose outside, but inside, Diana and I were snug and safe.

Until I heard it. A loud banging noise, barely audible between the cracks of thunder. I turned the volume down and froze as Diana growled.

'Sh...' I whispered, my blood already freezing. Had a part of the roof come off in the wind, barely hanging on its last hinges? Would there be a lot of damage? Would it make it through the night? It was only four p.m., but I couldn't see an inch from my own nose stuck to the glass as outside all hell continued to rage like in some old apocalyptic movie. But wait – there was a black fuzz on the horizon. And huge objects flying around in the air. A twister! I swallowed, now officially scared.

I'd heard a lot about Lipari's famously dangerous storms, so bad that not even the hugest ferries dared to make the crossing, and how the islanders often remained cut off from the mainland for days while the wind whipped entire trees around like breadsticks, ripping off roofs and beating fences to the ground. Was it going to happen to my home? Was I in danger?

I gathered my robe around me and stole upstairs, turning on every light along the way and checking every window, every door and – wouldn't you know it – it was the very last window in the attic suite up top, banging open and closed in a sharp cadence. I'd forgotten it this morning and now the floor was sopping wet. Good thing I had ceramic tile. With a sigh, I reached into the cupboard for a mop.

When I got back downstairs, Diana was waiting for me under the throw on the sofa.

'Coward,' I said to her and she licked my face. 'Yes, I'm still alive, no thanks to you.' I sat down next to her just as the news was finishing. And now what? A long evening stretched ahead of us. All I had to do was find a good movie, pray the roof wouldn't come off and remember to take a flashlight to bed in case there was a power cut.

And speaking of which – the lights flickered and the TV completely lost the signal, no matter how many ways I twisted the remote like in a *Mr. Bean* sketch.

So I popped in a DVD put couldn't stretch out as Diana was taking up half the sofa. Some life she had. Fed and loved within an inch of her life, she'd finally found her place in this world. We had a lot in common but for the loved part. Sandra had been right from the start. If you didn't manage to find a guy during the summer, the season of love, then you'd pretty much be hibernating on your own. I'd almost got the guy. But almost didn't cut it.

Wrapped in my robe, I huddled next to the roaring fire. Luckily I'd brought in enough wood for an all-nighter *and* the next day should the storm decide to continue. I never thought it could be this cold in Sicily in December. I could almost hear Sandra say

I warned you about winters on the Aeolian islands – about the loneliness, the cold and the hardships to come.

Diana pricked her ears at something outside the door and let out a staccato of furious barks that nearly raised the roof beams. And that's when the lights went out.

Bloody hell. I scrambled for the torch to reassure her that no one was there, that we were safe, but she seemed determined.

'See?' I said, shining the light at the door, not really feeling brave enough to open the shutters because, in effect, there were a whole lot of ghastly noises out there. And one in particular was really freaking me out. It was like a scraping sound, as if some school of goblins were trying to dig their way through the door. *Cut it out*, I told myself. *You're a grown woman, for Christ's sake. It's only the storm.*

I needed to prove it to myself, almost as much as I was afraid to open the shutter and shine my flashlight out beyond the glass lest I found a waxen, gnarled monster's face filling my window. The wind howled down the guttering and even up through the kitchen sink with ghost-like laments. Images of all the horror movies I'd seem in a lifetime flashed through my mind.

Great. Just because Diana was spooked didn't mean I had to be as well. *It's of the living you should be afraid of, not the dead*, my dad used to say to me. But as sure as it was raining, tonight there wasn't a living soul out there.

All the same – because you never know – I brandished the poker from the fireplace and opened the shutter a cinch to brave a look through the window.

Complete, utter darkness. It was like Dorothy and Toto alone in the farmhouse, looking out into the eye of the storm. Behind me the flames from the hearth reflected themselves in the glass pane and I saw myself, hovering against a black background, wondering how many hours this would last. All night, at least. And how many more nights like this would I have to face?

All lines were down. The power was dead. My cell phone had no signal, not even the 112 or 118 emergency numbers were available. The signal tower on Monte Sant'Angelo must've given up, meaning the entire island was now completely *incommunicado*, isolated from the mainland as well.

Even the house phone was dead. All dead. Complete, utter darkness. And then I suddenly remembered Mattia's battery-powered radio. I could've sent it along to him through Sandra, of course. But as long as it was there it felt like he was coming back.

The fire lit up that far corner of the room in dancing shadows and I easily snatched it up, turning it on and twisting the dial through all kinds of music and disturbances until I found something intelligible.

Radio Uno, the national radio station connected with the national broadcasting channel *Rai Uno*, was reporting on the devastation hitting Messina and Milazzo on the mainland and in particular the Aeolian islands that were now completely cut off. Total darkness hung on the horizon and up the mountains where the bright lights of Lipari usually shone. But not tonight. And then came the news of the twisters and Lipari town... oh my God – *flooding!*

My friends were down there. Sandra had Alfonso, but Maria? I hoped Leo was with her. I checked my phone again lest some miracle occurred. Still nothing. But I kept trying until I got a feeble signal. The tower must still be up then.

With shaky fingers I logged on but it was taking forever. Facebook was the only solution. So I tapped in on my Timeline, *State tutti bene?* Are you all okay? And waited. And waited. Until I finally got an answer from Susanna, one of Maria's daughters.

The town center, she informed me, was flooded, including the post office, and the roads leading up and out of town had turned into mud-rapids. The post office? That was at least six or seven steps up off the ground level! Oh my God, what was happening down there?

Up here, I was safe as the water washed downhill, but the town? It would have received all of the water gushing down the side of the mountain and into the valley with a vengeance.

I knew they were used to the islands being lashed by violent storms, but were they used to floods? Or were they, at this very moment, in big trouble? What could I do?

My Ape was diesel and better than a donkey, the way it clung to the sides of the mountains. I could make it down there in a little under an hour, in this weather. Bring dry blankets and stuff. People must be terrified, looking for shelter and somewhere slightly dryer.

And then another message from Susanna:

The streets are deserted, all the shops closed. I can't see the building opposite me. My uncle says he barely made it home because big boulders and mud are rolling down the hills into the roads, which are like rivers. I have to log off and save the battery in case we need it. Take care, Gillian. And a sad face.

You too, Susanna, Stay safe, I typed in.

Sandra was offline. And so was Mattia. He had better things to do, obviously. Well, at least I didn't have to worry about little Martina and Elvira. He was undoubtedly with them right now.

If, as Susanna had said, mud and boulders were rolling down the roads, there was no way my little Ape was going to make it. And if the power lines were down, most of the island would be in the dark. I'd probably drive off the road and the cliff. There was absolutely nothing I could do now. As soon as it was over I'd go down to bring supplies. Best to try not to worry. Diana and I had a very long night ahead of us.

But worry I did. Sandra had told me Mattia had gone to Salina for the weekend as usual. He was still planning on bringing little Martina here to Lipari. Dear God, I hoped the storm hadn't caught them in his boat, especially with her.

All sorts of horrible images of his boat tipping over assailed me and I had to breathe deeply to calm down. Silly. He's fine, warm and dry in Elvira's house in Salina. And the baby was wrapped up warm and safe. If he was there with them, they'd be okay in Salina.

Salina. If it were daylight I could see it from my window

above the kitchen sink. Possibly see Elvira's house from here. I wondered if he was looking out a window now, too, facing the coast of Lipari and trying to make out in the dark the shape of black mountains against a black sky, just a stone's throw away. It was highly unlikely that he'd be worried about me or looking for my lights. Weeks and weeks of radio silence from Mattia had made that clear to me. I was no longer his problem.

Diana had finally fallen asleep next to me. I got to my knees and gently placed a couple of more logs into the fire. They spit and popped, settling in to burn amongst the others and I knelt there for a while, thinking about how I could help my friends, but there was simply no way my Ape could make it. Even if it was strong, it was lightweight, and I could easily be blown off the cliff like a child blowing bubbles.

The windows rattled harder. All I could do was try to sleep and hope for better weather in the next few hours. Camp down here for the night, next to the fire. I pulled the throw over me and cozied down with Diana. My brand-new bed could wait another night.

Hour after hour passed. But I couldn't sleep, worried sick about the townspeople.

In the firelight, the room seemed much smaller, like the inside of an egg, warm and cozy. I only hoped it wouldn't be like this every night. I much preferred sitting on my terrace facing a starry night. Up here the stars were so close you could practically pluck them out of the sky. That is, most nights. Tonight was not one of them.

Okay, confession time. I'd been a bit gung-ho about sitting out the storm and all. Being alone *sucked*. As much as I loved Diana, she couldn't answer me except for in short, happy yaps, and she couldn't play board games. *Board games*. Must get some for my guests. If I wasn't too warm and lazy to get up and reach for a writing pad I'd jot that down. No, too tired. I'd just have to remember. Which of course I wouldn't. *Board games, board games*, I repeated to myself.

Through the haze of my sleepiness, a shaft of light shot up against the ceiling through the double-glazed stained-glass lunette above the front door. I sat up, confused. It was so bright surely there was a space ship in my front garden? Had I seen too many alien movies? Or maybe I was – of course – I was just dreaming. *Go back to sleep, Gillian…*

I would've, but there was a pounding on my door. I sat up again in a sleepy stupor. Aliens at my door? *Wake up*, I told myself. *This is just a nightmare.*

But someone really was pounding – like you've never heard before. At that rate it wouldn't take them long to knock the door down. Up here on this mountain, there was no one else around for quite a distance. Sandra had been right. Up here I was truly isolated. And suddenly I was afraid. Again.

I grabbed the poker from the hearth and slowly slid the tip into the fire, my eyes never leaving the door. Diana was now in full attack mode, bearing her teeth and barking and growling at the same time, so loud she almost – *almost* – covered the sound of the pounding and of the wind.

I froze, pulling Diana to me behind the sofa, all the while watching as the key turned in the lock, my hand still on the poker. Only Limping Man, the creepy locksmith, had the keys! That shifty bastard, giving me all those openly lascivious stares. Even Mattia had told him off. His presence had kept me on edge the whole time he was working here. You'd think I made sure he gave me all the copies of the keys. Luckily there was a bolt and – oh my God – I'd forgotten to bolt the door!

What could I do? Where could I hide? I'd never make it to the back door, not as the front door was almost fully open now. The room was much too long to make a break for it. I was trapped.

'Where are you?' came a fierce growl and suddenly he was filling the door, his limp even worse, if possible. All the same he whirled around, heading in the direction of my bedroom. Where I kept my safe. The operative word being *safe*. There was no way he was having my money. I'd worked and suffered too much to lose everything just yet. I wouldn't let him get away with this without a fight.

And with all my strength, I lunged for him, poker tight in my hands.

29

In the Eye of the Storm

He whirled around – just as I reached him – and wrenched the poker from me. Just like that. Now I was in trouble. Now I could see his face. *Mattia!*

'Gillian… sick!' he shouted into my ear above the thunder and before I could quite grasp his exact words, he pulled me to him and planted the fiercest kiss onto my mouth.

'Mattia…?' I gasped as his words sunk into my brain.

He'd been worried sick…?

'Are you okay?' he yelled over the racket, clearing my face of my hair that had come loose from my ponytail in the fight.

'What… what are you *doing* here…?' I yelled back, but he was holding me close to his chest, half suffocating me.

'I heard that roofs were being blown off and people injured up here…'

'You mean to tell me you jumped onto your Jeep, risking your *life* on these roads in this weather?'

A grin split his face. 'My Vespa wasn't going to cut it!'

'Are you absolutely nuts?' I cried. 'You could've got yourself *killed*.'

And on and on I went until he smothered me with kisses and *I'm sorrys* and *thank God you're okays*. It was like the end of some romantic movie, only I'd missed the part in between where the male lead acknowledges his feelings for the female lead.

'I tried calling you – I had to make sure you were okay,' he confessed between frantic kisses, lest the storm really ripped off the roof and blew us to kingdom come, ending everything right there and then.

'I had this crazy notion you were going to jump into your Ape and try and save the day!' he cried.

'Me? Go figure!'

'Yes – *you*. You are the most selfless person I know, sweetheart,' he said in between laughter and frantic kisses.

'Mattia, I...'

'Don't,' he said into my ear. 'I was unfair to not believe you and Claudio weren't – it was horrible of me. While I was driving up here I realized what you mean to me and how terrified I was of losing you like I already lost my parents and my brother.'

I kissed him and he grabbed the sides of my face. 'I was dead before you appeared, Gillian. Martina was the only reason I woke up in the morning.'

This was too good to be true. Give me some more! 'And now?'

'Now I have two reasons,' he shouted as he pulled me against his chest. 'I love you, Gillian...!'

My head snapped up and I searched his face. 'You *love* me...?'

He grinned and nodded. 'Ever since the night we found you, right here, when I tried to take Diana out of your arms. You just wouldn't let go. I realized how loving and tender you are and...' He kissed me again. 'I just... *knew* you were The One.'

He loved me? He loved *me*. Out of all the women in the world, this magnificent man loved *me*! And out of all the men in the world, this new and improved version of me loved *him*. How lucky could I get? I'd pined after something like this all my life – to feel special, to really feel important and loved. Some people are still waiting to achieve that.

Oh, but don't give up. There is someone out there for everyone. You just have to be willing to go back on yourself, take the right roads, take the most painful detours, cross land and sea (even if they terrify you) to discover territories unknown. But in the end it's all worth every arduous step.

And the best things will happen when you least expect them – without planning or stressing about it. Look at me – in the firelight, while the world outside seeming about to end, mine was just about to begin.

Meaning that, without thinking, planning or agonizing over it, as the storm continued to rage outside, indoors, safe and warm, *it* finally happened.

And it was unbelievably hot. I didn't for one second think of my wobbly bits, bingo wings or wrinkles, but of how great it felt to be in his arms, to feel so loved and special after so, so long. I won't go into any details because I'm still a little old-fashioned, but I will tell you this:

Mattia was *nothing* like I had imagined. He didn't bat an eye when the jammies came off. If anything, his eyes went even darker. And most of all, he was extremely considerate, passionate and hot, hot, hot. And he was *mine*.

A week later

'Gillian? There's a courier for you, *tesoro*,' came Mattia's voice. This endearment always managed to warm my heart.

A courier? I peered past Mattia out into the sun at the uniformed driver. And there it was… my *Sesame Street* trolley. Five months late. *Sicilian* late.

I signed the slip on his clipboard and followed Mattia who had retrieved it and brought it upstairs to our bedroom, placing it on the chaise at the end of the bed.

I eyed the bag as he left me to it. It looked all right on the outside. No breakages, no stains. Where the hell had it been all this time? In some depot, waiting for me to age and season before I got a piece of my life and hopes back?

I slowly unzipped it, a giddy feeling welling up inside me as if I was unpacking a long-lost gift. In truth, it was more like a time capsule. I gasped at the sight of my very favorite Monsoon cocktail dress (the one I was supposed to bowl Tony over with, remember?) lying on top of the heap.

Memories flooded back to me as if from another life. I'd bought it last year to look good on the fantastically romantic dinner I'd planned for Tony. Who'd sent me a text to tell me he would be dining with clients that evening. I remember the disappointment, the waiting for him all night, and how he'd collapsed fast asleep into bed five minutes after he'd crept through the door.

I caressed the silk material as tears pricked my eyes. But I wasn't going to cry anymore. I didn't need to hang on to old, musty memories. No more old stuff for me. From now on it was new, modern, clutter-free, heart included.

And, just for fun, I tried the dress on. Too big. I tried on another dress, just to make sure. And then another and another, happy to see that, somehow, in the space of five months, they were now *falling* off me. Where had I gone? Nothing of me was the same – my body, my hair, my heart, my disposition.

All that working like a mad dog in construction – the squats, the lifts, the hauling, pulling and pushing had actually resulted in something. It wasn't so much that I had shed a lot of weight as much as my body changing shape. I was now taut where I'd been saggy, flat (well, flatter) where I'd been bulgy. But best of all, there were the other changes I'd gone through, which weren't visible from the outside. This arsenal of seduction – I didn't need it anymore. But I knew someone who would appreciate it greatly and who deserved it more than anyone.

'*Ciao, arrivo subito,*' Maria mouthed discreetly as she checked out a large family of German tourists' groceries. I nodded and waited on the side, my huge Sisa bag in my arms. This family was completely pale, like they'd never seen a drop of sunlight in their lives, all bare skin exposed, no protection whatsoever. Just like I was when I'd arrived. I smiled to myself. They'd learn.

They picked up their bags, nodded to Maria and headed for the exit.

'*Ciao, bella!*' she cooed and hugged me.

'How are you? Did they clear out your basement?' I asked.

'Yes, thank God. Kilos and kilos of mud. We were lucky in the end.'

We had all been. The damages to the town were reversible and already Mattia was working with the town hall to rebuild part of the old harbor wall in Marina Corta.

'What's that?' She peered over the counter at my bag.

'I thought you might like to recycle some of this stuff. Almost all of it's new. Save you a shopping trip to the mainland.'

Eyeing me uncertainly, she opened the bag and gasped as my blue silk cocktail number tumbled out into her hands.

She looked up at me, eyes shiny. 'For me…? *E' bellissimo…*'

A funny warm feeling pervaded me. I didn't realize how much I wanted her to like them. It wasn't gratification for my taste, but because those dresses that had been so important to me were finally making someone else happy. They would allow her to dream and plan romantic nights that I'd never had.

'There's more – go ahead.'

She looked at me, then back at the bag as she reached in, her small hands delicate and caressing a cherry red dress. The one I'd bought for my previous birthday and never got to wear because Tony had developed a stomach ache. I hoped it would at least make her happy. It did wonders for her complexion.

'Gillian – thank you.'

I shrugged. 'You deserve them. Make sure they work their magic.'

At that, she turned beet red. Monsoon cocktail dress red. 'Well, actually… Leo's invited me to dinner tomorrow night. He said he has something very important to ask me.'

I gasped. 'Maria…!'

She circled the counter to come and hug me. I squeezed her tight. 'Thank you, Gillian. For the dresses. For everything.'

I planted a kiss on her cheek and turned to go before she could see the emotions bubbling to the surface.

'And now, are you ready for the rest of your life?' Mattia asked me as I climbed back into his Jeep.

I slid him a sidelong glance. 'Are *you* ready?'

'I'm always ready,' he drawled, leaning over to nuzzle my neck.

'Not that, silly. You have something to do first, remember?'

I'd managed to extract from him a promise that he'd make an effort to patch things up with Cosetta. I'd banged my strongest nail into him, i.e. that when Martina was old enough to understand, she'd never forgive him for keeping her away from her great-grandmother. And he would have to live with the fact that he'd acted no better than Cosetta. In the end he'd reluctantly agreed.

'Go,' I whispered when he parked in front of her house. 'I'll swing by later.'

With a brief hug, he disappeared into the palazzo that would hopefully become a place we'd be visiting often in the future.

Mattia and I may never have a child of our own, but Martina was as close as could be. I was finally at peace with myself and the world. And the second half of my life, the best yet to come, still lay ahead of me.

Sure, it wasn't going to be easy. I was a foreigner on a rock in the sea, living with a younger man. That alone was still news the locals had had a field day with. But I knew that whatever life threw my way, I wasn't alone. I had Mattia, Sandra, Maria, Cosetta and Martina and so many other friends. Even Elvira had warmed up to me in the end.

But most of all, I had me, Gillian Morana, formerly known as Gilly Wallflower – a new friend I was just getting to know. And I couldn't wait to discover what other marvelous, crazy adventures she had in store for me.

Epilogue

Six months later

Annie finally convinced Miles that it wasn't a crime to take a holiday, and they came over on long weekends – as did Martha and Brends.

Alfonso finally got his divorce and proposed to Sandra. She refused and is now seeing someone new – a single guy, this time.

Nadia Tomaselli, Tony's former lover, was now dating a man she'd known for ages, an old high school sweetheart, as local as could be. No more surprises for her, while Tony... who cared? He was alive, according to Annie, and looking for his next trophy wife.

As it turned out, Elvira eventually gave up pining for Mattia and she and Martina moved permanently from Salina and in with Cosetta, which was a double result. We all spent time together on a regular basis and soon Mattia's people and mine were one huge – and regular – happy gathering.

Maria's landscaper boyfriend Leo *did* propose and she joyfully accepted. Upon their return from honeymooning around a few European capitals (a wedding gift from Mattia and myself), they moved into my annex as I needed a professional gardener and maintenance man to take care of the property all year-round. With that kind of money, Maria wouldn't have to work and be at the mercy of hotel seasons.

All the same, she accepted the job of being my right-hand

woman and helping me with the upkeep of the business. *And*, most importantly, the daily baking of delicious Sicilian desserts, as I personally planned to stay *desserted* to my eyeballs in Sicily, for as long as possible.

'That's it, honey... keep doing what you're doing... *nice...*' Mattia urged me softly.

I looked up from the outboard motor and smiled as it came to life and sat back with a satisfied thump onto my seat. The sea and I had decided to bury the hatchet. We would be living together for the rest of our lives and might as well get to know each other a bit better.

Our first South to Sicily guests were due in a month, and I had finally managed to get my nautical license so I could take them on my little archipelago tours.

Mattia caressed my cheek. 'Now, you know what to do...'

I nodded and gripped the handle, gently steering my brand-new little dinghy through the bobbing corridors of neighboring vessels moored in Marina Corta. And slowly, gently, I brought her out into the open sea toward the infinite horizon.

Acknowledgements

Hello, my dearest readers! I can't tell you how grateful I am to you all for buying, reading, reviewing and recommending my little books among those of so many amazingly talented authors out there. The fact that you had given a then-new author a go touches me deeply. Who knew that when I started off with a tiny novella years ago, I would go on to write novels?

Many heartfelt thanks as always to my lovely editor Martina Arzu, everyone on the Aria Fiction Team over at Head Of Zeus, my amazing agent Lorella Belli and everyone at the LBLA, Lorella Belli Literary Agency who believed in me. I couldn't have done any of this without you all!

And of course, my family and friends who always joke about the fact that I live in two (or three or four) different worlds because I write more than one book at a time. Your support is indispensable! Also, to my dear friend Michele Nash who was with me in Lipari and will recognize many places – and dishes – in the book! And to my beloved husband Nick – here's to yet another dream come true! Thank you!

About the Author

NANCY BARONE grew up in Canada, but at the age of twelve her family moved to Italy. Catapulted into a world where her only contact with the English language was her old Judy Blume books, Nancy became an avid reader and a die-hard romantic.

Nancy stayed in Italy and, despite being surrounded by handsome Italian men, she married an even more handsome Brit. They now live in Sicily where she teaches English.

Nancy is a member of the Romantic Novelists' Association and a keen supporter of the Women's Fiction Festival at Matera where she meets up with writing friends from all over the globe.